D0958626

Also by Erica Spindler

Blood Vines

Erica Spindler

St. Martin's Paperbacks

This is a work of fiction. All of the characters, organizations, and events portrayed in this novel are either products of the author's imagination or are used fictitiously.

BLOOD VINES

Copyright © 2010 by Erica Spindler.
Excerpt from *Watch Me Die* copyright © 2011 by Erica Spindler.

Cover photograph of eyes © Katya Evdokimova/Trevillion Images
Cover photograph of vines © Imageworks/Getty Images

For information address St. Martin's Press, 175 Fifth Avenue, New York, NY 10010.

Library of Congress Catalog Card Number: 2009040234

ISBN: 978-0-312-36393-2

Printed in the United States of America

St. Martin's hardcover edition / March 2010
St. Martin's Paperbacks edition / February 2011

St. Martin's Paperbacks are published by St. Martin's Press, 175 Fifth Avenue, New York, NY 10010.

10 9 8 7 6 5 4 3 2 1

To those who nurture the vines and craft
"the drink of the gods" from their fruit.

Acknowledgments

Love at first sight exists. I know this because that's how long it took me to fall for California wine country. Knowing I *had* to set my next novel there took a few days longer and an innocent comment from winemaker Brian Fleury: "There are a dozen ways you could kill somebody during the wine-making process." As you can imagine, I was off and running.

So, of all the people I want to thank, I must begin with Brian. Huge thanks for first sparking my imagination, then for your time, explanations and tour—with detailed descriptions of the dangers of winemaking. And finally, thank you for your absolutely fabulous wine (www.fleurywinery.com).

I owe so many thanks to the Sonoma County Sheriff's Department, I don't even know where I should begin. So I'll begin at the top: Sheriff Bill Cogbill, thank you for opening your department to me and allowing me access to the facility and officers. I appreciate it and hope the book does your fine department proud.

Captain Dave Edmonds, what can I say besides you are, simply, terrific? Thank you for all the time you spent with me, the many questions you answered and for setting up the ride-along, instructing the deputy to help me "find places to dump bodies." (Thanks, Deputy Mike Mason. Great ride-along!)

Detective Sergeant Mitch Mana, thank you for giving me the Red Rooster secateur, the perfect wine country murder weapon! There's no doubt the book is better for it. Thanks also for the tour of the morgue and autopsy room and for the many after-the-fact questions answered.

Real estate agent Lisa Albertson, you're the greatest. Thanks for your time, your expertise, your point of view and setting up our tour at Seghesio. And for the fun, too. (In the book, you'll recognize our dinner at the girl & the fig.)

Ted Seghesio, big thanks for the tour and the most excellent wine. You'll find my favorite mentioned in the book!

To all the folks at Larson Family Winery, especially winemaker Carolyn Craig, thanks for making my Vocation Vacation research day so fabulous. It was truly terrific. I'll never forget climbing the wine barrels and into a fermenting tank—how many authors can claim that?

Vicki and John Faivre, thanks for hooking me up with your Salvestrin Winery friends. Hearing stories from wine country old timers was both fascinating and helpful. Didn't we have fun—and a lot of really good wine—in the process?

Final thanks to my assistant, Evelyn Marshall, who really did prove herself invaluable with this one; our wine country driver, Dennis Wulbrecht; my agent, Evan Marshall; my editor, Jennifer Weis, and the great St. Martin's team; my husband and kids and, lastly, my God for making it all possible.

Dear Reader,

Thank you for choosing *Blood Vines*. Loving wine almost as much as I do writing, I had a wonderful time working on this novel—I hope you enjoy reading it!

As a toast of "thank you" to my readers, I'm offering a free gift*—a custom *Blood Vines* drink coaster. Use it while sipping your favorite beverage. Just mail me your original store receipt or original packing slip receipt for the purchase of a new copy of *Blood Vines*, or any of my other novels, and the coaster is yours absolutely free.

While visiting California's wine country was a thrill, my next venture is set at home in New Orleans. Look for *Watch Me Die* in June 2011.

I love hearing from my readers. Please visit my website www.ericaspindler.com to drop me an e-mail, learn more about my special offers, and the latest book and tour news.

Cheers!

Erica

Mail to:
Erica Spindler, P.O. Box 8556, Mandeville, LA 70470

*Offer available only to U.S. and Canadian residents, age 18 or older, and gifts will only be shipped to addresses in the 50 United States, D.C., Puerto Rico, and Canada. One per person or household. Original store receipt, original electronic receipt or original packing slip receipt, dated February 1, 2011 or later, with purchase price circled, must be received by May 1, 2011. Offer valid only while supplies last. No copies of receipts or packing slips, or used book sales receipts accepted. Requests for gifts will be accepted by regular mail only. No telephone or e-mail requests will be accepted. You must purchase a new copy of *Blood Vines* or a new copy of any Erica Spindler novel to take advantage of this offer. Theft, diversion, reproduction, transfer, sale or purchase of receipts is prohibited and constitutes fraud. Erica Spindler is not responsible for late, lost or misdirected mail. Offer void where prohibited. Allow 6-8 weeks from close of offer for delivery.

Prologue

San Francisco, California
Tuesday, February 9, 2010
1:05 A.M.

Ex-husbands were like bad pennies, Alexandra Clarkson thought, arching her back as a wave of pleasure washed over her. They kept coming back. At least hers did. And she, horny, idealistic idiot, kept opening the door—and jumping into the sack with him.

But damn, he knew just the right things to say. And do. She moaned and rubbed herself against his hand. Yes, just the right things.

She wrapped her legs around him, urging him on as he slipped into her. She let her mind wander as sensation rippled over her. Suddenly, a series of images raced into her head, strobe light–like, one after another: A robed figure, face obscured by a hood; flickering candles, smoke curling upward; naked bodies, writhing together.

A faceless baby, screaming.

Alex froze, passion obliterated by fear. On top of her, her ex rocked, moaning, seemingly oblivious to the fact she was no longer participating in the act.

Fear became panic. She couldn't breathe. He was crushing

her. A primal, thundering beat filled her head. With it the certainty she was going to die.

She wedged her hands under his chest and pushed. "Stop. Don't." She meant to scream the words; they came out a choked whisper.

He didn't stop. She struggled then, pummeling his back with her fists. "Get . . . off . . . me!" The last came out as a shout.

"What the fu—" He rolled onto his back, breathing heavily. "Shit, Alex. What's your problem?"

Trembling violently, she sat up, pulling her knees to her chest. "My problem is you, obviously. Go away."

"Gladly, schizo." He climbed off the bed, grabbed his clothes and looked back at her. "You're one freaky chick, you know that?"

She was. Alex dropped her head to her drawn-up knees and closed her eyes. *Dear Jesus, what just happened?*

The bathroom door slammed shut and she drew a shuddering breath. What *was* her problem? Yes, he'd showed up at her door. But she'd invited him into her home *and* bed.

Why did she keep making a monumental mess of . . . everything?

Light sliced across the bed as Tim emerged from the bathroom. She lifted her head. He stood in the rectangle of light, a dark silhouette. She didn't blame him for being pissed.

"I don't know what . . . I'm sorry," she said softly. "I feel like an idiot."

"Are you okay?"

Was she? she wondered, even as she nodded.

"Is there anything I can do to help you?"

Yeah. Change her life. Fill the empty places. Turn her into an ordinary Jane who had a settled, ordinary life.

She wished he could do that for her. The desire had no doubt played a part in her marrying him.

Unfortunately, no one could change her life but her.

"Afraid not. Thanks for the offer anyway."

"This mistake was mine," he said, crossing to the bed. "I'll take the credit."

"Booty call gone bad," she murmured, looking up at him. "I warn you, it's going on your permanent record."

"We'll make this divorce work, I promise." He smiled slightly and threaded his fingers through her dark hair, then tucked strands behind her ear. "See you on campus."

He let himself out; she heard the lock click into place. Dammit. Who got involved with one of their professors? A psychology professor, no less. What a pathetic cliché. The girl with no father falling for an older, wiser guy. That just screamed "looking for Daddy syndrome." Worse, she'd married him. Then been surprised when he cheated on her.

Surprised, but not brokenhearted. That had told her everything she'd needed to know about their relationship. And things about herself she'd rather not have known.

She was, indeed, one freaky chick.

Alex climbed out of bed and, shivering, slipped into her robe. She wandered into the apartment's living room, to the large front window. Moonlight, cool and blue-hued, spilled over the street below.

San Francisco didn't sleep. Despite the hour, people populated the sidewalk below, some simply strolling, others rushing, bravely confronting the steep hill.

Alex touched the pane of glass. It was cool against her fingers. The image of the robed figure filled her head once more. Where had it come from? A book, maybe? Something from her research on religious ceremonies and sects? She didn't recall the specific source, but it made sense, especially since she had just recently returned to work on her doctoral dissertation.

But why had she thought of them at that moment? Why had they popped crystal clear into her head? And why had she reacted so violently to them?

Alex turned away from the window. Dammit. Things had been better. The nightmares that had once plagued her were gone. Neither insomnia nor depression had reared its ugly head in months.

She had her act together. As together as her act got, anyway. The bartending gig had afforded her the opportunity to finish the dissertation. She and her mother had settled into an uneasy peace—but peace nonetheless.

Now, this. She had never experienced anything like it before. Alex rubbed her arms, suddenly chilled. It'd been nothing. The trick of a mind actively engaged in research. Proof she had chosen the right time to return to her work. The moment made sense as well. She'd let go of the corporeal world, focused on sensation and allowed her mind to "float." Similar to the trancelike state used in shamanism, Buddhism and a number of other religions and rituals as a way to shut down the logical mind and unlock the truth.

She would backtrack, she decided. Go through her notes, locate the source of the images. Until she did, this thing was going to bug the hell out of her.

Chapter One

Sonoma Valley, California
Friday, February 12
10:05 A.M.

Violent Crimes Investigations detective Daniel Reed eased to the side of the road, stopping behind the Sheriff's Department cruiser. He swung out of his four-wheel-drive Tahoe, a small, rust-colored cloud forming as his boots landed on the dirt road. Before him, vineyards stretched across the gently rolling hills, the mustard in bloom, painting the rows yellow. The cheery yellow contrasted sharply with the dormant vines, standing like gnarled headstones in a cemetery that extended as far as the eye could see.

The Native American Miwoks had named this place Valley of the Moon. Their legend held that the moon had risen from the valley. Reed figured that's why so much crazy shit went down here. You had your bizarro religions, whacked-out criminals and a little dark cloud of weirdness that seemed to hang over the valley.

Blame the moon. It worked for him.

Today, however, his job was to figure out who'd buried what in this torn-up vineyard.

The CSI unit pulled up behind him. The Sheriff's

Department employed its own crime scene investigators, all sworn officers. The CSI guys—and gals—worked in tandem with the VCI, forming a two-lead partnership for each case. Jointly, they were held responsible for the case.

Tanner had drawn this one, Reed saw, as the attractive blonde stepped out of her vehicle. Barbara Tanner looked a decade younger than her fifty years and had a reputation for being driven. A reputation he, unlike a few of his fellow detectives, admired.

Of course, his reputation for being a cowboy wasn't always appreciated either. They made a good team.

He slammed the SUV door and sauntered her way. "Flying solo today, Tanner?" he called, grinning.

"Hell no, Reed. I've got you."

"Born lucky and beautiful."

"Tell that to my shrink, plastic surgeon and prick of an ex-husband."

He laughed. "Know anything about this one?"

"Not much. Somebody found bones."

"My bet's on a dog."

"Coyote, maybe."

They reached the inner perimeter. He greeted the patrolman standing watch with a clipboard. He signed the log and handed it to Tanner. "What's the deal?"

"Phylloxera infestation. The whole vineyard had to be ripped out."

Tanner made a sound of distress. "Breaks my heart to see old vines like these go."

"Tell me about it," the deputy agreed. "You feel it in the gut, you know?"

Reed glanced at the piles of thick, gnarled stocks and branches. Century-old vines. The older the vine, the less fruit produced, but the more intense the flavor of that fruit. Nothing tasted quite like the wine produced from them.

"I'm a beer man myself," he said.

The other two looked at him. Tanner shook her head. "You're a weird one, Reed. You know that?"

She said it with a smile, but it was true. Here, in this little slice of the world, it was all about the grapes, the wine produced from them. The wine's color. Its nose. The points awarded it by *Wine Enthusiast*. Here, invariably, idle conversation turned not to religion or politics, but to *viticulture* or *terroir*.

He'd turned his back on all that years ago.

He grinned at her. "Yeah, I know. But I wear the label well."

"That you do." She turned her attention back to the deputy. "The remains were found in the clearing process?"

He nodded and motioned to a group of fieldworkers sitting in the bed of a battered pickup truck. "The front loader unearthed a wooden crate, or what was left of one. Guys there figured they'd found buried treasure, got pretty excited. That changed when they got a look inside."

"You confirmed?"

"Didn't want to mess with the box. Took a peek, confirmed some sort of remains."

"Human?" Tanner asked.

"Not my area. It's damn creepy, though."

Tanner cocked a perfectly arched eyebrow, clearly amused. "Would that be your professional opinion, Officer?"

He laughed. "As a matter of fact it would."

Reed and Tanner ducked under the crime scene tape and picked their way to the discovery. The old vines had gone deep; ripping them up had created a mess.

Reed fitted on Latex gloves and squatted beside the find. The box was badly decomposed. In the fieldworkers' eagerness to pry off the top, it had partially crumbled.

"Wine crate," he said. "Or what's left of one. Rules out a coyote."

"Been buried awhile."

"Lid was nailed shut." He indicated the rusty nail that had fallen away from the crumbled wood. "Somebody gave a shit about Fido. Got a pen?"

She handed him one; he used it to lift away a corner of the heavy plastic sheeting. Reed prepared himself for a wave of odor that surprisingly didn't come.

Tanner got the first look and swore. "Holy Christ. Creepy doesn't quite cover it."

Not a dog or coyote, Reed saw. And not just bones. An infant, mummified.

"This is out of my area of expertise," Tanner said. "I'll need to call Sonoma State, get an anthropologist out here."

Reed nodded, a sinking feeling in the pit of his gut. This picture-perfect wine country day had just turned ugly.

Chapter Two

While Tanner called in reinforcements, Reed studied the infant's remains. The tiny body was partly skeletonized and partly mummified, intact save for head, feet and hands. The skeletonized hands and feet had disarticulated. The skull, he decided, may have dislodged in the excavation process. It lay in three pieces.

He sat back on his heels. True mummification took place when a corpse dried out. The fleshy tissue shrank to the bones, becoming leathery and brown like beef jerky. This was different. The body had saponified, becoming what was affectionately referred to as a soap mummy.

Reed peeled away the plastic, taking in the contents of the homemade coffin. Whoever had buried the infant had taken a good bit of care. The child had been wrapped in a blanket—pieces of the mostly decomposed fabric clung to the remains—then enfolded, envelope style, in plastic sheeting.

He frowned. The plastic and the depth of the grave, from what he could tell a good four feet, had probably been an attempt to prevent scavengers or regular vineyard maintenance

from unearthing the victim. If not for the phylloxera infestation, this little victim would still be buried.

Tanner returned. "Anthropologist is on his way. A new
kid. And Cal."

"California" Cal. One of the other CSI detectives. Termi-
nally cool, he bought into the whole Hollywood interpretation of the job. At least when it came to his closet.

Reed grinned. "I'll have to see if I can help him get his
Cole Haans dirty."

"Bet you five bucks, you can't."

"You're on." He motioned to the victim. "What're you
thinking so far?"

"This wasn't a case of SIDS, that's for certain. Look here."
She indicated the pieces of skull. Two of the pieces showed
signs of blunt force trauma. "I don't think there's any doubt
what killed this child. Poor little thing."

Reed looked at his partner. "How long have you lived in
the valley, Tanner?"

"Fifteen years."

"Ever heard the name Dylan Sommer?"

She thought a moment, then shook her head. "Any rela-
tion to Sommer Winery?"

"Yeah. Dylan Sommer was the owner's son. He was abducted from their home back in '85."

Reed returned his gaze to the gruesome remains. "It was
a huge deal around here. It challenged the valley's notion
about safety. The possible and impossible. The kid was
nabbed from his own bed while his two sisters, one of them a
teenager, slept right across the hall. Everybody figured it was
a kidnapping, but no ransom request ever arrived. He was
never found."

She tucked her hair behind her ear. "You're thinking this
could be him."

"Yes."

"This might not even be a—"

"Boy's remains? I think it is. Check it out." He pointed.
Trapped in a still taped fold of the plastic was a pacifier. A
blue one.

"My God." She sat back on her heels. "Doesn't mean it's Dylan Sommer."

"True. But we've got a male infant buried in a wine crate on land not far from the family's winery."

She drew her eyebrows together. "The parents weren't suspects?"

"No. Among other things, they had an airtight alibi."

"Which was?"

"They were having dinner with their best friends. My parents."

Chapter Three

Reed's stomach rumbled loudly. Beside him Tanner sympathized. There'd be no chance to eat for a while as this party was now in full swing, complete with contingents from VCI and CSI, the Coroner's Office, as well as both units' sergeants.

He and Tanner had conferred with their sergeants, who'd felt comfortable enough with their handle on the case to leave them to it. No doubt, they were on their way to lunch, Reed thought. Lucky bastards.

Tanner's CSI cohort, Detective "California" Cal Calhoon, chose that moment to arrive. He looked as if he'd just stepped out of a *GQ* spread—except for the Hazmat booties he wore over his shoes.

Shit. Reed thought. Bye-bye five bucks.

Calhoon stopped beside Reed, and looked up at him. At six foot four, Reed towered over the flashy detective. "Who's the kid?" Cal asked, motioning toward the anthropologist crouched by the grave.

"Pete Robb, PhD."

Cal smiled, revealing perfectly aligned, bright white teeth.

"Anybody but me think that anthropologist is too young to know his butt from that hole in the ground?"

"He's a pain in *my* butt," Reed said, "I'll give you that. He finally shows up, then asks us to stand around while he 'assesses the find.'"

"Give the kid a break," Tanner said. "We all started at the same place—wet behind the ears, overeager, do-gooders."

"Speak for yourself," Reed muttered. "Time's up."

Cal and Tanner fell in step with Reed. The anthropologist didn't even look up when they reached him.

"Before *I* mummify," Reed said, "you have any thoughts?"

"Actually, a classic example of saponification," the PhD corrected. "You've heard of the process?"

Oh yeah, Reed thought. *Really* young. "That's a mighty big word, Doc. Maybe you want to break it down for us?"

Cal grinned and Tanner shot Reed an amused glance. The anthropologist seemed oblivious. "It's a process aided by moisture, wherein the body's fat is turned to a soaplike substance called adipocere."

"Grave wax," Tanner said innocently. "Right?"

"Exactly!" Robb beamed up at her, the way a professor would his prize student. "It's great stuff. Really interesting. It can run the gamut from soft and soapy to hard, brittle and waxy. Like this one."

Reed gave the kid points for enthusiasm—and Tanner props for calling it.

"Under the right conditions—moisture, lack of oxygen, alkaline soil—fat turns to adipocere. Infants are a large percentage fat. They also lack certain digestive tract enzymes, a fact which aids adipocere production."

"Yet the hands and feet skeletonized," Cal said. "How'd that happen?"

"No fat, no adipocere."

"How old was he?" Reed asked. "Best guess anyway."

"Younger than two." The kid nudged his glasses higher on his nose. "The skull hadn't knitted together yet. Obviously, this child was considerably younger than that."

"Six or seven months old?" Reed asked.

"Maybe. I'll take long bone measurements back at the lab, that'll narrow it down."

"How long's he been buried?" Tanner asked.

"Years, judging by the decomposition of the crate. At least two."

"Why's that?"

"In conditions like these, adipocere begins forming a month or two after death and reaches completion within two years."

"Could he have been buried twenty-five years?" Reed asked.

"Maybe, sure."

Reed turned to Cal and Tanner. "I want to find out if that particular pacifier is still being made, and if it's not, when production stopped."

"I'll do the same with the diaper," Cal offered. "Nasty as it looks, the lab might be able to do something with it through material and design comparisons. Plus, the crate may be marked."

Tanner looked at Reed. "The lab may be able to extract some DNA from the bones. The adipocere might also be a source."

"Ditto the pacifier," Cal added.

"What's your next move?" Tanner asked.

"I have a pretty good idea who this land belongs to. I'll confirm and follow up."

"Sommer?"

Reed nodded and glanced at his watch. "Even if the land's not his, I'll need to talk to him."

"I'm sorry," she said simply, no doubt understanding how difficult that meeting would be for him, because of his personal history with the family.

"Me, too. Call me when you and Cal finish processing and are back at the Barn," he said, referring to HQ by its nickname. "We'll rendezvous then."

Chapter Four

Reed navigated the steep, winding road that led to the Sommer Winery from memory. He had traveled it hundreds of times, many of them much faster and more carelessly than now. How many of those times had he been under the influence? And not just the influence of drugs or alcohol—but of youth, machismo and his overinflated opinion of himself and his place in the world.

Reed smiled grimly. He barely recognized that person anymore.

He eased off the gas, thoughts turning to the task ahead. He'd skimmed the case files, reviewed statements from Sommer family members and friends and read the various accounts of the events of that day twenty-five years ago.

Some moments, however, had such impact they lingered in the memory, clear as the day they occurred. The morning he'd awakened to learn Dylan Sommer had been kidnapped was one of them.

August 17: a Saturday. He'd been ten, had awakened to sunlight streaming through the open windows. The sky had been a perfect robin's egg blue and the breeze wafting through the open window sweet.

And carried on the breeze, the sound of his mother crying.

He'd gone to investigate. And found the adults whispering among themselves, their expressions twisted with something he hadn't recognized. Not then, anyway. Now he would: Grief. Disbelief. Fear.

The police had arrived shortly after, then the FBI. He had eavesdropped—and learned about Dylan's disappearance, the discovery of blood near the Sommer Winery's caves, about the expectation of a ransom demand.

A demand that never came.

Life had changed after that day. His parents had begun to turn old. They fought more, smiled less. Their relationship with their friends—particularly the Sommers—had become strained as well. Life had lost its carelessness, certainly its simplicity. Doors were locked. Alarm systems installed. No more night games of hide-and-seek while their parents drank wine and lost themselves in adult conversations.

As a kid, he hadn't understood why. As an adult, he did. How did you bounce back from something like that? How did you manage to move on?

Harlan and Patsy Sommer hadn't. Their marriage had fallen apart. Patsy had left, taking her daughter, Alexandra, leaving behind not only Harlan and his daughter, but their friends and the life they had made together.

The house and winery came into view. Both rambled, modernized and expanded here and there over the years. And like many homes in the area, what made it spectacular was the location—two thousand feet above the valley, nestled among the bay, oak and eucalyptus trees. The view was breathtaking—vineyards sloping down the mountain, each elevation its own microclimate, perfect for producing a uniquely flavored grape.

Heaven on earth.

Reed parked his vehicle, climbed out, then started for the winery. Harlan Sommer was a good guy; Reed had always liked him. He hated that he had to be the one to open this old wound, but the job was his.

A man and woman emerged from the tasting room. "I'm sorry," the woman called, "the winery's closed."

Rachel Sommer, he recognized. Harlan's daughter. "Rachel, it's Dan Reed."

"Danny?" She broke into a smile and hurried to meet him. "I haven't seen you in ages."

He kissed her cheek. "You look wonderful."

She did. Tawny, shoulder-length hair, soft brown eyes, chamois-colored buckskin coat and boots. Five years his senior, he'd had a major crush on her when he was thirteen. To her credit, she had been kind.

"And you're as big and handsome as ever. Still not hitched?"

"You going to make me an offer?"

"I just might." She hugged him again, then turned toward her companion. "This is Ron Bell, our assistant winemaker. Ron, Dan and I practically grew up together."

"Practically?" He shook the other man's hand. "I think I spent more time here than home."

"Our parents were best friends," she said by way of explanation. "Dan's family owns Red Crest Winery."

"Good wines," the other man said. "Your '05 cab franc was excellent. Didn't it win the *San Francisco Chronicle*'s competition?"

"Yes, thank you. A gold. But it wasn't mine. My father and brothers'."

Rachel tucked her arm through Dan's. "Dan left the wine biz behind for the law."

"You're an attorney?"

"Cop," he answered, his lips lifting at the man's shocked expression.

"A rebel," Rachel said. "That's what he is."

They started for the house. "Dad's testing one of the '08 cabs. Come have a taste. He'll be delighted to see you."

"I'm not so sure of that. This isn't a social call. It's about Dylan."

She stopped short. She looked as if he had slapped her. "My God, Dan. You can't be—"

The last was cut off by Harlan Sommer calling out to her, "Rachel, who's that with you?"

"Little Danny—"

"Reed," Harlan finished, a smile stretching across his face. He strode toward them. "Good to see you, son." He reached him and clapped him on the back. "It's been too damn long."

Since Reed had last seen him, the man's hair had gone completely gray. And he looked thinner, more frail than he remembered. "It has. How have you been?"

"Wonderful. Just great. Treven and Clark are here. Come say hello."

"Dad, wait." Rachel touched his arm. "Dan's visit isn't social." She lowered her voice. "Something about Dylan."

Harlan stopped cold. "I see," he said stiffly, and turned to Ron. "Could you let my brother and nephew know I'll be a few minutes? They needn't wait."

Ron moved his gaze between them, then nodded and headed into the house.

"We've uncovered the remains of an infant," Reed began. "A boy."

"Where?" the man managed, voice thick.

"In one of your vineyards. The one with the phylloxera infestation."

Rachel brought a hand to her mouth. "The ancient vines. My God, that's just down the hill."

Harlan began to tremble. Rachel put her arm around him.

"We don't know if it's Dylan," Reed added. "The age appears to be right, and the fact the child was buried in a wine crate, in a location so close to—"

"I need to sit down."

Without waiting for a response, Harlan crossed to a group of benches clustered together near an outdoor brick oven. He sank heavily onto one. Rachel sat beside him and gathered his hand in hers.

Reed took the bench kitty-corner to theirs. "I need to ask you a few questions, Harlan." The man nodded and Reed continued. "Did Dylan use a pacifier?"

"Yes," he managed.

"Can you describe it to me?"

He shook his head. "It was blue. That's all I remember." He looked at his daughter. "After all this time. Can it be?"

"Do you remember, did he go to bed with it that night?"

"He always went to bed with it," Rachel answered for her father, voice strong, almost angry-sounding.

"Do you recall, was it missing the morning you discovered Dylan gone?"

"I don't know. I don't—" He rubbed his head, voice shaking. "It never crossed my mind."

"The infant we unearthed was buried with one. It was blue."

A sound passed the man's lips, low and feral, like an animal in pain. Rachel put her arms around him, rested her head on his shoulder. "I'm so sorry, Dad."

"I always hoped he was alive," he whispered. "Foolishly. It . . . helped me, it . . ." His words trailed off.

"We don't know for certain it's Dylan," Reed said softly. "The remains are surprisingly intact. Disturbingly so."

"I don't understand," Rachel said. "It's been twenty-five years . . . I was fifteen years old, for God's sake! What could be left?"

Reed quickly, and as gently as possible, explained the saponification process. "What's left is a mummy. I'm sorry."

Harlan said nothing, though he saw that his throat worked. Reed went on. "Was Dylan still in diapers?"

"Yes."

"Tell me about that night."

He clasped his hands together. "We went to dinner at your parents'. We drank too much wine. In those days we . . . we used to do that." He lowered his gaze. "She never forgave me . . . Leaving the children alone was my idea. I promised her they'd be fine."

"I was fifteen," Rachel said, voice shaking. "Old enough to babysit. If anyone was to blame, it should have been me."

"No," Harlan said. "I just thank God you were . . . if anything had happened to you . . . I don't think I could have gone on."

Reed turned to her. "If I remember correctly, Rachel, you and your stepsister slept through whatever happened."

"Yes," she whispered.

Harlan stepped in. "The police believed whoever took Dylan knew the children were alone. Knew the layout of the home, which bedroom was Dylan's. The FBI supported that theory. They were convinced it was a kidnapping for ransom."

"But no ransom demand came in."

"No."

Something had gone wrong. Perhaps. Or they had lost their nerve, killed and buried Dylan, then run.

He didn't share his train of thoughts with Harlan and his daughter.

Harlan shook his head. "We never thought something like that could happen here . . . not in Sonoma. We never even locked our doors . . ."

His words trailed off; Rachel stepped in. "When will we know if it's Dylan?"

"We're attempting to pinpoint the child's age, also to determine how long he's been buried. In addition, we may be able to retrieve DNA from the remains and positively ID him that way. If that doesn't pan out, we could turn to a forensic sculptor."

"Whatever it takes," Harlan said. "I'll pay. I have to know if it's Dylan."

"I'll need to speak with your ex-wife."

"I don't know where she is." At Reed's disbelieving expression, he shrugged. "I haven't spoken to her since she left. The loss of Dylan . . . she couldn't handle it."

Treven emerged from the house. The elder Sommer carried a bottle and two wineglasses. The man reached them, greeted Reed, then poured a glass of wine and handed it to his brother. "What's going on, Harlan?"

"It's Dylan." He struggled to clear his throat. "They may have found his remains."

"Good God. Where?"

Reed went through the story again. When he'd finished, Treven asked, "What do you know so far?"

The older brother's style was far different from the younger's. Businesslike. To the point. He wanted the facts.

Of course, it hadn't been his child who had been abducted and possibly killed.

"The remains suggest death by blunt force trauma to the head. He was buried in a wine crate, wearing a disposable diaper and wrapped in a blanket. His pacifier was buried with him."

Harlan's shoulders shook as he began to cry. Treven squatted in front of him. "This is good news, Harlan. All these years without knowing. Without justice. Surely this will reopen the investigation." He glanced up at Reed for confirmation. Reed gave it to him and he continued. "Think about it, justice for Dylan, at long last. A proper burial for his remains."

"When will we know?" Harlan asked.

"We'll move as quickly as we can," Reed assured him. "We're in the process now of excavating the remains and will transport them to the lab. I'll keep you informed."

Chapter Five

San Francisco, California
Monday, February 15
2:20 P.M.

Alex parked in front of her mother's Victorian row house, one of San Francisco's famed "painted ladies." She hadn't appreciated growing up here until after she was grown. Typical kid, she supposed. Longing for what she didn't have instead of enjoying what she did.

Alex set the emergency brake and climbed out of her Toyota Prius. She had spent the past six days searching for the source of her "vision," as she had come to refer to it. So far, she'd come up empty.

She re-cinched her caramel-colored trench and started up the walk. Although frustrated, she had gradually become less troubled over the incident. She'd told herself it'd been a one-time thing, an aberration of sorts. Certainly nothing to get worked up about.

Alex scooped up her mother's newspaper, then let herself into the home. The smell of oil paints and turpentine stung her nose. Her mother had been working.

"Mom," she called, "it's Alex."

"On the porch, honey."

Alex made her way down the central hallway. The living room and dining room were both a wreck. Furniture pushed to the walls; floors covered by drop cloths; easels with works in progress; canvases propped against every available surface.

Her mother had long ago given up any semblance of normalcy in the way she lived. Even before Alex had gone off to college, her mother's art had begun gobbling square footage, until nothing but Alex's bedroom and the bathrooms remained untouched. A sort of metaphor for her mother's mental illness—there were very few areas of their lives it didn't touch.

Alex dropped the newspaper on the kitchen counter and crossed to the doors to the patio. They stood open and she paused, the chilly air enveloping her.

Her mother, still a striking beauty at fifty-four, sat sketching at the café table on the patio, a pot of French press coffee and an untouched croissant beside her.

Alex resembled her—the same dark hair and fine features. The same almond-shaped eyes. But she had always seen herself as a watery reflection of her mother's dramatic beauty—her hair wasn't as inky, her skin not as alabaster, her eyes a sensible hazel instead of clear green.

Now, the sun fell across her mother's silky black hair, illuminating the inky highlights as her pencil flew across the pages, flitting almost frenetically from one sketch to another. She wasn't wearing a coat but seemed oblivious to the cold.

All the signs of a full-blown manic episode, Alex acknowledged. She stepped onto the porch, crossed to her mother, and dropped a kiss on the top of her head. "I see you've been working. Anything you loved?"

Her mother looked up at her. "Several things. It was a wonderful session. Just wonderful."

"Why don't you come inside? You'll catch your death out here."

Her mother waved off the concern. "These are the ones, Alex. The ones I'll be remembered for. Grab yourself a cup of coffee or a juice and take a look."

A moment later, glass of orange juice in her hand, Alex studied the works in progress. There were at least twenty of them, in various stages of completion. Swirling colors, brilliant. Organic shapes, vibrating with life. Stunning.

She gazed at them, a catch in her chest. Her mother could have been an important artist. Could have been. Hard to have a real career without a consistent body of work. Or when you committed to showings, then backed out at the last moment.

Alex sipped the juice. How long had she worked without stopping to eat or sleep? Twelve hours? Twenty-four? More than that? At least when Alex still lived here, she'd been able to coax her mother to eat. Had been able to keep tabs on her. Make certain she rested and took her medication.

"What do you think?" her mother called from the kitchen.

"Incredible," she called back, heading that way. She found her mother standing at the counter, newspaper spread open before her. She was humming as she read. "They're really wonderful, Mom."

Her mother smiled. "Some of my best work. Certainly the best in years."

How many times had she heard those same words from her mother? Too many to count. And each time it had ended the same way.

"May I have one of them?" she asked.

"Silly." Her mother's hands fluttered. "None of them are complete."

And most likely, they never would be. "I'd like one anyway. Would you mind?"

Her mother laughed. "Strange girl. But if it's that important to you, take any one you like." She snapped on the radio; Fleetwood Mac's late seventies rock classic "Don't Stop" filled the room. Her mother rocked to the beat. "This song brings back memories." She snapped her fingers. "I was quite the wild child. The Eagles, Peter Frampton, the Grateful Dead, I saw them all."

"You're not taking your medication, are you?"

Her mother frowned. "Don't start, please."

"You need your meds, Mom."

"I don't like the way they make me feel."

"They keep you even."

"If feeling like a zombie is 'even,' you can have it."

"We've talked about this before. Now you feel unstoppable, but—"

She waved off Alex's concern. "Nothing you say can pop my bubble today."

"Mother, plea—"

"No, no, no." She sank onto a chair and reached for Alex's hands. "I don't want to argue. Please, let's not."

"I'm just worried about you."

"No need, I'm on top of the world."

On top of the world now, Alex thought minutes later as she placed the canvas she'd chosen in her old bedroom. But the moment's lofty perch meant a steep plunge later.

She moved her gaze over the room's girlish furnishings and the small collection of works in progress she had stored here. She thought of it as an archiving method. A way to ensure that someday her mother would have a body of work to look back on, even if they were incomplete works.

She locked the door, then headed back down the wide staircase. Her mother stood at the bottom, gazing up at her. "You're a funny girl," she said affectionately.

Alex reached the landing. "I come by it honestly."

"That you do." She cupped her face in her palms. "My pretty, pretty girl. So different than—"

She bit the words back and spun away, humming, heading back toward the kitchen.

"Than who, Mom?"

Her mother stopped in the doorway. "Than everyone, silly."

Alex gazed at her mother, battling twin feelings of frustration and resignation. They had been through this a hundred times. At least. Her mother would hint at something or someone from their past, then refuse to say more.

She tried again anyway. "What's so horrible about my dad that you won't tell me about him?"

"I don't know who your father was. You know that."

Alex followed her into the kitchen. It wouldn't do any good

to argue with her. To plead and cajole. She had tried that. Nor would questions about her mother's family and past provide clues. All she knew was her mother's parents had disowned her when she'd gotten pregnant.

Alex snatched her purse off the table and slung it over her shoulder. "I have to go to work."

Her mother didn't respond. Alex crossed to the doorway, stopped and looked back at her. Something in the newspaper had caught her attention and she was gazing down at it as if she had already forgotten Alex was there.

What was the point of pushing? Of getting angry or wishing for something that would never happen?

The truth was, her mother didn't have the emotional wherewithal for an honest relationship.

"Goodbye, Mom."

Her mother looked up, her expression strange. "You're leaving?"

"Going to work."

She frowned slightly. Her bubble had popped, Alex realized. And she had begun her descent.

"All I've ever wanted to do was protect you."

"From what, Mom?"

But she'd already returned to the newspaper. Alex let herself out and crossed to her car. She slid inside and started it, only then looking back at the house. She half expected to find her mother standing at the window, watching her go. Instead, the windows were empty.

Empty. The way these visits always left her feeling. She pulled away from the curb, thinking again of her mother's words. *"All I've ever wanted to do was protect you."*

But from what? she wondered. From who?

Chapter Six

Alex was still asking herself those same questions as she called good night to her colleagues two days later. She exited the bar. Business had been slow, so she had clocked out a few minutes early. Located in the Mission district, Third Place was usually hopping weeknights until ten o'clock, when activity slowed considerably. Tonight had been a crawl; her feet and back ached from standing around doing nothing.

It'd given her too much time to think, as well. About her mother. Her illness and her secrets. And to worry.

As she neared her car, she saw Tim leaning against it, waiting for her. He always looked every inch the hip professor, from his shaggy threaded-with-silver blond hair to his Armani sweater and Ecco driving mocs.

Typical Tim. She had left him a message after leaving her mother's the other afternoon; instead of a call back, here he was at bedtime, tail wagging and puppy dog earnest.

She couldn't help but smile. Knowing exactly where she stood with him took the angst out of their relationship. For her, anyway. It also placed her in the driver's seat.

"Hey," she said as she neared him. "I thought you might have decided I was more trouble than I'm worth."

"Never." He kissed her cheek. Another woman's perfume, flowery and sweet, clung to him. "How was work?"

"Slow." She tucked her hair behind her ear. "One of those nights I had too much time to think."

"What's going on? You sounded pretty upset when you called."

"I needed someone to talk to."

"Your mother?"

"How'd you know?"

"Recognized your tone." He leaned forward, lowered his voice to the silky rumble she used to love. "What happened to us, Alex?"

"Where did *that* come from?"

"I miss you."

She placed her hand against his chest to keep him from moving closer. "Even if we forget that you couldn't keep your peter in your pants, we have nothing in common."

"Not true. We're both seekers. Both fascinated by the universal quest for meaning. What people will do to find it." He grinned. "And we were great together in bed."

"Not so great the other night."

"You were having head issues."

She winced at the way he casually tossed that out there. As if her "head issues" were a common occurrence, in the sack and otherwise. It struck a nerve—she lived in fear she had inherited her mother's mental illness, although at thirty it still hadn't manifested itself.

Was her "vision" the other night its first appearance?

"I know what you're thinking," he said softly. He covered her hand with his. "I didn't mean anything by that. You're not like her."

She searched his gaze. Should she tell him about her vision? Get his opinion, see if he could help her figure it out?

She opened her mouth to do that, but instead said, "The day I called, I'd stopped by to see her. She's not taking her meds and was in the middle of a manic episode."

"I'm sorry, Alex."

"Me, too. It's so frustrating." She heard helplessness in her voice and fought it. "Thanks for listening."

"You want to have a drink? My shoulder's available."

Alex was tempted, but suspected what that drink would lead to. And even though she knew she wouldn't find what she sought through sex, she wasn't that strong right now. "I don't think so, Tim. I'm back to work on my dissertation and keeping some late hours. I'm pretty tired."

"I could wake you up," he teased. "Plus, I'd like a chance to expunge my record."

She unlocked her car. "Sorry. Not happening."

"You know I still love you."

"Still not happening." She kissed him lightly on the mouth, slid into her vehicle, and drove away. When she reached the corner, Alex glanced in the rearview mirror and found he had already gone.

Probably into the bar in the hopes of convincing some other woman to give him the chance to prove himself, she thought. So much for love.

The light ahead turned red, and Alex eased to a stop. She dug her cell phone out of her purse and flipped it open. She had missed several calls and had a new message waiting.

All from her mother. The first had come in at 1:00 P.M., not that long after she had arrived at work. She'd left the voice mail a couple hours ago.

Alex punched in her password and her mother's voice came through the device.

"I have to talk to you, Alex. I have to—" She sounded horrible. Voice slurry, thick. With tears? Or from self-medication? Alex didn't know.

"I'll tell you everything. I promise . . . I—" Her mother drew in a shuddering breath. "I didn't mean for any of this to happen—I only wanted, I—"

The message clicked off. Had she hung up? Alex wondered, a catch in her chest. Or had the machine cut her off?

Either way, what had happened was obvious. The pendulum had swung back—mania had become depression.

At the blare of a horn behind her, Alex rolled through the intersection. She had to check on her, make certain she was all right.

Sighing, Alex turned onto Guerrero Street heading toward her mother's house.

Ten minutes later she braked in front of her mother's. The house was dark, not a sliver of light spilled from any of the windows. She climbed out of her car and hurried up the walk.

She let herself in. "Mother," she called. "It's Alex."

Only silence answered and she flipped on the light. Carnage greeted her. Her mother's beautiful canvases all destroyed. Some obliterated by paint, others scraped clean and a few slashed, as if in one final burst of despair or fury.

It hurt to look at them and she averted her gaze. The shades were all drawn tight and Alex wondered if she had even opened them to the day. It had rained earlier and she saw a puddle of water on the floor.

"Mom," she called again, heading up the curving stairs. "It's Alex."

She reached the second-floor landing and started for the master bedroom. She would find her in bed. Maybe sleeping. Maybe curled up under the covers, staring at nothing.

The glow from a streetlight fell across her mother's bed. She wasn't wrong, Alex saw. Her mother was there, lying on her back, blanket a jumble around her, as if she had been thrashing about.

Alex crossed to her. "Mom," she said softly, "are you awake?"

She didn't reply and Alex bent to straighten the blankets. Her hand knocked something to the floor. A pill vial, she realized, bending to retrieve it.

Seroquel. It was empty.

Her heart jumped to her throat. "Mom," she said, loudly this time. "Mom!"

Alex shook her. Her body was stiff. Her skin cold to the touch.

She shook her again, panicking. "No, no, no . . . you did not do this . . . Mom, talk to me. Wake up!" She caught her mother's hand, frantically pressed her fingers to the wrist, praying for even a flutter of a pulse.

Nothing. Nothing.

With a cry, she stumbled backward, fumbling for her phone. She found it, but dropped her purse, the contents spilling across the floor.

She punched in 911. "Hello? Oh my God . . . I think my mother . . . I can't get a pulse! I think she's . . . please, you've got to help!"

Chapter Seven

Alex's 911 call yielded a patrol unit and an investigator from the Medical Examiner's Office, who'd introduced himself as Investigator Hwang. Apparently, they couldn't take her word for it that her mother had killed herself.

The patrolman babysat her while the ME investigator looked at her mother. He explained that she had to stay put because the detective would need to ask her some questions.

Where did he think she would go? Alex wondered, struggling to keep hysteria at bay. Bar hopping? To visit friends?

"Is there someone you can call?" the officer asked gently. "A family member?"

"I have no . . . my mother was my only fam—"

Alex choked on the last. She saw the sympathy in his eyes. He was young, surname and coloring indicated Italian decent. Judging by his wedding band, he was married; he might even have a kid or two; and likely boasted an extended family that included aunts and uncles, cousins, nephews and nieces.

Young Officer Pagani couldn't understand what it felt like to be alone. To have no one. He couldn't understand it, but he could pity it.

"A friend then?" he offered. "A coworker?"

She nodded, retrieved her phone and dialed Tim's cell. It went directly to voice mail.

His cell was off. He must have found company for the night.

"Tim, it's me. I'm at Mom's. She's . . . oh my God, Tim, she killed herself. Call me when you get this, okay?"

She closed her phone and turned back to the patrolman. "Is it okay if I sit?"

"I suggest it. It may be awhile yet. Thirty minutes even."

He hit it on the button. Exactly thirty minutes later, the investigator, a trim Asian man with a no-nonsense demeanor, found her.

"Ms. Owens?"

"Owens was my maiden name. It's Clarkson now, though I've been thinking of changing it back." She was rambling but couldn't seem to stop herself. "I mean, since the divorce."

He nodded, took a small spiral notebook from his trench pocket. "I'm sorry for your loss."

"Thank you."

"Could you tell me how you happened to be here tonight?"

"My mother left a message on my cell. I was working. She sounded—"

"Where do you work?"

"I'm a bartender at Third Place. On Sixteenth Street."

"Nice place. How'd she sound?"

"Upset. She was crying. So I came to check on her."

Again he jotted a note. "Her message, what did she say?"

Alex struggled to think clearly. "She said she was sorry . . . that she was ready to tell me everything."

"Everything," he repeated. "What does that mean?"

How did she explain? Alex wondered. It didn't make sense, even to her. "Mom refused to talk about the past. My father. We argued about it—"

"When?"

"The last time I saw her. Though it wasn't the first time."

"When was that?"

"Day before yesterday."

"Monday?"

She thought a moment. "Yes. In the afternoon."

"And that's when you argued?"

Alex nodded. "She wasn't taking her meds. Another bone of contention."

"What kind of meds?"

"Valproate and Seroquel. She suffered from bipolar disorder."

"Why wasn't she taking her medication?"

"Didn't like the way it made her feel."

"I'll need the name of her prescribing physician."

"Dr. Connor. I can get her number."

"I'd appreciate it." He cleared his throat. "She didn't leave a note. Do you find that odd?"

Alex frowned. She hadn't even thought about a note until now. "I don't know, I . . . Do you think it means something?"

"Maybe. Maybe not. Statistically, overwhelmingly, suicide victims do."

"Oh." She frowned. "I just assumed . . . You don't think—"

Tim burst into the house. "Alex! I came as soon as I got your message!" She ran to meet him and he enfolded her in his arms. "Are you all right?"

She nodded and drew away. "This is Investigator Hwang. Investigator, my ex-husband, Tim Clarkson."

The two men greeted each other. "How well did you know the deceased, Mr. Clarkson?"

Her mother. The deceased. Alex curved her arms around her middle, struggling to hold it together.

"Dr. Clarkson," he corrected. "I'm a psych professor at State. And I knew her well enough to not be all that surprised she took her own life."

The investigator's eyebrows lifted ever so slightly. "Is that so?"

"She wasn't a stable woman. And she'd attempted it before. Twice."

Investigator Hwang looked at Alex as if for clarification. She gave it to him.

"Look, for those suffering bipolar disorder, depression isn't like what your everyday person experiences. The lows are really low, the darkness as black as you can imagine. It doesn't take that much to push them over the edge."

"Interesting choice of words, Professor." He turned his attention to Alex and motioned to the paintings. "What happened here?"

"She did this."

His eyebrows shot up in disbelief. "*She* destroyed her own artwork?"

Alex nodded. "She'd go on creative binges, then destroy what she created when she fell into despair."

The investigator noted the fact, then closed his notebook. "The state requires an autopsy on all unexplained deaths. This looks pretty cut and dried to me, but it's up to the pathologist to call it."

"An autopsy," she repeated, knees weak.

"The Medical Examiner's Office will notify you when her remains are released. In the meantime, if anything unexpected crops up, I'll call you. Again, Ms. Clarkson, I'm sorry for your loss."

Chapter Eight

Alex lay on her side on her old twin bed. She had slept little, instead had gone over and over in her head the previous days' sequences of events. Anguishing over what she could have done differently, if she could have stopped her mother.

Her mother. Her only family. She should have known. Should have sensed that this time was different.

Why hadn't she?

Alex choked back tears. Her eyes burned and her sides ached. How could she have any left? she wondered. She'd cried enough to last a lifetime.

From downstairs came the shrill scream of the phone. Again. Her mother didn't have an answering machine, didn't have caller ID, call waiting, or even a portable phone.

Just an old-fashioned, wall-mounted land line.

Sorry for your loss. The investigator had said it, so had Tim. No doubt over the next days and weeks countless others would utter those same words.

Alex balled her hands into fists, suddenly angry. She moved her gaze over her mother's half-finished paintings.

Incomplete. Abruptly ended. So much potential that had come to so little.

Oh, Mom . . . Why?

Alex dragged herself to a sitting position, then got unsteadily to her feet. She needed food. And coffee. Lots of coffee. Then she needed to get busy doing whatever it was a person in this position was supposed to be doing.

Notifying people, she supposed. But who? Alex pressed her fingers to her temple. Her mother had had few friends, if any. A handful of acquaintances. None she imagined who would even attend a service. Her own friends would, in an effort to show their support. She appreciated that, but why ask them?

Alex made her way carefully down the stairs, keeping her gaze averted as she passed her mother's ruined artworks. What of burial preparations? She had no clue what her mother's financial condition had been or if she had a will.

Alex reached the kitchen, and found it in disarray. She worked around the mess, making a pot of French press coffee, then grabbing a banana and a handful of grapes from the fruit bowl, acknowledging that they would soon go bad.

Monday's newspaper, she saw, was still spread out on the counter. She set her overfilled mug on it, spilling some of the brew. She grabbed a towel, wiped the mug, then blotted up the puddle of coffee. As she did, a headline jumped out at her:

Baby's Remains Found Amongst Old Vines

She gazed at the headline, a strange sensation moving over her. She scanned the brief piece—the remains of an unidentified infant boy had been unearthed in a Sonoma vineyard. A sad story, but what interested her was the fact her mother had circled the name and phone number of the detective investigating the case.

Alex frowned and reread the piece. Why'd her mother do that? She went over the possibilities. She knew the detective or his family? In her depressed emotional state, she had been moved to note the discovery? Or to follow up on it? Perhaps her mother had some knowledge of the case?

Could that be? She stared at the name: Detective Daniel Reed.

Without giving herself the opportunity to lose her nerve, she opened her cell phone and punched in the number.

The detective answered immediately. Only then did she realize she hadn't a clue what to say to the man.

"Detective Reed," he said again. "Can I help you?"

She cleared her throat. "Yes, hello. This may sound strange, but I found a newspaper story with your name and number circled." He was silent, waiting. "In my mother's house."

"I see," he said, though his tone suggested he didn't. "So, how can I help you, Ms—"

"Clarkson," she answered, feeling ridiculous. "Alex. I guess, I just wondered why she—" Alex bit the thought back. "Never mind. I'm sorry I've wasted your ti—"

He cut her off. "Not at all. What news story?"

"About the remains, the baby's, found in the vineyard."

"Is this Alexandra Owens?"

A wave of disbelief rolled over her. Her mouth went dry. "Yes?" she managed.

"Alex, it's Dan. Danny Reed. We played together as kids."

"Could you hold a moment?" Light-headed, she found a chair and sank onto it. She drew a deep, steadying breath. "You say we played together as children?"

"You don't remember me." He sounded disappointed. "It's not that surprising, I suppose. You were only five years old when you left."

"Left where?" she asked, heart pounding.

He was silent a moment, "Are you all right, Alex?"

"No, I . . . please, where was I living?"

"Sonoma."

She digested that bit of information. *Sonoma*. She had zero recollection of living there. She had visited a couple times, doing the whole wine tour thing. She'd found it charming. Beautiful. Otherwise, it hadn't made an impression on her.

Could it be? She cleared her throat again, excitement bubbling up in her. "How long did I live there? What about my dad? Is he still there?"

"I'm sorry, Alex, but your mother called me yesterday. She said she had information about the case. Are you with her now?"

Alex struggled to come to grips with what he was saying. "What? I'm sorry, I—"

"Your mother, Alex. Can I speak to her? I tried her back but never got an answer."

"My mother's dead. She killed herself sometime yesterday."

Chapter Nine

Reed had suggested to Alex they meet. She'd agreed, seeming relieved when he offered to come to her. Just over an hour later, he glanced at his in-dash GPS. The positioning system had him arriving at Patsy Owens's San Francisco address in six minutes. He had made good time.

Reed turned his thoughts to the meeting ahead. Patsy Owens had called him, claiming she had information about the baby's remains. Now Patsy was dead by her own hand. Alex had been in the dark not only about the call but her years in Sonoma as well.

What did it mean?

They'd made little progress so far on the identification. They were still awaiting word on the pacifier pattern and the diaper had proved no help—there simply hadn't been enough left for an identification.

His cell phone sounded. "Reed here."

"Investigator Hwang, SFME."

"Thanks for returning my call. I understand you investigated an apparent suicide last night. A Patricia Owens."

"That's right. Looks pretty clear-cut. Self-administered

overdose. Had a history of mood swings and two previous suicide attempts. My office is performing an autopsy tomorrow morning. Why the interest?"

"The woman called me yesterday afternoon, said she had information about a case I'm working."

"Sucks. Sorry I can't give you more."

"Call me if anything changes."

He agreed and hung up. Minutes later, Reed eased to a stop in front of Patsy's home. A slim, dark-haired woman waited on the front porch. She stood as he climbed out of the car; he saw she was dressed casually in blue jeans and a bulky white sweater.

She had grown into an attractive woman. In fact, she bore a striking resemblance to her mother. For a split second, it threw him. As if he had been transported back in time. He chalked it up to having refreshed his memory by looking at some old family photos before driving down.

He reached her and smiled. "Alexandra? Detective Daniel Reed. It's good to see you after all these years, though I wish the circumstances were better."

She silently studied him a moment, as if attempting to dredge up recognition. She frowned slightly. "Me, too, Detective. Come inside."

He followed her in. Beautiful old place, he thought, moving his gaze over the interior, taking in both the big picture and the details. Canvases everywhere. Photos on the mantel.

The place had a chaotic feel. It wouldn't be a comfortable place to live. Or grow up. He wondered if it had always been this way.

"Let's talk in the kitchen."

The kitchen was a sunny room. Less cluttered. A couple cups in the sink, plants in need of watering. A newspaper open on the counter.

She saw his gaze. "I left it where I found it."

He nodded and crossed to it. *The San Francisco Chronicle*: Bay Area/State News. Short piece. His name and numbered circled.

"I tried her back several times," he said, "it just rang."

"Mom didn't believe in answering machines. Can I get you anything? Water, coffee?"

"Nothing, thanks."

She poured herself a cup of coffee and carried it over to the café-style table. They sat, facing each other. "Thank you for coming," she said. "I have so many questions."

"Actually, that's my job." She smiled. He went on, "I'm sorry about your mom."

The pain was fresh; tears flooded her eyes. To her credit, they didn't spill over. "Thank you."

"I spoke with Investigator Hwang. He said your mother had a history of mood swings and had previously attempted to take her own life."

"Yes. She was . . . troubled. When you knew her, what was she like?"

"I was only ten."

"You must have some recollection of her."

He thought a moment. "She was kind. Gentle. She seemed happy."

The tears welled again, this time spilling over. She wiped impatiently at them. "You say I was five when we left Sonoma. Was I happy?"

"You seemed to be. You were a pistol, always into everything. A chatterbox. You used to drive Rachel crazy, the way you followed her around."

"Rachel?"

"Your stepsister, Alex." He said it gently, giving her a moment to digest the information, then leaned forward. "Alex, your mother called me the same day she took her life. She said she had information about the baby from the news story. Do you have any idea what that information may have been?"

A bitter sound slipped past her lips. "Actually, I was hoping you could tell me that."

He studied her a moment, looking for a trace of deception. "I think she was wondering if the baby we found was Dylan."

He saw her stiffen slightly. Saw the combination of fear and curiosity race into her eyes. "Dylan?" she asked, voice shaking.

In that moment, he wondered if she could be playing him, then rejected the thought. She really didn't know.

"Your brother," he said softly. "Dylan Sommer was your baby brother, Alex."

Chapter Ten

Nothing he could have said would have rocked her more. She simply stared at him, unable to find her voice.

"Actually, Dylan was your half brother. I'm sorry."

A half brother. She'd had a half brother and a family in Sonoma. How could she not remember? People couldn't just forget things like that, could they?

The detective was looking at her strangely, as if she was some sort of freak for not knowing these things. She didn't blame him; she felt like one.

"Tell me about him," she managed, voice small and choked.

"He was abducted from his bed. Your mom and Harlan had left you with his fifteen-year-old daughter."

"Rachel?"

He nodded. "Nobody knows for sure what happened. Someone entered the house and took Dylan. No ransom demand arrived, and he was never found. Your mother's marriage ended. She took you and left."

Alex clasped her hands together, imagining her mother's anguish. What would it be like to lose a child that way? To never know what happened, if he was alive or dead. If he had suffered and cried out for her.

"She never told you any of this?" he asked.

She shook her head. "Mother was always . . . secretive. I always wondered why. I always thought . . ." She let the words trail off.

He picked them up. "Always thought what?"

She met his gaze. "That she was hiding something. But I never imagined it was something like . . . this."

"And you have no recollection of your time in Sonoma or your brother?"

Alex shook her head again. How was it possible she had blocked it all out? "Do you have any photographs of him? Or any of my stepfamily?"

"My parents do. Harlan does." He cleared his throat. "I hate to ask, but could I have a look around? I'm hoping whatever your mom wanted to tell me didn't die with her."

Alex followed while he searched. They didn't speak, and truth be told, she was there in body only, her thoughts on the things he'd said, sorting through the way she felt about them.

"I'm sorry I couldn't be of any help," she said, when he had finished and come up empty-handed.

"Here's my card. If you think of anything, some comment your mother made, anything at all, call me."

"I will." She walked him to the door. "You'll let me know if that baby turns out to be my brother?"

"Of course." He held out a hand. "It was nice seeing you again, Alex."

She took it. "You, too, Dan."

"Call me Reed. Everybody does these days."

A moment later he was across the porch and down the front steps, heading to his car. She watched as he climbed in and drove away. For a long time after he had gone, she wandered the house, thoughts whirling.

Anger and betrayal rose up inside her. She'd had a brother. A stepfather and stepsister. Her mother had kept them from her. Why?

If only she'd picked up that last call. Her mother had been ready to tell her everything. From her own lips, with explanations.

Now, she would never know why.

Fury took her breath. She wanted to scream, strike out at someone or something, kick and wail. How could her mother have done this? This was *her* history, *her* family. Whatever had occured had happened to her as well.

Of course. She started to pace. Something missing, she'd always felt that way. As if she had an empty place inside her that she'd kept trying to fill up.

A place that had once held a brother she loved—and who had been stolen from her.

Literally. And figuratively.

How had her mother managed to keep his existence hidden from her all these years—

Hidden.

Photographs. Mementos, official records. Dylan had been her child, she wouldn't have destroyed all that remained of him. She couldn't have done it, even in her deepest despair.

Alex moved her gaze over the room. If she had kept a box of mementos, where would she have hidden it? Here in the house, no doubt. A place she could easily access, but Alex didn't frequent.

Or wasn't allowed.

Her mother's bedroom. Of course.

Alex ran up the stairs. Like the rest of the house, her mother's bedroom had become part art studio. She picked her way around drawings in progress, laid out on the floor, crossing to the dresser. Beginning with the top drawer, she rifled through them, tossing the contents into a heap on the floor.

Nada. Nothing.

Undeterred, Alex moved on to her mother's closet, then bathroom, the vanity drawers, tearing them apart. From there she moved from one room to another, until she had searched every drawer, closet and compartment.

Still she came up empty.

Her mother destroyed her art, why not all physical

remnants of her son? The thought planted and Alex stopped, heart racing. No. She refused to believe that. Somewhere in this house her mother had stashed a record of her son's short life.

The attic, she thought. The only place left.

She made her way there, pulled down the attic steps, then climbed them, cold air swirling around her as she ascended. When she reached the top, she yanked the cord attached to the single lightbulb.

Weak light illuminated a lifetime of stored stuff. Brown cardboard boxes, dozens of them, stacked one on top of the other. A cry rose in her throat. Where did she start? It would take her days to go through every box.

Whatever she had to do. One step, one box at a time.

She began at the front right. Her progress was slow; between the cold and the dust, her nose began to run. It'd be smart to go grab a coat and gloves, but she refused to stop even for the few minutes that would take.

Her gaze fell on a large steamer trunk, the kind people had used in the 1800s for cross-Atlantic travel. It was locked, she saw. Secured with a combination lock, the kind she had used on her high school locker.

Heart thundering, she made her way to the trunk. She gazed down at the only thing between her and its contents.

She tried a couple obvious combinations: her mother's birthday, her own birthday, consecutive numbers. When those didn't work, she looked around for something to break it open with.

Her gaze landed on an aluminum baseball bat propped up in the corner. Alex retrieved it, lifted and swung. On the third whack, the lock gave. She removed it, released the hasp and opened the trunk.

Her breath caught. Inside, her mother had carefully stored photographs and letters, stuffed animals and baby toys. A christening gown, she saw. Several unbearably small, blue outfits. A binky. Booties.

Alex caressed each item, rubbing the soft fabric between her fingers, then against her cheek. She buried her face in a

Teddy bear's fuzzy belly and breathed deeply. Was it her imagination or did it still smell of baby powder and formula?

Her chest tightened and tears stung her eyes. A brother— *her* brother. One day she had awakened and he was gone. How had she processed it? She must have been frightened and confused.

Alex wiped the tears from her cheeks and gently laid the bear back in its makeshift bed. She chose a small photo album next, opened it and stared transfixed at the first photograph.

Her mother. Young and lovely. Smiling—no, beaming— for the camera, a baby cradled in her arms. And beside her, gazing up in adoration, was her three- or four-year-old self.

She'd never seen her mother happy, Alex realized. Manic, yes. But never like this—glowing with joy.

What part had the loss of her child played in the woman her mother had become? What part had it played in her illness? Her violent mood swings?

With a sense of desperation, Alex flipped through the album, soaking in the images of people she didn't know, studying their faces, expressions, body language. Everything. Longing to remember.

From downstairs came the sound of the front door slamming. She swung toward the stairs. "Hello?" she called.

"Alex? Where are you?"

"Tim! I'm up here! In the attic."

Moments later he appeared at the top of the stairs. "Alex? What the hell—"

"I had a brother," she said, voice shaking. "A stepsister, too. Come look."

Chapter Eleven

Together they carried the trunk from the attic to the living room. They sat on the floor, and words tumbling one over the other, Alex told him about finding the news story, the detective's name and number being circled, calling the number and finally about the detective's visit.

When she'd finished, she held out the photo album, open to the picture of her mother holding Dylan, Alex at her side.

For long moments he studied the photo, then lifted his gaze to hers. "Unbelievable. It makes me wonder what else she was hiding."

"What else *could* she be hiding? My God, Tim." Alex tucked her hair behind her ear and leaned toward him. "This is it. What I always felt was missing. I thought it was not knowing my dad. Or my mother's emotional distance. But it was the brother who was taken from me."

"Literally missing." Tim nodded. "It makes sense, from a psychological standpoint." He flipped through the photo album, expression thoughtful. "The creation of art is a type of birthing process. The destruction of that very personal creation a form of self-hatred."

"You think her cycle of painting, then obliterating what she'd created was tied to the loss of her son?"

"I think it makes sense." He stopped on a photo and gazed intently at the image. "She represses her emotions—her anger, guilt and despair. But repressed emotions have a way of erupting, coming out sideways, directed at something or someone else. This is classic avoidant coping strategy."

"Guilt?" Alex said, frowning. "I understand anger and despair, but why would she—"

"Feel responsible? Come on, Alex, put yourself in her shoes. A mother's supposed to protect her children, keep them from harm's way. A mother's instinct is 'supposed' to kick in, alert her to danger. And what did she do? She left her children alone. And the unthinkable happened."

Alex rubbed her arms, cold. "How could I have forgotten, Tim? I was five years old. I had a baby brother, then I didn't. Surely I would have remembered him?"

He caught her hands and rubbed them between his. "Your mother took you away from all the people who knew Dylan. She packed away all physical reminders of him. Children are sponges. They pick up on everything. You quickly learned that asking about your brother was met with disapproval. Maybe even tears. Or a spanking. Perhaps when you asked about him, she denied his existence."

He squeezed her hands, then released them. "You complied. You simply 'forgot.' Truth is, it probably didn't even take that long."

Alex blinked against tears. "Okay, I get all that. But why can't I remember now that I—"

She bit the last back. *A faceless baby, screaming.*

She did remember.

"Oh my God, Tim. It makes sense now."

"What does, hon?"

"The other night, when we were in bed together, I had this weird vision. It's what got me so freaked out. In it there was a faceless baby. The baby was screaming."

"Textbook symbolism, Alex. The baby has no face, therefore no identity. Your subconscious was screaming at you to remember."

Her tears spilled over and he scooted to her side and wrapped an arm around her. She buried her face in the crook of his neck.

He allowed her to cry, saying nothing.

After a time, her tears slowed, then stopped. "It's so horrible," she whispered. "All of it. What happened to my brother. My mother denying his existence. What that denial did to both of us. How could she not have seen how destructive it was?"

"If it helps, no, she probably didn't see how destructive it was. She was trying to spare you more pain and ease her own."

They fell silent. She leaned against him, comforted by his steady breathing and the rhythmic beat of his heart. When he shifted away from her, she was cold and drew her knees to her chest and hugged them.

"How old was your brother when he was abducted?" He picked up the photo album and thumbed through it.

"I don't know. I didn't think to ask."

"How old were you when your mom married this guy?"

Again, she didn't know. She frowned. "Why?"

He tapped one of the photos. "This man, standing beside your mother, was this her husband?"

"I don't know. I found these pictures after the detective left. But my guess is yes."

"You look like him, Alex."

He handed her the album. Alex studied the photo, heart in her throat. He was right. She *did* resemble him. What was it? She cocked her head. The chin. The broad forehead and widely spaced eyes.

Could he be her father? she wondered. Was it so far-fetched? If she'd been an infant when they married . . .

But why would he claim Dylan and not her? His reputation, maybe? A previous marriage that hadn't yet officially ended?

"Seems there are still a lot of questions you need answered."

"An understatement."

"Have you eaten? We could go grab a bite?"

She hadn't. All day, she realized. But she wanted to stay and go through the rest of the things in the trunk. She told him so.

"I could pick up some Chinese? Or a pizza? Unless you'd rather be alone?"

"No, stay. If you have the time."

He said he did and they ordered pizza from a local place that specialized in New York–style, thin crust pies. While he went to pick up their food and a bottle of wine, Alex sifted through the remaining contents of the trunk.

At the very bottom, nestled in the folds of a baby blanket, Alex found a ring. She held it to the light. Unusual, lovely and delicate, it consisted of twisting strands of gold. Like writhing snakes.

Or grapevines, she realized, as she ran her finger over a small cluster of petite rubies.

"Got it!" Tim called as he let himself into the house a half an hour later. "Picked up a really nice bottle of zin. Dry Creek Valley old vine."

"Perfect." She slid the ring onto her pinky finger and got to her feet. "I'm starving."

They ate in the kitchen over the pizza box, not bothering with plates but drinking from Riedel crystal, glasses specifically crafted to enhance an individual wine's bouquet and flavor.

This wine, with its bold flavor and high alcohol content, instantly buoyed her with a false burst of energy and well-being. The tension flowed out of her and she held out her glass for a refill.

"Where'd that come from?" he asked, indicating the ring.

She glanced at her hand. "I found it in the trunk."

"Different. May I see it?" She slipped it off and handed it to him. He turned it over in his fingers, then held it up to the light. "Did you see? It has an inscription."

"I didn't." She took it from him, squinting to read it. "BOV—1984. I wonder what BOV stands for?"

"Initials maybe?"

"Not my mother's. Maybe her husband's? Maybe a gift from him?"

"Initials of the person who gave it to her? That'd be different."

"Maybe it's an acronym?"

"Works for me." He downed the rest of his wine, then poured the last of the bottle in his glass. He held up the empty bottle. "That's it! Bottle of vino, 1984. Must have been a really good year."

"I hope you're not planning to drive home."

"Is that an invitation?"

"An observation."

He leaned toward her, a familar gleam in his eyes. "What do you think, Alex?"

"That I have a lot of questions I still need answered," she said, being deliberatively obtuse. "That maybe I should drive to Sonoma and see if I can get some answers."

"Not that. What do you think about tonight?" He reached across the counter and caught her hand. "Maybe I should stay?"

"Please tell me you are not turning this into a booty call."

"Give me some credit, Alex. I'm worried about you. I'm thinking you shouldn't be alone."

"Isn't that sweet?" She leaned across the pizza box and kissed his cheek. "It's total bullshit, but sweet."

"It's not. I care about you. I am worried. But if we happened to end up in the sack having wild, monkey sex, I wouldn't complain."

"You're a pig. You know that?"

"I'm a guy, what do you expect? Besides, my motor's still running from the other night. You left me hangin'."

"Poor baby." She grabbed her purse and dug out her wallet and twenty bucks. "This should cover my part of the pizza and wine."

He gazed at the money a moment, then lifted his gaze to hers. "That's a no, then?"

"It's a no."

He pocketed the twenty. "How about I check on you to-morrow?"

"Don't bother. I'm planning a trip to wine country."

Chapter Twelve

Friday, February 19
8:10 A.M.

Reed filed into the interview room. He had arranged this early meeting with Tanner and Cal to go over what he'd learned from his visit with Alexandra Clarkson.

Tanner, he saw, had beat him there. She looked tired. "Hey, Babs. Bad night?"

"Long. Cakebread Cellars was having a tasting. My ex was there. Me, my ex and free wine are an explosive combination."

"Fireworks?"

"Mmm." She yawned and curved her hands around her venti-sized coffee. "But not necessarily the kind you're thinking of."

Before he could ask what kind she figured that was, Cal arrived. He carried a box from Tan's Donuts.

"Sustenance," she said. "Thank you, Jesus."

Cal grinned. "I've been called a lot of things, but never Lord and Savior."

"She had a bad night," Reed said. He opened the bakery box and peered inside. "What'd you get?"

"Glazed, filled, chocolate and plain."

Tanner frowned. "No crullers?"

"Nope."

"No bear claws?"

"Nope. Glazed, filled, chocolate and plain. If you'd wanted something else, you should've stopped yourself."

"Kiss my ass, Cal."

"Only if you kiss mine first."

Reed polished off a pastry and grinned. "Okay, kids, how about we talk about my interview with Patsy Owens's daughter?"

"I'd rather Tanner here kiss my ass, but—"

"But," she jumped in, "knowing that'll *never* happen, did Alexandra Owens have anything interesting to offer?"

"Name's Clarkson now. The most interesting thing about the interview was what she *didn't* have to offer. Clarkson has no memory of her brother or her years in Sonoma."

"Bullshit," Tanner offered, wiping a glob of raspberry filling from her mouth. "Her mother—"

"Wiped their lives of all evidence of their time in Sonoma, and Dylan."

"Okay, that's just weird." Cal dunked a chunk of donut in his latte. "You believed her?"

"I did."

"How old was she when Dylan disappeared?"

"Five."

Tanner shook her head. "I remember my fifth birthday party and she forgot her *brother*? How could that be?"

"I wondered that myself." Reed eyed the pastries, then went for a second. "I got in touch with the on-call shrink. He thought it could be a form of traumatic memory loss. Like what's seen in post-traumatic stress disorder and repressed memory."

Cal jumped in. "I worked a case a couple years ago that involved PTSD. The one where the kid witnessed his brother being shot to death right in front of their house. He was there, at the scene. Couldn't recall what happened."

"Exactly. Shrink said Clarkson's memory loss would have been aided by her young age and her mother's influence. Obviously, the former Patsy Sommer wanted her daughter to forget."

Tanner drained her coffee. "Sorry, but that's really fucked up."

"No joke." Reed crumpled his napkin, then sent it sailing toward the trash. "So here's what we have. Patsy sees the article about Baby Doe. She wonders if it's Dylan and calls me. Her call to me came in at three P.M. She leaves a message. Sometime later that day, she ingests a bottle of pills."

Tanner leaned forward. "Why not wait for you to return her call?"

Cal stepped in. "Consider this. Patsy *knows* it's Dylan. She calls you to confess. She can't reach you, and overwhelmed with guilt, kills herself."

"Are we certain she killed herself?" Tanner asked. "What about a note?"

"No note. But I spoke with the SFME." Reed opened his spiral. "An investigator Hwang. He called it a clear case of suicide. In addition, she had a history of depression and had attempted suicide twice before."

Tanner finished off her donut, then licked the sugar from her fingers. "Is it that surprising? Something like that happened to my kid, I'm not sure I wouldn't go nuts."

"Autopsy's happening today, pathologist will call it then."

"Got word back on the pacifier," Cal offered. "That particular pattern was available from 1982 to 1986."

Reed nodded. "It could have belonged to Dylan Sommer. What about the wine crate?"

"Trying to piece together what's left." Tanner slid a manila folder across the table. "Robb's report. Long bone measurements indicate the child was no more than six months old."

Reed skimmed the report. Another marker that pointed toward Baby Doe being Dylan Sommer. "Remains on their way to the state lab?"

Tanner said they were, then added, "Has it occurred to you that big sister's traumatic memory loss occurred because she saw or heard something that night?"

It had. The problem would be recovering those memories. If they even existed.

"I read the files," he said. "She was questioned at the time. By the Sheriff's Department, the FBI and a social worker. She was scared and confused, but seemed well adjusted. None of the interviewers felt she had seen anything she wasn't sharing."

Before either could respond, his cell phone buzzed. "Reed," he answered.

"Detective, a woman is here to see you. One Alex Clarkson. Says it's about Baby Doe."

"I'll be right down." He ended the call and looked at his colleagues. "Be available. This may get interesting."

"What's up?" Tanner asked.

"Big sister's downstairs."

Chapter Thirteen

Friday, February 19
9:10 A.M.

Alex paced while she waited for the detective to come and collect her. She'd slept little the night before. But instead of tired, she was wired. She couldn't stop thinking about the things she had learned from him or the confirmation of them she had gotten from the items in the trunk.

A brother. She'd had a brother. And a stepfamily. Years of her life she had no recollection of.

She wanted to know why.

She had brought the photo album with her. As proof. And in the hopes Reed, or someone else in Sonoma, could put names to faces in the pictures.

She turned to find him crossing the lobby toward her. "Alex," he said when he reached her, "is everything all right?"

"Yes, fine." She cleared her throat. "I had some questions . . . I hope just showing up like this isn't a problem."

"Not at all. Can I get you some coffee? Or a soft drink?"

"No, thanks. I've been up most of the night, caffeine's the last thing I need."

He cocked an eyebrow, expression bemused.

"That sounds a bit counterintuitive, doesn't it? What I meant is, I've been drinking coffee all night. Another cup and I might jump out of my skin."

"That'd be a sight." One corner of his mouth lifted. "Let's not do that, then."

He was a cop. A detective. Yet he seemed so laid-back. Sort of aw-shucks, with an edge. Could he really be so unassuming, or was it an act? Some sort of cop schtick, meant to lull her into complacency?

"I found some photos," she said. "I hoped you would look at them, help me put some names to faces."

"I'll be happy to try. Let's go up to my office."

His office consisted of a cubicle in the Violent Crimes Investigations unit. He moved a stack of folders from a chair so she could sit, then took a seat himself. The other detectives, busy with their own cases, hardly glanced their way.

"You say you found some photographs?"

"Yes. I went searching. I found them in a locked trunk, in the attic." Alex realized her palms were sweating, rubbed them on her thighs, then retrieved the photo album from her tote bag. She opened it to the first photo and laid it on the desk so they could both see it. "That's my mother," she said. "Me by her side. I presume that's Dylan in her arms?"

"I would think so. And that"—he tapped the man standing beside her mother—"is Harlan Sommer."

"My stepfather?"

When he nodded, she studied the image. He wasn't a tall man—only a couple inches taller than her mother—but was powerfully built. She wouldn't describe him as handsome, but even in the photograph he exuded a commanding presence. She could see why her mother had been attracted to him.

She lifted her gaze to Reed's. "How old was I when my mother married him?"

"I remember you were young, but not an infant."

Not an infant. "Was I walking yet? Talking?"

He lifted his shoulders. "Sorry."

"And when my mother took me away? How old was I then?"

"Five or so."

"And Dylan? How old when he disappeared?"

"Not quite six months. What are you getting at here, Alex?"

"Just trying to fill in the blanks. Create a time line."

"Have you remembered anything? Since your memory's been jogged?"

Alex thought of her strange vision, which had occurred before all this, and shook her head. "No, nothing."

"You hesitated, Alex."

"Did I?"

"Yes." He searched her gaze. "You're certain?"

"Absolutely. If I do, believe me, you'll be the first to know." She flipped forward several pages in the album, stopping on a big group shot. "How about these people?"

Reed studied the image. "I'm not certain of everyone, but that's my mom and dad." He tapped the photo. "And this is Harlan's brother, Treven. His wife. May I?" he asked, indicating the album.

She said yes and he flipped through it, stopping when he recognized someone to point out, including himself. "That's me. And your stepsister, Rachel." He turned to a group shot of children, all outfitted in their Easter finery—girls in dresses and bonnets, boys in suits and ties. The younger children clutched the handles of baskets.

"The Sommer egg hunts," he murmured, lips curving into a smile. "God, how we kids loved them. There you are," he said. "You're holding Dylan."

She was, her Easter basket on the ground beside her. She looked so proud of herself, Alex thought. So happy.

His smile faded. "That was the last egg hunt. After Dylan disappeared, they stopped them."

A knot formed in her throat; she swallowed past it. "A lot of the photos seem to have been taken in the same place. Any idea where?"

"Sure. The winery."

"Winery?"

"The Sommer Family Winery. Back then, Harlan ran it. Sommer wines are well known in oenophile circles."

"He doesn't run it anymore?"

"His brother does. Took over after—"

"Dylan disappeared," she guessed.

"Yes." He glanced at his watch. "The trunk, were there any other mementos of your brother?"

"Yes." She looked away, then back, sudden tears stinging her eyes. "A Teddy bear and a christening gown. A couple outfits. Booties. A pacifier."

He looked up from his notes. "Did you say a pacifier?" She nodded. "Do you have it with you?"

"No. It's at my mom's."

"Hold a moment." He unclipped his phone and dialed. "Tanner? It's Reed. Do we have a photo of the pacifier? Great. I've got Alexandra Clarkson here, I'm going to bring her down to take a look at it."

He ended the call, reholstered his phone and met her gaze. "Think you might be able to recognize that pacifier? We found one with the remains."

"I might, yeah."

"Do you mind taking a look?"

Instead of answering, she made a request of her own. "I'd like to contact my stepfamily."

He gazed at her, eyes narrowed. "That's an old, nasty wound. You might not get the reception you're hoping for."

"I'm willing to take that chance."

He studied her a moment before replying. "I'm not sure they will. Look—" he spread his hands. "They're a prominent family, they suffered a horrible tragedy and are wary of strangers."

"I'm not a stranger. I'm family."

"It's been twenty-five years, Alex. You were a part of the family only for a couple years, ones that ended badly."

He said it gently, but it rankled anyway. She looked him straight in the eyes. "I want to know why my mother hid them from me. I want to know about my years here. And since she's dead, I have nowhere else to turn for answers."

"These people are my friends. Good friends of my family. They're nice people who had something really awful happen to them."

"And I didn't?"

"All I'm saying is, let me speak with Harlan first. Prepare him for seeing you. Surprising him might get you exactly what you don't want."

"Which is?"

"Shut out. I can't make any of them talk to you, Alex."

She hadn't considered her stepfamily might refuse to meet with her. She had imagined a tearful reunion, complete with an invitation back into the fold.

But real life rarely resembled the stuff of daydreams.

"Maybe there's a good reason she kept all this from you. Have you thought about that?"

"What exactly are you saying?"

"Do you know anything about traumatic memory loss?"

"A little. Why?"

"I'm wondering if you saw something the night Dylan disappeared. Something more than you told the police at the time."

Alex frowned, a chill moving over her. "I doubt that."

"Why?"

"I just do. Surely I was questioned. Someone would have picked up on it?"

"I've interviewed young kids before, it's a whole different ball game in terms of their reactions to traumatic events. They can easily confuse fantasy and reality, truth and fiction. I had a six-year-old witness confuse a crime she witnessed with a TV show."

"I've forgotten because I was so young," she said, an edge in her voice. "Because my mother encouraged it by separating me from everyone who knew him and everything that would remind me of him."

At his pitying expression she stiffened her spine. "How much do you remember from the fifth year of your life?"

"Quite a lot, actually. Certainly my family members."

"With the help of being reminded of them every day. Take that away, would *you* remember?"

"You've got a point." He stood. "Let's go take a look at the photo, then I'll call Harlan Sommer and try to set up a meeting for you as soon as possible."

Chapter Fourteen

True to his promise, Reed had called Harlan Sommer but had been unable to reach him directly. He'd left a message, then promised to call Alex on her cell phone the moment he heard back. Having learned that the Sonoma County Library was located in Santa Rosa, not five minutes from the Sheriff's Department, she had decided to pass the time until she heard back from Reed researching news stories from the year her brother disappeared.

She parked her Prius, climbed out and started across the parking lot. The detectives had shown her a photograph of a pacifier. Alex couldn't get the image out of her head—stained from being in the ground, awash in God only knew what.

She didn't want to know the specifics, the hows and whys of chemical reactions and decomposition. She had only to look at the photo and compare it to the pacifier in her possession and see the horrific.

The two were identical. Same shape, color, design. Reed and his colleagues had been excited about that, though they had kept it low-key.

The library was a single-story brick building. She entered and crossed to the information desk. The woman manning it had shoulder-length gray hair and a dusting of freckles across her weathered face. She had the look of someone who had decided going natural beat the hell out of Botox, fillers and serums.

"Good morning," Alex said. "Could you direct me to the microfilm?"

The woman looked up and smiled. "Certainly. I'll get you set up." She came around the desk. "What are you look-ing for?"

Alex fell in step with her. "Newspaper stories from 1985. Local papers."

"We have that. Any stories in particular?" she asked. "I've lived here all my life."

"The disappearance of Dylan Sommer."

Her steps faltered. She made a sound, soft and distressed. "A terrible thing. Awful. Arguably the worst crime ever in this valley."

"Did you know the family?"

The librarian stopped. Her expression changed from open and friendly to wary. "May I ask why you're interested in the case?"

Alex hadn't anticipated this. In the big city, librarians didn't care what you read, researched, or why.

She hesitated a moment, then said, "I'm Patsy Sommer's daughter. Dylan's sister."

The woman's eyes widened. "Little Alexandra! My God, look at you . . . all grown up. Patsy and I were friends."

"You knew my mom?"

"We were really close in our young, wild days. If she ever talked about Rita Welsh, that's me." She shook her head. "You can't imagine the trouble we got into."

Rita shifted her gaze over Alex's shoulder. "Is she here with you? I'd love to see her."

"No, she passed away recently."

"Oh, no." Rita hugged her. "I'm so sorry."

Alex saw tears in her eyes and caught her hands, suddenly excited. "Rita, do you have time to talk to me?"

"Now?"

"Yes. I'd be so grateful."

Rita glanced at her watch, then back at the information desk. "It's early for my break, but it should be fine. I'll let my assistant know."

A short time later, they sat across from each other in the employee break room. Unable to contain her eagerness, Alex leaned toward her. "When did you and my mother meet?"

"We were barely twenty-one. Both single." Her eyes sparkled. "I was attractive back then. And despite my librarian image, wild as a billy goat.

"We were both working the tasting room at Robert Mondavi. It was in '78 or '79. Oh, the parties Magrit used to host. They were incredible. Lavish beyond anything the valley had ever seen before."

"Mom worked in a tasting room?"

"She didn't tell you? I'm surprised." Rita sighed. "That's where she met your father."

Alex's heart skipped a beat. "You knew my father?"

She shook her head. "All I really knew is she met him at one of the parties. She wouldn't tell me his name."

Alex's disappointment was so acute she could taste it.

"Little by little she stopped going out with our group, stopped partying. She spent all her time with him—or sitting home waiting for him. Next thing we knew, she was pregnant."

"You must have had some clue who he was." Alex winced at the desperation in her tone. "You must have speculated about his identity."

Alex's urgency wasn't lost on the librarian. "We did, believe me. He had money, we were certain of that. When she began to show, she quit Robert Mondavi and he supported her. Put her up in an apartment."

"He must have been married," Alex murmured, as much to herself as the other woman.

"That's what we figured. We wondered, too, if he was a public figure, afraid of a scandal. Or the cost of a divorce."

Alex's upset must have shown because the woman reached across the table and squeezed her hand. "The affair ended after you were born. She was brokenhearted. But truthfully, I thought it was for the best. That's no way to live. She deserved a man who would honor her by making her his wife."

"And she found him," Alex murmured, thinking of her mother's obvious joy in the photos from the album.

"Yes." Rita checked her watch, then continued. "She went to work in the Sommer Family Winery's tasting room. That's where she met Harlan.

"He was an important man here in Sonoma and their courtship was quite public. I used to babysit for you sometimes, so they could go out. It was like watching her come back to life, and I was so happy for her."

"Then he proposed? Did they have a big wedding or—"

"They ran off to Vegas." She laughed, the sound girlish. "It was the talk of the valley."

"How old was I then?"

"A year, I think. Just past."

"And he was good to me?"

Rita looked surprised. "He doted on you. In fact, if I hadn't known the whole story, I would have thought you were his own."

Alex recalled the photo from the album and Tim's comment about how much she had looked like the man pictured. That man had been Harlan Sommer.

She tucked that away for later. "What happened to them after Dylan disappeared? Why'd they break up?"

"Broken hearts. Too much pain between them. Too much anger."

Alex remembered what Tim had told her about her mother's feelings, the guilt she had probably suffered at having left her children alone that night. "He couldn't forgive her, could he?"

Rita looked surprised. "She couldn't forgive him. He insisted they go out that night. He promised her you and Dylan would be fine with Rachel."

This time, Alex knew, she was the one who looked surprised. Which was it? she wondered. Guilt or anger?

Her phone vibrated; she saw it was Reed, excused herself and answered.

"I spoke with Harlan," he said. "He can meet with us this afternoon, after the winery closes at four. I'll pick you up."

"Where?"

"Sonoma town square. In front of the girl & the fig."

She ended the call and found the librarian staring at her hand, her expression odd. "What?" she asked.

"Your ring. It was your mother's, wasn't it?"

"It was." Alex glanced at it, then back at Rita. "Do you happen to know where she got it?"

"I don't know. Sorry."

An awkward silence fell between them and Alex sensed that Rita wasn't telling the truth. She leaned toward her. "Was my mother happy, Rita? Before Dylan disappeared?"

"Yes. Very happy."

"Did she suffer from depression or any other emotional disorder? Anything like that?"

"Patsy? Goodness, not that I ever saw." Rita shook her head, as if for emphasis. "She was down sometimes, like we all are. But nothing that seemed . . . *clinical.*"

"How old was I when she became pregnant with my brother?"

"Three, three and a half." She glanced at her watch. "I'm sorry, but I've already been away from my desk too long."

She stood. Alex followed her to her feet. "Thank you so much for taking the time to talk to me, Rita. My mother didn't talk about the past."

"Too painful, I suppose." She sighed. "People change as they age. Especially when they've suffered horrible losses. Come, I'll get you set up with the microfilm."

They exited the break room. The readers' film files were located on the far north wall. Rita quickly loaded the *Press Democrat* reels for her, then gave her a hug. "I'm so glad you came in today. I've thought of you and your mother so often over the years. If you want to talk again, just call me. Here or at home, anytime."

She jotted her name and number on a slip of paper and handed it to Alex. "Anytime," she repeated.

Alex thanked her again, then, thinking of a last question, stopped her at the door. "Harlan Sommer's first marriage, when did they divorce?"

"They didn't," she said softly. "She died in a tragic accident at the winery."

Chapter Fifteen

Hours later, eyes burning and head throbbing, Alex still sat at the microfilm reader. She had begun her search with Dylan from his birth and christening to his abduction. Story after story repeated the same facts: he had been stolen from his bed; the expected ransom note that never came, the family's despair and public pleas for his safe return.

The stories had been devastating to read. The accompanying photographs had broken her heart.

When she simply couldn't take any more, Alex had turned her attention to Harlan's first wife, Susan. The accident that killed her had been both tragic *and* gruesome. During a process called punching down, she had been overcome by the fermenting wine's high CO_2 content, tumbled into the tank and drowned.

She hadn't been wearing the safety harness required by CALOSHA of all persons working on the catwalks above the tanks. Her brother-in-law and another winery worker had seen it happen and rushed to save her, but it was too late.

Exactly nine months after that had come the first local news blip about her mother and Harlan.

Alex sat back and rubbed her temple. It seemed odd to her. Nine months seemed a short time to mourn a wife and the mother of your child. How could the man suddenly appear, all smiles, with her mother on his arm?

Alex backtracked. Read the gossip columns and society news, looking for a hint of marital problems between Harlan and Susan. Even the whiff of a rumor of an affair. She found none. Indeed, in each of the published photos they looked happy.

A happy family. The way the photos with her mother all looked.

The Sommer family's story read like a script for a made-for-TV tearjerker. They had suffered so much tragedy, it was as if a dark cloud hung over them, beginning with Harlan's father's generation. Accidents. Unexpected deaths. Broken marriages.

A kidnapped child.

Alex realized she was trembling. She glanced at her watch, shocked to realize how late it was. She collected the copies she had purchased, a stack over an inch thick, and stood.

What did it all mean? she wondered, sliding the copies into her tote. Nothing? Everything? Was this why her mother had stripped these years from their lives? To outrun the cloud of tragedy?

But she hadn't outrun it, had she? She had dragged it along with her.

Alex hurried toward the exit. As she passed the information desk, she glanced that way. Rita was on the phone. When she saw Alex's glance, she quickly turned away, as if she didn't want Alex to see her.

Frowning at the thought, Alex stepped out into the brilliant day, squinting against the light. She rummaged for her sunglasses, found them and slipped them on.

Guided by her GPS, Alex made it to the Sonoma town square and the girl & the fig—wolfing down a sandwich on the way—arriving only a few minutes late.

Reed was waiting for her, leaning against the front fender of his vehicle, arms folded across his chest, face lifted slightly

to the sun. He might've been sleeping. Cat quiet, she thought.
Absolutely still with the ability to pounce without warning.

The sunlight caught the gold and red highlights in his
chestnut-colored hair and she was suddenly struck by how
ruggedly good-looking he was. She wondered how she had
missed that before.

Alex parked beside him and climbed out. "Sorry. I lost
track of time."

"No problem." He straightened. "Sightseeing?"

"Researching. Would you believe, I met someone who was
a good friend of my mother's?"

"Yeah, I would. It's a small world around here." They both
climbed into his car. "Who?" he asked, after they had buckled
their seat belts.

"Rita Welsh. A librarian at the main branch."

He backed out of the spot. "Learn anything interesting?"

"Several things. She said my mother was happy. And that
Harlan doted on me."

"He did." Reed flashed her a smile. "But you were pretty
darn adorable."

She felt herself flush, but didn't know if it was his smile or
the comment that caused it. "She didn't know who my father
was. Mom was very secretive. She met him at a Robert Mondavi party. She worked there, in the tasting room."

"Why so secretive, do you think?"

"My guess, he was married. Maybe in the public eye as
well."

"A classic story," he murmured.

She angled in her seat so she could clearly see his face.
"Rita told me that Harlan's first wife died in an accident."

"That's true."

When he didn't offer anything else, she frowned. "She
drowned in a wine vat."

"Asphyxiated, yes. What are you getting at, Alex?"

Did she just come out with it? Tell him she wondered if
Harlan Sommer was her dad? Or mention the fact the man had
gone from "happily married" to madly in love with her mother
pretty damn quickly?

Instead, she shrugged. "It seems the Sommer family's had more than their share of tragedy."

He looked at her oddly. "They have. But I don't think I'd bring that up when you meet them."

"I'm not a complete idiot."

"I don't think you are, Alex. Far from it."

They fell silent. She gazed out the window. Under different circumstances, she would have marveled at the natural beauty before her. The eucalyptus, madrone and oak trees. Rolling hills of dormant vineyards. The narrow, serpentine road, spiraling upward.

Circumstances didn't get much more different than these, she acknowledged, chest tightening. In a matter of minutes she was going to meet the stepfather two days ago she hadn't even known she had. In fact, these circumstances were so far out of her frame of reference, she had no idea what to expect.

Would he like her? she wondered. Would he look at her and see the little girl she had been? Or had he forgotten everything about that girl? Did it really matter to her either way?

Could Harlan Sommer be her father?

She cleared her throat and folded her hands in her lap. "What did he say when you told him I wanted to meet him?"

"Harlan? He agreed. Isn't that enough?"

"That excited, huh?"

"Can you blame him, Alex?" He glanced quickly at her, then back at the road. "It's been a long time. We're talking some pretty painful territory."

She was a physical connection to the loss of his son and the end of his marriage. No doubt he'd have preferred never to see her again. It hurt, but how would she have felt on his side of the situation? "I appreciate him doing the right thing."

"What if it's not?"

He asked the question in such a matter-of-fact way, she thought she had misheard him. "Excuse me?"

"One person's blessing is another's curse."

"Maybe you should have become a philosopher instead of a cop?"

"Maybe so." His mouth turned into a sheepish grin as he

navigated the narrow road. "Think about it this way. Refusing to allow the past to be dredged up by refusing to see you would've been a hell of a lot easier. Harlan's not an 'easy way' kind of guy."

"He let my mother go. He let me go."

"Maybe he didn't have a choice?"

Maybe, she thought, turning her gaze once more to the window. She would just have to see.

Chapter Sixteen

Friday, February 19
4:15 P.M.

A short time later, as Alex gazed into Harlan Sommer's cool gray eyes, she acknowledged she might never know what choices Harlan Sommer had made or what they had cost him. He would most probably never let her close enough for that.

"Alexandra," he said, "it's been such a long time. It's hard to believe it's you, all grown up."

Time had not been kind to him, Alex thought, comparing him to the robust man in her mother's photographs. Not handsome, no. But full of self-confidence and swagger.

"Thank you for agreeing to speak with me," she said.

"Of course I would." He smiled, though the smile didn't reach his eyes. "Let's sit down. I've opened one of our 2004 cabs. Do you enjoy red wine?"

"I adore red wine."

"Very good."

He poured them each a glass. Reed, she noticed, abstained. Harlan handed her one and sat. The awkward silence she had anticipated—and dreaded—ensued.

After several moments, it was broken by an attractive brunette rushing into the tasting room. "Where is she?" Her gaze landed on Alex and she broke into a huge smile. "Oh my God, it is you! My annoying little shadow!"

She crossed to Alex and hugged her hard. "I wondered if I would ever see you again."

Tears stung Alex's eyes and she blinked against them. "You must be Rachel."

"When Dad called and said you were in Sonoma, I couldn't believe it. Tell me everything that's happened to you in the last twenty-five years. Absolutely everything!"

Her father handed her a glass of wine. She tasted it, then nodded. "The '04. I continue to be impressed with this one." She turned back to Alex. "Are you married?"

"Divorced."

"Children?"

"Let the poor girl take a breath," Harlan said. "This isn't an inquisition."

"Sorry." Rachel smiled. "I'm a little nosy. And bossy."

Reed chuckled. "A little?"

"Stuff it." She turned back to Alex. "So, do you . . . have children?"

"No. What about you? Husband? Kids?"

"Neither. Beautifully unencumbered." She laughed. "Except for this freaking albatross of a business. Sorry, Dad." She bent and kissed his cheek, then took the chair across from Alex. "I love my position here at Sommer, but it's all the responsibility I want just now. How about you, Alex? You must work."

"I'm working on my PhD right now, tending bar to pay the bills."

"A PhD?" She looked at her father. "Dear God, she's an academic. I never would have guessed that."

She turned back to Alex. "What are you studying?"

"My thesis explores the role of belief systems in the human experience."

"Belief systems?" Her eyebrows rose. "As in?"

"Studies suggest we're actually hardwired to believe in a

creator, a controlling creative force we pay homage to through ritualistic acts. That's why we see again and again, across all cultures, a search for meaning through religion."

"Sounds like the Catholic Church to me," Rachel quipped.

"Judeo-Christian beliefs represent only a fraction of the world's belief systems," Alex said softly. "Paganism is actually the world's oldest religion, with literally an endless number of variations. Some of the earliest artifacts are clearly items of pagan worship . . ."

Alex let her words trail off. The room had gone stone silent and its three other occupants were staring at her. "Sorry, I get a little carried away with my work."

Rachel's eyebrows shot up and she leaned forward. "Mary Mother of God, you left the church, didn't you?"

"What church?"

"The Catholic Church, of course. Father would've killed me if I'd tried. Believe me, some Sundays I think I would have preferred death."

"Was I Catholic?"

Rachel looked stunned. "Your mother was a *rabid* Catholic."

Alex struggled to process what her stepsister had just said. She and her mother had never attended church, not even on Christmas and Easter. Nor had her mother ever mentioned having been a Catholic—even after Alex had begun studying world religions.

Reed spoke up. "Rabid, Rachel? Interesting word choice."

Rachel ignored him. "How long are you here for, Alex? We could go to lunch. Get reacquainted."

Rachel, Alex decided, was like a small tornado. She'd spun into the room and sucked all of them into her vortex. "Just today. I have to get back and begin making arrangements for my mother."

Rachel sat on the arm of her father's chair. She laid a hand on her father's shoulder, as if to comfort him. "Reed told us about your mother. We're so sorry."

"Thank you." To her horror, she choked up. She struggled for composure. "Excuse me, I . . . It's still fresh."

Rachel handed her a purse-pack of tissues; Alex pulled one out and dabbed at her eyes. "Mom battled depression for years," she said when she found her voice. "She attempted suicide twice before . . . I guess third time was the charm."

She heard the bitterness in her voice and regretted it. These people, despite the past they all shared, were strangers. They knew nothing about her and her mother's relationship. That revealing glimpse felt wrong.

She shifted her gaze to Harlan. "Did my mother . . . did she suffer with depression while you were married?"

He shook his head. "Not until after Dylan disappeared . . . but I thought that was to be expected. We all—" His voice thickened. "We were all different after."

It was obvious how much the loss of his son had hurt him. How much it hurt him still.

"Why are you here, Alexandra?"

Alex realized she was shredding the tissue and wadded it into a ball. "Until two days ago, I didn't know anything about you. About my early life living here, or even that I had a brother."

He frowned, but didn't comment.

"Mom never spoke of her early life or my father. She insisted we were it, that we had no other family. No grandparents, aunts or uncles. I accepted that but always felt . . . felt something was missing in my life. Frankly, I thought the feeling was brought on by my mother's mental illness. Now, I think it's this. You, my time here. But mostly I think it was the brother my subconscious knew I'd had."

Rachel gasped softly. "That's so awful," she said. "How could she do that to you? How could she pretend Dylan never existed? I'm sorry, but that just seems cruel to me."

Alex fought falling apart. Her thoughts exactly—which was why the words hurt so much.

This time it was Harlan who attempted to comfort by laying a hand on his daughter's arm. Alex noticed it shook.

"Dylan was a sweet little boy. Happy. Hardly ever fussed. Slept through the night from his third week. A joy."

He looked away, as if gazing deeply into the past, then

met her eyes once more. "You doted on him. So did Rachel. His mother and I, of course. We all took it hard, but Patsy the hardest. Somehow, she blamed herself. For going out that night. Not being there. She didn't bounce back."

"You tried to make the marriage work?"

"Of course. Tried everything I could think of. Time. Counseling. Gifts. The truth is, I loved her, but she couldn't get beyond her grief"—he cleared his throat—"to love me back." He sighed. "I don't know what else to tell you."

"Do you have any pictures?"

Rachel stood and crossed to an ornately carved desk. She selected a framed photo and brought it to her.

The photo depicted a young girl—Rachel, Alex presumed—holding a beautiful, cherubic infant. Alex lightly touched the glass. "I found a photo album in the attic," she said softly. "Hidden away in a trunk. It held a photo similar to this one, only I was holding him."

"It took me years to be able to bring that out," Harlan murmured, "to look at it without falling apart. I thank God that I'm able to now. It seems unfair to his memory to pretend he didn't exist."

Again, tears burned Alex's eyes. Ones of grief—and anger. At her mother for having done this—it was an affront to Dylan's memory.

She blinked them away and held out her hand, displaying the ring. "You mentioned gifts. Did you give this to my mother? I found it in the trunk with Dylan's things. It appears to be grapevines and a sna—"

"No," he said quickly. "I don't recognize it."

"You're certain you've never—"

"Yes, I'm certain." He paused a moment as if to give her time to come to grips with his words. When he spoke again, his voice held a note of finality. "Is there anything else I can help you with, Alexandra?"

"Yes. Do you know who my father is?"

She held her breath; his expression altered slightly. "I don't. I'm sorry."

"But you were married, surely she—"

"It wasn't important to me. I loved her."

He said it simply and in a way that left no doubt he really had loved her mother. But it didn't answer her question. "I appreciate that. But I find it hard to believe she never talked to you about him."

"Alexandra," he said gently, "I don't think she knew who your father was."

Alex thought of the things Rita the librarian had told her about her mother's love affair. He knew more than he was saying, she thought. He knew what he'd just said was a lie. But why keep the truth from her?

Maybe because he was her father?

"She was young," Rachel murmured. "Things happen. You know that."

"But why wouldn't she just tell me the tru—"

She didn't finish the question, hearing how inane it sounded—she'd already revealed how much her mother had kept hidden from her.

"It didn't matter to me," Harlan said again. "I fell in love with her. And with you, Alex."

His words washed over her in a bittersweet wave, and she struggled to speak. "Then why . . . all these years . . ."

"When it became obvious Dylan wasn't coming home, Patsy took you. Legally, you were her daughter, not mine, What could I do?"

"She wanted nothing to do with any of us," Rachel said. "She left *us,* Alex. All of us."

There was no denying the edge in the other woman's voice. For the first time it occurred to Alex that Rachel had lost two mothers—and how painful that must have been.

"We never forgot you. But as Dad said, what could we do?"

What indeed, Alex wondered, reaching for her wineglass and bringing it to her lips, only then realizing she had already emptied it.

"It's so odd." Rachel went on. "You've forgotten it all. Even your own brother. I'd have thought all that trauma would be burned onto your brain. I know it is mine."

Reed stepped in. "Maybe that's the very reason she forgot."

They fell silent. The fire hissed and crackled. The mantel clock struck the hour.

When the sixth chime faded away, Harlan leaned forward in his chair. "Is there anything we can do for you, Alexandra?" he asked. "Anything you need?"

She stiffened at the question, and at the pity in his eyes. "I wanted to meet you, learn what I could about my brother. That's all." She stood. "Thank you."

Their goodbye moment felt as awkward as their hello had, maybe more so. At least with hello had come expectation.

But of what? she wondered, gazing out the car window. A warm family reunion? A shocking revelation?

Certainly not for what she'd gotten—surprise, sympathy and a small dose of suspicion.

"Would you like to get something to eat?" Reed asked.

She realized they had reached the Sonoma square and the girl & the fig. "I don't think so, no. But thanks."

"Are you all right to drive? It's been a big day."

She smiled slightly, appreciative of his empathy. "I'm fine. I need to process."

He nodded, then indicated the restaurant. "If you come back, you'll have to try the place. It's really good."

She glanced at the front window, saw past the Help Wanted sign to the bar and dining room beyond. Warm-toned wood, tiny amber lights, small, white linen–covered tables, nestled together, bistro style. Charming.

"I will."

"I'm going to have a crime scene tech come by and collect the pacifier. Maybe some other things as well."

"I'll get them back?"

"Of course."

"Thank you for everything, Detective Reed." She held out her hand. "Please let me know what happens with the identification."

"I will. Absolutely." He released her hand. "Goodbye, Alex."

She watched him drive away, then climbed into her own vehicle for the long drive back to San Francisco.

Chapter Seventeen

"Morning, Tanner," Reed said, parking himself in the doorway of her cubicle. "How's life?"

"Not bad. For a Monday." She picked up her coffee cup. "Crime lab has the pacifier."

"And?"

"Said there's a slim chance they'll be able to retrieve any DNA from it. Marginal at best, their words."

"But a chance, nonetheless."

"Exactly."

Reed yawned. "Spent the weekend reviewing interview transcripts in the Dylan Sommer case. Specifically interviews of Alexandra Clarkson." He crossed to her desk and dropped a manila folder on it. "Basically got nothing new. One social worker found her to be unusually 'dissociative.'"

Tanner opened the folder and began scanning his notes. "But everyone else described her as a happy, talkative and well adjusted child."

"True. Although, when asked if she knew where her brother was, she said he was 'sleeping.'"

"Interesting." She tapped the notes. "Kids are tough interviews. You can only push so hard."

The VCI receptionist stuck her head in the door. "You two need to take a ride. Hilldale Winery. The B&B."

"What's up?"

"Someone mutilated a baby doll, left it strung up in the vines."

Thirty minutes later, Reed and Tanner stood side by side at the scene. Neither spoke, just gazed at the baby doll. It was incredibly lifelike. So lifelike that when they'd approached, Reed had been certain it was a real baby.

Apparently, Mrs. Dale had been taking a group of her guests on the tractor tour, a woman had spotted the doll and screamed. And no wonder. In a weird way it was Baby Doe number two.

"I've seen some seriously twisted shit," Tanner muttered, "but this beats it all."

It did rank right up there, Reed thought, taking in the gruesome display. What should have been a beautiful child's toy had been violated in a very ugly way. Strung up like a sacrificial lamb, arms and legs stretched wide and fastened with cord to the foliage wire. Its body had been sliced open and smeared with what appeared to be blood. Its eyes were wide open; the mouth had been violently punctured to form a hideous gaping hole.

Tanner coughed, clearly struggling to steady herself. "A response to Baby Doe?"

Reed nodded. "Some bored kids thinking they were being funny. Maybe."

He moved his gaze slowly over the area. The doll had been strung up in easy view from the tractor paths that ran alongside the vineyard. The spot was located within eyeshot of the B&B and the main road.

The road wasn't highly traveled, but it wasn't remote. Placing the doll here would have presented problems for the perps. They had to have done it at night and been especially quiet.

"They didn't hide it, that's for sure." Reed squatted in front of the find.

Tanner joined him. "Whoever left this wanted it found."

"That'd be my bet. But why?"

"To get a reaction, of course."

Baby Doe number two. The press could have a field day with that. Uneasiness settled in the pit of his gut. He looked at Tanner. "Think it was a sick joke?"

"Normally that'd be my guess."

"But?"

"But this isn't a doll somebody picked up at Walmart. "It's an Ashton Drake collectible. They go for a bill and a half."

"A hundred and fifty dollars? For a doll?"

"Yup."

He frowned. "And how do you know so much about collectible dolls?"

"My sister's kid. She's gaga over 'em and there's nothing my sister won't spend on her. She's spoiled her rotten. And I do mean rotten."

"How old's your niece? Maybe she's our prankster?"

"Eight. Give her a few years."

"Wow," he murmured, expression deadpan, "such a doting aunt."

"That's what my sister says." Tanner motioned to the desecrated doll. "My point is, that's a lot of money for a doll you're going to destroy in a prank."

"Yet using this doll is what made it so effective."

"Which means our pranksters thought it out."

"Maybe. Or they're selfish brats who don't give a crap about how much their parents spent on something. Just plucked it off one of their shelves."

"Which would mean a girl's involved." He retrieved a glove from his coat pocket, fitted it on and carefully examined the bloodied polyfill spilling out. "How about it, Tanner. Is it blood?"

"It's not ketchup or paint, that's for damn certain. But it could be theatrical. There are home recipes that look pretty authentic."

"Let's photograph and bag it. Find out if it's blood."

"And if it is, is it human?"

"Right," he said, disgusted. "When kids pull these stunts, they don't think about the manpower it takes to clean them up. I hope this is the work of some stupid kid so I get a chance to scare the shit out of him."

"Hey." Tanner wagged her finger at him. "Stop with the sexism. A female could be behind this, you know. Equal opportunity stupid fucks."

Chapter Eighteen

Alex sat in her mother's living room, what was left of her mother's work set up around her. Ten days had passed since her trip to Sonoma. In that time she had taken care of her mother's remains. The arrangements had been exhausting, even though they had been relatively minor. Her mother had wanted to be cremated and because she'd had few friends, Alex hadn't seen a need for a memorial service. She had contacted the *Chronicle* with obituary information, picked out an urn, and worked on processing the fact that her mother was gone.

That wasn't the only fact she had been processing. And sadly, it wasn't the most disturbing. What kept her up at night was a lifetime of lies and secrets.

"Talk to me, Alex." Tim sat across from her, expression concerned. "I'm worried about you."

"I'll be fine."

He didn't buy it, obviously. "What about finances?"

"I'll be fine," she said again. "Mom didn't have any life insurance, but she was debt-free. She owned the house and her car outright. If I have to I'll sell the house."

She may want to, she thought, moving her gaze over the room. So many bad memories.

She motioned to the paintings. "They're beautiful, aren't they? Even unfinished."

"Yes," he said. "It's good you saved them."

"Yes. Good." She frowned and brought a hand to her temple, massaged at the tension there. "I can't stop thinking about her other life. In Sonoma, before Dylan disappeared. She was happy, Tim. Everyone I met said so. You saw the pictures, she looked like a different person."

"Tragedy changes people," he said softly, mimicking what he'd said after she'd shared everything she'd learned with him.

It wasn't enough, she thought. Not nearly.

"I want to know who she was, Tim. I *need* to know."

"You need to move on, love."

She met his gaze evenly. "Move on to what? I don't know who I am anymore."

He leaned forward. "You're the same person you were the day before your mother died."

She shook her head. "Think about it. It's like a piece of a puzzle's been forced into the wrong spot. The picture that emerged around it is wrong. Warped."

He stood and crossed to her. Kneeling in front of her, he gathered her hands in his. "You're grieving. You lost your mother, your only family."

She stared at him, frowning. What she was experiencing didn't feel like grief. It felt like betrayal. Anger and uncertainty.

And it felt like a gnawing urge to *do* something. Right now, sitting still wasn't an option.

"I quit my job," she said.

Something like alarm raced into his eyes. "Now's not the time to make life-changing decisions."

"How important a life decision was it, Tim? I was a bartender."

"You have your dissertation to finish. Your PhD to earn. That's important to you. I know it is."

She gently eased her hands from his. "It is important. But so is this."

"What?"

"Finding out who I am."

"I want us to get back together."

She stared at him, certain she must have heard him wrong. Certain it wasn't panic she heard in his voice.

He pressed on. "It's just grief, I promise you. I'll love you through this."

"It's not, Tim. And you can't."

"I can." He drew her to her feet. "We were good together once. We will be again."

She shook her head. "Tim, I don't—"

He tightened his fingers over hers. "I need you, Alex. What will I do without you here?"

It was all about him, she realized. His needs. Same as when they'd been married. That's why at the first bump in the road, he'd cheated on her.

"What about what's good for my life?" she asked softly, extricating herself from his grasp. She crossed to one of her mother's paintings and gazed at swirls and slashes of color.

After a moment, she glanced back at him. "I'm thinking of moving to Sonoma."

"Sonoma? You can't be serious."

"More than thinking about it. I found a house to rent." He didn't reply and she went on. "It'll be a temporary move. Just until I get the answers I need."

"You may never get those answers, Alex. What then?"

She refused to consider that an option and pressed on. "I'm subletting my apartment to a friend from the bar, furnishings and all. The place I'm thinking of renting is furnished. And Sonoma's the perfect place to work on my dissertation."

"I can't talk you out of this, can I?"

"Nope. Sorry."

"I don't want you to be hurt, Alex."

"I'm already hurt, so bad it's sometimes hard to breathe. How could it hurt more?"

He crossed to stand behind her and gently turned her

toward him. "I've been thinking a lot about this whole thing. About what happened to your brother and what your mother did. Your mother took you away from there for a reason. She wiped that time from your memory, for a reason."

"Grief," Alex said. "Guilt."

"Maybe," he said, searching her gaze. "But what if it's more?"

"What if? That was twenty-five years ago."

"What about your vision? The screaming baby? What if you *did* see something you don't want to remember?"

Uneasiness stole over her. She shook it off, firming her resolve. "Then, maybe, I'll help unearth my brother's killer."

Chapter Nineteen

Sonoma Valley, California
Friday, March 5
4:40 P.M.

Alex sat at a window table at the girl & the fig, gazing out at the Sonoma square. Tourists meandered from shop to shop, moms with strollers ambled in the park while a group of young people loitered on benches. They looked a bit more hippie throwback than twenty-first-century Gen-Ys, though their Starbucks cups gave them away.

She had noted already that unlike San Francisco, people didn't rush here. The living was relaxed. The atmosphere laid-back.

Was it the influence of the landscape? Alex wondered, lifting her glass. Or the grape?

She held her wineglass to her nose and breathed in the zinfandel's full-bodied, spicy bouquet. It was a Sommer wine. She'd seen it on the wine menu and ordered it despite its ridiculous per glass price.

She sipped the wine, held it on her tongue a moment before swallowing. It was worth every penny, if not for its superior quality then for the fact seeing it on the menu and sipping it now was like a sign. She had done the right thing.

She thought of Tim. He had begged her to reconsider this move, was convinced she was making a bad decision. One motivated by grief. He was frightened for her.

Too late to second-guess yourself, Alex.

Way too late, she acknowledged, taking another sip. Thirty minutes ago, she'd signed a six-month lease on a charming cottage just a block and a half from here.

She couldn't turn back or chicken out now. She had committed herself.

A knock on the picture window jerked her from her thoughts. Reed, she saw. He smiled in greeting and she motioned him inside.

A moment later she invited him to join her. "I'm surprised to see you this time of day," she said. "Shouldn't you be off detecting?"

"Maybe I am?"

"Cryptic. That fits."

He motioned the bartender, ordered a Coke, then turned back to her. "Word was, you were back in Sonoma."

"Really? Do you have spies everywhere, Detective Reed?"

"It's a small town."

"And you're not going to tell me more than that?"

"Reveal my sources? No way." The waitress delivered Alex's appetizer, a display of fruits and artisanal cheese, and his soft drink. She sent Reed a conspiratorial glance, then walked away.

"One of your sources?" Alex asked.

"Could be. Neely knows most everything that goes on around the square."

"Is that so?" She smiled. "She tell you I rented a house around the corner? The little yellow one?"

His eyebrows shot up in disbelief. She laughed and shook her head. "I'm not kidding. I'm moving in Saturday."

"You don't think that's a little rash?"

"Not for me."

"What about your job?"

"I'm good for a few months without one. I intend to finish

my dissertation. This'll be the perfect opportunity. And the perfect place to do it."

"You never heard the advice about not making snap decisions when grieving?"

She thought of Tim. "Just the other day, in fact. Problem is, I'm not very good at taking advice."

"Independent thinker? Or ODD?" She cocked an eyebrow in question and he grinned. "Oppositional defiance disorder. My brother has a kid tagged with that. Makes life interesting."

She spread brie on a piece of baguette, took a bite and murmured her approval. "Independent or oppositionally defiant? Depends on who you're talking to."

He laughed. "Good enough. So, next Saturday's the day."

"No, this Saturday."

"Tomorrow?"

"The house is furnished so all I'll need is clothes, personal items and my research materials."

He digested that for a moment, then leaned toward her. "But why, Alex? What do you hope to gain by this?"

"Answers."

"To what?"

"I would think that's obvious. Why my mother ran away, why she hid the past from me. To what happened to my brother."

"What if there are no answers?"

"There're answers. I just need to dig them up."

"I wish you luck, Alex." He stood, seemed to come to a decision and met her eyes. "Think you'd have the energy to go to a party Saturday night? My family's launching their '08 Bear Creek Zin."

"Are you asking me out, Detective?"

"I suppose I am." He smiled. "I'll introduce you to my mother. Maybe she can help you get some of those answers you're looking for." He laid three dollars on the bar. "I'll pick you up at eight."

"Dress?" she asked.

He grinned. "Anything goes here. I'll see you then."

Alex watched him exit the restaurant. It occurred to her as she lowered her gaze that he'd probably be fabulous in bed. Would "anything go" there as well? she wondered.

She'd better watch herself around the handsome detective, Alex thought. She had a history of not using the good sense God had given her.

Chapter Twenty

Reed picked her up at eight. He wore blue jeans and a soft-looking chambray shirt. The battered leather jacket he wore over that was obviously an old friend.

Alex felt terribly overdressed in her little black dress.

"Wow," he said.

"I should have realized it was casual when you said anything goes. I'll change," she said. "It'll only take a minute."

"Don't. Mother will approve. Hell, I approve."

"Your mother? I didn't realize it'd gotten so serious between us?"

"Really serious." He laughed. "Just for the record, you had a major crush on me when you were five. Ask anyone."

She shook her head, amused. "I'll get my coat."

"Nice place," he said. "Cozy."

"I like it. It's a little weird to be sitting on someone else's couch, but I'll get over it."

"Here, let me help you with that." He held her coat for her. "The move went okay?"

She slid into the garment. "Piece of cake. A couple suitcases. My toothbrush. Margo."

As if on cue, Margo emerged from the kitchen, meowing. She wrapped herself around his ankles and he bent and scratched behind her ears.

"Careful, she bites."

He jerked his hand back and she laughed. "Love nips is all. But they tend to startle."

"A watch cat," he muttered. "Is there anything ordinary about you?"

"Nothing, actually. But tonight I'll take that as a compliment."

They stepped out into the clear, cold night. He helped her into his SUV.

She buckled in, then angled toward him. "Who told you I was in Sonoma?"

"The truth? I recognized your car and plate number. It's a cop thing."

So much for her conspiracy theories. She smiled. "How's the investigation going?"

"Nowhere, actually."

"The pacifier—"

"No good. Any biological matter that might have been available was too degraded to use."

"I'm sorry," she said.

He eased into traffic. "Some cases, all the pieces fall together, just like that. Others take time and coaxing. And some have so few pieces, there's nothing to build on."

"And they go nowhere," she murmured, thinking aloud. "Just fade away."

"No," he said, sounding suddenly fierce. "Baby Doe will not go unidentified. I won't let that happen."

"Because he may be Dylan?"

He met her eyes briefly, then returned his gaze to the road. "Because no child deserves that."

She studied his profile, her chest tight with emotion. She couldn't imagine being in his position, seeing the kind of ugliness he did, day in and out, and feeling the responsibility to somehow make it right.

He changed the subject. "How about I fill you in on who you'll meet tonight?"

"Perfect. Thanks."

"First, you'll meet my mother and father. Dad's a crusty old bastard, a fact Mom mostly ignores. She's a class act, hence her approval of your dress."

"Siblings?"

"Two brothers. Joe and Ferris."

"And where do they fall in the Reed lineup?"

"Joe is the oldest, Ferris the youngest—"

"And you're monkey in the middle?"

"Something like that. They both work for the family winery."

"But not you. Why?"

"Long story." He swung onto Sonoma Highway. "I expect the entire Sommer clan will be in attendance. Our families are close, but also in competition. A little industrial espionage is always in order."

She laughed. "You're joking, right?"

"Not really. You're sure to meet Treven tonight, Harlan's older brother. He runs the Sommer outfit. He has two sons. Clark's the older, Will the younger. Both are also in the business."

"Rachel will be there?"

"Almost certainly." He shot her a quick grin. "She's a hoot, isn't she?" When Alex agreed, he added, "But don't be fooled. She's as sharp as they come. Smart and ambitious. She lives for that winery."

"What does she do?"

"Head winemaker." He made a sharp right onto a private road. The iron gates were open, but judging by the card reader and keypad, that wasn't always the case. "It's a big deal, actually. Traditionally, the title of head winemaker has been a man's domain. Only recently have women begun making names for themselves. Helen Turley, Mia Klein, Heidi Barrett—and Rachel Sommer."

"I'm impressed. And frankly, intimidated."

"In her case, you can check that at the door. Rachel is real people."

"But the others aren't?"

He pursed his lips, as if in thought. After a moment, he said, "Some are. But there are plenty of egos in that group. And plenty of bullshit."

"Should I have worn boots tonight?"

"Hip waders."

She laughed just as the house came into view. The large stone structure sat on a hill. Light spilled from the windows. The surrounding trees had been laced with tiny white lights. Jazz floated on the cold night air, at once earthy and elegant.

"More impressive than the Sommer place, isn't it?"

It was. The house was grander. More manorlike. In light of the fact he'd wanted no part in the business, the obvious pride in his voice surprised her.

Interesting, she thought. No doubt there'd been a lot more to his opting out of the family business than he'd let on.

He parked and they climbed out. Alex was happy to see she wasn't the only one in a dress. But Reed hadn't been exaggerating—attire ran the gamut from grunge to bling.

Obviously, Reed had warned his family she would be his date this evening. One after another they approached her with some version of "Little Alexandra, I can't believe it's you!"

His brothers found them first. They were both dynamic, though in very different ways. Joe commanded and Ferris charmed. Their personal styles reflected that. Joe's hair, silvering at the temples, was close-cropped. He wore a button-down shirt, open at the throat, and a pair of dress trousers. His shoes were polished to a shine that rivaled the glint of the Rolex watch on his wrist. Ferris's hair was shaggy, his smile open and disarming. His choice in clothing: casual hip.

Reed resembled neither, with his thick, chestnut-colored hair, light eyes and rugged build.

After Reed introduced them, Ferris caught her hand and brought it to his lips. "Danny didn't tell us you were gorgeous," he teased. "Hoping to keep you all to himself, selfish bastard."

"Typical Dan." Joe held out his hand and smiled. "Wonderful to see you again after all these years. My brother told you about his reputation with the ladies, I'm sure?"

"Actually, he didn't." She smiled back at the man. "However, he did remind me I had a raging crush on him at five."

The two men burst out laughing. "Way to go, Bro. Smooth."

To his credit, Reed seemed unfazed by their ribbing. "Laugh your asses off, guys. I'm still the one introducing *you* to the lady on my arm."

Joe threw up his hands. "Hey, I'm out of this. Hitched. Ferris, on the other hand, needs some serious help."

Considering the way he lingered over her hand, Alex seriously doubted that. As they left the brothers moments later, she leaned toward Reed. "Ladies' man? And here I thought you were busy working the streets, not the sheets."

He grinned down at her. "Funny. Nice play on words."

But no denial. Alex tucked that fact away for later.

Wine, tonight's zinfandel and in general, was the evening's star attraction. As they moved through the party, talk revolved around it: the weather, grapes and current growing season, which wines were worth tasting and which ones weren't. Everybody, it seemed, was an expert.

Alex was torn between finding it fascinating and totally affected. Reed had no such conflicts—as he led her through the party he kept up a running, sometimes irreverent, sometimes outright sarcastic monologue of who was who and why they thought so.

As he exchanged her empty glass for a full one, he said, "Here comes my father. Prepare yourself."

She followed the direction of his gaze. She saw immediately where Reed had gotten his looks. He was a big man, with a head of thick silvering hair, whose gait—his very countenance—shouted, *I'll do it my way, thanks.*

Now she knew where Reed had gotten that as well. And perhaps why he had opted out of the family business.

"Dad," he said stiffly. "Good to see you."

"Son. Glad you could make it."

The tension between the two was palpable, Alex noted.

"Where else would I be tonight?"

"You tell me. It's only wine, after all. Not life or death."

Alex felt Reed stiffen beside her. She held out her hand. "Hi. I'm Alexandra Clarkson."

The older Reed turned to her, pinning her with his piercing blue eyes. Only then did he take her hand. "Patsy's girl."

"Yes."

"Wayne Reed." He released her hand. "I hear you rented a place in town."

"I did."

"You'll not be bothering Harlan."

She bristled. "I had no plans to."

"Good. Enjoy the party." Without another word he turned and strode off.

She watched him go, working to recover her balance. "That went well," she muttered.

Reed laughed. "I told you he was a crusty bastard."

"In some cases, crusty is charming."

"Not Dad's. But you know that now."

That she did. "You didn't tell me there was such bad blood between you two."

"Just disappointment." Before she could comment, he added, "Here comes Mom. Big surprise."

His mother, Lyla, proved to be the epitome of elegance and hospitality. Alex realized instantly that she played peacemaker between father and son. Or rather, she tried.

As Reed had predicted, she approved of the dress. "Don't you look lovely!" she exclaimed, catching Alex's hands and looking her over. "Little Alex, grown into a beautiful woman."

"It's wonderful to meet you, Lyla."

"To meet me? Why, we're old friends." She linked their arms. "Come, let me show you something."

Alex glanced at Reed, who shrugged, his expression amused. He followed as his mother led her through an alcove into a large, paneled room. The room was richly but comfortably furnished, the walls hung with photographs, some of celebrities and politicians, framed medals and certificates. A scent lingered in the air, at once woodsy, sweet and somehow familiar. A fire crackled in the massive stone hearth. A video monitor played a promotional piece about the making of the Bear Creek Zinfandel.

"Trophy room," Reed said.

"Our family history room," she corrected, leading Alex to a grouping of photographs. "Our Marvale Pinot was served at the White House." She indicated a photograph of a man who looked remarkably like Reed standing with President and Nancy Reagan. "That's Wayne's father."

She pointed to another photograph. "Joe and Ferris with Governor Schwarzenegger. And here, Wayne and his father with Robert Mondavi. But that's not why I brought you in here. Look."

A photograph of Lyla and Patsy, both smiling for the camera, her mother very pregnant. They held up glasses of wine. Apparently, the picture predated the Surgeon General's warning about consuming alcohol while pregnant.

Or maybe it didn't. Here in wine country, Alex suspected, people wrote their own rules about such things.

"I missed your mother terribly when she left. We all did."

"Were you close?"

"Very." She sighed and lightly touched the glass. "We loved Harlan. He and Wayne were best friends from the time they were in short pants—as Wayne likes to say. I was close to Susan, his first wife . . . such a terrible tragedy." Her voice thickened and she cleared it. "Poor Harlan, he has endured so much."

She paused as if in thought. "Patsy made him so happy. You, too. Then, when Dylan was born . . . Those were joyful years."

Alex imagined those years. In a strange way, as Lyla Reed led her through a series of photographs, she *almost* remembered them.

Lyla stopped on a picture of Harlan and Patsy, swinging Dylan between them. "That was right before—" She bit the words back, overcome with emotion.

Alex gazed at the image, then looked away. A log dropped in the fireplace, sending a shower of sparks up the flue. She turned back to Lyla. "I don't understand . . . why did she leave?"

Lyla looked surprised. She glanced at her son, then back at Alex, obviously distressed. "I thought you knew about Dylan."

"I do. Now, anyway. But I'm having a hard time understanding the way she picked up and left. And an even harder time reconciling the woman she appeared to be in these photos and the mother I knew. Here, she seemed so happy, and all my life—"

"You're not a mother," Lyla said sharply. "You can't truly understand until you are. His loss destroyed her."

A young girl poked her head into the room, "Grandma, Pop-pop is asking for you."

"Thanks, sweet pea. Tell him I'll be right out." She turned back to Alex. "If it had been one of my boys, I don't know what I would have done. Or how I'd have gone on."

She gave Alex's arm a reassuring squeeze. "Take all the time you need. We have photo albums from those years. Dan will show you."

Chapter Twenty-one

Alex hadn't wanted to see any more photographs. Instead of answering her questions, what she'd seen had posed more. Not only that, it hurt to look at them. She couldn't stop thinking about her mother, the smile she'd worn in each picture, and comparing that to the woman who had been so despondent she had swallowed a bottle of pills.

Maybe Lyla was right. Maybe she couldn't understand because she wasn't a mother.

"Are you okay?" Reed asked.

She forced a smile and held up her glass. "I'm empty. And hungry, I think."

They found the buffet and filled their plates. The spread was incredible, everything California and that paired with zinfandel, all fresh, natural and arranged beautifully.

There they ran into Rachel. She was talking wine with a journalist, but paused to give Alex a hug and kiss on the cheek. "We're going to lunch on Monday," she said. "You can't say no. Noon at El Dorado Kitchen."

Next, she met Treven Sommer. Although she knew Treven

to be several years older than Harlan, he looked a decade younger.

"Alexandra," he said warmly, gathering her hands in his, "Harlan told me you had been by to see him. He told me about Patsy. She was an exceptional woman. I'm so sorry for your loss."

"Thank you," she managed, voice thick. "I'm certain she would have appreciated you saying that."

"Did she ever do anything with her painting?" he asked. "She was quite gifted."

"She was painting back then?" Alex asked, surprised. No one else had mentioned it.

"Yes, indeed. The painting in our tasting room, behind the bar, is one of hers. I believe Harlan has several. There are a few in the collections of friends in the valley. Come by the winery before you leave."

"She's going to be around awhile, Dad. Haven't you heard?"

She turned to the man who had come up behind them. Fortysomething, she guessed. Trim and fit—almost too trim. She would bet he was a runner. He had that look about him, tightly coiled, the kind of guy who pounded the miles as a release.

"My son, Clark."

He held out his hand. "Alex. Good to see you again."

"You, too." She took his hand. "Though I wish I could say I remember you."

"I heard about that. Think being here might jog your memory?"

"I can hope, though it hasn't yet."

They chatted awhile; others came and went. Her glass was refilled—several times. Suddenly, she needed fresh air. While Reed took a call, she headed out onto the patio.

She breathed deeply though her nose, the cold air clearing her head. The sky was brilliantly black, dusted with stars. Laughter floated on the night air. At the back of the property, the lit entrance to the wine cave created a welcoming window in the darkness.

And it beckoned. Why not? she thought. The caves were open for tours tonight, and truthfully the idea of them fascinated her. If she had explored them as a child, like everything else, she didn't remember.

She stepped off the patio and onto the gravel path that led to the cave. Considering the wine she'd consumed and the impracticality of her strappy sandals, she probably shouldn't be doing this alone, she thought. Of course, she'd never let pragmatism stop her before.

The walkway wound through the gardens. She glanced back at the house, at the dark path behind her. Beyond it, a circle of light spilled from the house into the gardens. Music mingled with the laughter on the night air, though the nearer she drew to the cave, the more muted the sound.

The area directly inside the cave served as a sort of welcome center. A table had been set up, complete with some brochures on tonight's Bear Creek Zin as well as the Reeds' other wines and the winery's history. On the table, also, stood an open bottle of wine and a display of glasses. Above the table hung a magnificent candelabra constructed out of a wine barrel.

If someone had been manning the table, they were gone now. Perhaps giving a tour, she thought. Pouring herself a glass of wine, she waited for their return, using the time to take in the cave's interior. The walls were relatively smooth, the corridors narrow. Although a good thirteen feet high, the ceilings' barrel shapes made them seem considerably more closed in.

Three arms extended off the welcome area and Alex wandered toward the center one. The only light was provided by a ceiling-mounted row of bare lightbulbs. Racks of stacked wooden barrels lined both sides of the tunnel.

A cooled-by-nature place to age wine, she thought. Purely functional. None of the glamour of the welcome area or inside tasting rooms.

She wandered deeper, as if propelled by an unseen force. As she did, a strong sense of déjà vu came over her. She had been here before, she was certain of it.

She headed deeper into the cave, excited by the possibility that she was finally remembering.

A sound behind her caused her to stop and look back. The tunnel behind her was empty. "Hello," she called.

Her voice echoed back at her. She frowned. How far from the welcome area was she? Not far, she decided. Not so far she wouldn't hear activity there.

She pressed on, her heart beating heavily. Drumlike, it filled her head. She hesitated, glancing over her shoulder again, torn between the urge to push on and head back.

Pushing forward won out.

The smell of incense, sharp and sweet, stung her nose. Her steps faltered. She glanced around her. Where, she wondered, was it coming from? Up ahead, the tunnel split into two. She reached the fork, then stopped and listened. She heard the faint strain of voices. Laughter.

A tour in progress, she thought. To the right.

She started off that way. The voices grew louder. Men and women, she heard. Laughter. Other sounds, as well. Ones she couldn't quite identify but that made her feel uncomfortable.

Not a tour. A group had moved the party out here. They were having themselves a really good time. They wouldn't appreciate her interruption.

Time to head back, Alex.

She hadn't paid attention to where she was going, she realized. But how hard could it be? A left would take her back toward the entrance. Maybe.

She tried it. But instead of taking her away from the partying group, it seemed to bring her closer. The voices grew louder; the smell more intense.

She turned back the way she'd come, then took the right instead. But again, the sounds grew louder.

She stopped, confused and fuzzy-headed. She took a deep breath, trying to focus, cursing herself the last couple glasses of wine.

"Hello?" she called out. "Is someone there?"

Instead of a response came the rise and fall of laughter.

Louder still, she thought. How could that be? Was she walking in circles? Was the cave playing tricks on her?

Panic came upon her suddenly. With it the sense that the cave was closing in on her. She struggled to control her runaway pulse, to breathe deeply and slowly.

Stop it, Alex. There are people nearby; Reed will come looking for you. Someone will find you.

Somewhat calmer, she took stock of her location, then told herself to keep moving. Put one foot in front of the other. She did, counting her steps, acknowledging that the tunnels all looked exactly the same—lined with barrels, the single row of bulbs seeming to stretch on forever.

And then they went out. Total darkness engulfed her. Her knees went weak. The glass slipped from her hand, hitting the floor and shattering. She felt the spilled wine splash her ankles.

The sound of the partiers grew louder, though nearly drowned out by her thundering heart and ragged breathing.

"I'm still in here!" she cried. "Wait!"

More laughter reached her ears. Strange grunting noises. A howl that sounded part human, part animal. She backed away, bumping into a stack of barrels.

"Hello!" she called again, hearing the desperation in her own voice. "Please, someone!"

"Alex! Alex, where are you?"

"Reed!" she cried. "I'm here!"

A beam of light swept crazily over the floor and walls, then pinned her.

It seemed ages until he reached her, until he drew her into his arms and against his chest. "My God, you're shaking."

Alex clung to him. "I got turned around. I called out, but no one—" She buried her face in his chest. His shirt was soft against her cheek, the beat of his heart reassuring. He smelled of soap and a subtly spicy aftershave.

Except for their breathing, it was silent. No more clandestine party animals.

"I guess we broke up that party," she murmured, easing out of his arms, feeling more than a little bit foolish.

"We didn't have much to do with it. Once the caterer packs up the bar, the fun's always over."

She realized he meant the wine launch. "Not that. There was a group out here. Carrying on. Burning incense."

"Incense?"

She realized how outrageous that sounded. "That's what I thought at the time, but maybe they were smoking weed." He frowned and she went on, "Whatever they were up to, it hadn't been for public viewing."

The lights snapped on. A moment later, Reed's younger brother, Ferris, appeared at the far end of the tunnel.

"Bro," Ferris called, "what's the deal? I thought I heard someone scream."

Reed turned toward his brother. "Alex got turned around, then the lights went out. It scared her. No big deal."

Alex stepped away from Reed, frowning. She hadn't screamed. She opened her mouth to tell them, then shut it, confused. Or had she? Obviously they'd both heard a scream.

Not good, Alex. Definitely not good.

Ferris grinned. "Okay then. Sorry to interrupt your knight in shining armor thing."

"Get a life, little brother," Reed shot back, "that's everyday for me."

"Give *me* a break. And look, flip the lights and lock up when you go."

"Wait!" Alex called. "There's a group deeper in the cave. I heard them partying."

"Are you sure? I did a sweep of the tunnels earlier—"

"I know what I heard. And smelled."

"She thinks they might've been smoking weed," Reed said.

Ferris swore. "Punks. This has happened before."

Reed looked back at her. "When the lights went out, could you still hear them?"

"Right before, yes."

He frowned. "There's only one way in and out of the cave, Alex. When the lights went out, that's where I was. I heard you scream, grabbed the flashlight and came looking for you."

"And I was right behind you, Reed," Ferris said. "One of us would have run into a group exiting."

"Then they're still here. I'm certain of it."

Reed gazed at her a moment, then back at his brother. "Alex and I will take a look. Ferris, hang out in front, would you? The last thing we want is a group of kids using this as their personal party pad."

Ferris agreed, and together, Alex and Reed searched the cave. Designed in a fan shape, with dozens of pockets off each arm and a reception area at the far corner, it took better than thirty minutes to complete. And in the end, they found no sign of anyone else or a clandestine party.

"Sorry, Alex," Reed said.

"I don't understand. I know what I heard."

A small group had gathered at the cave entrance. It included Reed's mother and father, Rachel and Treven.

"Anything?" Ferris asked. Reed shook his head.

Rachel rushed forward. "Are you all right, Alex?" She grabbed her hands and rubbed them. "They're so cold! Poor thing."

"This is so embarrassing."

"Nonsense!" Rachel exclaimed. "Those caves are creepy even when the lights are on. I wandered into one when I was ten, got lost and wasn't discovered for hours. I still shudder when I go in."

Lyla joined Rachel. "Ferris said you thought you heard voices?"

Before she could respond, Reed stepped in. "We did a search. Came up empty."

The older Reed made a sound of sympathy. "Funny the way sounds carry at night."

"Indeed," Treven agreed.

Alex bit back a denial. She'd heard voices nobody else had and hadn't heard the scream everybody else had. Arguing would make her look more ridiculous than she already did.

It might even make her look crazy.

Just like her mother.

Chapter Twenty-two

Saturday, March 6
11:22 P.M.

They didn't speak on the drive back to her house. When he'd parked in front of her cottage, they both climbed out and walked to her front door. Alex's hands were shaking so badly Reed took the house key from her fingers and unlocked the door for her.

"Are you going to be all right?" he asked, pushing the door open.

"I'm fine."

But she wasn't. She was embarrassed and shaken. Angry that no one believed her. Angry with herself for her own doubt. Determined to prove herself.

She met his gaze. "I didn't imagine what I heard. I didn't."

"You'd had some wine and—"

"I had a lot of wine," she corrected. "But I wasn't drunk."

"Voices carry on the night air."

"I was deep inside that cave. How could sounds from the party reach me there?"

"Look, Alex, you've been dealing with some big issues.

Nobody's going to point fingers if your behavior's a little erratic."

"Excuse me?"

"I didn't want to say that, but it's true. Honey, you've been through some terrible—"

"Don't call me honey." She pushed the door the rest of the way open and strode inside. He followed her. She tossed her coat on the sofa and swung to face him. "And I am not crazy."

"I'm not saying you're crazy."

"Maybe my time line is wrong? Maybe I heard some folks carrying on and it got stuck in my head. They were partying. Burning something. I smelled it."

"Why'd you scream, Alex?"

She wasn't about to tell him she hadn't. Or even that she didn't remember doing it. She already looked a brick short of a load. "It was involuntary. I was already turned around, and when the lights went off . . . I must have . . . screamed."

"Must have?"

"Never mind." She folded her arms across her chest. "I don't know why I'm justifying myself to you."

"I didn't ask you to, Alex." He crossed to her, laid his hands on her shoulders. "You've been through a lot. Your mother's death, the shock of learning about Dylan and now the move here. Cut yourself some slack."

She tipped her face up to his, ready to argue. Their eyes met and the words caught in her throat.

"Don't hold back, Alex. You look like you want to say something. Go ahead."

Go ahead. Don't hold back. Aware of the warmth of his hands on her shoulders, the stirring of his breath against her cheek, those words took on a new meaning.

His gaze dropped to her mouth. The air between them turned electric. Her face heated, the heat spread.

Dammit. She had wanted to avoid this. Had wanted to keep things platonic.

He moved one hand to the back of her neck, threading his

fingers through her hair. She felt the subtle movement, the whisper soft caress of his fingers, deep in her belly, at the apex of her thighs.

He lowered his mouth to hers, rubbed his experimentally against hers. Alex laid her palms against his chest. Beneath her right, his heart pounded.

"A mistake," he murmured against her mouth, voice thick.

"Yes." She curled her fingers into his shirt, holding on.

"Should I go?"

"God, no."

Groaning, he caught her lips and cupping her derriere, lifted her. She wrapped her legs around his waist, rubbing against him as he carried her to the bedroom. They fell onto the bed, only separating long enough to loosen and remove clothing, cursing garments that clung, tearing at those that resisted. She exploded in orgasm as he entered her, with a force that had her crying out and bucking against him.

Afterward, they lay side by side, damp, winded. Alex stared at the ceiling, thoughts racing. She'd left this part of her life behind years ago. This mindless search for fulfillment through sex. It'd been a stage, one that had been self-destructive and ultimately humiliating.

He touched her cheek, dragging her away from her own thoughts. She turned her face to his.

"Wow," he said.

"Yeah." Her lips curved up. "But . . . never mind."

"What?" He propped himself on an elbow and gazed down at her.

"I'm thinking this wasn't such a good idea."

"Then stop thinking."

She couldn't help but smile. "It was just sex, right?"

"Great sex," he corrected. "Come here."

He pulled her into the crook of his arm. Alex rested her head against his shoulder and her hand over his heart.

Moments became minutes. He yawned. "I suppose I should go."

"Whenever you need to."

He yawned again. "Soon."

She rested her head against his shoulder. "What's the long story?"

"About?"

"You and your dad. Why you didn't join the family business."

"Nosy, aren't you?"

"Impatient. I'm not good at waiting for what I want."

"I noticed." He fell silent. When he spoke again, all traces of amusement and the afterglow of explosive sex had disappeared from his voice. "If you asked my old man, he'd tell you I didn't have the balls."

"Interesting. But I'm asking you."

He rubbed his jaw against the top of her head. "I didn't want to fight my brothers for it. Dad pitted the three of us against each other. I thought it was bullshit."

"So you opted out."

"I opted out."

She doubted it had been anywhere near as simple as that. "And your brothers?"

"Fell right in line. They fought each other for Dad's 'attaboy.' He decided who they would be, like it or not."

She had picked up on the family dynamics enough to have recognized them as he was talking. The elder Reed ruled over the family business with an iron will—if not an iron fist as well. Joe was the favored son. Father's confidant and CEO in training. Obviously singled out to take the company forward. Ferris had been relegated to the voice of Reed wines. Head of sales and marketing.

"Where would you have fit in the family circus?"

"Dad had pegged me as the winemaker."

"And?"

"Nobody was going to pick my career for me."

"You didn't love it?"

"Not enough to sell my soul to it—or to Dad."

His cell went off. "Reed here," he answered.

Alex sat up, bringing the sheet with her. She watched his expression tighten.

"Where?" He paused. "Son of a bitch. On my way."

He climbed out of the bed, bent and grabbed his jeans. "I've got to go." He yanked them on, then snatched up his shirt. "Sorry."

He didn't look at her. An uneasy sensation settled in the pit of her gut. "What's going on, Reed?"

"A murder. Someone from the party tonight."

"Who?" she asked. "Was it someone I met?"

"Don't think so." He shrugged into his shirt, then buttoned it. "A guy named Tom Schwann. His roots went deep around here."

Dressed, he crossed to the bed, bent and kissed her. "Sorry about this. I'll call."

She watched him go, thinking about roots that went deep and wondering if he would call.

Chapter Twenty-three

Sunday, March 7
2:35 A.M.

Schwann had been found on a gravel T-bone off Thornsberry Road, the narrow road that led to his family winery. The T-bone was hardly even a drive. Tucked back that way, cars could have driven by all night long and not seen him.

Reed moved his gaze, taking count of the vehicles at the scene. Tanner and her team had already arrived. The scene lights lit up the night like an urban parking lot. In addition, a patrol car and a banged-up Honda Civic sat by the roadside.

Schwann and his wife both drove big-ass sedans. So, how had Tom ended up here, dead?

Reed shoved his hands into the pockets of his bomber jacket. His breath made frosty pillows on the air. He couldn't help thinking this was a damn rude ending to what had been a pretty spectacular night.

Wow hadn't quite covered it.

He signed in, then ducked under the crime scene tape. His boots crunched on the gravel path and Tanner turned and looked at him. She didn't have to say a thing; he knew what she was thinking.

This was going to blow the valley's tight-knit wine community apart.

His comment to Alex about Schwann's family roots had been spot-on. Tom's great-great-grandfather, Albrecht Schwann, had settled here and begun growing grapes before the Reeds, Sommers or Mondavis and their effort had helped bring California wines to international prominence. Tom had been a patron of the arts and a local philanthropist as well. And he'd had a lot of friends in this town. Reed's brother Joe had been one of his closest.

"Who found him?" Reed asked, squatting beside the body, grimacing at the gruesome sight. Someone had planted a secateur in Schwann's throat, then yanked, nearly decapitating him.

Known by the brand name Red Rooster, the small curved blade implements used for cutting clusters of grapes from the vines were as common as quarters in the valley. Pretty much every field hand had one on him, whether in the field or not.

Conveniently, the killer had left his Red Rooster behind.

"Meri Calvin. Worked for him. Said he called and asked her to come get him."

Reed nodded. "Where is she?"

"Keeping warm in the patrol unit." As if reminded of the cold, Tanner stomped her feet to warm them. "Unfortunately, she's not covered in blood."

"That'd be too damn easy," Reed muttered, studying the bloodied plastic handle. It'd been a clumsy job. And a messy one. He glanced at Tanner. "Depending on the exact strike point, blood spray would have been significant."

"Like puncturing a high-pressure hose."

He nodded and carefully scanned the ground around the victim. Even with the scene lights, the blood trail would be a bitch to follow. Gravel, leaves and other debris made evidence collection a game of hide-and-seek. "Whoever did this didn't walk away clean, that's for sure."

He straightened. "Doesn't look premeditated. Perp didn't think it through. I'm guessing there'll be prints all over the weapon."

"Wallet's cleaned out," Tanner offered, indicating the wallet on the ground, a foot from the body. "Watch is gone. So is his wedding ring. Crime of opportunity."

"Or crime of passion, made to look like a robbery." Reed glanced at his partner. "I saw him tonight. A wine launch party. At my folks'."

"What time did you last see him?"

"Eleven or so. Right before I took Alex home." Her eyebrows shot up at the woman's name. "What?" he asked.

"You have something going on with her?"

"None of your damn business. She's not a suspect."

"She may be a witness."

To a twenty-five-year-old crime she didn't remember. "Just introducing her around," he said. "Trying to jog her memory."

"Bullshit, partner. But it's your ass." Tanner motioned to the victim. "Was he drinking?"

"Ask a better question, Tanner. Like, was he drinking heavily?"

"Was he?"

"Of course. The wine was free."

"Who was he with?"

"His wife. I saw them together at one point."

"So where is she now?"

"That's a very good question. Maybe Ms. Calvin knows the answer."

He found the young woman in the back of the patrol car, wrapped in a blanket. The door stood open and he bent down and introduced himself. She burst into tears.

"I can't believe this has"—she sucked in a sobbing breath—"that this has . . . Oh, my God! Tom's dead!"

He handed her a tissue. She blew her nose and lifted her tear-streaked face to his. "What do I do now?"

"What do you mean?"

"I'm going to have to find a new job. Another place to live. How am I going to do all that?"

He didn't respond, directing her to the events of the night. "I need to ask you some questions, Meri. Do you think you can remain calm enough to answer?"

She still looked a hiccup away from total hysteria, but she nodded. "I'll . . . I'll try."

"Good." He spoke slowly, keeping his tone as nonconfrontational as possible. "Tell me how you happened to be here."

"I told the other officer—"

"I need to hear it from you. I hope you don't mind?"

"Okay." She shredded the tissue he'd handed her. "He called me. He said he needed a ride home."

"What time was that?"

"About midnight."

"Why did he call you?"

"What do you mean?"

"Why you? Instead of someone else?"

"I work for him."

"You're an awfully dedicated employee, to come out at midnight. I'm impressed."

She shifted her gaze. "I like my job . . . and I want to make certain I . . . keep . . ."

Her words trailed off, as if she knew how lame they sounded. As gently as possible, he said, "You weren't just Tom's employee, were you?"

She shook her head. "We were friends."

"Friends?"

She started to cry again, though this time softly. "More than friends," she whispered.

"You were lovers, weren't you?"

She nodded. "He and his wife were splitting up."

Doubtful, Reed thought. He had heard that Tom had a weakness for women nearly half his age. If the rumors were true, young Meri here was just one in a long line of Tom's dalliances.

He kept that to himself. "He was at a launch party with his wife tonight. Right up the road. Red Crest Winery."

"It wasn't fair! She got to go to all the really cool places and events, while I stayed home and waited for him to call."

Reed didn't point out that as Schwann's wife, that was her right. Nor did he mention all the crap the woman obviously put up with. Seemed to him both women had been getting the short end of the stick. "Tell me what happened tonight."

"I was already in bed when he called. He said he and his wife had had a huge fight and she'd kicked him out of the car."

"What did they fight about?"

"He didn't tell me."

"And you didn't ask?"

"I figured I'd ask when . . . I didn't get the chance."

"How long between when he called and you arrived here?"

"Maybe an hour." She hung her head, looking miserable. "I was really mad. I figured he could wait, that it'd serve him right."

"When you arrived, did you see anyone? A car driving off? Anything like that?"

She hadn't, and after exacting her promise to call if she remembered anything else, Reed decided his next move had to be a face-to-face with Schwann's wife.

Chapter Twenty-four

Sunday, March 7
4:10 A.M.

Tom and Jill Schwann lived in a big house on Arrowhead Mountain. Reed had gone to school with Jill; they'd been in the same high school graduating class. He couldn't imagine her getting pissed off enough to kill her husband, but what did he know? The brutality of the human animal continually surprised him.

He brought a couple uniformed deputies along with him, just in case he needed assistance.

Reed reached the front door, rang the bell. A dog started to bark, one of those high-pitched, yappy barks that brought to mind celebrities Paris Hilton and Britney Spears.

Jill answered the door looking totally wrung out. Marriage to an asshole had that effect; he'd seen it time and again. She wore a wrap robe, her feet were bare. Her blond hair had mostly come out of its chignon and hung in hanks around her face. Obviously she had been crying: her nose was red and mascara had created dark tracks down her cheeks. A small white dog growled and bared its teeth at him.

"Dan?" She shifted her gaze to the officers behind him and frowned. "What's going on?"

"I've got some bad news, Jill. Can I come in?"

She scooped up the dog. "Pinot," she admonished, moving aside, "shush, baby."

Reed stepped into the foyer, the deputies behind him. He took in the area—the white carpeting, the marble foyer, the silk wall coverings—looking for a trail, smear or drop of blood. He knew the deputies behind him were doing the same.

"Maybe we should sit down?"

"You're scaring me, Dan. What's—"

"Tom's dead, Jill. I'm sorry."

For a split second her expression went totally blank, a moment later it lit with fury. "I get it. That son of a bitch. He put you up to this, didn't he? To teach me a lesson. Prick."

"Jill, that's not why—"

"Save it, Danny. He thinks this is all right. That it's okay for him to fuck anything that moves and I should take it because he pays the bills." She strode to the large, open living room, dropped Pinot on the couch and swung back to face him. "Well, it's not okay. I kicked his two-timing, drunk butt out of the car. Told him to get his latest piece of ass to give him a ride home. I don't deserve this."

"Jill," he said quietly, "Tom's dead. He was murdered."

Several different emotions raced across her face. Shock and disbelief. Horror. She opened her mouth, then shut it. Her throat worked. The dog growled.

"This isn't a setup?" He shook his head. Again she looked at the deputies, as if she needed further confirmation. "I left him just an hour or two ago."

"Are you certain about the time?"

"No, I—" She brought a hand to her throat. Reed saw that it shook. "I was drinking. We argued . . . It's all a blur now."

"Why don't you sit down?" She nodded but didn't move. She swayed slightly, face ashen. He caught her elbow and led her to the couch. She sank onto it. Pinot hopped onto her lap.

"Can I get you some water?" he asked. "Anything else?"

She shook her head, threading her fingers in the animal's silky fur. "Tom's dead?"

"Yes. I'm sorry."

"How?" she asked. "Who?"

"We don't know who. His throat was slit."

"Oh my God!"

"Can we call someone for you?"

"My mother."

He remembered Jill's mother. Very involved in her daughter's life. Ambitious for her. He wondered if she had known about her daughter's marital troubles.

"I'll have someone pick her up and bring her over. How's that?"

She nodded, throat working. Reed instructed one of the deputies to call it in, then turned back to her. "While we talk, may my deputies take a look around? We'll need to check your car as well."

She looked surprised. "Look around? Here? Sure, but I . . . I don't understan . . ." But then she did; the realization crossed her face. "You don't think I had anything to do with his . . . death?"

"Of course not," he said gently, taking a notebook and pen from his jacket pocket. "But it's standard operating procedure. You were his wife. Maybe the last person to have seen him alive. Is it okay if they look around?"

She nodded and began to cry. Reed instructed the deputies to get started, found a box of tissues, then sat beside her, waiting, giving her time.

After several minutes had passed, she blew her nose, then looked at him. "You probably think I'm an idiot. Crying over a man who treated the dog with more respect than he did me."

"I don't think you're an idiot, Jill. Far from it."

"I loved him." She snatched another tissue from the box. "At least I did, once upon a time. Lately, I mostly hated his guts."

Reed laid a hand on her arm. "Jill, anything you say can be held against you. You know that, right?"

"And I have a right to have a lawyer present. I know. I watch TV."

"This isn't television. It's real."

She laughed, the sound also equal parts sob and hiccup. "I

have nothing to hide, Reed." She curved her arms around her middle. "Thank God we didn't have children. Thank God."

"Jill, I need you to think carefully about the time. It's important." He paused to let his words sink in, then pressed on. "What time did you leave the party?"

"I don't . . . I know it was after midnight. Because I remember looking at my watch and thinking it was Sunday already and mass wasn't that far off. We left maybe a half hour after that."

"And he was drunk?"

"Totally inebriated. Disgustingly sloppy."

"What happened next?"

She looked away, then back, expression tight. "He was acting all sexed up in the car. Like, com'on, baby, pull over and do me. Give 'Big Tom' a honk."

"A honk?"

"Blow job. I told him to blow himself."

"That's when you fought?"

"Oh yeah. We fought. I pulled off the road. Told him to get the fuck out. He was so drunk, I don't think it occurred to him that I was the one who was driving."

"Did anyone else see him get out of the car?"

"No."

"There was no one else, no other vehicles, anywhere around?"

She shook her head. "I saw him on the phone as I pulled away. I figured he was calling his little whore." She flushed, as if suddenly realizing who she was talking to.

He made a note. "Who is she? Do you know her name?"

"She works for him. At the winery." She pulled another tissue from the box and balled it up in her fist. "It's not about her. She's just one of his many . . . indiscretions."

"Do you know her name?" he asked again.

"Meri," she whispered. "Like I said, she works at the winery."

"After you kicked him out, did you make any calls?"

She shook her head. "No."

"He was robbed. His wallet emptied, his watch and

wedding ring taken. Did he have any other valuables on him, that you know of?"

She shook her head again as her mother arrived, sweeping into the room, the deputy trailing behind. Jill cried out and leaped to her feet and ran to her. "Mom, I can't believe this happened!"

"My God, Jill! The deputies told me Tom—"

"He was murdered, Mom. Murdered!"

The tears flowed again. Reed left the women alone, using the opportunity to confer with the deputies: the search of the house and vehicles had turned up nothing, no blood, bloody clothing or evidence of a cleanup.

He also learned that Jill's mother had been deeply asleep when the deputy called for her. Her live-in boyfriend had been in front of the TV, also asleep. Neither of them had been out that night. And both had been convincingly shocked and horrified by the news of Tom's murder.

"Who could have done this?" Jill's mother demanded, when Reed rejoined them. "How could this have happened here in Sonoma County?"

Reed figured she wouldn't appreciate the truth—that crimes like this happened every day, here in Sonoma County and everywhere else, that this one only felt unique and impossible because it had touched her.

When he left a short time later, he acknowledged a sense that before it was all over, this case would personally touch many more in this small valley. And he sensed, also, that it was going to get ugly.

Chapter Twenty-five

Back in his SUV, Reed let out a long breath. That had been particularly unpleasant. There were things you just didn't want to know about neighbors or old classmates.

Reed gazed a moment at the horizon, the first glimmers of light announcing the new day had arrived, like it or not. He flipped open his phone and punched in Tanner's number.

She answered almost immediately. "Please tell me the wife did it. That the evidence was not only overwhelming but she spilled a full confession."

"Sorry, Babs. No evidence, no confession. Just a tearful widow who'll be so much better off without her prick of a husband."

"You're no damn fun at all."

"Tell me about it. According to her, they left the party together around twelve thirty. They fought about his latest girlfriend and she kicked him out of the car. Says he was drunk on his ass and only too happy to escape her bitching."

"That's where Meri Calvin comes in."

He heard the fatigue in her voice. "How's it going there?"

"Slow. There's a lot of blood to collect. We've got footprints, tire tracks and debris to sift through." She sighed heavily. "It'll be awhile."

"You have my sympathy. I'm going to swing home, shower, change and eat, then head to the Barn. You got Schwann's cell phone?"

"Bagged and tagged."

"Wife said when she pulled away he was already on it. My guess is he called Meri. But you never know."

"I'll get you the call record ASAP."

"And here I thought you'd call me a demanding bastard."

"Give me a minute."

He laughed, told her to keep in touch and hung up.

A little over an hour later, Reed arrived back at the Barn. Schwann's cell phone call record was waiting for him on his desk. A yellow Post-it attached read: *As usual, you owe me.*

He grinned. As usual, he did. He tossed the Post-it, sat and studied the list.

Schwann had made four calls between twelve forty-two and twelve fifty-nine. The first, third and fourth had been to the same number. Meri Calvin's was his guess. And easy enough to check.

Reed swung toward his computer terminal, fired it up and tapped in the appropriate code. The responding officer would have taken her contact information; he should have already inputted his report.

Sure enough, he had. Reed scrolled through the information, stopping on Calvin's entry.

Her cell number matched the one Schwann had dialed three times the night before. Made perfect sense, Reed decided. He'd called her first, cooled his heels, then being his impatient demanding self, had called two more times. And in between he had called someone else and been on with them two and a half minutes. Who?

Maybe the person who had killed him.

He opened his cell phone and punched in the number. It connected and rang; he counted fifteen rings before he ended the call. So much for the quick and easy way. He made a note to expedite getting the information from the phone company.

"No rest for the wicked, man."

Reed looked up. A sleepy-looking Cal stood at his cubicle door. "What's up, dude? Why not out at the Schwann scene?"

"Got called off." He yawned. "Wanted to let you know, we got that analysis back on the doll late yesterday. Tested negative for blood."

"Okay." Reed inclined his head. "Looks more like a stupid prank now. I would have had a hard time picturing a couple spoiled teenagers slaughtering a farm animal for a joke."

Cal yawned again, and backed out the door. "Wish me luck staying awake."

"What's going?"

"More weird Sonoma Valley shit. Somebody's built their own little church up by Castle Road. Got ourselves an altar and all sorts of crazy symbols. Biker called it in."

"Our corner of the world at its best."

"No joke. We got our Bohemian Grove in Monte Rio, the Manson Family in San Francisco and Shambhala up north. Why not a bit of animal sacrifice in Sonoma?"

He started off; Reed stopped him. "Did you say animal sacrifice?"

"Yeah, maybe. That's what the biker thought, but who knows?"

"If you confirm that, let me know. I might want to check it out."

Less than an hour later, Cal confirmed and Reed headed up to the site. The spot had been an observation point and picnic area. It not only overlooked the valley, but on a clear day, offered a view of the Golden Gate Bridge.

"What's the nearest winery?" Reed asked.

"Bart Park. Up and around the bend. Ceased public tours two years ago. Looks like this spot was a casualty."

Reed could make out the peak of a roof through the stand of oak trees. "Casualty is right," he muttered. "Not quite what tourists come for."

"Come on, my brother," Cal said, "what's a day in wine country without a little alternative religion?"

Reed crossed to the altar. It sat in a six-foot circle that had been created with rocks. What had been a concrete picnic table had been transformed into the altar. On its top, the remnants of black candles, sitting in pools of dried wax. Inverted letters, stars and a pentagram had been drawn on the top and sides. Greenery had been collected and arranged around the altar, notably grape stalks and vines.

Reed frowned. Sure, the thought of some nut job up here burning black candles and scribbling pentagrams was unnerving, but the unmistakable stain on the table and ground below was downright disturbing.

Blood. And plenty of it.

Reed studied the stain. Blood had an unmistakable quality to the way it ran and puddled. The dark reddish-brown color it turned. And the rancid way a pool of it smelled as it sat in the sun decomposing.

"This was a fair amount of blood," Cal said. "We're not talking a chicken here."

Reed agreed. "An adult human has what, five, six liters?"

"Yup. An infant about one."

"A small dog, maybe? A cat?"

"How long ago, do you think?"

Cal drew his eyebrows together in thought. "Rained three days ago. So, since then."

"No sign of the carcass?"

"None. Did a search of the area, fifty feet in all directions. But another animal could have dragged it off."

"Or our nut job could have taken it with him. Or her," Reed murmured, starting off. "Keep me posted, all right?"

"You got it. Say, Reed?"

He stopped and looked back at Cal.

"Why so interested?"

"A hunch."

"Thinking our ceremonial friend here also strung up the baby doll."

Reed gave him a thumbs-up, climbed into his car, then

called back, "I have a friend who studies religious cults and rituals. I might have her take a look, see if she knows what we're dealing with."

Moments later, on his way back to the Barn, Reed thought again of Alex. Interesting how things worked out. Somebody constructs a crazy altar and begins sacrificing animals just about the time an expert on such things arrives in town.

Reed glanced at his watch and frowned. But contacting Alex about it had to go way down on his list of priorities. At the top of the list was discovering who'd killed Tom Schwann.

Chapter Twenty-six

Sunday, March 7
9:40 A.M.

Alex awakened with a start. She moved her gaze around the room, disoriented. She'd been dreaming, she realized. One of those disjointed dreams that left her feeling vaguely uneasy.

She untangled herself from the sheet and sat up, struggling to recall what the dream had been about. She'd been moving toward the sound of voices. There had been a strange light. The smell of incense, like in the cave.

The incense. She recognized the scent, Alex realized. But from where?

On the bed stand, her cell phone went off. She snatched it up. From the display, she saw it was Tim. "Morning," she said.

"Way to answer your phone. I called three times last night. I was getting worried."

"You did? I never heard it ring."

Probably because she had been in the middle of a mind-blowing orgasm.

She squirmed, remembering how loud she'd been. *Damn, Alex, could you be any classier?*

"Are you okay?"

"Sure." She cleared her throat. "Why?"

"Just thinking about you. What'd you do last night?"

She supposed, *Went to bed with an incredibly sexy guy I hardly know, had some of the best sex of my life and now want to crawl under a rock and hide* wasn't appropriate, so she told him the other truth.

"Went to a fabulous wine launch party."

"What wine?"

She climbed out of bed and, phone propped to her ear, headed to the bathroom. "The new Red Crest Bear Creek Zin. Fabulous. Hold on, would you?"

She relieved herself, then went back to her cell. "You still there?"

"Yeah, I'm here. And green with envy. You have room in that rental for two?"

She pictured Reed and Tim in a staredown. "Sorry."

"Seriously, you're okay? You need anything?"

"Some help analyzing a dream I had last night would be nice."

Tim had done his doctoral dissertation on dream interpretation. While they were married, he'd analyzed plenty of them for her.

"Shoot."

"I was watching some sort of religious ceremony or ritual."

"Part of the worshippers?"

"No. On the outside. Looking on."

"Spying?"

"Maybe."

"Do you remember how you felt while looking on?"

She thought a moment, then shook her head. "No. But I woke up disoriented and uneasy."

"Go on."

"I was inside, but it wasn't a traditional church. I remember feeling closed in. Or surrounded."

"Trapped?" he asked.

She thought a moment. "No."

"What else do you remember?"

"Nothing." She squirted toothpaste onto her brush, ran it under the water, then stuck it in her mouth.

"It's not much to go on, but here goes. Your dream's clearly about ceremony and commitment. It's your subconscious urging you to cling to what's deeply important to you. On a physical and spiritual level." He paused. "Me."

It took her a moment to realize what he had said. When she did, she laughed, nearly choking on toothpaste foam.

"No, listen to me," he said. "Clearly, you're longing for me and the comfort of our marriage."

She laughed again, then spit. "Goodbye, Tim."

"It's true," he said. "You're crazy about me."

"Goodbye, Tim," she said again, ending the call. She rinsed her toothbrush, then her mouth. Truth was, she did miss him.

She just didn't miss being married to him. Tim was a better friend "with benefits" than he had been a husband.

Some guys just weren't meant to be married.

Alex grabbed the hand towel to wipe the sink and vanity top, then stopped, her gaze settling on what appeared to be a drop of blood on the rounded lip of the sink. Dried but distinctive.

She looked at both her hands, palms and backs. No cuts or scrapes. It hadn't been there yesterday, she was certain of that.

Maybe Reed, she thought, from the night before. She didn't remember him using the bathroom . . . but it wasn't like she had been thinking all that clearly.

Reed. Damn. She dampened the towel and wiped away the spot. *Another expertly executed move on her part. Way to think it through, Alex.*

Think it through, that's what she needed to do. But she definitely needed coffee to make that happen.

A short time later, mug of coffee cupped in her hands, she sat in the swing on her small front porch. She breathed deeply, working to quiet her mind and focus her thoughts. On what her first steps would be, what she wanted to accomplish.

The task should have been be easy. Instead, her thoughts kept circling back to the same three things: the bizarre dream she had awakened to, her panic in the wine cave the night before, and making love with Reed.

Quite a way to start off her stay here in Sonoma; not quite the "bang" she had hoped for.

Alex rolled her eyes at her own crude play on words. Other than her making an ass of herself in front of her former family, what had happened in the cave the night before? She knew what she had heard and smelled. Others had been in the cave and had somehow slipped out before Reed and his brother came along.

But that wasn't what was really bothering her. It was her panicked reaction to being lost. Her absolute terror when the lights went off.

Neither was like her. She had been mostly taking care of herself all her life. She remembered being in grade school and getting herself up, fed and ready for school, then walking alone to the bus stop, remembered coming home in the afternoon and finding her mother still in bed, too depressed to participate in her daughter's life. Many times she had prepared them both dinner, then gotten herself put to bed. No hand-holding or night-lights for her.

The amount of wine she'd drunk, Alex decided. Fatigue. Grief. The newness of her situation. A potent mix that had upended her typically self-confident and fearless self.

Alex sipped her coffee, picturing the smiling, obviously happy woman her mother had been in Lyla Reed's photographs. She couldn't lose focus, Alex reminded herself. That woman was why she was here. To discover what had happened to her.

Maybe, as Lyla had suggested, the loss of Dylan had destroyed her. Maybe, because Alex wasn't a mother, she couldn't understand.

Even if that was true, she wanted to know *that* Patsy. The woman who had smiled and laughed and taken pleasure in being alive. She was hungry to know her.

Coffee mug empty, she stood and headed back into the house. After being out in the fresh air, she noticed a subtle, sour odor inside. She wrinkled her nose, trying to identify the smell. She couldn't and decided it must be something that had drifted in the night before.

Chapter Twenty-seven

Sunday, March 7
11:50 A.M.

Reed met his brother Joe at the second-floor elevator. Joe and Tom Schwann had been friends since grade school and had run in the same pack as teenagers. With Joe was another of their lifelong friends, Carter Townsend.

"I can't believe it, Dan," Joe said, voice thick. "Tom had his faults, but he was basically a good guy."

"I'm really sorry, Joe." He gave his brother a quick hug. "I know how close you were."

Reed turned to Carter. "Sorry, man. How're you holding up?"

The man looked stricken. "Best I can. Like Joe, I can't believe Tom's dead."

"Let's find a quiet place to talk."

Reed led them to an interview room. They sat. "I'm glad you came in. You were both good friends of Tom's; do you have any idea who could have done this?"

"Maybe Jill," Carter offered. "They fought all the time."

"Jill is currently not a suspect. Is there anyone else? A former lover? Business employee?"

The two men looked at each other, then Joe turned back

to him. "I can't imagine anyone who knew Tom doing this. He was an okay guy, not perfect, but who is?"

"Not perfect, can you elaborate?"

The two looked at each other; Joe took the lead. "What you already know. He was a notorious hound dog and drank too much, but as far as I know, he was a straight-up businessman. Didn't screw with his suppliers or clients. Paid his bills and was generally the life of the party."

Carter spoke up again. "The newspaper said he was killed with a secateur. How . . . I mean, where—"

"We're keeping that part out of the press for now. But I can tell you, it was a bloody, gruesome mess." Reed threw that out there so he could judge their reactions.

They passed with flying colors. Joe looked sick. Carter went white and clasped his hands together.

Carter broke the uncomfortable silence first. "I read about that altar being found up off Castle Road."

"Yes?"

"It's got me spooked," he said.

Reed frowned. "Why? The two aren't related."

"You don't remember," Joe said. "You were really young." He stopped. "Never mind."

"Bullshit, Bro. I was too young to remember what?"

"There was a whole rash of that crap," Joe said. "Around the time Dylan disappeared."

"Rash of what kind of crap?"

"Altars popping up around the countryside. Animals disappearing."

"Animals?"

"A couple dogs. A lamb and goat. Chickens. Not all at once, but over the course of months."

Carter jumped in. "I remember people talking. You know, wondering if . . ."

His voice trailed off. Reed looked from one man to the other. "If what?"

"If Dylan had been taken as a . . . human sacrifice."

The words landed grotesquely between the three. Reed cleared his throat. "I've never heard any of this."

"You were young. Remember, I was a teenager." His brother's voice shook. "I heard everything."

"There's more," Carter stepped in. "Another murder, by secateur."

"When?"

"Not too long after Dylan disappeared."

"Who?"

"Some guy. A fieldworker. I don't remember his name."

"Why are you telling me all this, Joe?"

"What if history's repeating itself? I have kids of my own. What if something happened to one of them? I couldn't take it, Dan. It'd kill me, I know it would."

"Joe, look"—he leaned forward—"Dylan was not the victim of some bizarre cult ritual. The Sheriff's Department did a thorough investigation. So did the FBI. They determined he was kidnapped."

"But no ransom—"

"Recent findings may explain why. Trust me on this, Joe. Dylan was kidnapped, but something went terribly wrong."

"And the other murder?"

"Every Tom, Dick and Harry carries one of those Red Roosters around. I can't tell you how many times I've been called to a scene where one drunk field hand has pulled his secateur on the other. You remember this so clearly because it occurred so soon after Dylan's disappearance. I'll check it, though. Let you know if anything turns up."

A short time later, Reed had a name: the Sommers' groundskeeper, Alberto Alvarez. He had been considered a strong suspect in Dylan's abduction—he had been seen on the property that night, then afterward failed to show up for work—until he turned up dead.

Murdered by secateur to the throat.

The murder had gone unsolved, swallowed up by the furor over Dylan.

Reed frowned and leaned back in his chair. It seemed obvious that Alvarez had either seen something and been murdered because of it, or had been part of the plot and murdered when it went south.

And yet, as he dug, he found no records of an active search for a link between the two crimes. A search for the man's killer, yes. But no suspicion that his death had been linked to Dylan Sommer's disappearance.

How had they missed this? It represented shoddy, irresponsible police work. Why hadn't the FBI followed the lead?

Reed drummed his fingers on his desktop. Who, if anyone, was still on the force from back then? His captain was only an eighteen-year veteran of the force. He dug his department directory out and began scanning. Names of a few old-timers popped out, guys who'd been around thirty or so years.

"Why so serious?"

He looked up at Tanner. She stood in the doorway, a carton of yogurt in her hands. "Alberto Alvarez, ever hear that name before?"

"Nope." She took a spoonful of the yogurt. "Why?"

"He was a groundskeeper for the Sommers. Took a secateur to the neck shortly after Dylan's disappearance. Before his murder he was considered a strong suspect in the abduction."

"Then he turned up dead." She wandered across to his desk. "Who killed him?"

"Never solved." He turned his computer monitor to face her.

She scanned the report, eyebrows drawing together. "How'd you find this?"

"My brother. This shouldn't have flown under our radar."

"It's a twenty-five-year-old crime. What bothers me is the ignored no-brainer here."

"The link between this murder and Dylan Sommer's disappearance."

"Exactly."

"Here's another weird fact, according to my brother and his buddy Carter Townsend. Around the time of Dylan's abduction, there was a rash of reports of ritual sites and animal sacrifice. There was talk that Dylan had been taken by one of these groups."

"You verified any of this?"

"Not yet."

"Let's do it."

Chapter Twenty-eight

A search of old reports had verified his brother's facts. Reed and Tanner had decided to wait until the following morning to bring it to their superiors.

They met at eight thirty sharp. Tanner had brought him a venti-sized dark roast. "Thanks," he said, taking it.

Together they headed for Jon MacIntyre's office. When they reached it, Reed tapped on the open door. "Morning, Mac. Have a few minutes?"

The sergeant waved them in. Jon MacIntyre had been on the force eighteen years, the last four as the VCI sergeant. His Teddy bear demeanor belied an iron will and fierce intellect.

Now, he fixed that sharp gaze on the two detectives. "What do you have?"

Tanner began with their progress so far. "Processed the scene. We've got a boatload of possible evidence to sift through. No viable prints on the weapon. Could've been wiped or the perp may have been wearing gloves."

Reed took over. "Jill Schwann's story checked out. So did the girlfriend's. Cell phone numbers verify both witness accounts. We're running the list of all calls made the twenty-four hours before and after his murder."

"Good. Your report indicated Schwann had been robbed."

Reed nodded. "Watch, wedding ring, contents of his wallet."

"Autopsy?"

"Scheduled for tomorrow."

Mac looked from one to the other of them. "Is that it?"

"Not quite. Ran across something interesting. Another Red Rooster murder. Unsolved."

The sergeant frowned. "Where?"

"Here in Sonoma County. Twenty-five years ago."

"You think it's relevant?"

"Let's just say I'm not ruling out its relevancy yet." Reed handed Mac the file of printouts he'd prepared, then filled him in on the details. "What struck both of us were the lapses in the initial investigation."

The sergeant scanned the reports. "Astounding lapses."

"I'm thinking that between unearthing Baby Doe and seeing this, we should officially reopen the Dylan Sommer abduction case."

He studied Reed a moment, then picked up his phone and dialed their lieutenant.

"He's free now. Let's take a walk."

Moments later they sat in the lieutenant of detectives' spacious, light-filled office. Lieutenant George Torres came from the school of hard knocks. The son of a vineyard worker and housekeeper, he had fought his way up to highest ranking Latino in the Sheriff's Department. He often said that anybody who said racism didn't exist in this country was either blind or a liar. He also said that anybody who used it as an excuse was a fool.

He'd cried when Barack Obama won the United States presidency. The doors, he'd said, were finally opened for all.

Mac filled the man in; when he finished, Torres narrowed his eyes. "This pisses me off. I remember this murder. The victim was Latino."

"Yes, sir."

"First a suspect, then a victim.. And the ball was completely dropped. I was a rookie deputy at the time."

"Who was Sheriff?" Reed asked.

"Oscar Beulle. Retired not too long after. Maybe a year."

"He's still alive," Mac offered.

Lieutenant Torres nodded. "Right. Moved to Calistoga to be near his daughter. Grows a few grapes. Pops in every now and then to 'check on us.' "

"I think we should question him. See what he remembers."

"I agree."

"Do we officially reopen the Sommer case?" Reed asked.

"Talk to Beulle first."

"What about your counterpart from back then?" Tanner asked the lieutenant. "Maybe he'd remember—"

"He was killed in the line of duty. I was a rookie. I remember because it shook me up pretty bad. I had a wife and a new baby. Frankly, I thought about a career change."

"Dig a bit," Mac said. "See if the detectives in charge of the investigation are still active. Maybe there's more here than we're seeing."

If there was, Reed discovered after several hours, he wasn't going to learn it from the detectives who had worked the case. Everybody who had touched the Sommer disappearance or Alvarez murder had either relocated or was dead.

Which left former Sheriff Beulle.

Calistoga, an old western-style town with more than a touch of eccentricity and known for its natural hot springs, was located in Napa Valley.

Reed found the man at home, tending the patch of vines he had in his backyard. Folks did that around here, used an available back- or side yard to grow grapes, then used them to make a few cases of wine. He'd thought about it himself, but figured it'd be too weird, considering his family history. Besides, when would he have time to tend the vines? He was never home.

"Sheriff Beulle?" he said, crossing to the man's garden gate. "Detective Reed, Sonoma County Sheriff's Department." He held up his shield.

The man smiled, waved him in, then went back to pruning his vines. "What can I do for you?" he asked when Reed neared him.

"I wanted to ask you a few questions about an old case."

"That so?" he said without stopping his work. "What case?"

"Dylan Sommer and Alberto Alvarez."

Beulle stopped, looked up at him. "Thinking about re-opening them?"

"Yes, sir."

He nodded and motioned Reed to follow him. "'Bout time for a break anyway."

"How do you do with your vines?" Reed asked as they made their way to the back of the house.

"Pretty well. Seventy pounds of grapes last year. Got two cases of merlot out of it." They climbed the stairs to the back porch. "It's a tasty little wine, too. I'll pour us a glass."

"None for me."

Beulle grinned. "Good man. But I'd only have reported you if you'd had a second."

He slid open the glass door; Reed followed him inside. It was a simple home, without any fussy, homey touches. Apparently there was no Mrs. Beulle.

True to his word, Beulle poured himself a glass of his house merlot, then a splash in another glass and pushed it across the counter.

Reed swirled the sample, then tasted. Beulle was right—it wasn't bad. He told him so.

The older man thanked him, then swirled the liquid. "So why now?" he murmured, more to himself than Reed, "twenty-five years later?" He answered his own question. "The remains of that baby. You're thinking it's little Dylan Sommer."

Reed didn't confirm, just let Beulle go. "And you're reopening Alvarez, because of Schwann. Same manner of death, secateur to the throat. Only Alvarez had nothing of value to steal."

"Except his life." Reed cocked an eyebrow. "You seem privy to facts we haven't released, Sheriff."

Beulle laughed. "Don't play naive, Detective. I still have

plenty of friends in the department; what I don't get from the news, I get from them." He sipped the wine, expression thoughtful. "Is the ID on the boy positive?"

"No. But it's looking strong." Reed sensed that the older man wasn't just curious but hungry for information. "I've got a question, Sheriff. Why didn't you investigate a possible connection between the Alvarez murder and the Sommer boy's disappearance?"

Beulle stiffened. "I had my best men working on the case. They didn't see a reason to."

"Maybe it's just me, but it seems like a no-brainer. The man was considered a suspect, then turned up dead."

"So?"

"So, it's a red flag. Maybe he was in on it and was killed to keep him quiet. Or maybe he saw something and was killed because of it."

"If he'd seen something why not say so, especially when we had his feet to the fire? As for being part of it, Alvarez was a migrant farmworker. He spoke almost no English. He'd come for harvest, gotten hurt, so the Sommer family had taken pity on him and let him stay on."

Beulle shook his head. "Dylan Sommer was abducted from his bed. The perpetrator was smart and prepared. He slipped in while Harlan and Patsy were out and the other children were sleeping, and stole the boy."

"Not that smart," Reed murmured. "Not that prepared."

"No? He got away with it, didn't he?"

Reed leaned forward. "Depends on how you define 'getting away with it.' If the remains we found belong to Dylan Sommer, the perp didn't get far with him. Why do *you* think he did it, Sheriff?"

"Ransom. Something went wrong. Or they got scared. And they killed the child, buried him and ran."

"Maybe what went wrong was Alvarez got a look at them. That's why he was killed."

"With his own secateur?" He shook his head. "No. Alvarez was killed by one of his own kind."

"His own kind? Another human being?"

Beulle ignored that. "Autopsy found alcohol in his system. A lot of it. My detectives believed he had been out drinking and gotten into a fight that ended up going terminal."

"And that's it?"

"That's it."

"What about the rumors that Dylan had been abducted to be part of a ritualistic sacrifice?"

A mottled red crept up Beulle's cheeks. "Rumors, Detective. Ugly and destructive. We never found anything to suggest such a thing."

"No evidence in the area of ritualistic activity?"

"You've obviously read the activity reports. This area is known for that ritualistic crap. It comes and goes. It's not against the law and most of it is harmless."

"Most of it?"

"Yeah. When they start harming animals, it crosses the line. But in most cases, that line isn't crossed."

Reed narrowed his eyes. "Since you're still plugged into the department, you heard about the altar up by Bart Park?"

"I did."

"They crossed the line with that one."

"Like I said, it does happen. I don't know what you want from me, Detective."

"Did you question Alvarez's family?"

"He had none."

"His friends or close associates?"

"The ones we could find. Asked around in the community, nobody had a clue who would have harmed Alvarez."

"And he didn't confide in anyone?"

"No one."

"You've got a good memory, Sheriff Beulle."

He narrowed his eyes. "Dylan Sommer's disappearance was the worst case I ever faced. I retired when I did because I couldn't clear it. You don't forget cases like that, Detective. Just because you leave 'em behind doesn't mean they leave you alone."

Reed experienced a moment of sympathy for the man. "I thought if I spoke with the case detectives, something might jump out at me. I saw that Detective Hurst was killed in the line of duty. What about the other detective?"

"He relocated," Beulle said, and stood. "The Chicago area, I believe. Left police work. Had simply had enough of it."

"Do you have any idea how I could contact—"

"Sorry. I haven't heard from him in years." He held out his hand, indicating their meeting was over. "Tell Lieutenant Torres I said hello."

Reed shook his hand. "I will. And if you think of anything pertinent—"

"I'll call." Beulle showed him back to the door he had entered through. "I hope you can prove the remains are Dylan Sommer's, so that family gets closure."

Chapter Twenty-nine

Alex knew of the El Dorado Kitchen. Located in the El Dorado Hotel on Sonoma's town square and helmed by up-and-coming chef Justin Everett, it was consistently named by critics and foodies as one of *the* places to eat in wine country.

Rachel had already arrived and was waiting for her at a table in the courtyard. She looked like a million bucks in her earth-toned brocade blazer and Alex wished she tried a little harder than her jeans and denim jacket.

The waiter was at the table, opening a bottle of wine. Alex raised her eyebrows. Apparently, people here drank wine with every meal, no matter the day of the week.

A moment later, Alex reached the table. Rachel smiled brilliantly up at her. "You did remember! I was worried you wouldn't."

The waiter held out the chair for her. Alex returned the smile and sat. "You're not the only one. I half thought the wine had prompted the invitation, which you had then immediately forgotten you made."

Rachel laughed. "I never let the wine talk for me. And

I never forget." She waved the waiter off and poured them both a glass of wine. "It's a Russian River Pinot."

Alex tasted. "Mmm, yummy. Thank you."

"No, thank you. I'm so glad you agreed to have lunch." The waiter delivered a basket of bread and Rachel dug in.

"How was your morning?" she asked, spreading herb aioli on the sourdough bread. "Did you explore a bit? Hunt down some of your mother's old friends?"

"Much less exciting, I'm afraid. I spent the morning working on my doctoral dissertation."

Rachel looked utterly disappointed and Alex laughed. "Don't worry, I plan on striking out this afternoon. But no caves. Maybe never again."

"I'm so sorry that happened. How're you feeling today?"

"Frankly, embarrassed."

"Don't be. We're used to drama around here. Goes with the wine."

"I don't know how I got so turned around. My sense of direction is usually pretty good. And I know what I heard. There were people partying in there."

"That's what really worried Joe and Ferris. They've had problems before. Kids smoking pot, stuff like that. It's a huge liability. Like I said, those caves creep me out, too. You should see the caves at our winer—" She bit the words back and shook her head. "I keep forgetting, you have seen the Sommer caves."

"But I don't remember, so it's sort of like I haven't."

"I find this whole amnesia thing of yours fascinating and weird." Rachel broke off a piece of her bread and popped it in her mouth.

Alex could have been offended. But she found Rachel's honesty refreshing. She laughed. "Want the truth? I find it really weird myself. Not so fascinating."

"You don't remember any of this?"

"Nope. Nothing."

The waiter arrived with food. "I hope you don't mind, I ordered several of my favorites apps for you to try. Fried egg pizza, fennel sausage and Fourme d'Ambert."

"Not at all. It looks wonderful." Alex helped herself to a little of each. "Why should I see the Sommer caves?" she asked. "How are they different?"

Rachel leaned forward. "The Reed caves are modern, ours are original. Dad likes to say Francis Reed had a case of extreme cave envy, so he had theirs dug."

"But isn't a cave a cave?" Alex gave in and broke off a piece of sourdough bread. "How are they different?"

"Try as different as a Disney jungle and a real one." Rachel selected a portion of the pizza, then went on. "The first caves, like ours and the Schramsberg caves, were dug by hand in the late 1800s. They're living caves, complete with mossy lichen hanging from the ceilings. They can be . . . atmospheric. If you can screw up your courage, I'll give you a tour sometime."

Alex shuddered. "No thanks."

Rachel smiled. "To give you an idea, we have forty thousand square feet of caves and Schramsberg has fifty. Red Crest, where you got lost last night, is only fifteen—Don't look now, there's Joe and Ferris. Oh shit, they saw us."

Alex turned. Sure enough, Reed's brothers were heading toward their table. The same as the other night, she was struck with how different in looks the three Reed brothers were.

Rachel stood. "Joe," she said warmly, offering her cheek for a kiss from them both. "Ferris. You remember Alex."

How could they forget? Alex stood and greeted the men. "I'm so embarrassed about Saturday night. I'm usually not so excitable."

"Don't worry about it," Ferris said, smiling.

"It's understandable," Joe murmured. "Ferris told me you thought you heard voices?"

"Yes, but I—"

"She and I were just talking about that. Wondering if being lost in there might have jogged a childhood memory."

Alex looked at Rachel in surprise. The woman winked at her, then turned back to the two men. "Seems I even remember something like that happening to you, Ferris. How old were you? Six? Seven?"

"Six." He looked at his older brother. "A joke perpetrated by Joe and Clark."

"And their group of evil henchmen."

"Reed swooped in to save the day," Joe drawled, though his playful words didn't match his expression. "Already playing hero. We'll let you get back to your lunch."

When the two had gone to their table, Rachel leaned toward her. "Daddy's boys, the both of them, I can't stand either of them, though I find Mr. CEO Joe particularly loathsome. At least Ferris can laugh at himself once in a while."

Alex was shocked. Rachel must have been able to tell, because her lips lifted in a self-mocking smile. "How's that for honesty? Clark's the same way. They're their fathers' puppets."

Rachel pushed away her plate and reached for her wineglass. "I have a lot of respect for Reed. Walking away like he did."

"What about you? You didn't walk away."

"I couldn't." She smiled. "Cut me open and I bleed cabernet sauvignon."

Alex laughed. "So you love the work, but they don't?"

"They covet it, there's a difference." She drained her glass and poured another. "Clark and Will both strut around like a couple of peacocks. Sommer Wines are the plumage. They can strut all they want, but I'm an equal shareholder. And you know what? Without me, those feathers aren't nearly so fine."

Rancor for her cousins was obvious. Alex supposed this was what Reed had been talking about.

Rachel motioned with her glass and the garnet-hued liquid dipped and swayed. "Until Dylan disappeared, Dad ran Sommer Wines, not Treven." She leaned closer and motioned Alex to do the same. "But Dad was Grandpa's favorite. So he put him in charge."

She stopped, then shook her head. "His favorite, that sounded awful, didn't it? I should say, Grandpa recognized Dad's gifts. And he and Grandpa had the same vision of how to move the company forward."

"And Treven's differed from theirs?"

"Oh yes, world wine domination, bottle by cheap bottle."

"I don't understand."

"Expansion and profits, by whatever means necessary." Rachel started to say something else, then caught her breath. "Oh my God. That was your mother's ring, wasn't it?"

"You remember the ring. Any idea what BOV stands for?" Alex slipped the ring off and handed it to Rachel. "The inscription. I'm curious."

She studied it. "No clue. You know who you could ask? There's a jewelry store on the square, the Golden Bow. They specialize in wine country designs, they might know something."

Rachel handed it back. "I just had the most completely morbid thought. If they hadn't dug up that grave, we wouldn't be sitting here together."

Alex had thought the same. Many times over the past days she'd thought of how those remains had changed her life. And sometimes as she lay in the dark, she wondered what changes still awaited her.

"Do you think it's him," Alex asked softly. "Do you think it's our . . . brother?"

Instead of answering, Rachel said, "The grave was in one of our vineyards. One of the Sommer family's first. We produced a small production of old vine zinfandel called Two Brothers."

"Two Brothers? For Harlan and Treven?"

"Actually, for the two Sommer brothers who founded the winery. The first Friedrich and Oliver." Rachel picked up her glass and twirled it. The wine caught the light and Alex found herself mesmerized by it.

"Great wine starts with good fruit. The right amount of sun and water, temperatures that are neither too hot nor too cold. Soil that has just the right combination of minerals." She laughed. "You see why I don't have children; every year I give birth."

Alex smiled. "What happened to the Two Brothers vineyard? Didn't they find the grave while ripping it up?"

"We had no choice. The vines became infested with phyl-loxera." At Alex's expression, she explained. "It's a louse that attacks the root of the vine. You don't know you have a problem until it's too late."

Alex frowned, recalling something from a wine tour she had taken years ago. "I thought the phylloxera problem had been solved?"

"Mmm. After nearly totaling California's wine industry." She drained her glass. "Now, they graft a phylloxera-resistant root stock to the scion. But these were century-old vines."

A note of reverence in her tone hinted that ripping up those vines had torn a piece from Rachel's heart—as if she was physically attached to them.

She'd said it a moment ago: the wines were her babies.

Rachel reached across the table and caught her hand. "But if the vines hadn't had to be torn out—"

"The grave wouldn't have been found."

"Yes. And we may never have seen each other again." She paused. "Would you like to see it? The vineyard where the body was found? His grave?"

Even as "No" sprang to her lips, she said, "Yes."

Rachel insisted on paying for their lunch. It occurred to Alex as they buckled into Rachel's work truck that they'd polished off the entire bottle of wine and that Rachel shouldn't be driving.

They took Sonoma Highway north to Moon Mountain Road. The road gently snaked upward, and Alex partially lowered her window to let the spring air blow against her face. For all her worries about Rachel's driving ability, she handled the road with what seemed like effortless expertise.

Twenty minutes later, Rachel eased to the side of the road. They climbed out of the truck and silently crossed into the vineyard, stopping beside an area that had been staked off. It wasn't a neat, clean hole, the way Alex had imagined it would be. Instead, it had the look of an eruption. As if something violent had taken place here, as if the earth had rejected the tiny body and forced it out. A sort of reverse birthing process.

"Ugly, isn't it?"

Alex couldn't find her voice and nodded.

"I think the body . . . that it was Dylan," Rachel whispered, answering Alex's earlier question. "I just do. I guess I feel it here"—she pressed her fist to her stomach—"deep in my gut."

They fell silent. Alex gazed at the grave, tears welling in her eyes, swamping them. The breeze ruffled her hair and a crow flying overhead screeched.

Her brother. Why couldn't she remember him? She'd loved him desperately. Even without his memory, she knew it was true.

"I wish I could remember," Alex whispered.

"I wish I couldn't," Rachel said, voice thick. She looked at Alex. "Let's get out of here."

Silently, they returned to the truck and climbed in. Alex saw that Rachel was crying and reached across the seat and caught her hand.

Rachel curled her fingers tightly around hers. "No one should have to go through that. No one."

Alex wasn't certain whether Rachel was talking about what Dylan had endured—or what she had. In the end, she supposed it didn't really matter. The pain was the same.

"Do you want to talk about it?" she asked.

Rachel looked almost startled at the sound of Alex's voice. She glanced her way, shook her head. "Nothing was ever the same again."

Not for any of them, Alex realized. All their lives had been violently, irrevocably altered.

Rachel freed her hand and wiped the tears from her cheeks. "Maybe your mother had the right idea. Bury it all. Forget about it."

Some things couldn't be buried or forgotten. They made themselves known, coming out twisted and foul.

"No," Alex said. "It destroyed her."

"I think it destroyed us all." Rachel made a face. "I didn't plan for this to become a sobfest." She flipped down her visor and peered into the mirror. "Look at me! I'm a mess!"

"Raccoon Woman," Alex said. She lowered her own visor, peered into the mirror and laughed. "And her sidekick."

Rachel handed her a tissue and they took a minute to clean themselves up. They rode in silence back into town. Alex had walked to the restaurant, so Rachel dropped her at her rental.

"I'm really glad you're back, Alex," Rachel said. "I think you being here is going to help us all heal."

Tears stung Alex's eyes. She blinked against them, uncertain what to say. Rachel reached across the seat and squeezed her hand. "I know that's pretty heavy, but you're a piece of the puzzle from that time. And you were taken away from us."

Moments later, Alex watched her stepsister drive off. It *was* like a puzzle, she thought. But because of the individual frame of reference, everyone's piece was overlapping but unique. She wondered where hers fit in.

Chapter Thirty

Monday, March 8
6:40 P.M.

Alex spent the rest of the day in downtown Sonoma, introducing herself to some of the old-timers, asking questions and following leads. At the jewelry store Rachel had told her about, the owner had admired her ring and given her the name of an artist who'd been making original wine country–inspired jewelry for forty years. She'd thought it looked like his work.

Alex had decided to wait until the next day to contact him. She was hungry, tired, and needed to process.

As she approached her front door, she heard Margo mewing. Poor baby must be hungry, she thought, unlocking the door. As she opened it, the cat darted out.

"Margo!" Alex scooped her up. But instead of the passive animal she was accustomed to, the cat struggled in her grasp. Alex frowned. "What's up with you, silly cat?"

Alex tightened her hold and carried Margo into the house. The moment they were inside, the cat leapt out of her arms and darted off.

She shut the door, wrinkling her nose. Maybe the smell was getting to her? It'd definitely grown stronger in the time she'd been out.

Alex flipped on a lamp and looked around, tired and annoyed. What was the deal? She'd eaten only a handful of meals since moving in and had taken the trash out.

She stopped in the center of the living room. Backed-up sewage was a possible answer. Or an animal that had gotten trapped in the attic or walls and died there. Alex followed her nose; the smell grew stronger as she headed to the back of the house.

She stopped outside the bathroom. Margo sat on the throw rug, staring intently at the cabinet located under the sink.

Alex studied the cat. She sat stone still, as if every fiber of her being was focused on that closed cabinet door. The way she did when hunting.

Suddenly, the cat yowled. Alex jumped, chill bumps racing up her spine.

Something was in that cabinet. Something Margo didn't like.

Swallowing hard, Alex entered the bathroom, crossed to the cabinet and knelt in front of it. She reached for the knob and eased the door open.

The stench hit Alex hard. Her stomach clenched and she covered her nose and mouth with her hand. At least now she knew where the smell was coming from.

But what was causing it?

She peered into the cabinet. A plastic bag, she saw. Black.

She didn't want to reach her hand in there. Her every instinct recoiled from the thought. But she had to.

Grabbing a hand towel to hold over her nose and mouth, Alex grasped the bag and dragged it out. She noticed the flies then. Dozens of them. The contents of her stomach rushed to her throat.

Choking sickness back, Alex opened the bag. An animal, she saw. Or what was left of one.

With a cry, she released the bag and stumbled backward. Getting to her feet, she ran for the front of the house and out onto the porch. She reached the edge, bent over the rail and vomited.

Trembling, she squeezed her eyes shut. But instead of

forcing the image out, it filled her head. Matted fur. An eye winking up at her.

She breathed deeply and slowly through her nose, fighting for calm. To slow her thoughts so she could think.

Who'd done this? She searched her memory. The creature hadn't been there when she moved in, she was certain of it. So when had it been placed there?

Saturday night. It must have been. While she was out? When she was sleeping? Sunday morning was the first time she'd smelled—

The drop of blood. On the vanity.

Not hers. Not Reed's. The creature's.

And then she realized: somebody was messing with her. Wanting her to be afraid. To run.

Sick bastard. She didn't scare that easily.

Anger kicked in. Sucking in a sharp breath, she marched back into the house. She rinsed her mouth, then retrieved her cell phone and punched in Reed's number. He answered right away. It sounded like he was eating.

"It's Alex. Am I interrupting your dinner?"

"If you call a burger at my desk dinner. What's up?"

"There's something here I think you should see. Someone left a . . . someone was in my house and left a dead animal under my bathroom sink."

For a long moment he was silent. When he finally spoke, he simply said, "I'll be there in thirty minutes."

True to his word, he pulled up thirty minutes later. She was waiting on the front porch, Margo in her arms.

"The bathroom?" he asked as he approached her.

"Yes. I'll wait here, if you don't mind?"

He said he didn't and a few minutes later, he returned. He was on his cell phone. When he hung up, she looked at him in question. "One of the CSI detectives is on their way over to collect it."

She nodded.

"Can you answer some questions?" When she nodded again, he said, "Tell me how you came to discover the animal."

She did, starting with noticing the spot of blood on the vanity, then the subtle smell later that same morning, to arriving home tonight to find Margo acting strangely.

"The smell had gotten much worse and I started to search for what was causing it. When I found Margo in the bathroom staring at that cupboard I . . . knew."

"That the smell was coming from in there?"

"Yes." She rubbed at the chill bumps on her arms. "I saw the bag, pulled it out and—" She drew a deep breath. "What kind of animal was it?"

"A lamb. Very young."

Her stomach rolled. "How did it . . . what happened to it?"

"It was sliced open."

Alex brought a hand to her mouth. "A sacrificial lamb," she whispered.

"What did you say?"

She repeated it and looked at him. "Why?" she asked. "Why hurt that poor creature and . . . why bring it here? I don't understand."

"You noticed the smell the first time Sunday?"

"Yes."

"And the drop of blood on the sink, also Sunday?"

She nodded. "I remember looking at my hands, for a cut, then thinking maybe you—"

"I didn't use the bathroom."

"I didn't think so, but I couldn't remember for sure."

"And then?"

"I wiped it away and forgot about it."

He was looking at her strangely, as if he was trying to figure something out. "What?"

"You're awfully calm."

"Is there something wrong with that?"

"It's a little surprising, that's all."

"I suppose I should be frightened and feel violated. Maybe I will later, but right now I'm pissed. Really pissed." She looked away, then back. "The bastard wants me afraid. I'm not inclined to give him what he wants."

He continued to look intently at her. "Him?"

She met his gaze. "Or her."

"Any idea why someone would target you this way?"

"None." He cocked an eyebrow and she made a sound of irritation. "You're the detective, piece it together."

The CSI unit arrived. Alex recognized the woman: Detective Tanner.

She greeted Alex, then she and Reed headed into the house. This time she followed them inside, opening windows as she went. She'd rather the cold than the smell.

She moved from the front of the house to the back. As she neared the bathroom, she caught snatches of their conversation.

"—a little odd," Tanner was saying, voice low. "I find it difficult to—"

Reed murmured something she couldn't make out, then, "to the site—reaction—don't you think?"

As if aware of her proximity, they went silent. Alex hurried past, to the kitchen. She unlocked the single window above the sink and slid it up.

"Are you okay?"

She turned to Reed in the doorway. "Trying to get rid of the smell."

"Tanner's going to take care of the animal. Dust for prints."

"Great."

"There's something I'd like to get your opinion on. It'll mean taking a drive."

"Now?"

"As soon as Tanner's done. You up for it?"

She was, and thirty minutes later, they were in his Tahoe, traveling the narrow, vineyard-lined road. They had driven in silence for several miles when he spoke again. "A biker discovered a makeshift altar yesterday. I thought maybe you could tell me something about it." He glanced her way. "Your area of expertise, right?"

"Right. Why tonight?"

"Why not? I was there, you were there—"

"Brought together by a dead animal found sliced open and stuffed into the cabinet under my bathroom sink."

"Yes."

"One I called a sacrificial lamb."

"You did."

"And you're thinking the creature may have been used as a sacrifice on the makeshift altar we're going to see."

"I didn't say that."

"But it's a possibility."

He didn't respond, though he didn't have to—they both knew it was true. They fell silent. Alex gazed out the window, her thoughts turning to the other night and their love-making.

Odd how she hadn't thought of it until now. She wondered if he had.

They arrived at their destination. Reed opened the glove compartment and brought out a flashlight, then reached around to the backseat for a second. As he did, his coat opened and she caught a glimpse of his gun.

Her mouth went dry. They were in the middle of God only knew where. Pitch-black, the only illumination from the stars and slim crescent moon, the only sign of civilization a house they had passed a mile down the road.

He was a cop. She trusted him. Enough to have had sex with him, for Heaven's sake.

So, why the unease?

He turned back and handed her the light. She took it and shook off the question and the crazy thoughts that had prompted it. She opened her car door and stepped out into the night. She snapped on the light. Its bright beam sliced through the dark, landing on the altar. She moved the beam over the site, taking a quick, visual inventory.

This site didn't look that different from ceremonial sites she had seen over the years. And she had seen many. Been witness to many religious rituals, from the routine Catholic mass to the truly bizarre and sometimes frightening. Most she had attended as an academic, a chronicler of culture.

And as one with a thirst to *understand*. To figure out what drove the human animal's search for meaning. What inside humans cried out for an overarching belief system.

She moved closer, taking in the scrawled symbols, the black candles, the evidence of animal sacrifice.

Reed came up to stand beside her. She glanced at him. "So, I was right about your reason for bringing me up here. You think the lamb in my bathroom could be the animal slaughtered here."

"What do you think?"

"That it's a crazy idea."

"Why crazy?"

She looked at him. "Frame of reference. What possible connection could there be between this"—she swept her flashlight beam over the tableau—"and me?"

He didn't answer. "Tell me about what you see. Who did this?"

"By that you mean who philosophically?"

"Yes. What group."

She shook her head. "Don't know if it was a specific group. What I see is more like a kitchen sink approach."

She pointed her flashlight toward the ground, the series of stones that had been placed around the altar. "Let's start here. The altar's been placed in a ritual circle, also referred to as the sacred circle. The circle forms protection from evil. Pretty standard stuff."

She moved the light beam yet again. "Look at the symbols. The pentagram is used in all forms of paganism but also, when inverted, in Satanism. The moon and stars we see in Wiccan ceremonies."

She settled the light on double jagged lines. "In Satanism, the double Z symbol represents the destroyer. It could also depict thunderbolts, which were the weapon of Zeus. The cross is an obvious Christian symbol but also seen in pagan worship and Santeria, which absorbed many of the Catholic rituals, symbols and saints. An inverted cross is seen in Satanic worship."

She indicated the clusters of foliage and grapevines arranged on the altar. "These represent a reverence for nature, which we see in all forms of paganism."

"You're avoiding the obvious."

He meant the sacrifice. She corrected him. "Not avoiding. Getting around to it. It's the deal breaker."

"Deal breaker?"

"You simply don't see it in paganism. That eliminates a whole slew of belief systems. Wicca, Shamanism, Odinism, Neo-Hellenism, among others."

"Which leaves?"

"Santeria. Satanism. Early Christianity and Judaism. Like I said, you've got a kitchen sink here, Reed. Or a Louisiana gumbo."

He frowned. "Why sacrifice an animal?"

"As an offering. In thanks. Reverence. As an atonement for sins. Or in a show of power."

"You think this is for real?"

"What do you mean, for real?"

"Was whoever built this serious about . . . the whole thing? The ceremony, the offering? Or is it a gag? A stage set?"

A stage set, she thought. Interesting. She cleared her throat. "Some people believe all religion is a gag. A hoax perpetrated on the stupid and gullible. Some call all religious ceremonies a form of theater, with churches, synagogues and altars like these simply places to perform."

He studied her, eyebrows drawn together. "What about you, Alex? What do you believe?"

She turned her gaze back to the altar and its symbols. "I believe worship is an intrinsic part of the human condition. That it's as elemental as the need for food and drink." She glanced back at him. "We're hardwired for it, Reed. We're hardwired for worship."

"You're saying I don't even have a choice in that?"

She nodded. "The choice you do have is in what you believe. What or who you choose to worship."

"And this? A single wacko or a group? Legitimate or not?"

She shoved her hands into her jacket pockets, suddenly cold. "There are cults and sects with only a handful of followers. Look at it this way, if I get the idea I'm the living God, or His chosen prophet, all I have to do is convince one other person it's true and I have a following. I'm legitimized."

"And there are people out there willing to believe anything."

"Aching to," she corrected. "Because of this basic, hard-wired need."

He seemed to digest that. "And the symbols, the animal sacrifice and black candles?"

"It's not an assembly line creation, Reed. It's somebody's personal doctrine." She motioned with her flashlight. "They're incorporating it all."

"The kitchen sink approach."

"My opinion only."

"This doesn't scare you at all?"

"No. Should it?"

"You're the expert."

"And you're the detective. Does it scare you?"

He smiled slightly. "Me? Scared?"

"There's a reason you brought me out here."

"Answers, Alex. And connections. That's what detectives are always looking for."

"You didn't answer my question. Does this scare you?"

His smile widened. The laid-back good old boy.

"You've got this all wrong, Alex. Detectives ask the questions, they don't answer them."

Their gazes held. In that moment, it was there between them. The memory of their lovemaking, the remnants of their passion, still smoldering between them.

He lifted a hand as if to touch her, then dropped it. "Let's get out of here."

They climbed into his SUV. He started back down the mountain road. Moments ticked past. The silence felt awkward—elephant in the middle of the room awkward. She wondered if he felt it, too.

And if he was as aware of her as she was of him.

"Maybe we should talk about it?" she offered.

"It?"

"The other night. You don't have to feel weird about it."

"I don't."

"Good." Alex laced her fingers together in her lap. "And I don't expect you to say anything about it."

"No?"

"That's the only reason I'm bringing it up. I mean, it just occurred to me that you—" She made a fluttering motion. "It happened. We move on."

"Very cosmopolitan of you. Nobody gets their knickers in a twist."

"Exactly."

His lips lifted slightly. "One problem. I want it to happen again."

She hadn't expected that. Had secretly wished for it. Maybe. But certainly not broached in that way. Alex searched for a response that wouldn't totally blow her cover.

He beat her to it. Again.

"Thanks, by the way. I had a great time."

She smiled. She couldn't help herself. "Okay, so if we're being embarrassingly honest, I did, too."

A short time later, she stood on her porch, watching him drive off. He had insisted on walking her up, then doing a quick check of her home. They'd closed the windows; he'd helped her light a fire in the fireplace. Then he'd said good night.

So that was that, she thought. No more sex talk. No suggestion of when it might "happen" again. Not even a brush of his mouth against hers.

Frustrated, Alex stepped inside the house and locked the door behind her. She wished she had left the elephant unmentioned in the middle of the room; it'd be a lot easier to deal with now.

She changed into her pajamas, poured a glass of wine and curled up with it in front of the fire. She was emotionally and physically drained. Yet her thoughts raced. So much had happened in such a short span of time. It was overwhelming.

Gazing at the fire, she sipped the wine, holding it a moment on her tongue, enjoying its complex bite. Similar to the Reeds' Bear Creek Zin, though not quite as good. A log dropped in the fireplace, sending a shower of sparks up the flue.

Suddenly, Alex remembered. She straightened, nearly spilling her wine. The Reeds' trophy room, the scent that hung in the air. It had been familiar.

Woodsy and sweet. The same as the incense in the cave. The same as in her dream.

She set aside her wine and collected her phone. She dialed Reed; he answered immediately, sounding alert.

"It's Alex," she said, sounding breathless to her own ears.

"Is everything all right?"

"Yes. This is going to sound a little nuts, but in your family's trophy room, what was that scent? It was subtle, but at the same time—"

"Sandalwood," he answered. "It's my mother's favorite. Why?"

"That was the smell, in the cave that night."

"Sandalwood? In the cave?" He sounded doubting. "I didn't smell anything, Alex."

He hadn't. Nor had she after he found her. And that stuff didn't dissipate in the blink of an eye. Maybe she *had* imagined it.

Crazy, crazy girl.

She ignored the quiver of fear the thought sent through her and pressed on. "Did your mother always like it?"

"As long as I can remember. She uses sandalwood-scented soap, too." He paused. "What are you thinking, Alex?"

"I don't know," she answered truthfully. "Good night, Reed."

She ended the call and sagged against the sofa back. What did it mean? she wondered. Could the memory of the scent have triggered the episode in the cave? And what of her dream? Was some long buried memory trying to emerge? Or was her subconscious simply playing a nasty trick on her?

Chapter Thirty-one

Tuesday, March 9
9:10 A.M.

The Sonoma County Coroner's Office was located in Santa Rosa, not far from the Barn. Reed entered the building, called out a hello to the receptionist, then headed to the autopsy viewing room. In addition to the Coroner's detective, both the lead VCI and the CSI detectives were required to attend the autopsy of every homicide case they worked.

Because of Schwann's position in the community, the pathologist had pushed him to the front of the line. Reed glanced at his watch. And he was late.

He stepped into the room. It was narrow, joined to the autopsy room by a door and a window that spanned the rest of the wall. In front of the window, a counter and stools. Like a bar.

Step right up, folks. Get yourself some.

His counterparts had already arrived; the autopsy had begun. Bob Ware, the Coroner's detective, sat on one of the stools, his McDonald's breakfast on the counter before him. Tanner sat on the adjacent stool, eyeing the McMuffin meal.

She glanced his way. "Can you believe he eats that garbage? If I ate that, I'd be in a grease coma within thirty minutes."

"You're just jealous," Bob responded. "I'm the picture of health."

"He's got a point," Reed said, crossing to the coffeepot.

"On the outside. I bet his arteries are a fright."

Bob didn't argue with that.

Reed poured himself a cup of the hot beverage, then held out the pot. "Anybody else?"

Not surprisingly, the two detectives held out their cups. It was cold in the viewing room, though nothing compared to the chill in the actual examination room. Ditto for the smell, a sort of antiseptic laced with death.

He refilled them, then crossed to the counter and sat. "What'd I miss?"

Like all seasoned cops, they were desensitized to the process. The body on the stainless steel table had ceased being a human being and had become, simply, evidence. The most important piece of evidence they had. No body, no murder.

Bob looked over at him. "External examination of the body," he said around a mouthful of hash browns. "Other than the neck, no outward signs of trauma. Nails were clean. Nothing unusual."

"Except for the tattoo," Tanner corrected.

"Tom had a tatt? That surprises me."

"On the bottom of his foot."

Reed crossed to the door that separated the room from the autopsy suite. He opened it and stuck his head in. "Kath, did you get a picture of that tattoo?"

She sent him an irritated glance. "This isn't my first dance, Detective. In the future, maybe you should try a little harder to be on time?"

Tanner and Bob snickered. Unfazed, Reed grinned. "Anything else you want to share with me?"

"Yeah. Sit down and shut up so I can get this done."

"Love you, too, Kath."

An autopsy always followed the same procedure: top to

bottom, outside to in, head last. Since Kath had already finished the external examination, she was preparing to open the vic up. She made a series of incisions that formed a Y and opened him from breastbone to groin. Next, she cut through ribs and cartilage to reveal the heart and lungs, which she removed. All organs would be measured and weighed, then sliced into sections to evaluate damage.

Reed glanced at his watch, anxious to move on. The autopsy process took two hours, give or take, and was as tedious as it was exacting. Some were more enlightening than others, but for the most part Reed found them a major time drain.

He stifled a yawn, his mind wandering to the previous night, to the things Alex had said about the altar. A kitchen sink approach, she had called it. He recalled her exact words: *"Look . . . if I get the idea I'm the living God, or His chosen prophet, all I have to do is convince one other person it's true and I have a following. I'm legitimized."*

Power grew out of the act of being legitimized. That newly crowned wacko could decide God was telling him to commit murder. Or that he must "save" his flock through death. The Jonestown massacre came to mind. As did the Manson Family's killing spree.

A dead lamb left in Alex's rental. Who had done it? And why?

Her connection to the past, he thought. Other than it having been completely random, what other reason could there be?

She remembered more than she was letting on.

His cell vibrated; he saw it was HQ. He answered to the buzz of the bone saw cutting open Schwann's skull. "Reed here."

"Detective, Officer Trenton, front desk. There are two gentlemen here to speak with you. A Harlan and Treven Sommer. They say it's about Baby Doe."

An interesting twist. "It's going to be about another hour here."

"They said they would wait as long as necessary. I just wanted to alert you."

Reed thanked her and hung up. He found Tanner looking at him. "The Sommer brothers want to talk to me about Baby Doe."

"Sweet. Any idea what's up?"

"None."

"How did the altar visit go last night?"

"Productive." He looked back at the autopsy in progress. The pathologist was weighing Schwann's brain. He returned his gaze to Tanner's. "She couldn't attribute it to a particular group. Called it a kitchen sink approach." He went on, describing what that meant, then added, "Apparently anybody can start their own religion, all you need is a belief system and somebody who buys into it."

"Rogue worshippers."

He smiled at that, gaze on the autopsy. "I asked; she found it nonthreatening and pretty routine."

"Why am I not surprised by that?" He glanced at her in question and she went on, "She seemed pretty calm when I arrived last night. How was she when she called you?"

He thought back. "Not panicked or crying. Voice wasn't shaking. Told me what had happened, asked if I could come over."

"Why you?"

"I'm a cop. She knows me. That's human nature."

"Maybe."

He drained the last of his coffee, though it had grown cold. "I found her composure odd, as well. I asked her about it. She told me that whoever had done this wanted her to be afraid and she refused to give them what they wanted."

"Good for her," she said. "That takes some iron-clad cojones."

It did. Reed knew how Tanner's mind worked and where it was going. "You think she killed the lamb, stuck it under her bathroom sink to marinate a few days, then called me?"

"It's possible."

Anything was possible. They'd both been cops long enough to know that. "Why do it?"

"Attention. Yours. The Sommer family's. Maybe even police attention." She turned to meet his eyes. "Maybe she knows more than she's let on."

His thought from earlier. But why the charade? Why the Byzantine scenario?

"Or maybe she's a total whack job?" Bob offered, as if he had heard Reed's unspoken questions and answered them.

They both looked at him. He shrugged. "Just can't ignore the obvious."

Tanner leaned toward Reed. "Has it occurred to you that since she arrived, there's been some severely weird shit going on? Weird shit she's well versed in."

"Yeah, it has."

"And with this animal, the happenings physically connect to her."

"Suggestions?"

"Stay close. Be suspicious. If she's responsible she might be crazy enough to be dangerous, and not just to small animals. And if she's a target—"

"She may be in danger," he finished.

They both turned their full attention back to the autopsy, and for the next thirty minutes, Reed struggled to keep focus. The secateur had sliced open Schwann's throat and the carotid artery and he bled out. It would've happened fast: with that injury in that location, about two to three minutes.

"No surprises with this," Tanner said a short while later as they crossed the parking area. "Poor bastard."

They reached her vehicle. She unlocked the door and climbed in. "Let me know what the Sommer brothers have to say."

"Will do. See you back at the Barn."

Reed crossed to his own vehicle, slid inside and started it up. But instead of heading out, he sat, turning his and Tanner's conversation over in his head.

Could Alex have killed the lamb and left it for him to find? If she had, she was one seriously twisted chick. One for whom the lines between reality and fantasy had become blurred.

He didn't peg her that way. She seemed relatively grounded.

Like she was rolling with the punches pretty well, considering.

Still, she'd lived through an awful trauma. A brother disappearing. Her life upended. The bizarre excision of that brother from her memory. Her mother's suicide.

Enough to psychologically tweak even the most stable individual.

His cell phone sounded. "Reed," he answered.

"Investigator Hwang, SFME. I've been meaning to call, about the Owens autopsy. The findings were consistent with suicide. Seroquel in her system. No outward signs of a struggle."

"Thanks for letting me know."

"No problem. There was one odd thing, though."

Reed shifted into drive and eased out of the parking spot. "What's that?"

"Her right pinkie finger was broken."

"I'm sorry, did you say her pinkie finger was broken?"

"I did."

"Could it have happened when she was being transported?"

"Pathologist didn't think so because of bruising to the area." He cleared his throat. "From the chaotic state of her home and paintings, she experienced a violent manic state prior to ingesting the Seroquel. Our theory is she broke it then."

Reed nodded, shifted into drive and headed out of the lot. "Nothing else that might indicate a struggle with an assailant?"

"Nothing."

Reed thanked the man, hung up and turned his thoughts to Harlan and Treven Sommer waiting for him at HQ.

Chapter Thirty-two

Tuesday, March 9
11:30 A.M.

Fifteen minutes later, Reed crossed the large lobby to where the brothers stood. Rachel, he saw, had joined them.

"I appreciate you waiting," Reed said as he reached them. "How can I help you?"

"Is there somewhere more private?" Treven asked tersely.

"Of course. Follow me."

Reed led them upstairs to one of the interview rooms. He closed the door behind them as they sat. No one spoke.

Harlan broke the heavy silence. "I want to see him," he said, voice shaking. "The baby."

"The remains," Treven corrected.

Reed moved his gaze between the two men, then shifted his attention to Rachel. She looked at her father, her expression naked with pain. In that moment she looked like the teenager whose life had been shattered. Truth be told, she may have been the one hurt most by Dylan's abduction.

"I can't bear not knowing." Harlan's voice thickened and both his brother and daughter laid a comforting hand on his. "Finding that baby . . . Seeing Alexandra . . . it's brought it all back to me. I can't stop thinking about him . . . I can't stop wondering . . .''

He lifted his stricken face to Reed's. "I can't sleep. I have no appetite. I have to know. Please . . . I *have* to."

Reed cleared his throat. "I understand, Harlan. And I have no problem with you viewing the remains; however, they've transferred them to the lab at Sonoma State and I'm not certain where in the process the forensic anthropologist is. In addition, I'm worried you're expecting more from what we have than you'll get."

"I don't care, I have to see them."

"I have photos," Reed said. "If that will do, I'll arrange it."

"Harlan," Treven said, turning toward his brother, "I beg you to reconsider. Don't put yourself through this. You won't be able to tell if it's Dylan, so what's the point?"

"I agree, Dad," Rachel said. "You're upset enough already."

Harlan didn't waver. "And do you think burying my head in the sand will change that?"

Treven looked at Reed. "Don't let him do this, please."

Reed was torn between sympathy and duty. Times like these, he hated being a cop. "It's his decision. I'm sorry." He turned to Harlan. "I want you to be prepared. The remains aren't pretty. In fact, they're shocking."

"I have to do it."

Treven snorted, obviously frustrated. Harlan laid a hand on his brother's arm. Interestingly, when he spoke his voice no longer shook. "I know you're trying to protect me, but nothing I could see with my eyes could match the horror of my nightmares."

He shifted his gaze to Rachel. "Are you with me on this, honey?" She nodded and Harlan turned back to Reed, suddenly appearing the strong, confident man he had been all those years ago. "Let's do this."

"All right. It'll take me a few minutes to assemble the photographs. Drink machine and restrooms are down the hall."

He slipped out of the room. Rachel followed. "Dan, wait!"

He stopped and she caught up with him. "Question?" he asked.

"I wanted to . . . I just—" She looked away, then back. "It feels like the world's splitting apart at the seams. Same as it felt back then, after Dylan disappeared."

"Your dad's been through a lot, Rachel. He'll get through this."

"It's not just Dad. I heard about that altar, off Castle Road in Bartholomew Park. And about the doll in Hilldale's vineyard." She lowered her voice. "And I heard about that animal . . . how somebody planted it at Alex's. What the hell's going on?"

"How did you hear?"

"We hear everything that goes on in the valley, Dan, you know that."

He understood the first two, because the wine community was as close knit as it was competitive. Information, especially juicy rumors, spread faster than a wildfire in the High Sierras.

But Alex was most certainly not hooked into the local grapevine.

"But who'd you hear it from?" he pressed.

"Clark." She searched his gaze. "Why?"

"How news spreads interests me, that's all."

She didn't believe him. He saw it by the speculative gleam in her eyes. He also knew her well enough to know that she wouldn't hesitate to throw her cousin under a bus if the opportunity presented itself.

"I don't know what's going on," he said, answering her original question. "But I will. I promise you that."

He watched her as she walked back to the interview room, thinking of his promise, wondering if he would be able to keep it.

Reed gathered together the photographs. He instructed Harlan to take a seat, then laid them out.

Harlan stared at them, throat working. He grasped the arms of his chair so tightly his knuckles were white. Seconds ticked past. No one spoke. Harlan seemed not to even breathe as he gazed at the images, his expression twisted with pain.

"It's him," he said finally, the sound broken. "It's my baby. My Dylan."

"How can you be so certain, Harlan?" Reed asked as gently as possible.

"A father knows his own son."

Reed glanced at Treven's stunned expression, then at Rachel's horrified one, before turning back to Harlan. "I hate to do this to you, but look again. It's been years, these remains are—"

"I know my own son! My Dylan . . . my sweet, sweet boy."

He broke down sobbing. Rachel put her arms around him, her own tears flowing.

Reed collected the photographs. "We're trying to establish if there's any viable DNA—"

"We'll pay for any tests," Treven offered, "if that will give us the proof—"

Harlan turned on him. "What more proof do you need? I was his father. I know my son!"

"This is too important to make a mistake on. What if you're wrong and he's not dead? What if he's—"

"Uncle Treven," Rachel said sharply, "that's enough! I'm taking Dad home."

He went with her without resistance. As soon as the interview room door had shut behind them, Treven turned to Reed. "I don't care what it costs, we need proof that's Dylan."

"I understand completely, Treven. But it simply may not be possible."

"Nothing is impossible. That's been my lifelong credo. There must be something you can do."

Reed thought a moment. "We could turn the skull over to a forensic sculptor. The re-creations can be uncanny. However—"

"Yes, let's do it."

"However," he continued, "the best reconstructions are still generalized, and baby skulls are exceptionally difficult because the facial features aren't fully formed yet. Our best bet is still DNA, if we're able."

"I want it all, every test. We'll pay."

"I appreciate that. But at this point, it's not about money."

"It's always about money," he said. "My brother needs closure. If this will give it to him, I'll do everything in my power to make it happen."

"Harlan expressed conviction," Reed said softly. "It seems to me that it's you who needs the closure, Treven."

"My brother's an emotional mess. I think we can agree on that. An hour from now, he'll be doubting himself. You wait and see."

Reed thought of Rachel, her pain. And then of Alex. Her mother. The entire community. Closure, he thought. A funeral. A way for the family to move completely past this.

"I'll see what I can do. There are procedures that need to be followed."

"Harlan ID'd him. So the remains are ours now. Isn't that the way it works?"

"It's not that simple. Or that immediate."

"I'm Treven Sommer. I can make it simple."

Reed held on to his temper by reminding himself of what this family had endured. "The remains cannot be released to you or anybody else until forensic testing is complete. When that's happened, I'll see what I can do."

Reed could see Treven wasn't happy with his answer. Obviously, when you were Treven Sommer, you weren't accustomed to waiting.

"All right, Dan. But just so you know, I'm prepared to sue the department if it comes to it."

Chapter Thirty-three

Tuesday, March 9
4:00 P.M.

The jewelry designer Alex had been pointed toward lived in a California-style cottage on Brockman Lane right here in Sonoma. He had agreed to meet her and take a look at her mother's ring.

He came to the door, a charming gnome of a man in a red plaid flannel shirt and pants held up by suspenders. "Max?" she asked.

He broke into a broad smile. "You must be Alexandra. Come in . . . come in."

She followed him into the cottage. She found it as charming and unique as the man, filled with all sorts of art, from traditional to contemporary. "Thank you for agreeing to see me, Max. I appreciate you taking the time."

"Nonsense. I have lots of time. Too much." He motioned her to follow him. "I don't get many visitors. And certainly not ones wanting to talk about my designs. That was a lifetime ago. Come, I've made us some tea."

In the kitchen, Alex watched as he set about pouring. She noticed that his hands shook badly.

"Would you mind?" he asked, indicating the full cups.

"Not at all." She carried them both to the small kitchen table, then went back for the milk and sugar. They both sat.

While she doctored her tea, he talked. "When my friend Janice called me about you, I was delighted. As you can see, I can't design anymore." He looked at his shaking hands. "I used to do such delicate work."

"I'm sorry. That must be very distressing for you."

"You would think." He chuckled. "But God has surely blessed me. Talent and success as a young man and an old age surrounded by love. May I show you something?"

He was obviously not in a hurry to get to the reason for her visit, which suited her fine. She stood and let him lead her to the center hallway, which was decorated with framed photographs. She smiled as he pointed out himself as a young man and commented on a picture of his late wife, calling her the love of his life.

He stopped on a family portrait. "My daughter, Angie, and her three girls. How could I complain?"

"They're a lovely family."

He gazed at it. "In the end, it's all about family. That's all we have that means anything."

His words hit her hard. She struggled to keep it from showing, but lost the battle.

"I've upset you," he said. "Forgive me."

"It's okay," she said. "I lost my mother recently. And she was . . . it's been difficult."

He patted her hand. "Tell me about the piece you brought me."

"It was my mother's." Alex slid it off her finger and handed it to him. "I found it in her things after she died. It's so unusual, I wondered—"

"It's not mine," he said curtly.

"Excuse me?"

He handed it back. "It's not one of my designs."

"Oh." Confused by his change in tone, she wasn't certain how to respond. "Is there anything you can tell me about the design or materials?"

"I'm sorry, I can't help you."

Alex frowned and held it out again. "The inscription, *BOV*, I wondered if that could have been a local organization or—"

"I'm sorry, but I really can't tell you anything about it." He stuck his hands in his pockets and she noticed he wouldn't even look at the ring. "But I wish you luck."

Disappointed, Alex slipped the ring back onto her finger. "Any suggestions where I might look or who I might contact?"

"No. I've never seen . . . I would remember. It's an unusual design."

He knew more than he was letting on, she felt certain. But why keep information from her?

She laid a hand on his arm. "Please, Max. It was my mother's and now she's gone. I'm just trying to learn more about her. About her life here. She was my only family."

His expression softened. "Some stories aren't meant to be known. Maybe this is one of them."

"Please. Her name was Patsy Sommer. You may have known her." He looked as if she had struck him. "You did know her," she said.

"Everyone did after that horrible thing with her baby. Sweet little boy. How anyone could . . ." He let out a heavy-sounding breath. "I'm tired now. You have to go."

He herded her toward the door. When they'd reached it, she opened her mouth to ask him one more time if he was certain he knew nothing of the ring's design or inscription. He stopped her by gripping her hands tightly.

"Be careful, Alexandra," he said. "And remember what I said. Some stories are meant to be left untold."

A moment later she was outside, the door snapping shut behind her. He hadn't given her a chance to do more than mumble another "Thank you." He had wanted her out of his house, and as quickly as possible.

Why? She walked slowly to her car, thoughts whirling. What did he know that he wasn't telling her? And how could she get him to change his mind?

Chapter Thirty-four

Tuesday, March 9
9:03 P.M.

Turned out, Alex didn't have to do a thing. Max called her as she was putting on her PJs. "Max," she said, surprised.

"I apologize for calling so late."

"No problem. Not at all."

He cleared his throat, but didn't speak. She waited. When he still didn't speak, she prodded him. "Max, what is it? Have you remembered something about my ring?"

"I think so, yes." He spoke so softly she had to strain to hear. "But not on the phone. I can show you—"

In the background she heard a doorbell chime. "That's probably my Angie. She stops by some nights with a treat."

"That's so sweet. When should I come by?"

The bell chimed again. "Anytime. I've got to go—"

"I'll be by first thing in the morning. Will that be all right?"

"That'd be good. But Alexandra, don't tell anyone."

"Tell anyone?" she repeated. "That we're meeting?"

"Yes. Or even that we spoke." He let out a breath and she could tell that he was anxious to go. "And what I share with you is for your ears only. You have to promise me."

The hair on the back of her neck stood up. "Max, you're scaring me."

"I've got to go. Remember, not a word to anyone. See you in the morning."

Chapter Thirty-five

Wednesday, March 10
8:20 A.M.

Max didn't answer his bell. Alex stood at the front door, shivering, bag of muffins clutched in her gloved hand. She tried knocking. "Max," she called, "it's Alex Clarkson."

When he still didn't answer, she peered through the side-light. A big gray cat sat in the foyer, blinking up at her. A light spilled through from the open kitchen door.

Frowning, she checked her watch—8:25. She'd told him she would be by first thing. Surely, it wasn't too early? From her experience, the elderly weren't late sleepers.

Besides, he'd been expecting her.

Even as Alex told herself he was in the shower or out for a walk, she began to worry. It didn't feel right. If he'd had a change of heart, he would tell her so, face-to-face.

He could have hurt himself and be unable to answer. Or have fallen ill and need help.

Don't tell anyone. Why had he been so insistent on secrecy?

Alex shook her head, fighting the sense that something was wrong. Just a lonely old man. Any excuse for a bit of drama.

She knocked again, loudly. When she didn't get an answer, she tried the door. Finding it locked, she went around back. She crossed the small deck to the rear entrance and peeked through the windows. Neat as a pin, she saw, save for the teacup and saucer on the counter, carton of milk and sugar bowl beside it.

Clearly, he was up. He had been making his tea.

Where was he now?

She rapped on the door, once, then twice. When he didn't answer, she tried the knob. It turned.

She stepped inside. "Max," she called, "it's Alex. Are you all right?"

The absolute quality of the silence panicked her. Even as she told herself she was overreacting, that she appeared to be the one in need of drama, urgency pushed her on.

"Max," she called as she moved through the small cottage, first the living room, then the single bathroom, followed by the first, then second bedroom.

The master, judging by its size. And by the slippers beside the bed, the clock, Bible and photographs on the night table. Max's room.

She gazed at the neatly made bed. The waiting slippers.

"Remember, Alex, not a word to anyone."

He hadn't slept in the bed. He'd called her, then disappeared.

Get a grip, Alexandra. Just because you let hours—or even days—pass without making your own bed doesn't mean everyone's such a mess.

Any moment he was going to arrive home and ask what the hell she thought she was doing in his house. Besides, he'd been making tea.

Arrive home. Of course. He'd run to the grocery. Or to see his grandchildren. He'd forgotten she was coming. There could have been an emergency.

She laughed to herself, though even to her own ears the sound rang false. She quickly headed back to the kitchen. As she started out the door, she stopped and looked back at the tea.

Telling herself she had rocketed past overreaction and into the territory of obsession, Alex turned and crossed to it. She touched the kettle. It was cold. The milk carton warm. The tea had never been brewed.

Sleepy Time tea, she saw.

A bed that hadn't been slept in. Tea that hadn't been brewed. And a meeting that hadn't been met.

"Don't tell anyone."

She turned and ran. Out the back door and around to the front of the house. The garage door stood halfway up. She ducked under it, blinking at the sudden darkness. She looked frantically around for the light switch. Instead she found a pull cord attached to a single bulb.

She pulled it; a dim glow illuminated the space. An ancient-looking, convertible VW Beetle sat squarely in the center of the garage. An equally outdated push mower. Gardening tools.

What looked to be a work or storage room in back. A sliver of light shone from beneath the closed door.

Heart thundering, she approached. "Max?" she said. "It's Alex."

What the hell was she doing? she wondered, as she grasped the doorknob and twisted it. The door eased open, knocking against something heavy, pushing it.

As she stepped through, she saw what. Max, hanging by the neck, eyes bulging, face swollen and purple. A stepladder on its side under him.

A cry flew to her lips. She stumbled backward, hand to her mouth, unable to tear her eyes away from the gruesome sight.

She bumped into the door, turned and ran. Reaching her car, she clawed open the door and fell inside, slamming it shut behind her. Pressing down the lock. She sat, shaking, teeth chattering. Wishing she could force the image from her head.

Alex hugged herself. He'd been such a sweet man . . . Why had he . . . he'd seemed so content . . . this didn't make any—

"But Alexandra, don't tell anyone . . . You have to promise me."

She brought her trembling hands to her face. No, this didn't have anything to do with her. How could it?

Reed. She had to call Reed.

She found her cell phone, punched in his number. When he answered, she cried out with relief. "Thank God! It's me, Alex!"

"Alex? What's wrong?"

"He killed himself. Oh my God, he—"

"Who? Where are you?"

"Max Cragan. He hung . . . I'm at his house. On Brockman Lane."

"Hold on. I'm on my way."

Chapter Thirty-six

Reed found Alex huddled behind the wheel of her Toyota Prius. She stared straight ahead, only turning to look at him when he tapped on the window. She opened the door but made no move to get out.

"Where is he?" he asked.

"Garage," she whispered. "In back."

He turned to the deputies waiting at their cruisers and motioned them that way, then turned back to her. She had swung to face him.

"Are you okay?" he asked.

She shook her head. "He was such a sweet man. I can't believe . . ."

Her words trailed miserably off. He squatted in front of her, caught her hands and rubbed them between his. "What were you doing here, Alex?"

"My ring. He was going to tell me about my ring."

"Your ring?" he prodded.

"The one that was my mother's. I found it in the storage trunk. With Dylan's things." She lifted her gaze to his. "This is two. Mom and now . . . I don't understand."

"Some things just can't be understood, Alex. I'm so sorry."

She nodded, eyes filling with tears.

He squeezed her fingers, then released them. "Can you wait here a couple minutes? I need to ask you a few more questions after I take a look."

She nodded again and he stood. "I'll send one of the deputies out. If you need anything, just ask him."

A few moments later, Reed entered the workroom at the back of the garage.

Not a pretty sight, he thought, studying the victim. Most times, the victim of a hanging actually suffocated. The drop from chair or step stool wasn't sharp enough to snap the neck; instead, the rope cinched the windpipe. Both oxygen and blood flow cut off, the blood began to pool above the rope, which accounted for the discoloration and swelling in the victim's face.

Reed lowered his gaze. A small stepladder lay on its side under the man's dangling feet. The rope had stretched and the old man's toes just brushed the floor.

Another classic mistake. Choosing a nylon or cotton rope that had too much give.

Poor bastard. It would have taken about ten minutes for death to be complete. Horrible minutes. He would have fought for life. No matter how much they wanted to die, they always fought for life.

Reed fitted on Latex gloves and moved closer. He examined the neck, the gouges made by the victim clawing at the rope. Reed lowered his gaze to the victim's hands. Sure enough, the tips were raw and bloodied; there appeared to be matter under the fingernails. On the dusty workshop floor, scuff marks from his flailing feet.

Reed sighed. He'd known of Max Cragan. He'd been a Sonoma institution, a onetime member of wine country's inner circle. Nationally acclaimed jewelry designer. The inside, go-to person for special event, one-of-a-kind pieces.

His mother had one. A brooch in an organic scrollwork design set with semiprecious stones.

The Coroner's detective arrived. "Hey, Reed. What've we got?"

He yanked off his gloves and turned to the other man. "Looks like standard issue suicide."

Ware nodded. "Who's the babe?"

"Babe?"

"In the car."

"She found him."

Ware nodded and set to work. Reed stuffed his gloves into his jacket pocket and headed back out to Alex, passing the CSI team on the way. He nodded, but didn't comment. Neither Tanner nor Cal had pulled this one.

Alex saw him crossing to her and climbed out, expression hopeful. Human nature, he thought. To hope she had been wrong. That she hadn't seen what she thought and old Max Cragan wasn't really dead.

"I'm sorry," he said softly.

Her face fell and she looked away, blinking.

"Let's go over the events that led you here this morning, step by step. Are you up to that?"

She drew a deep breath, then let it slowly out. "I got Max's name from a shop owner on the square."

"The name of the shop?"

"The Golden Bow. I was trying to track down where my mother got the ring."

"Why?"

"I was hoping it might lead to my father. There are initials engraved on the band, I'm guessing they're his."

"Go on."

"She called Max for me; I made an appointment to go by."

"This morning."

She shook her head. "No. I went yesterday. We had a nice chat until . . ." Her voice trailed off and she frowned, as if remembering something that bothered her.

"Until what, Alex?"

"He saw the ring. He seemed flustered. Even upset. He told me he wasn't the designer, had no idea who was or what the initials stood for."

She clasped her hands together. "He called me last night, told me he'd changed his mind. He said that he might know something about the ring, after all. I agreed to stop by this morning."

"And that's it?"

"No." She looked down at her hands, then back up at him. "He . . . he made me promise not to tell anyone we'd talked."

Reed kept his expression neutral. "That sounds a bit melodramatic, don't you think?"

"I did. But he was serious. He said what he was going to share with me was 'for your ears' only. I swear."

At the last, she lost him. When someone "swore" something was true, it was almost always false. But why would she lie about this?

"And that's it?" he asked.

"Pretty much. Someone was at his door. He thought it was his daughter and said he had to go."

"What time was this?"

"I don't know for certain—Wait, my cell will have it." She retrieved the phone from her car, accessed the call log and handed him the device.

9:03 P.M. He noted the time and returned the phone. He motioned to her right hand. "Is that the ring?"

She looked down at her hand. "Yes. Would you like to see it?"

He said he would, and she slipped it off her finger and handed it to him. He gazed at the slim, gold ring. At the twisted vines, snake and gemstones. It was beautiful work, delicate and ornate.

But its beauty wasn't what had the hairs standing up on his arms. He had seen this design before. This combination of vines and snake. But not on a piece of jewelry.

On the bottom of a dead man's foot. In the form of a tattoo.

Chapter Thirty-seven

"You say this was with your mother's things?" he said, turning it over in his fingers.

"In the trunk with her mementos of Dylan and her life here."

BOV–1984. The year before Dylan disappeared. He frowned. "I hate to tell you this, Alex, but I'm going to have to keep this for a while."

"Keep it? Why?"

He wasn't ready to tell her about the tattoo. Not yet anyway. "It's evidence. You'll get it back. I promise."

"Evidence? But—" She bit back what she had been about to say and made a sound, a cross between a whimper and a laugh. "It seems everybody's interested in this ring."

"What do you mean?"

"At least a half dozen people have asked me about it, including your mother and Rachel."

He made a note to question them about the ring. "Who else?"

"Rita Welsh, my mother's friend, the librarian. A few others, names I don't even know."

He closed his notebook. "I'm done for now. Are you going to be okay?"

"No problems."

"Do you need me to call someone to sit with you?"

"Of course not." She jammed her hands into her pockets. "I'll be fine."

As she turned to go, he caught her arm. She looked at him. The naked vulnerability in her gaze blew her tough girl act to smithereens. In the next moment, it was gone.

"What?" she asked.

"Call me if you need anything. Okay?"

She said she would and climbed into her car. He watched her drive off, then headed back into the scene. Ware was examining the body.

"What do you think, Bobby?"

"I think you nailed it. Suicide. Poor old bastard."

"What about TOD?"

The man sent him an irritated glance. "Can't give you a time yet. You know that."

"Yeah, I know. I still want it."

The man began to hum the Rolling Stones classic "You Can't Always Get What You Want." At the appropriate moment the CSI team sang out, "But sometimes, you get what you need!"

Reed bit back a guffaw, glared at the three, then pointed at the Coroner's detective. "Call me, Ware. I need that TOD."

Moments later, he slid behind the wheel of his Tahoe. He dialed Tanner. "Where are you?"

"Barn. What's up?"

"You have the Schwann autopsy photos?"

"Nope. But the Coroner's Office uploaded them, along with Kath's report."

"Great. I'm on my way in. I need to get a look at the tattoo on the bottom of Schwann's foot."

"I'm not even going to ask. See you in a few."

A short time later, Reed gazed at the computer image of Schwann's tattoo. The design was a mirror image of the ring's—grapevines and a snake.

"Want to tell me what you've got?" Tanner asked.

"Better than that, I'll show you." He handed her the ring.

She studied it, then swore softly. "Where'd you get this?"

"Alex. It was her mother's. She found it in the same trunk she found Dylan's pacifier."

"BOV. What does it stand for?"

"She didn't know. She thought they might be her father's initials." He explained about Max Cragan, how Alex had found him and why.

"What I find interesting is that once again, Alexandra Clarkson's at the center of trouble."

"It does seem to be following her."

"And her reaction this time?"

"Shook up. Very." He drummed his fingers on the desktop. "The question is, why Tom Schwann and Patsy Sommer would both be in possession of the same, rather unusual image."

"Coincidence?" she offered. "It's unusual but not so off the charts it couldn't happen. This is wine country, and the image reflects that."

He agreed. "Dylan disappeared in '85. Schwann would have been seventeen at the time. Alex five."

"That eliminates the possibility of his being her father."

"But their families would have traveled in the same circles." Reed grabbed his jacket and stood. "This just got a bit more interesting. I'm going to pay a visit to Schwann's wife, see what she knows about the tatt, then maybe a few of his friends."

After speaking to Jill Schwann, who knew nothing about the tattoo except that it was something he'd done when young and that she'd found it hideous, Reed paid a visit to his brothers.

He made his way into the winery's offices. "Hey, Eve," he called to the receptionist. "Either of my brothers in?"

The woman, who had been with the winery since Reed was a toddler, smiled. She used to keep a jar of candy on her desk just for when he, Joe and Ferris came around. Which had been often.

"They're together. In Joe's office."

"Double trouble," he said. She returned his grin and he headed down the hall, passing his father's closed office door, stopping at Joe's.

He heard them arguing. Not a big surprise. This time about the replanting of a vineyard from cabernet grapes to pinot noir.

"You're so full of shit!" Ferris exclaimed. "The fact is that vineyard produces inferior cab grapes; its northern exposure is perfect for pinots. You know it and I know it."

"The cost of ripping up and replanting is too great for the return we'll see. Plus, we're known for our cabs."

"Good cabs! Not the blended crap those grapes—"

Reed tapped on the partially open door, then stuck his head in. "Wow, what a touching moment. I ask myself, why didn't I go into the family business?"

"Kiss my ass, Dan," Joe said, coming around his desk to greet him. He clapped him on the back. "This is a surprise. How the hell are you?"

Ferris didn't give him a chance to respond. "Talk some sense into this low-rent, penny-pinching jackass, would ya?"

"Impossible. I've tried before." He hugged his younger brother. "Sorry to interrupt, but I need to ask you a couple of questions about Tom."

"Fire away," Joe said, returning to his chair.

"What do you know about the tattoo on Tom's foot?"

"Tom had a tattoo?" Ferris made a face. "Mr. Conservative?"

"From the old days," Joe said. "He and Carter got a wild hair one summer. Got matching tatts."

Reed turned toward Joe. "You know where they had 'em done?"

"Local place, I think. Ask Carter."

"I will. You know anything else about it?"

"Sorry, Bro." He folded his hands on the desk. "Why the interest?"

"Following up every lead, that's all."

"How's Alex doing?" Ferris asked. "I heard she found old Max Cragan dead."

"News travels fast."

"Small town."

Ferris shrugged; Joe stepped in. "She's a little nuts. Like her mother."

It shouldn't have, but the comment got Reed's back up. "How do you figure?"

"You saw her the other night. Hearing voices, screaming. Nuts."

"Cut her some slack," Ferris said. "She'd been drinking and got turned around. It happens."

Joe rolled his eyes. "Not to me."

"Of course not," Ferris shot back. "Because you're perfect."

"That's right, little brother. And don't forget it."

Reed decided it was time to exit. Middleman in one of his brothers' arguments was a thankless place to be. Been there, done that. Besides, if he was lucky he could catch Carter before lunch.

He said his goodbyes and left Red Crest, thoughts already on the interview ahead. Carter Townsend had also left the wine industry, though he hadn't strayed far. He'd earned a law degree, specializing in corporate law, then settled right back here in Sonoma County. Carter represented a number of wineries, including the Reed and Sommer outfits.

Walton, Townsend Johnson & Associates law firm was located in Santa Rosa, not far from the county courthouse. As Reed stepped off the elevator and crossed to the firm's double glass doors, he decided that Carter must be doing well. Beyond the doors he could see gleaming dark wood and shiny brass fixtures.

He crossed to the reception area and the perky blonde sitting there. In Reed's experience, every law office was a cookie-cutter version of every other law office. Not in size or furnishings. In atmosphere. Hushed, like a library, with a certain "tiptoe" quality.

Law offices, even when luxuriously outfitted, were not warm, fuzzy places.

"Good morning," the woman said, smiling. "How can I help you?"

"Is Carter Townsend in?"

"Do you have an appointment?"

"Detective Reed." He held up his shield. "Is he in?"

She looked startled. "He may have left for . . . lunch. Let me see."

He hadn't. Several moments later, the man crossed the reception area to greet him. "Dan, what the hell? Scared my girl here to death with all that official badge crap." He shook his hand. "Next time, just tell her Danny Reed needs a moment."

"I'll do that." Reed smiled. "Could we speak in private?"

"Absolutely. Come on."

He led Reed to his office. Richly decorated. Mahogany desk, leather chairs. Pictures of the wife and kids.

"Nice family, Carter," Reed said, picking up one of the photos—a family shot complete with his four kids.

"Shelley, that's my oldest, she's starting high school this year."

Reed set down the photo. "That's crazy. I remember us being that age not that long ago."

"Seems like a lifetime ago to me. Give yourself another ten years, a wife and four kids. It'll make you old fast."

"I had a question about when you and Tom were kids. About those matching tattoos you got."

"Where'd you hear that?"

"Joe mentioned it."

He leaned back in his chair, hands behind his head. "That was random. What's up?"

Instead of answering, Reed asked another question. "Why the vines and snake?"

He blinked. "Pardon?"

"What did the image symbolize? Most people get tattoos that have some special meaning to them."

Carter shook his head, expression rueful. "I'm sure it meant something at the time. Hell if I remember what."

He was lying. "How'd you come up with the image?"

Carter frowned. "Tom did. I was just along for the ride."

"And that's it?"

"Pretty much. We were young and stupid. Completely loaded that night."

"How old were you?"

He rubbed his jaw. "Eighteen. Maybe. We had to show our IDs."

"Anybody else with you?"

He hesitated, then shook his head. "I don't remember."

"You don't remember? You'll understand why I find that unbelievable?"

Carter stiffened. "I was drunk. It was twenty-some years ago. A lot's happened since then."

"Sure," Reed said easily. "You're right. I was out of line."

Carter glanced pointedly at his watch and stood. "I hate to rush you, but I have an appointment."

"No problem." Reed followed him to his feet. "Where's yours?"

Carter looked surprised. "My lunch appointment?"

"Tattoo."

"I had it removed. Ten or fifteen years ago."

"Really? Why's that?"

He looked suddenly irritated. He motioned to the family photo. "I wasn't like Tom. I had kids; what they and my wife think is important to me."

Reed held out his hand. "Thanks, Carter. I appreciate your time."

Carter shook it, then walked with him to his office door. "Can I ask, why the interest in Tom's tattoo?"

Reed decided to throw him a nugget of information and see how he reacted. "It may be linked to another crime."

For the space of a heartbeat, the man's expression went curiously blank. The moment passed, and he morphed once more into the affable family man. "Holy shit, Dan. That's unbelievable."

Reed waited a moment, then agreed. "You're not going to ask?"

"Ask what?"

"What crime Tom's tattoo might be linked to."

He laughed, the sound forced. "Of course not. I knew you wouldn't tell me."

"Right you are." Reed smiled. "Thanks again, Carter. I'll be in touch."

He started down the hall. Carter stopped him. "Have you talked to Clark? He and Tom were friends back then. Big buddies."

Interesting, Reed thought moments later, as he climbed into his SUV. For a lawyer, Carter hadn't been very smooth. He'd done a poor job of hiding his unease. And of lying. Getting a tattoo, a permanent mark on your body, was a significant event. And Carter had forgotten why he'd done it, what the vines and snake had meant and if any other friends had been in on it? Right. Even fall-down drunk that memory stuck.

Reed backed out of his parking spot, then eased out of the lot. Interesting, also, how in an attempt to divert attention from his relationship with Schwann, he'd thrown Clark under the bus.

What did he know that he didn't want to tell?

No time like the present to find out, he decided, and reached for his cell phone.

Several inquiries later he located Clark at the El Dorado Kitchen. He and Treven were having lunch.

The older man looked up and smiled. "Dan. Good news, I hope."

"Actually, I don't have anything on the facial reconstruction yet. I need to have a word with Clark."

"Have a seat. Wine?"

Reed chose the chair across from Clark. "On duty. Thanks."

"So, what's up, buddy?" Clark asked.

"You and Tom were good friends. Am I right?"

"Absolutely. Since we were kids."

"Then you were aware he had a tattoo?"

"Sure. Adolescent prank. He and Carter. Idiots."

Leaning back in his chair, Treven laughed. "Carter and Tom got tattoos?"

"Yeah." Clark shook his head. "I went with them, all fired up to get a tatt. I wasn't eighteen, so the guy wouldn't do it. I was so pissed."

Treven shook his head. "This is the first I'm hearing of all this."

He glanced at his father, lips lifting in amusement. "Didn't think you needed to know all my drunken exploits, Dad."

Treven chuckled. "I suppose I should be grateful. The exploits I *did* know about are responsible for this hairline."

"What hairline?" Reed offered.

Clark guffawed. Treven shot his son an irritated glance. "Exactly. Have yourself a couple kids, Reed. Get back to me when they're teenagers."

"No, thanks. Why do you think I'm not a parent?"

Clark lifted his glass. "Because you can't find a woman willing to have your kids."

"Finding willing women isn't *my* problem, Clark."

This time it was the father who burst out laughing. Unruffled, Clark took another sip of his wine. "So, Reed, why the interest in the follies of my misspent youth?"

"Following a lead, my friend," Reed murmured, watching Clark intently. He noticed that his hand shook slightly as he set his glass back down.

"An adolescent tattoo is a lead?"

He glanced at Treven and found him frowning slightly as he gazed at his son.

"You never know." Reed spread his fingers. "Speaking of, what was with the snake and vines?"

"We thought it was hot."

"We?"

"All of us guys."

"Who besides you, Tom and Carter?"

"Joe. Terry Bianche."

Terry Bianche had died a number of years back, an ugly

motorcycle wreck. Most folks around the county figured he'd died the way he'd lived: ugly, under the influence and going way too fast.

"My brother Joe?"

"The very one. Also saved by a law-abiding tattoo artist."

"So, you thought the vines and snake were hot. Who came up with it?"

Clark looked at him blankly.

"It's an unusual design. Ornate and quite beautiful. I imagine it would translate well into jewelry."

Something flickered behind Clark's eyes, Reed saw. Was it fear?

"The beauty was lost on me, man. I was seventeen and thought it was cool."

"So, you don't know where it came from?"

"As far as I know, it was one of the tattoo artist's designs."

"You never went back for yours? Why?"

"The moment had passed." Clark smiled, though it didn't reach his eyes. "We were over it."

"Thank God. Horrid things." Treven leaned forward. "Any closer to finding the animal who killed Tom?"

"We've got some leads, Treven. That's all I can say right now."

"I heard he was robbed," Clark offered. "I'll bet it was a field hand. Probably didn't even speak English."

Reed stiffened at the slur. "Thanks for your time, guys. Sorry I interrupted your lunch."

They all stood, shook hands. "Anything we can do to help," Treven said. "Everybody's on edge over this thing."

"Wondering who's next," Clark said.

Reed frowned. "Why would anyone assume there'll be a next?"

Clark looked surprised. "Not assuming, just—"

"Afraid," Treven offered. "Francine hasn't slept well since it happened."

"I understand. And I promise you, we're doing all we can."

"We know that. Thank you, Danny."

After another round of goodbyes, Reed walked away. When he reached the doorway, he glanced back. It looked like the two men were arguing.

Chapter Thirty-eight

Wednesday, March 10
5:10 P.M.

Alex swung open her front door. Rachel stood on the other side, expression concerned.

"I heard," she said. "About you finding Max Cragan. I thought I'd better check on you."

"I'm okay." Alex swung the door wider. "Come on in."

Rachel stepped inside, then held up two bottles of wine. "I brought some liquid painkiller."

"A two-fisted drinker?"

"I didn't know how much pain we were in."

Alex grimaced. "Two bottles might not be enough."

While Rachel opened the wine, Alex put together a plate of cheese and fruit. They carried it all to the living room and sat.

Rachel didn't waste any time. "Tell me what happened."

Alex did, recounting how she had taken Rachel's advice and paid a visit to the Golden Bow, how the shop owner had put her in touch with Cragan, their first meeting and then his call the night before. "This morning," she continued, "when he didn't answer the door, I knew something was wrong, and I—"

The image of the man's bloated face filled her head and, overcome with emotion, she bit the words back and looked away.

Rachel reached across the sofa and squeezed her hand. "It must have been awful."

Alex struggled to find her voice. "It was. He . . . was in his garage. He'd hung himself. He . . . his face was—"

She couldn't say any more. Rachel seemed to understand and didn't press her. They sipped their wine in silence. Minutes passed, but strangely, the silence wasn't uncomfortable. If anything, she found it almost soothing.

"Thank you," Alex said finally.

Rachel refilled their glasses. "For what?"

"For being here." She brought her glass to her lips, then lowered it without sipping. "I found my mom, too. It was totally different, but I feel a little like Typhoid Mary."

"Waiting for the other shoe to drop?"

Alex laughed, feeling the first of the wine's buzz. "Don't even say it."

"A toast!" Rachel said, holding up her glass.

Alex frowned. "A toast?"

"To the earth's gift of the grape, the gods' gift of wine and its magical, healing properties. And to sisters."

Alex tapped the other woman's glass. "You're a little nuts, you know that?"

"I do, indeed. But so are you."

She couldn't dispute that, though she wished she felt at least a niggling doubt it was true.

"It's what we lived through," Rachel said. "How could we not be a bit left of center?"

How indeed? Alex thought of Rachel's childhood, the traumas she had lived through, and ached for her. "I'm sorry about your mom," she said. "Your real mom. It must have been rough for you, losing her that way."

Rachel stiffened. "What do you know about that?"

Alex was taken aback by the ferocity in her tone and expression. "I didn't mean to upset you. I heard about the accident, how she drowned in a fermenting tank and I just . . ."

I'm really sorry. I know what it's like to lose your mother too soon."

"Right," Rachel snapped. "How old are you? Thirty? And she's been gone a whole month?"

"But I lost her long before that. She was with me physically, but in every other way she was absent."

The other woman visibly pulled herself together. "She didn't drown. She asphyxiated."

Rachel got to her feet and walked to the fireplace. She stared down at the hearth, though what she was seeing with her mind's eye, Alex could only guess.

"In winemaking there's a process called punching down. It's basically pushing the grape skins back into the fermenting wine with what looks like a giant potato masher. It'd be no big deal, except for the amount of CO_2 produced in the process. One whiff too many, you take a header into the tank and it's all over."

Alex frowned. She had seen the catwalks around the tanks, had even been allowed to walk on one during a wine tour. She remembered the tour guide talking about the dangers of the CO_2. "That's what happened to your mother."

"Yes." Rachel rubbed her arms. "It still happens, even with all the new equipment and safety standards."

"No one tried to save her?"

"They had to hold Uncle Treven back."

"Hold him back! I don't understand—"

"He would have been overcome as well. And in the time it would have taken to harness him, she would've been dead already. None of them were properly rigged," she added bitterly. "Dad made excuses for them. For not being harnessed."

Alex didn't know what to say, so she said nothing.

"I suppose I understand. They both grew up on a winery. They'd been around the equipment and process from the time they could walk . . ."

Her voice trailed off and she swung to face Alex. She shook with fury. "No, I don't understand! She shouldn't have been up on that catwalk! What the hell was she thinking? No harness? No safety line? She was a mother. I needed her. She was—"

Rachel stopped, struggling, Alex thought, for control. She flexed her fingers. "She was pregnant. Did you know that?"

"Oh my God. No, I didn't—"

Rachel sighed, a cross between anger and grief. "Three months along." She swiped angrily at a tear. "It was a boy. We didn't learn that until the autopsy."

"How horrible. I'm so, so sorry."

"You see why my dad's the way he is? It's so easy for Uncle Treven to be strong. He didn't lose two wives and two sons. It's easy for Clark and Will to strut around as if they owned the world. They don't know what it's like to lose . . ."

Anger made her tone brittle. So brittle Alex thought it would break. "Their mother is still alive. Still married to their dad. Still . . . Shit! I hate being like this!"

Alex crossed to her and touched her shoulder. "I'm so sorry, Rachel."

"They're not like us, Alex," she whispered. "None of them."

A lump formed in her throat. Rachel was right. The two of them were bound by shared pain. Losing their brother. Losing their mothers.

She and Rachel truly were sisters.

Alex put her arms around her. Rachel resisted, but only for a moment. She turned into Alex's hug and hugged her back.

Neither cried. They simply stood that way, holding on to each other—and holding each other up.

As the minutes ticked past, Alex realized how much she had needed this. A sister. A shared past. Someone who understood.

Maybe Rachel had been right the other day when she'd said that Alex being here would bring healing. Hers had already begun.

"I feel like such an idiot," Rachel said finally, stepping away. "I come over here to comfort you and end up with you comforting me."

"What's a sister for?"

Tears filled Rachel's eyes. "And here I hated your guts when you were five."

"I have a lot to atone for."

She swiped at a lone tear that rolled down her cheek. "Hardly. I was a pain in the ass teenager. I owe you."

"Payback begins now," Alex teased, and held up her glass. "Time for a refill."

Rachel laughed. "I've got this, you stay put."

Alex heard her rummaging around, then the distinctive sound of a cork being released from a bottle. *Had they polished off the first already?*

Moments later, Rachel appeared in the doorway. In one hand she held the now opened bottle of wine, in the other the stainless steel chopsticks—designed by a well-known San Francisco artist—that Tim had given her for her birthday a few years before.

"Wicked-looking sticks." She tapped them together. "Very cool."

"They were a gift. From my ex. He loved sushi."

"Typical man. Gives *you* a gift of something he loves."

"I never thought of it that way before."

"Now you have, so you won't make that mistake again." Rachel made her way back into the living room. "Speaking of mistakes, I want to hear all about him."

"Tim?"

"Yes, him." Rachel refilled their glasses, then sat cross-legged on the floor.

Alex held up her glass. "Speaking of my ex, he'll be so jealous when I tell him about this wine. It's spectacular."

"It should be. It's a limited production reserve. A really good vintage. From my private cellar." She tapped the chopsticks together. "I take it you still talk to your ex."

"I still sleep with him sometimes." Alex slapped a hand over her mouth, acknowledging that she needed to stop drinking *now*. "I can't believe I shared that."

Rachel giggled. "Tell me about him."

Alex did. She shared how they met, why they divorced and about their current relationship. Rachel followed suit, and as the evening progressed and the bottle emptied, they talked, at times as giggly as teenagers, at others fiercely serious.

Alex discovered they had similar beliefs and political

views, the same sense of humor. Likes and dislikes. Some-time during the passing hours, it occurred to Alex how alike they were for two people who didn't share blood.

Or maybe they did. Maybe Harlan Sommer really was her father? She started to wonder it aloud, then decided against it. As close as she felt to Rachel at this moment, she was un-certain how the woman would respond to the question.

Rachel frowned suddenly. "Where's your ring?"

Alex looked at her naked hand. "Reed took it."

"Reed took it?" she repeated, words slurring slightly. "Why?"

"He said he needed it for the investigation."

Rachel leaned against the couch, legs stretched out on the floor in front of her. She'd long ago taken off her boots. She wiggled her stocking-clad toes. "That doesn't make sense."

Alex blinked, simultaneously realizing two things: she was completely inebriated and she couldn't feel her tongue. "What d'you mean?"

"Max killed himself. Right?"

She nodded. "Right."

"What could your ring have t'do with that?"

Alex gazed at her, struggling to think clearly. "That's why I was there. T'see if he'd designed it."

"I'm just saying, Reed's got some other reason to hold on to it."

She frowned. "What?"

"Hell if I know." Rachel looked down at her empty glass and giggled. "Wine's gone. S'pose I should go now."

"O'no you're not." Alex got unsteadily to her feet. At least the room wasn't spinning—yet. "What kind of sister would I be if I let you drive now? You're sleepin' on th'couch."

Chapter Thirty-nine

Thursday, March 11
4:55 A.M.

They wore hooded robes. She struggled to see their faces, but couldn't. The robes concealed their bodies as well. Even so, she recognized them as male. Sensed their violent arousal.

The circle tightened around her. A drumming beat filled her head. She looked wildly around, fighting panic. Looking for an escape. A way out.

Suddenly, she was in a forest. Crouching in underbrush. Someone was speaking. Threatening, the voice high, feminine. No, male. Angry. She struggled to make out the words. To understand. But as hard as she tried, she couldn't make sense of it. The words were garbled, nonsense.

An acrid scent stung her nose. Sandalwood. She couldn't breathe, let alone scream. But screaming, she knew, was the only way out.

Scream, Alex . . . Scream—

Alex sat bolt upright in bed, eyes snapping open as her scream echoed off the walls.

Her bedroom door flew open. Light tumbled in. "Alex? Are you all right?"

She blinked, confused, still trapped in the circle of men.

"Alex, honey, you screamed."

Rachel. The night before. She'd stayed.

"A nightmare," Alex managed, gathering the sheet and blanket to her chin. She realized she was trembling. "I . . . I'm sorry I woke you."

"Waking me wasn't the problem, scaring the crap out of me was."

Alex reached for her bedside lamp and snapped it on. "Shit. Sorry."

Rachel crossed to the bed and sat on the corner. "You want to talk about it?"

She shook her head. "I just want to forget it."

"Okay, no problem." Expression hurt, Rachel started to stand.

Alex caught her hand. "I have nightmares. I've had them all my life. They come and go. Right now, I'm in a bad patch. That's all."

Rachel squeezed her hand in acknowledgment of what it had cost Alex to share. "I didn't mean to pry."

"You weren't. It's just me, I—" Alex smiled ruefully. "I'm sorry I blasted you out of bed."

Rachel returned the smile. "What a pair we are. You going back to sleep?"

Alex glanced at the clock. "What's the point? It's almost five anyway."

"I'll make coffee?"

"That sounds like heaven. Everything's in the cabinet above the pot. I'll be right out."

Alex took a minute to throw on sweats and brush her teeth. She found Rachel in the kitchen, back in the clothes she had worn over the night before, staring at the coffee as it dripped into the carafe.

"Slowest coffeepot on earth," Alex murmured.

"I see that." She looked over at Alex. "How's your head this morning?"

"Hurting, though it could have been worse. How about yours?"

"It's punishing me for my excesses. But I had it coming."

Alex smiled. "Coffee will help."

"I've never suffered with nightmares, I'm happy to say."

"One of those who sleeps like a baby? I'm seriously jealous."

Rachel laughed. "Now, I didn't say that. I've got my own demons, nightmares just don't happen to be one of them."

Demons, Alex thought. She would bet she had them.

"Do you really want to hear about my nightmare?"

"Only if you want to share."

"I need food first."

Working together, they whipped up some scrambled eggs and toast. Just as the meal came together, the coffeemaker burbled its last. They sat at the table and began to eat. Rachel didn't hurry her or push, which Alex appreciated.

It was only after she had scraped the last bit of food from her plate and refilled her coffee cup that she began.

"Like I said, I've had nightmares for years. As far back as I can remember. Lots of the typical being chased and running for your life variety. But recently, they're . . . different. More specific."

"Like tonight's?"

"Yes. Tonight I was surrounded by men. Trapped in the middle of their circle. I knew they were aroused, and I felt threatened. Really afraid."

Rachel's eyes widened. "My God. Could you see their faces?"

Alex shook her head. "They wore hooded robes. Dreams are like that, your subconscious plays a game of peek-a-boo with you."

"They meant to rape you."

"That's the obvious interpretation. But dreams are rarely about the obvious. The men, the circle, not being able to see their faces, feeling trapped and threatened were all symbols for something else."

"What?"

"Dunno. And this morning, I'm too tired to think about it." She felt a little guilty at the half truth. The complete truth was, if it was Tim sitting across from her, hungover and exhausted or not, she would be eagerly digging in. She wasn't ready to share her soul with Rachel. Their relationship was just too new.

"I've got just the fix for that!" Rachel exclaimed, jumping to her feet. "Manipeds."

"Manicures and pedicures?"

"I know I can get us booked. It may take a bottle of my best reserve, but I can do it. What do you say?"

"Don't you have to work?"

"Screw work, I work all the time."

Alex looked at her hands. Her fingernails were a mess. Her toes were worse.

"We'll buy a new lipstick, too," Rachel said, collecting their breakfast plates and carrying them to the sink. "And eyeshadow. Both in some hideous color we'll never wear."

Alex laughed. It sounded like fun. The kind of fun she hadn't had in . . . well, in forever. "I'm in."

Rachel rubbed her hands together. "Goody. I have to get cleaned up and check in at work. I'll call you after."

Chapter Forty

Alex pulled up in front of the modest home. She shifted into park and shut off the car. She let out a pent-up breath and flexed her fingers on the steering wheel. Her newly painted nails caught her eyes, and she smiled, thinking of the afternoon's antics. Rachel was crazy; she made her laugh. A lot. And she'd drawn Alex out of herself. They'd been silly, acting more like teenagers than grown women.

Case in point, the color of her fingers and toes: Shocking Pink. Rachel had chosen Darling Clementine—an orange bright enough to make Florida proud. As for their lipstick choice, in true BFF form, they'd picked the same impractical but surprisingly flattering red. The way they'd carried on, Alex was surprised the salesperson hadn't called security.

Alex swung open her car door, stepped out, then retrieved the basket of flowers she had stowed on the back floorboard. Oddly, her time with her stepsister had given her the courage to do what she had been considering ever since finding Max Cragan dead. Pay her respects to his daughter.

And maybe unearth answers as well.

She took the walkway to the front door and rang the bell. A dark-haired, dimple-cheeked little girl opened the door. Alex recognized her from the picture Max had proudly shown her—the youngest of his three granddaughters.

"Hello," Alex said. "Is your mommy home?"

The child nodded, stuck her thumb in her mouth and ran off, leaving Alex standing there and the front door wide open.

Uncertain what to do, she poked her head in. "Hello," she called "Mrs. Wilson, are you home?"

A moment later a woman appeared, daughter in tow. Or rather, it appeared the child had her mother in tow.

Angie Wilson looked like a woman in pain. Grief harshly etched her features, creating a sad clone of the woman Alex had seen in Max's photograph.

"Can I help you?" she said.

"I'm Alex Clarkson." She held out the flowers. "I'm so sorry about your dad."

Angie looked at the basket, then back up at Alex, eyes wet with tears. "Thank you. Come in."

She took the basket and led Alex inside. The house looked as if a bomb had gone off in it. She supposed in a way, one had.

Angie cleared a space on the couch. Alex sat, then cleared her throat. "Your dad loved you and your girls so much . . . He told me how God had blessed him."

Understanding crossed the woman's face. "You're from his church."

When she said she wasn't, the woman frowned. "Do I know you?"

"No, I . . . I only met your father once, but he touched me deeply. He was a sweet, sweet man."

Angie began to cry. The child, who had been at her mother's feet flipping through a picture book, climbed onto her mother's lap, expression stricken. "Don't cry, Mommy. Poppy's in Heaven."

"You're right, sweetie." She hugged the child. "Could you go get Mommy a tissue?"

The girl scrambled down, then trotted off to do as her mother asked.

Angie looked at Alex. "You're the one who found him."

It wasn't a question; she answered anyway. "Yes."

"Why were you there?"

"I have a ring . . . it was my mother's . . . he may have designed it."

She nodded. The girl returned with the tissues. Alex waited as the woman took them, praised the child, then wiped her cheeks and blew her nose.

"Thank you for the flowers. I . . . If you don't mind, now's not a good time."

"I know. I'm so sorry." She reached across and touched the woman's hand. "It will get better. Give it time. I understand how your—" Alex drew a deep breath. "My mother died recently. She . . . took her own life."

Angie stiffened. "Excuse me?"

"I'm just trying to say, I know how you feel."

"My dad didn't kill himself."

Alex couldn't hide her shock. "I'm . . . the police . . . I—"

"My dad did *not* commit suicide. He was happy. Content. Even after Mom passed away, he never—"

She stopped and fisted her fingers, as if in frustration. "You saw how frail he was! How do you think he did it?"

Alex blinked. "I don't know. I just—"

"His hands shook so badly he had trouble picking up his cat. How could he have pulled it off? Set up the stepladder, hung the rope from a beam and tied the slip knot? It's laughable."

She hadn't asked any questions, Alex realized. She had taken the scene at face value. Just as she had her mother's.

But her mother hadn't been happy and content. Her mother had attempted suicide before.

Alex cleared her throat. "Had your dad ever attempted this before? Had he ever talked about killing himself?"

She already knew the answer. The man who had trumpeted his blessings to a perfect stranger wouldn't have hung himself.

Even if he had been physically able to do it. Which was questionable.

As that realization struck, so did another: *If Max hadn't killed himself, then he'd been murdered.*

Her hands began to shake; she met Angie's eyes. "Did you talk to the police? Tell them what you just told me?"

"Of course," she said bitterly. "They treated me like I was a naive child."

Alex could see that happening. The cops knew what they knew, and that was it. But in this case, maybe they were wrong?

"You want me to talk to them? I know Detective Reed, maybe if I explain—"

"Why would you do that for me?"

It was a fair question. One she was certain she would have asked if she'd been in Angie Wilson's shoes.

But she was certain saying she felt somehow responsible wouldn't go over well. The other reason would.

"I liked your dad. A lot."

"I already spoke with Detective Reed, he wasn't too interested in my opinion."

"Let me see what I can do."

Alex stood. The woman followed her to her feet. "Thank you."

She walked her to the door. There, she asked, "Did you ever find out if Dad designed your ring?"

Alex shook her head. "I guess I'll just have to find out another way."

"Why does it matter?"

Alex looked away, then back. "She's gone and I don't . . . have anyone else. I hoped that maybe it'd be a clue to her past. That somehow it'd lead me to my father."

"My dad kept a portfolio of his designs. I'll look for it."

Chapter Forty-one

Thursday, March 11
7:40 P.M.

"Hello, Son."

"Dad." Reed looked past him, expecting to see his mother or his brothers. His father rarely visited without external prodding of some sort. Make that never. But today the porch behind him was empty.

He returned his gaze to his old man. "This is a surprise."

"May I come in?"

Reed swung the door wider. "Sure. I was making dinner. Let me go take it off the stove."

His dad stepped inside. He'd inherited the cottage from his maternal grandmother, a good thing because he'd never have been able to afford it on a cop's salary. Not that it was large or lavish, but Sonoma County real estate trended toward outrageously pricey.

"You've got the place fixed up nice," his father said, looking around the 1940s Arts and Crafts–style cottage with a scowl.

"A compliment? Wow, I didn't think I'd live long enough."

His father didn't comment. Reed headed to the kitchen, turned off the burner and covered his soup. When he returned to the living room, he found his dad pacing. "Have a seat."

"No, thanks. What I came to say, I can say standing." He looked Reed dead in the eye. "I hear you've been hounding our friends. Interrupting business, stirring up bad memories."

Apparently, he'd struck a nerve. Enough of one to send out the infantry, guns blazing. "Hounding, Dad? Funny, I call it doing my job."

"You know how I feel about your career choice."

"You've never made a secret of it. Though as we both know, how you feel about my job has zero to do with what I need to do."

"All this over some silly tattoo."

"That 'silly tattoo,' as you call it, is a link between two crimes."

"I'm going to ask you to drop this."

"Can't do it." Reed held his old man's gaze. "What's the significance of the vines and snake?"

"It's nothing."

"If it was nothing, you wouldn't be here. We both know that."

"I'm here because you're making our friends uncomfortable."

"Who called you?" Reed asked. "Treven? Clark? Carter? All the above?"

"I know what you have. This link between crimes, as you call it. Tom's tattoo and Patsy's ring."

"You know about the ring?"

"I do. And I noticed her daughter wearing it."

He put subtle, caustic emphasis on the word *her*, making his disdain for Patsy obvious. "What's the significance, Dad?"

"Not what you think, I'll tell you that. And certainly not a link to a murder."

"What do I think?"

"Don't play games with me, Danny."

"You're the one playing games, Pops. Not me. We may not have always agreed, but you've always been a straight shooter. Be straight with me now."

For a long moment, his father stood frozen. Then, sighing heavily, he crossed to the couch and sank onto it. For a long moment he stared at his folded hands, then lifted his gaze. "The boys were all part of a secret club."

Reed cocked an eyebrow. "A secret club?"

His dad averted his eyes. Reed frowned. His father was always the take-charge guy in the room. He handled every situation, was the one who made the power play.

Not today. Reed had never seen him look so uncomfortable. Reed took a seat across from him and waited.

"This is very difficult to talk about. Very difficult." He passed a hand over his eyes. "At the time, I had no idea what was going on. When I learned . . . it was such a betrayal. I felt as if my heart had been ripped from my body."

He balled his hands into fists. "Being a parent is about protecting and nurturing. You try to surround your child with all that's good. And when evil touches—" His voice cracked.

Reed saw evil every day; he knew it existed. But coming from his dad, delivered in such high, dramatic form, he had to laugh. "Not Academy Award material, Dad, but from a guy like you, almost convincing. But frankly, I can do without it."

"This is nothing to laugh about."

"What kind of secret 'evil' club?"

"An initiation club."

"Into what?"

"Sex," he said, expression harsh.

"And Patsy—"

"Was the initiator. She fucked them. They each got the tattoo after. Some of them were as young as fifteen."

Reed struggled to come to grips with what his father was telling him, and to jibe the Patsy Sommer he remembered with the sexual predator his father described. An adult having sexual relations with a minor was a crime. Didn't matter if the minor was a male and willing participant.

"You didn't go to the police?"

"No. I . . . we wanted to keep it out of the press. We felt

exposing our boys to that notoriety would make it even worse."

"Who was involved?"

"Which boys?" Reed nodded and he went on. "You know several already. Tom, of course. Carter. Clark. Joe. Terry Bianche. That other kid, they called him Spanky."

"The one who committed suicide ten or fifteen years ago?" His dad nodded and Reed wondered aloud, "You're saying my brother Joe was involved. He doesn't have the tattoo."

"What was going on came to light before he got his, thank God."

"Mom knows?"

"No. We decided that the boys' mothers be kept in the dark."

"And Harlan?"

"He didn't know and still doesn't. We'd like it to stay that way."

Reed stood and crossed to the pair of windows on the far wall. They looked out over an old vineyard, dark and overgrown. He'd always wondered why anyone would just let it go wild that way. The land was so valuable.

Reed looked over his shoulder at his father. "She had sex with them. That was it, the extent of the club?"

"Not quite. The initiated would watch the new initiates. Cheer them on. Then they'd all take turns with her."

Reed dragged a hand through his hair, thinking of Alex, wondering how he would tell her. "How did you find out?"

"Joe. After Dylan disappeared, he was completely traumatized. Confessed it all." His lips curled in distaste. "It still makes me sick to think of it."

Reed held himself stiffly. He'd seen and heard much worse. And he'd long ago reconciled himself with the ugliness the human animal was capable of. But this sickness had touched his family. His sheltered little circle.

"And the ring?" he asked stiffly. "Was it a gift? Or did Patsy have it made—"

"For herself. Yes. Max Cragan created the design. Of course he knew nothing about the symbolism."

Reed saw that his father's forehead gleamed with sweat. "To think, all those times we socialized with them, treating her as one of us, one of our inner circle, she was . . . doing that."

His father's expression puckered with grief and guilt. "I should have seen it. Should have somehow—" He bit the words back. "She was a whore. She preyed on our sons. How could I not have known? Not have seen something? But none of us suspected a thing."

"Do you know who Alexandra's father is?"

He shook his head. "It could have been anyone."

"And Dylan?"

His father looked up, surprised. "What about Dylan?"

"Who was his father?"

"Harlan was, of cour—" He bit the words back as if realizing for the first time that Dylan could have been fathered by someone other than Harlan. Considering what he and the other men had learned she was up to, Reed found that odd.

His father must have realized how odd it was as well, because he quickly backtracked. "We all assumed, never questioned his . . ."

He cleared his throat. "You have to understand, before this came to light, we were friends. The best of friends. They seemed like a loving couple. And I'm not even certain when her insanity began."

Reed frowned. "Insanity, Dad?"

"What would you call it? Define it for me." He launched to his feet, flushing. "Having sex with the sons of her friends, it was . . . craziness. Sick!"

"It was criminal," Reed corrected. "You should have gone to the police."

"We didn't! Dammit, we did what we thought was best!" He brought his hands to his face, a gesture Reed had never seen from his father.

When he dropped his hands, his eyes were wet. "She didn't leave on her own. We forced her to go. Dylan was gone. Alexandra wasn't Harlan's. God forgive us, we never wanted Harlan to know. When we confronted Patsy, she threatened to tell him. If we didn't offer her a settlement. She would need a nest egg, she said. We gave it to her. She took Alex and left, with the promise to never darken Harlan's door again."

His father reached a hand out. "I'm here, Dan. Hat in hand. I need your help. Let this tattoo thing die. If you don't, innocent people will be hurt. Think of Joe's kids. My God, if it got out . . ."

He was too close to this situation, Reed acknowledged. This wasn't some stranger asking for his help, it was his father. The unbending man who had accepted his decision not to be a part of the business with a terse "Go on, then. Who needs you?"

That man needed him now.

Some secrets were best left unearthed.

"I'll see what I can do. But I can't make any promises."

His father looked relieved. "Thank you, Son. It's the right thing to do, I promise you."

"Be aware, if something emerges that strengthens the connection between—"

"It won't. The ring and tattoo have nothing to do with Tom's murder."

For a long time after he left, Reed went over what his father had told him. He thought of Alex. Of his brother. Clark and the others. He thought of Patsy Sommer.

Who'd she been? Reed wondered. The woman he remembered: always kind, offering a smile, the picture-perfect mother and wife? The bipolar artist who had great talent but suffered fits of despair so deep they turned violent? Or the criminal temptress his father described, who seduced underage young men?

"The ring and tattoo have nothing to do with Tom's murder." Perhaps not, Reed thought. But could they have something to do with Dylan's?

He experienced a prickle of excitement, an *aha* moment. If Patsy had been as promiscuous as his dad described, Dylan could have been someone else's child, not Harlan's. A fact which, if learned, could have rocked a number of people's worlds. The actual father's. Harlan's. If the father was a minor, that minor's family.

Some secrets were best left unearthed.

Son of a bitch, he thought. This changed everything.

Chapter Forty-two

Thursday, March 11
9:00 P.M.

Reed dialed Tanner. She answered; he heard music and conversation in the background. "Where are you?" he asked.

"Tony's. What's up?"

Tony's, a bar not far from the Barn, served as one of the department's favorite after-shift watering holes. "We need to talk. Stay put."

Twenty minutes later he entered Tony's and crossed directly to the bar. "Tony" was actually an attractive, unpretentious, thirtysomething Antonia. She called her place "the anti–wine country alternative." Although wine was on the menu, decent quality even, more emphasis was put on the twenty-two different beers on tap and the mixed drink category. However, at Tony's call brands were out, well brands in. The bar sported two flat-screen TVs, the pool table in the back room was battered but level, and peanuts, pretzels and popcorn could be had for free, 24/7.

"Reed," she said as he approached, "long time no see." She drew him a Poppy Jasper amber ale and set it in front of him.

"The bad guys have been keeping me busy."

"Me, too." She grinned. "Tanner asked me to let you know she's playing pool."

"Thanks." He paid for the beer and headed for the back room. Sure enough, Tanner, Cal and a couple of rookies from Property Crimes were deep into a game of eight ball. It looked like Tanner and Cal were kicking their asses.

Typical. Tanner was wicked good with a stick.

Tanner bent over the table, readying her shot. She looked back at him. "Enjoying the view, Reed?"

"I have to say I am."

She grinned. "Good. Glad I still have it."

She took the shot, drawing the stick back smoothly, following through with unflinching accuracy. The cue ball struck its target—the fifteen—and it shot into the corner pocket. She ran the rest of the table, then called the eight ball. A moment later, the grumbling rookies were heading out front for a round of beers.

She pulled a stool up beside his. Cal followed suit. "What do you have?" she asked.

Reed quickly filled them in on what his father had told him, beginning with what Patsy Sommer had been doing, who had been involved, then finishing with how the boys' fathers had responded.

Cal whistled. "Being initiated by an older, experienced woman is every adolescent boy's wet dream. She'd have to be hot, though. You know, in that Mrs. Robinson sort of way—"

"Get a grip, Cal," Tanner snapped. "I'm not interested in your version of an adolescent wet dream."

"Some of the boys were as young as fifteen," Reed said.

"That's statutory rape. At the very least, carnal knowledge of a juvenile."

Reed agreed and went on. "Seems the initiation included some weird group action. An audience to cheer them on, then sharing the sloppy seconds."

"And thirds." Tanner made a face. "That's some sick shit. Certainly not the way I'd want my son to learn about sex."

"That's what the dads thought."

"All of them?" Tanner asked, tone skeptical.

Reed frowned. "What do you mean?"

"Our society tends to put a stamp of approval on a boy's sexual initiation at the hands of an older, hot woman. Case in point, Cal's comment."

"But with a girl of the same age," Reed murmured, "it's called a crime."

"Yes." Tanner frowned. "I could even see some fathers shrugging it off, no harm, no foul."

"They didn't go to the police," Cal agreed. "Which would seem to validate Tanner's thinking."

"Just sent her on her way. With a nest egg, even." Reed took a swallow of his beer. "They didn't want anyone to know what was going on. Especially Harlan. They even kept it from the boys' mothers."

The rookies returned with the beers. Tanner declined another game; Reed thought the younger of the two looked relieved. They wandered back out front and Reed turned again to Tanner and Cal.

"My dad wants to keep it that way. He asked me to drop my questioning about the tattoo."

"Of course he did," Tanner murmured. "Look at who was involved, the Sommer, Reed, Townsend, Schwann and Bianche families. Unarguably Sonoma's most prominent wine families. They don't want their names connected to a sex scandal. One that would surely reignite the furor over Dylan's disappearance."

"Plus," Cal jumped in, "the dads would be barbecued in the media for the way they swept it all under the rug. Different times now. People are a lot more aware of abuse and its tragic effects."

"My dad insists there's no connection between this club and Tom's murder."

Tanner cocked an eyebrow. "And you believe him?"

"I believe he's telling his truth. And I think he may be right about Tom's murder. What interests me is how this might have affected the investigation of Dylan's disappearance."

"What was the timing?"

"Dylan disappeared. Investigation was under way. One of the kids came to his dad, spilled it all."

"And the dads told no one, not even the mothers." Cal scratched his head. "The information might have blown the investigation wide open."

Tanner agreed. "It certainly would have widened the suspect pool."

"It still does," Reed said. "Only now we have remains."

They fell silent. For his part, Reed sifted through the possibilities. An angry parent. A betrayed husband. A jealous teenager. Fertile stuff.

"My bet's on the husband," Tanner said. "Finds out what his wife's been up to, that the kid's not his, goes berserk."

"Patsy and Harlan were having dinner with my folks the night Dylan disappeared."

"So they said."

Tanner was right. That's the way investigations went. If one secret was uncovered, one untruth exposed, more remained to be found out. One lie was never enough, secrets bred secrets.

Nothing that had come before could be trusted now. This little nugget could be just the tip of the iceberg.

"Son of a bitch," Reed muttered.

"No joke." Tanner pursed her lips. "Where do we go from here?"

"Open it all back up. Start at the beginning. I'm thinking the kid who spilled the beans."

Before either of his colleagues could respond, his cell phone sounded. "Reed," he answered.

"It's Alex. Can we talk?"

"About what?"

"Max Cragan's death."

He glanced at his watch. "When?"

"Now?"

"I'm in Santa Rosa. It'll take me twenty-five minutes to get there."

"I'll be waiting."

She hung up and he reholstered his phone. He looked up at Tanner and Cal. "Alexandra Clarkson. She wants to talk about Max Cragan."

Chapter Forty-three

Thursday, March 11
10:45 P.M.

Alex waited for Reed on her front porch. She had spent the time since leaving Angie Wilson's home studying the situation and attempting to decide what she believed. What Angie said made sense: Max hadn't been strong enough to accomplish what the police believed he'd done. Plus, the man had been happy with his life. A devout Catholic as well, one who believed taking your own life was an unforgivable sin.

But murder?

Alex rubbed her arms, chilled. Someone had come to Max's door while they were on the phone. He had said so; she had heard the bell sound. Not Angie, as he had thought that night. His killer? Probably.

She shivered again, though the night was mild. How could she even consider this? Who would kill such a sweet old man? Why?

Her ring. To keep him quiet.

Could it be? It sounded crazy, but her gut told her she was right anyway.

She had to convince Reed. She couldn't let whoever did this get away with it.

Headlights sliced across her line of vision. She turned and watched as Reed eased to a stop in front of her cottage. He stepped out of the SUV and slammed the door behind him. She lifted her hand in a silent greeting, then waited.

"I know it's late," she said when he reached her, "but I had to talk to you tonight."

"No problem."

She motioned him to follow her inside. When he did, she closed the door behind them and faced him. "Max didn't kill himself."

"Okay. You have proof of that?"

"Yes." She clasped her hands together. "Not exactly. I mean, you may not call it proof, but—"

"You're convinced," he finished for her. "And you believe you can convince me."

"Yes." She held out a hand. "Just hear me out, please. Two things."

He sighed and shrugged out of his jacket. "Can we sit down? It's been a long day."

Without waiting for her response, he headed into the adjacent living room and sank onto the couch. He looked drained.

"I'm sorry," she said.

"For what?"

She spread her hands. "This. Calling you so late. Not considering that you might be tired."

"Your tax dollars at work. Shoot."

She took the chair directly across from his. "When I met Max," she began, "I was struck with how content he was. How at peace he was with his life, even with his physical limitations." She cleared her throat. "He showed me a photograph of his daughter and granddaughters. He called himself blessed."

"Alex—"

"I can't stop wondering, why would a man who described himself as blessed take his own life?"

"That's the first thing?"

"Yes." She laced her fingers. "Here's the second: how'd he do it, Reed?" She leaned toward him. "He was weak. His hands shook so badly he couldn't carry his own teacup without spilling."

"You spoke with his daughter, didn't you?"

"Yes, but—"

"I understand how difficult this is for her," he said softly. "How difficult for you, because of your mother."

"That's not it."

"I've seen suicides play out this way, over and over again, Alex. Family members never want to accept their loved one chose to take their life. It's too painful. They feel it's a personal rejection. Or somehow a reflection on how good a spouse, parent or in this case child they were."

"No." Alex shook her head. "Someone was at his door that night, while he was on the phone with me. I heard the doorbell ring. It wasn't Angie. You need to ask the neighbors, maybe someone saw who it was. It could have been his killer."

"Alex—"

"What about his doctor? Have you even spoken with him? Have you asked if, in their opinion, he had the strength to hang himself?"

She saw by his expression that he hadn't. "You should, because I don't think he could. Why would an old man like him choose that way to die? He'd do what my mother did, take a handful of pills and . . . I can't stop thinking"—tears blurred her vision and she blinked to keep them from falling—"I can't stop thinking that he was murdered because of me. Because of the ring. So I wouldn't find out who'd had it made."

He stood and crossed to her. "No." He caught her hands and drew her to her feet. "It didn't go down that way."

"It can't be a coincidence that just hours after he called me about it, he was dead." Her voice rose. "He was so weird about it. He made me promise not to tell anyone we'd talked."

He tightened his fingers over hers. "I promise you, Max Cragan was not killed because of you or your mother's ring."

"How can you be so certain? How?"

"There's something I have to tell you. Something I just learned."

She searched his expression. Something in it, some regret, had her backing away from him. "I don't want to hear this, do I?"

"It's about your mother. I'm sorry."

Alex turned away from him, crossed to the fireplace. She laid a hand on the old pine mantel and breathed deeply through her nose, trying to calm herself.

She wanted to know, she told herself. Whatever it was, she could handle it.

"Okay," she said softly, "what is it?"

"Max did design the ring."

She turned slowly and met his eyes.

"It wasn't a gift. Your mother had it designed for herself."

She felt some of her tension slip away. "How did you find that out?"

"Some people who knew her well." He looked away, then back. "I was interested in the ring because I'd seen the design before."

"Where?"

"A tattoo. On the bottom of a man's foot."

Her heart leapt to her throat. *Her father. Of course. It had to be.*

"Who is he?" she asked, voice shaking. "Does he know about m— Of course he does. Was he married? Is that it? Is that why they couldn't acknowledge each other?"

"No, Alex. This is difficult, so I'm just going—"

"It's Harlan, isn't it? It makes sense that he—"

He laid his hands on her shoulders. "Your mother initiated young men into sex. The sons of her and Harlan's friends. Some of them were as young as fifteen."

She stared disbelievingly at him. "What did you . . . you didn't just say—"

But he had, she realized. She started to tremble.

"I'm sorry, Alex. Maybe you should sit down?"

She shook her head. "It's not true."

"The boys got tattoos afterward, in a vines and snake image."

"No. You're lying."

"After Dylan disappeared, one of the boys went to his father, confessed everything. The fathers got together and ran her—and you—out of town."

Alex felt ill. She brought a trembling hand to her mouth. "It's not true. It's not!"

"I got it directly from parties involved. Parties I trust."

Her father had been just some guy her mother had fucked. She had always told Alex she didn't know who he was; Alex had preferred to believe she'd been lying.

It hurt so bad she could hardly breathe. Everything she had ever imagined about her father and the past her mother kept hidden had just been shot to hell.

She lashed out at Reed. "That makes me, what? The whore's kid? Not even conceived in love?"

"What she did or was has nothing to do with you."

"What a joke my coming back must be to them all. I can imagine what they're saying. How they're snickering behind my back."

"Why would they?" He tried to take her into his arms.

She fought against him. "No. No! Don't touch me."

Her stomach rushed to her throat and she turned and ran for the bathroom. She made it just in time, heaving over the commode, heaving until she was empty. And broken. The way she felt inside.

"I'm sorry, Alex," Reed said softly from the doorway.

She flushed the toilet and stood. "Leave me alone."

"Can't do it."

"Then hand me the mouthwash. It's in the medicine cabinet." He did and she rinsed her mouth and spit once, then again. "You don't have to worry I'm going to freak out or something. I'm not."

"I wasn't worried. Sit."

She flipped down the commode lid and did as he asked. He wet a washcloth and handed it to her. "Hold that on the back of your neck. You'll feel better."

She did as he suggested. "This is just great," she said. "Simply fucking wonderful."

"Feel better?"

"Than what?" She handed him the washcloth. "You're calling my mother a whore. And a . . . my God, a child molester?"

"Technically, since the boys were all older than fourteen, it's considered statutory rape or carnal knowledge of a juvenile."

"I feel so much better now."

"I'm sorry."

She stood. "If you say you're sorry one more time, I swear to God, I'm going to lose it."

He let that pass. She stalked out of the bathroom and to the kitchen. An open cabernet sat on the counter. She poured herself a glass. "Want one?" she asked.

"I'd rather have a beer."

"Sure. Help yourself." She sipped the wine and made a face at the taste.

"I was going to warn you about mixing a good red and mouthwash, but figured you'd have tried it anyway."

He was right, she would have. Stubbornly, she took another sip. This time, the taste was more tolerable. She looked at him. "Who are they? The young men my mother . . . initiated?"

"Does it matter?"

"To me, yes." When he didn't respond, she pursed her lips in thought. "Family friends, you said. As young as fifteen. Let me guess. Your brother Joe. Clark Sommer. The rest shouldn't be too hard to figure out." She narrowed her eyes. "The guy who was murdered. What was his name?"

"Tom Schwann."

"Right. Him." She thought of what Rachel had said, that Reed had more of a reason to take her ring than just Max's suicide.

"He had the tattoo that matched my mom's ring. Of course. That's what got you asking questions."

She nodded to herself, confirming her own thoughts. "Your questions either jostled someone's memory or upset an apple-cart or two and . . . voilà, Patsy Sommer, defiler of young men, is exposed."

"Alex—"

"Who'd you hear it from?" She tapped the stem of her wineglass, considering the options. "Your dad, I'll bet. Am I right?"

She saw from his expression that she was and went on. "Too bad you were only ten. You missed out on all the fun."

"Stop it, Alex."

"But that's not quite true. You had a piece of the whore's daughter, so in a way—"

"Stop it," he said again. He crossed to her, took the wineglass from her hand, then caught her by the shoulders. "Don't do this."

"Is it in the genes, then? Is that why I—" Sudden tears flooded her eyes. Dammit, she didn't want to cry! She preferred anger or even bitterness.

But the tears spilled over anyway. And he caught them with his fingertips, then lips. Kissing her, he dragged her to his chest and into his arms.

He carried her to the bedroom and there, in a frenzy that obliterated grief and transformed anger to passion, they made love.

Afterward, he didn't release her, instead held her tightly in his arms. She pressed her face to his damp chest. His heart thundered beneath her cheek and she pressed closer.

She thought of all the men she had been with, the therapy sessions she'd had, trying to figure out why. The answers had varied: she'd been looking for love, for Daddy, to rewrite history, as a way to complete or validate herself.

Did it all come down to genetics? Was she just like her mother?

Fear licked at her and she shuddered. Did the same future await her?

Reed stirred; he cocked his head to see her face. "Don't like what you're thinking," he murmured.

"So, now you're both cop and mind reader?"

She said it lightly, but he didn't bite. Instead, he drew her up so they were nose-to-nose. "You're not like your mother."

She frowned. "I'm here with you, aren't I?"

"I'm not young or uninitiated. And you didn't seduce me."

It hurt to look at him; she shifted her gaze and stared blankly at the wall. "It hurts," she said finally, softly.

"I know." He kissed her shoulder. "I'm sorry."

She turned to meet his eyes. "Don't say that anymore, okay? I'm tired of people telling me that. I've heard it so many times. Not just since Mom's death, but all my life."

"What would you rather hear?"

She searched his gaze. "No clue. I just know pity's not cutting it."

Chapter Forty-four

Friday, March 12
7:04 A.M.

Sunlight spilled across the bed. Alex opened her eyes. It all came crashing back. Reed. The night before. The things he had said about her mother. The way they had hurt. Their desperate lovemaking.

She moaned.

"Morning, sleepyhead."

Alex shifted her gaze. Reed stood at the door to the bathroom. He wore his jeans and a towel looped around his neck. His hair was wet. "I took a shower. I hope you don't mind?"

She told him she didn't, watching as he toweled his hair, then disappeared into the bathroom, emerging a moment later without the towel.

She sat up, pulling the blanket to her chin. "What time is it?"

"Just after seven. I've got to hit the road."

"I'll make coffee." She moved to climb out of bed.

"Stay put. I'll grab a cup on my way." He crossed to the bed, retrieving his shirt from the floor on the way. He pulled it over his head, then grinned down at her. "The drive'll be a lot more pleasant imagining you here and naked."

"It'd be a lot more pleasant *here*, if you'd call in sick and climb back in bed."

"Wish I could."

"Prove it."

"Is that a challenge?"

She let the blanket slip away, revealing her naked torso. "You tell me."

He bent and kissed her, softly at first, then deeply. Alex arched up to meet him, rubbing, hungry. Desperate.

She didn't want to be alone.

He caught her hand and brought it to him. "See?" he murmured against her mouth. "I really do wish I could stay."

"So, stay."

He groaned and set her away from him. "Can't. Sorry."

"No problem. Your loss." She tossed aside the covers and climbed naked out of bed. She stretched, then slipped by him on her way to the bathroom. She stopped in the doorway and looked over her shoulder at him. The view was having an obvious effect on him. "Be careful out there, Detective"—she lowered her eyes—"you've got a loaded weapon."

He grinned. "I know what you're doing, Alex."

"Really? And what's that?"

"Putting off the inevitable."

"The inevitable?"

"Dealing with what I told you last night. About your mother."

He was right, dammit. Not that she was about to let him know that. "First off, take a little more credit. A girl doesn't need an excuse to want to have sex with you. Secondly, there's nothing to deal with." She tipped up her chin. "Because it's not true."

He studied her a long moment. To his credit, she didn't read pity in his expression. "It all makes sense now, Alex. Her guilt. Her self-hatred. The way she hid the past from you."

It did make sense. She hated that it did. "You don't get it. She was my mother. Not perfect. Not even close. But she was mine, the only one I'm ever going to have."

"Yeah, I get that, Alex. And I'm sorry. But all that doesn't change what's true."

A knot of tears settled in her throat. "Not buying it."

But she was. She knew it—and so did he, she could tell by his expression.

"Are you going to be okay?"

"I'm fine. You don't have to worry about me."

He nodded, started toward the bedroom door, then stopped. "Can I call you later?"

"If you want to."

He didn't respond and a moment later she heard the front door snap shut.

Alex used the bathroom, then crawled back into bed. She propped the pillows up behind her, leaned back and stared up at the ceiling. A long, thin crack ran from the room's far right corner to the center light fixture.

She gazed at the imperfection. How had he known? How had he seen so easily through her? She had wanted him to stay so she wouldn't be alone with her thoughts. To put off the inevitable, just the way he had said.

No putting it off now, she thought. No distractions. Just her, the things Reed had said about her mother, and the way those things made her feel.

Alex plucked at the blanket. Her mother had seduced her friends' sons. Seduced? That was too nice a word for what Reed had described. Too soft.

Her mother had fucked them. She had fucked them individually and in a group. She had stolen their innocence. Initiated them into sex in a way that was perverse. Twisted and sick.

And she had lied to everyone: her husband, friends, her own daughter. Alex curved her arms around her middle. She'd been an adulteress. A user and a liar. Morally corrupt.

Tears flooded her eyes and she fought them off, angry. What did that make her? She had asked Reed that question, lashing out in pain. But it was true. Who was her dad? Some guy her mother screwed? A one-night stand? Hell, maybe some pimply-face teenager who hadn't known any better.

What did that make her? she wondered again. She thought back on her life, on the number of guys she had been with, how for a time she had turned to sex for answers. To everything. Boredom, anger, rebellion, powerlessness.

Is that what her mother had been doing? Looking for answers? Filling up the empty places? Had she finally recognized how self-destructive that behavior was, the way Alex had?

Alex looked down at her hands, feeling helpless and disingenuous. If she'd learned so much, what was she doing sleeping with Reed? They didn't have a relationship, they barely knew one another. Hell, she'd gone to bed with him when a handshake would have been appropriate.

No wonder he could so easily accept the story about her mother.

Alex realized she was crying and fisted her fingers. Why did her mother even have her? Alex wondered. Why have one baby, then another? It didn't make sense.

Angry, she swiped at her tears. She wished she hadn't come here. She wished she had never found the trunk with all its bittersweet mementos, never seen the photograph of her mother beaming as she held Dylan in her arms. Smiling with adoration at her husband. Looking for all the world like the perfectly content wife and mother.

Perfectly content. In love. Adoring of her husband and baby.

She couldn't have faked that, Alex thought. Even the most accomplished actress couldn't fake it one hundred percent of the time. Not in candid shots. The camera didn't lie.

Candid photographs.

Lyla Reed, she remembered. The wine launch party. On the walls of "the trophy room," as Reed had called it. His mother, offering her the opportunity to thumb through the family photo albums.

Alex wondered if that offer was still good. Acknowledging there was only one way to find out, she climbed out of bed and hurried to dress.

Chapter Forty-five

Friday, March 12
8:20 A.M.

Reed made his way through the still smoldering remains of Max Cragan's cottage. The irony of the situation hadn't struck him until this moment—he'd left his and Alex's still smoldering fire to be routed to this one.

The fire had begun sometime after midnight. Though the firefighters had been unable to save the house, they had kept the fire from spreading to neighboring properties. A feat considering the dry conditions and brisk wind.

An accelerant had been used to start the blaze; the fire investigator had officially called it arson and it'd become the Sheriff's Department's baby.

Reed frowned. When a home was deliberately torched, it was typically for one of two reasons: insurance fraud or an attempt to hide a crime. Several other motivations cropped up from time to time, like revenge, racial hatred, or pyromania.

So why did somebody torch the old man's cottage?

Something shiny winked up at him from the blackened debris and he bent and picked it up. He turned it over in his hands, a feat made difficult by the bulky protective gloves he wore. An eyeglass lens.

Tanner had arrived and finished suiting up. The protective gear swallowed her, but without it neither of them would have been able to investigate the scene for hours.

She made her way to his side. "What's it looking like?" she asked, voice muffled by her respirator.

"Arson investigator found a fuel can in back. Looks to him like that was the point of origin."

"Any victims?"

He replied that there hadn't been and held out the lens. "Found this just now."

She took it. "The old guy wear glasses?"

"Don't know, though it wouldn't surprise me."

"What're you thinking?"

"That maybe Alex and the old man's daughter are right. Maybe Cragan didn't kill himself after all."

A high, thin wail of grief pierced the morning air. Reed turned and saw Angie Wilson being consoled by a man he didn't recognize. Her husband, Reed guessed.

He looked back at Tanner. "Do your thing. I'll catch up with you later."

He picked his way through the blackened rubble, heading toward the sobbing woman. When he had cleared the scene, he removed his helmet and respirator.

The daughter caught sight of him and broke away from her husband's grasp. "You!" she cried, stumbling toward him. "Do you believe me now?"

Reed faced her stoically. "I'm sorry for your loss, Mrs. Wilson."

"To hell with that! I told you! You wouldn't listen! Are you listening now? All my father's things . . . our family photographs, all his designs . . . everything I had left of him, gone now!"

The man slipped his arm around her. "Honey," he said, "calm down. It's only stuff. Just things."

"To you!" She struggled free of his arms. "He was my

father, I grew up here. All my childhood photographs and my memor—" The words caught on a sob. "Do you believe me now, Detective Reed? My father didn't kill himself, he was murdered!"

She broke down then. Sobbing against her husband's chest, obviously heartbroken. The man met Reed's eyes. In them he saw apology—and condemnation.

"I'm Sean, Angie's husband. Do we know yet, was this accidental or—"

"It was deliberately set. What we don't know is who did it or why." He turned his gaze to the woman. "Mrs. Wilson, do you have any idea who might be responsible for this?"

"Whoever killed him. They did this."

He tried another tack. "Did your father have any enemies?"

"None that I know of. Everybody liked him." She looked up at her husband. "Right, Sean?"

"Right," her husband agreed, then looked at him. "Did you ever meet him, Detective?"

"I'm sorry to say I did not."

"If you had, you'd understand. He was loved by everyone."

"What about his house. Any idea why someone would want to torch it?"

"I don't know."

"Could he have been involved in something illegal?"

The question elicited vehement denials from them both. Reed tried again. "The house's contents, anything of great value? Perhaps the fire was used to cover up a burglary?"

The two looked at one another in question, then simultaneously replied in the negative.

"No art or jewelry? Rare coins or books?"

"My dad lived on his Social Security, Detective. To do that, he needed our help from time to time."

"Help we were happy to offer," her husband added. "He was always there for us, to help with the girls, whatever."

"You believe strongly he was murdered, yet you say everyone liked him. Somebody torched his house, yet you can't think of a reason why."

"Maybe it was just some wacko," she offered. "Some sick stranger. It happens, right?"

"It does, Mrs. Wilson, but frankly it's rare. Murder is a crime most often committed by a friend, family member or an acquaintance."

She started to cry again and pressed her face against her husband's chest. He wrapped his arms protectively around her. "Tell us what to do, Detective Reed. Anything that might help."

He wished he had something to offer them, something that would give them a sense of purpose. He had nothing. "If you think of anything later, even if it seems like nothing, call me."

He said he would and Reed started off, then stopped and looked back. "Did your dad wear glasses. Mrs. Wilson?"

"Yes," she whispered. "He was blind as a bat without them."

Twenty minutes later, Reed approached the medical group's receptionist. He provided his shield for her review. "Detective Reed, Sonoma County Sheriff's Department. I need to have a word with Dr. Whitney."

The woman studied the badge, then lifted her gaze to his. "He's with a patient right now. Could I help you?"

"Afraid not. I'll need to speak with him directly. When he's finished, could you let him know I'm waiting?"

She said she would, and as often happened, he didn't wait long. The badge served as an automatic bump to the front of the line. He received several unhappy glares as, moments later, the nurse called his name.

The doctor stood as Reed entered his office. "Dr. Whitney," the physician said, extending his hand.

Reed took it. The other man had red hair, thinning at the temples. Even so, he didn't look much older than thirty. "Detective Daniel Reed. Thank you for seeing me so quickly."

"I have a full book today, so if you don't mind getting to it?"

"Of course. You had a patient named Max Cragan?"

"Still do, as far as I know."

"He died Tuesday night. I'm investigating his death."

The doctor blinked and cleared his throat. "I had no idea. How did he . . . I'm sorry. I'm just so surprised."

"When was the last time you saw Mr. Cragan? Professionally."

He thought a moment. "I'd have to look that up to give you an exact date, but it wasn't that long ago. Less than a month."

"What was his condition?"

"I'm sorry, Detective, but I'm bound by patient privacy laws."

"Let me ask you this instead. In your professional opinion, was Mr. Cragan strong enough to hang himself?

He looked startled. "He hung himself?"

"That surprises you."

"Yes. He was a delightful man. Always positive, with a kind word for everyone."

"And physically? Could he have set up a stepladder, climbed it, looped and fastened a rope over an exposed beam, then slipped the noose over his head and kicked the ladder away?"

The physician thought a moment, then slowly shook his head. "In my professional opinion, no. Can I say absolutely no or that it would've been impossible? No, I can't." He leaned toward Reed. "The truth is, every day I'm humbled and awed by the power of the human spirit over the limitations of the body. Everyday miracles, Detective."

Chapter Forty-six

Friday, March 12
10:30 A.M.

Three hours later Lyla Reed opened her front door and greeted Alex warmly. "You called on just the right day," she said, grasping Alex's hand. "The rest of the week I've had board meetings and luncheons. It's endless, really."

She led Alex inside the grand home. Today it smelled of flowers and lemon polish. "Thank you so much, Lyla," Alex said. "I really appreciate you letting me do this."

"I'm happy to, really. I told you how close your mother and I were."

Alex opened her mouth to ask for assurances, then closed it fearing her desperation would show. That she would say something to raise the woman's suspicions.

"Are you settling in?"

"Very nicely."

"I heard about you finding poor Max. It must have been horrible."

"It was. I'd gone to ask him about my mother's ring. The one with the grapevines and snake."

"I don't recall her having a ring like that."

"But you commented on it at the party."

Lyla looked startled. "I did?"

"Yes. I'm certain you did."

She frowned slightly. "You must be confused."

"I must be," Alex said. "Several people commented on it . . . I guess I just . . . I thought you . . ."

She let the thought trail off, feeling a little silly. But she *was* sure Lyla had been one of those who had noted the ring.

Lyla patted her arm. "No worries, dear. You know, I have one of Max's designs. A brooch. He was so talented and our families were friends. Here we are."

They entered the room. Lyla crossed to bookshelves on the right. She selected three leatherbound volumes from one of the shelves. "These are the Patsy years, as I call them. Some of the happiest times of our lives."

She set them on a table in front of the velvet couch. "If you don't need me—"

"I'm fine. Please, go. You have things to do."

Lyla smiled and squeezed her hand. "I'll come check on you in a bit."

"Wait." Alex held on to her hand. "Lyla, you and my mother were such good friends. Did she ever mention my father?"

The woman's gaze went soft with sympathy. "Never. I always wondered about him. I even hinted around the subject, but she simply wouldn't go there."

"Why?" Alex asked. "Why so secretive? If the relationship was in the past, what difference would it have made?"

"I decided he must have hurt her badly. She was happy and wanted to leave that time of her life far behind."

But Alex had been the creation of that part of her life. Where did that leave her?

As if reading her thoughts, Lyla squeezed her hand again. "I'm sorry. She loved you very much, I promise you. We all saw how much."

Alex sat and reached for the first volume: *1982*. Working to keep her hopefulness in check, she opened it.

The photographs looked decidedly old-fashioned. The hair and clothes. The furnishings and events.

She flipped through. Interesting how, in the short time she'd been here, she had learned who all the players were. Reed and his older brother. Clark and Rachel. Max Cragan, she realized, recognizing him from the photograph that day at his house, in his hallway.

The pages crackled as she turned them. She found herself riveted by the beautiful, smiling people. And the story the pictures depicted. Of a close-knit group. One that spent a lot of time together partying—she couldn't really call it anything else. It was the rare photograph that didn't include someone—or several someones—with a glass in their hand. In many of them they were hugging one another, laughing or mugging for the camera.

Obviously feeling no pain.

Alex studied her mother. She had been a beautiful woman, certainly the most beautiful of their circle. The youngest, as well. She'd been only twenty-four then, Alex realized. Younger than Alex was now, and already married and a mother.

Not that she was in any way matronly, Alex thought, as she landed on a photo of the group poolside. Her mother wore a skimpy bikini and in several shots was draped over a couple of the other husbands.

A knot settled in her stomach. Alex turned the page. There she was again, this time in a cover-up, sitting on Treven's lap. She was laughing; he looked irritated.

The things Reed had said raced around her head. She pushed them back. But she wasn't alone. The other wives were carrying on as well. No one looked scandalized.

As Alex moved on to the second album, then the third, the photos evolved. Her mother seemed to become less carefree and more introspective. Candid shots caught expressions of worry, unguarded anxiety, furtiveness.

Alex passed a hand over her face. Or was she imagining it all? Had Reed's story caused her to look at the photos differently? Change her presumption about her mother's life?

"Hey, Alex. This is a nice surprise."

Reed's younger brother, she saw. Alex smiled and closed

the last album. "Hey back, Ferris. Your mother offered me a peek at the family photo albums."

"Still trying to catch up on your past?"

"Yup, still trying." She stood and carried the three albums back to the bookcase. She reshelved them, then turned to find him standing directly behind her, close enough to lift her hand and touch.

"Any luck?" he asked.

Uncomfortable with their proximity, she inched backward. "Truthfully? Not a lot. But it was fun seeing them."

"Would you like to go out to dinner?"

"Dinner?"

"Yeah. Tonight?"

"I don't think that'd be a good idea. Thanks anyway." She stepped around him and crossed back to the couch to collect her purse.

He followed, not looking at all bothered by her answer. She wondered whether he was one of those guys who was always putting the query out there, or if he had heard the stories about her mother.

"I knew it," he said. "You have something going on with Dan."

"I didn't say that."

"You didn't have to." He grinned. "Say, if you want to see some more memorabilia from those days, you should pay a visit to the Sommer Winery, they have a museum area, the walls are covered with photos. In fact, I think they have one of your mother's paintings in the tasting room."

Treven had told her that as well. She had forgotten.

"I could even take you—"

"Ferris, your brother is waiting for you out in the conference room."

Wayne Reed stood in the doorway, frowning at his son. Ferris straightened. "Duty calls. Good seeing you, Alex."

When he reached the doorway, he stopped, murmured something to his father that she couldn't make out and left.

Wayne Reed turned his attention to her. "Stay away from my sons."

"Excuse me?"

"You heard me. They've been hurt enough."

To say she was shocked would be an understatement. "I don't understand why you would say that to me."

"I think it would be pretty obvious, considering what your mother was."

Angry color flooded her face. "How dare you."

"How dare you," he countered. "Go back to San Francisco. There's nothing for you here."

She supposed she could have been hurt or intimidated. She was spitting mad instead. "I didn't have any part in what you say my mother was involved in. Which, frankly, I don't believe is true."

"Oh, it is true." He advanced on her, stopping so close she felt his breath stir against her cheek. "What do you think it's like for them? For all of us? Being reminded of—"

He leaned closer; it took all her strength of will not to back away. "Your mother didn't just fuck our sons. She fucked them up."

He turned on his heel and strode to the door. When he reached it, she stopped him by calling out, "It's not true."

He froze, then turned slowly to look at her. "Excuse me?"

"What you said about my mother. I know it's not true. And I'll prove it."

He narrowed his eyes. "You're no longer welcome here, Ms. Clarkson. I'll have one of the staff escort you out."

"Don't bother." She strode past him and through the door, passing so closely he could have grabbed her. And for one crazy moment, she wondered if he would.

He didn't, and minutes later she collapsed in her car, trembling so violently she gripped the steering wheel for support.

She'd be damned if she would run and hide. Scurry back to San Francisco and pretend none of this had happened. The way her mother had. No. What they were saying about her mother wasn't true. She didn't know how she would prove it, but she would.

Chapter Forty-seven

Friday, March 12
3:30 P.M.

Alex took Ferris's suggestion and headed for Sommer Winery. There she discovered that she had arrived in time to make the four o'clock tour, the last of the day. The for-a-fee tour took in both the winery and caves, then ended in the tasting room to sample several Sommer wines.

She bought a ticket, then was directed to the museum for the winery's history and a short video on winemaking. She made her way there; a half dozen others already waited. Catching parts of various conversations, she learned the Sommer tour was considered one of the best in wine country.

Covered with photographs and other memorabilia, the museum walls served as a visual history of the winery, from its early days making inexpensive jug wine to now, an internationally renowned name in California wine.

But what captured her interest were the labeled photographs. Harlan and Treven as boys, then young men. Harlan's first wife. Rachel, from infant to the winemaker she was today. Treven's wife, his son Clark—again glorifying his ascent from childhood athlete and young scholar to company president.

But not a single photograph of her mother or Dylan. None of her.

She must have missed something, Alex thought. She quickly walked the room again, scanning the clusters of photographs.

She hadn't. It stung. Her mother and Dylan hadn't even registered as a blip on the Sommer family timeline.

The guide arrived and called them all to join her. The group had burgeoned to twenty-one, Alex saw. She also noted she was the only person traveling without a companion.

The tour began in the crushing area. The guide described the grape-sorting process, how those grapes were mechanically transported to the crusher-destemmer. The machine's blades and chewers created free-run juice. Nobody stomped grapes with their feet anymore, the guide informed them— only as part of demonstrations or winemaking history lessons.

They moved on to the fermenting tanks. Stainless steel, the tanks stood twelve feet tall and each held three thousand gallons of fermenting wine.

"Notice the catwalks," the guide said, pointing to them. "The fermenting juice is accessed there for a process called punching down. The process is actually quite dangerous. Every year there are a number of deaths—"

Alex stared at the tanks, at the catwalk, mouth dry, heart pounding. She pictured Susan Sommer, overcome by CO_2 and tumbling into the tank. What had her last thought been? For the baby she carried in her womb? For the daughter she was leaving behind?

"Are there any questions?" the guide asked.

"Wasn't there an accident like that here?" Alex called out. "Many years ago?"

The guide looked at her strangely. "Not these tanks. The fermenting area has been totally upgraded and modernized since then."

"Someone died?" a young woman asked, eyes huge.

"Yes," the guide answered. "A member of the Sommer family. It was a terrible tragedy, and one we prefer not to talk about."

"What about the other tragedy?" Alex asked, unable to stop the question from springing from her lips. "The kidnapping I read about? That little boy?"

A murmur went through the group. The guide looked uncomfortable. "Dylan Sommer," she said. "He was abducted from his bed in 1985. The Sommer family has never given up hope that he's alive and one day will be home."

Of course they had, Alex thought. Everybody had moved on. There wasn't even a picture of him in their museum.

The guide cleared her throat. "Now, if there are no more questions, let's move on to the highlight of our tour, the wine caves. The Sommer caves are some of the oldest and largest of the wine country caves, rivaled only by those at Schramsberg."

The guide talked while she led them from the fermenting area to the caves. "These were hand-dug which, with twenty-six thousand square feet of tunnels, is simply amazing.

"Caves," she continued, "are the original green solution to refrigeration. The interior keeps the wine at a comfortable fifty-eight degrees with seventy percent humidity. We store approximately two thousand barrels in ours."

They reached the cave entrance. Alex's thoughts flooded with the memory of the other night, of being lost, of panicking.

The smell of incense. The sound of laughter. Her chest growing tight, her heart racing. Panic grabbing ahold of her.

No, she told herself. This moment has nothing to do with that one.

"Prepare yourself," the woman continued, "between the insufficient lighting and the lichen growing on the ceiling and walls, it's pretty creepy. But don't worry, as far as I know, there are no ghosts."

But there were, Alex thought. Ghosts of the past. Of the life she should remember, but couldn't.

"Are you all right, dear?"

That came from the woman beside her, a kindly looking

senior. The rest of the group, she saw, had entered the cave. Alex forced a weak smile. "I have trouble with closed-in spaces. Is it that obvious?"

"It is. You're white as a sheet."

"I'll be fine."

The woman patted her arm. "That's the spirit. Just stick with me. I was a nurse, back in the day."

They caught up with the group. The tour guide was describing the original process of cave formation. "Chinese laborers were used to dig these caves out of the side of the mountain. You'll be surprised by the . . ."

Alex worked to focus on the guide's words, to slow her heart and breathe evenly and deeply.

". . . use only French oak barrels. The barrels cost anywhere from five hundred to two thousand dollars each."

The group chattered excitedly. Her Florence Nightingale had wandered back to her husband. Blindly, Alex followed the guide, concentrating on putting one foot in front of the other.

She began to sweat. The clammy sweat of panic. Her heart beat so high and fast it felt as if it had climbed up into her throat.

Why was this happening to her?

Get out, find the exit.

". . . high humidity reduces the amount of evaporation from the barrels. Now stay with me," the guide called, "it's easy to get disoriented in here."

Dylan. As her brother's name popped into her head, so did his image. A beautiful dark-haired baby. Cooing up at her. Smiling.

Then screaming.

Alex stopped. She brought a hand to her mouth. The smell of incense filled her head.

She looked wildly around her. The group had rounded the bend and disappeared from sight. Alex took a step backward. Then another. And another.

Not backward, she realized. Sideways. She was pressed against the cave wall, surrounded by the stacked oak barrels.

The fingers of lichen brushed against her face and scalp and she pushed at them, a cry rising in her throat.

The smell of incense grew stronger. It burned her nose. She opened her mouth to call out to the group, to call for help. Her head filled instead with a wild thrumming.

She flattened herself against the wall, even as she was dragged into a long, musty tunnel. Her vision narrowed until it consisted of a small, round opening at the end.

The light flickered crazily. Not lights, she realized. Flames dancing around her. Crackling, their bright, hot tentacles reaching out to her. Surrounding her. The howls of creatures, writhing within the fire. Being consumed by it.

One of the creatures grabbed her arm, its bony fingers like claws digging into her skin.

"Miss? Are you all right? Miss?"

A security guard. She blinked, coming fully back into reality. He had a round, pleasant face. He was looking at her with a combination of concern and suspicion. As if she had sprouted horns.

In a way she had.

"Get me out of here," she managed. "Please."

Hand on her elbow to guide her, he led her out of the cave. She stepped into the fading sunlight and greedily sucked in the fresh air, as if she had been deprived, suffocating.

What the hell was happening to her?

"I need to sit down."

He led her to a bench not far from the cave entrance. She sat and lowered her head to her knees, breathing deeply, fear fading and her resolve returning.

She straightened. "How did you find me?"

"Ma'am?"

"Did I scream?"

He looked at her oddly. "No, ma'am."

"I have claustrophobia," she lied. "It's something I'm working on."

"Can I see you to your vehicle? Get you a glass of water or—"

"No. The tasting room, which way is it?"

By his expression she could tell that in his opinion, wine was the last thing she needed. What he didn't know was, wine was the last thing on her mind. She meant to get a look at her mother's painting.

Chapter Forty-eight

Alex arrived in the tasting room at the same time as her group.
They rushed the bar en masse, ready to enjoy their prepaid
samples.

Alex hung back, gaze going to the large painting behind
the bar. Her mother's work, she would have recognized it anywhere. The swirling use of paint, the lively, rich color.

Only this piece possessed a quality the later ones had
lacked: a joie de vivre, a hopefulness. Looking at it made
her ache.

"See," the kindly nurse said, coming up beside her, "you
did it."

Alex didn't bother correcting her. "How about that?" she
said.

The woman followed her gaze. "It's fetching," she said.
"I wonder who the artist is?"

"Patsy Sommer."

"A family member?"

"Yes. She was married to Harlan Sommer. His second
wife and mother of the child who—"

"Alexandra? This is a surprise."

Alex turned. Clark Sommer stood behind her, smiling warmly.

She thought of the story Reed had told her, the things his father had said: *"Your mother didn't just fuck our sons. She fucked them up."*

A whisper of unease moved over her. "Hello, Clark. Just playing tourist."

"Excellent. "He turned to the nurse and smiled. "Clark Sommer. Are you enjoying your visit?"

She gushed that she was. He handed her a business card. "Give this to Cathy at the bar, tell her I said you and your companion should have a taste of our Stone Hill Reserve Cabernet. On me, of course."

"That was nice of you," Alex said after her new friend had hurried off.

"Good PR and it costs me nothing. There's an open bottle of it behind the bar and we're closing in thirty minutes."

"Okay," she said, softening her words with a smile, "not nice. Calculating."

"Could I have a moment? In private?"

"Sure."

Clark took her arm and steered her out of the tasting room and across the walkway to the museum. Tours had ended and it was deserted.

"What's up?" she asked.

"The question I was about to ask you."

"I don't understand."

"When I walked up, what were you telling that woman?"

Alex frowned, working to recall. "I was admiring my mother's painting; she asked who painted it."

"So you were telling her."

"Yes. Is there something wrong with that?"

"Let's make something perfectly clear, your mother is no longer part of this family's history."

"You can't rewrite history, though"—she motioned around them—"I see you've tried. There's not one picture of her or Dylan."

"Do you blame us? Do you think we want to remember either of them? Or you, for that matter?"

Alex counted to ten before she spoke. Lashing out at him—in anger or hurt—would prove nothing. "You're entitled to your opinion."

She started past him; he caught her arm, stopping her. He leaned closer; she smelled wine on his breath and realized he had been drinking.

"Take your hand off me."

"Your mother," he said softly, trailing a finger across her cheek, "was a beautiful woman."

Alex jerked away. "I asked you not to—"

"Exciting. Full of life. You're just like her, aren't you?"

She made a move to leave, he grabbed her and pushed her up against the wall. Fear turned the inside of her mouth to ash. She worked to keep him from seeing it.

"Aren't you just like her?"

Alex wedged her hands between them. "Dammit, Clark! Don't do something you'll regret. Let me go!"

"Don't talk to me about regret." His mouth tightened. "You think I don't know how that feels? Or what it's like to wonder . . . every day—"

He weaved slightly, as if suddenly off balance. "Mike Acosta killed himself. Did you know that?"

"I don't know who Mike is."

"Spanky, we called him. He hung himself."

Like Max. She searched her memory for a Mike and came up empty.

"Couldn't take it." His words slurred slightly. "Terry's dead, too. How does that feel?"

"I don't know either of those men. Now, I suggest you—"

"You want to know what your mother was, Alexandra?" His gaze dropped to her mouth, then breasts. "You want to know so bad, I'll show you."

His words reverberated through her. Sudden, deep and debilitating panic took her breath. She fought against his grip.

"Let me go," she cried. "Now!"

"You like to fuck for an audience?"

"No!" she cried. "Let me—"

"Clark!"

He jerked around, so quickly he lost his balance. Treven stood in the doorway, face pinched with fury.

"Dad!" He cleared his throat and steadied himself. "I didn't . . . this isn't—"

"Son, I'm going to give you ten seconds to get the hell out of here. One second more than that, and I swear to God I'll kill you."

He meant it, Alex thought. Clark must have thought so, too, because he didn't hesitate. He slipped off without another word—or glance—for either of them.

Treven crossed to her. "Are you all right, Alexandra?"

She couldn't find her voice. Tears filled her eyes and she nodded.

"He didn't hurt you?"

"No," she managed, voice shaking.

Though, the truth was, he had hurt her. Down deep, a mortal wound she wondered if she would ever fully recover from.

"Come, let's get you a glass of wine."

When he steered her toward the tasting room, she resisted. "I don't want to see anyone right now."

"They're all gone," he murmured. "The winery's closed."

He was right. One lone winery worker remained, cleaning the bar area. Treven motioned for him to leave, then pulled two chairs together. "Sit."

She did and lifted her gaze to her mother's painting. How could someone as morally corrupt as they said her mother was have created something so beautiful, so full of life and hope?

"I came to see her painting," she said softly.

"I'm so sorry." Treven handed her a glass of red wine, then took the chair opposite hers. "I don't know what's gotten into him. Ever since—"

He didn't finish the thought. It hung in the air between them and she looked at him. "Ever since what?"

"You got here." His expression softened with regret. "Try the wine. It'll help. That's what it does."

They sipped in silence. The fruits and spice filled her mouth first, followed by the tannins that coated her tongue, the alcohol that warmed her belly. She felt its effect steal blessedly over her.

"Legend has it," he said softly, "that Ikarios and his daughter Erigone were the first humans to taste wine. Dionysus, the god of wine, shared it with them, then instructed them to make the fruit of the vines known to all. But when Ikarios did, the fellows gulped it down and became drunk.

"Observers, thinking Ikarios had poisoned their friends, beat him to death. When his daughter discovered his body, she hung herself in grief."

Alex laughed weakly. "That's a gruesome story, Treven. One I don't understand why you're telling me."

He motioned to her glass. "The history of wine is intertwined with the history of the world. It has been a tumultuous pairing. Wine has soothed the heartbroken, fueled both ecstasy and violence, and incited responsible men to act like idiots." He paused. "Case in point, my son."

She appreciated his apology and told him so.

"Not an apology," Treven corrected. "He's too damn old for that. An explanation. Perhaps a request for understanding."

Alex nodded and he went on. "History is populated by tragic stories. Our lives, too."

He glanced up at her mother's painting. She followed his gaze. Her mother's life. Her own. Those who had loved her.

Or been abused by her.

"Who was Mike?" Alex asked. "Clark said he hung himself."

"A good friend."

"When did he—"

"He was twenty. Clark found him."

"My God."

"Another of his childhood friends is gone, as well. Terry Bianche. Terry battled drug and alcohol addiction. He died in a motorcycle accident."

Treven held the glass slightly aloft and swirled the liquid, studying it. She sensed he did it from habit. He shifted his gaze to hers.

"I understand Reed spoke to you about your mother's actions with our sons. I also hear that you're having a difficult time accepting it. I don't blame you."

She flushed, uncertain if he meant he didn't hold her accountable for her mother's actions or that he didn't question her loyalty to her mother.

"Mike was one of the boys. So was Terry. They were sixteen and seventeen at the time."

"I don't know what to say."

He cradled the bowl of the wineglass in his palms. "We handled it all wrong. Everything. I share the blame for that."

He sighed, the sound heavy. "The boys should have had counseling. She should have been held accountable. But after Dylan . . ."

Alex looked away.

He laid a hand over hers. "I'm so sorry, Alexandra. None of this was your doing. After all, we can't help who our parents are."

Her parents. Mother and father. She turned back to meet his eyes. "Do you know who my father is?"

"I'm sorry." He released her hand and stood. "I wish I could help you."

She lifted a shoulder and followed him to his feet. "Someday, I'll ask someone and get a different answer."

"I hope so, Alex. I really do."

Chapter Forty-nine

Friday, March 12
8:45 P.M.

Alex sat huddled under a blanket on the end of her couch, unable to get warm. After leaving Treven Sommer, she had climbed into her car and driven aimlessly, on roads that wound through picturesque towns, past rolling hills dotted with sleeping vineyards.

Traffic had occasionally slowed to a crawl, then opened back up, with no particular rhythm.

No wonder she was cold, Alex thought. She'd driven with her window down, using the sting of the cold breeze to connect her to the physical while her mind raced with the events of the day.

"We can't help who our parents are."

"You want to know what your mother was, Alexandra? You want to know so bad, I'll show you."

"Stay away from my sons."

Alex shivered and huddled deeper into the blanket. Needing reassurance from someone who had known her mother, she had called Rita Welsh at her home, then the library. She learned that Rita had retired and moved to Oregon to be near her grandchildren. They refused to give her a forwarding address or phone number.

She thought again of what Wayne Reed had said to her: *"Stay away from my sons."* What would Wayne Reed think if he knew what she and his son had shared?

Maybe he did know. Maybe that was part of the reason he had passed along her mother's sordid story. And why he had been so hateful to her.

Reed. He hadn't called, though she wasn't sure how she felt about that. A part of her wished he had. The part that enjoyed his company—both his character and the mind-blowing sex. But the other part thought it was for the best. Too much history. Too many secrets. His worldview too conventional, hers too unconventional.

History. Secrets. She turned her gaze to the framed photo resting on the table beside her. Her mother holding Dylan, smiling for the camera. Her standing there, beaming up at them both.

She reached for it and gazed at her mother's image, pain curling through her. *What were your secrets? What they're telling me about you, is it true? Is that why you kept the past hidden from me?*

She shifted her attention to other aspects of the photo. It'd been taken at Sommer Winery. The cave entrance, she saw, stood in the background.

She stared at the shadowy opening, her head filling with the memory of her vision from that afternoon. The flames licking at her. The smell of incense. Her very real response: fear and panic.

Alex fisted her fingers, determined not to succumb to either. Her mother hadn't wanted Alex to remember. But what, specifically? Their lives here? The horrible loss of her baby brother?

Why? In an attempt to shelter Alex from pain? To shield herself from the painful reminders? Because of guilt? Fear?

Alex stopped on the last. *Had her mother been afraid? For herself? Or her remaining child?*

Her gaze refocused on the photograph, the shadowy cave entrance. Something happened in that cave. To her. Something awful—horrible and frightening.

Something fighting to get out.

Dear God, she thought. Had the terrible thing happened to her? Or had she witnessed it happening to someone else?

Dylan.

Her phone vibrated and she jumped. She answered, voice shaking.

It was Reed. "Hey. I said I'd call."

She thought back; that morning felt like a lifetime ago. She struggled to remember what he'd said, how they parted. She couldn't.

"I'm on your front porch. I've got a pizza and some beer. If you're in the mood for some company—"

She was. She tossed aside the blanket, hopped to her feet and hurried to the door. All the reasons why they shouldn't be together evaporated as she swung the door open. She wanted him. She needed to be with him. Now, this moment.

He stepped inside, nudging the door shut with his hip. "I brought my favorites, Boont Amber Ale and a 'Works' pie from the Red Grape."

Wordlessly, she took the six-pack and set it on the entryway table, then relieved him of the pizza box. She dropped it, then pushed him up against the door.

"Don't say anything," she whispered against his mouth. "Just . . . be with . . . me." She tore at his clothes, yanking his shirt over his head, greedily struggling with his belt, fumbling in her hurry.

He lifted her and turned them around so her back was pressed against the door. "Hold on, baby," he said, then speared into her.

She cried out, digging her nails into his back, arching and bucking against him. Waves of pleasure washed over her, mingling with the events of the day. Stay away from my sons . . . you want to know, Alexandra . . . she hung herself in grief . . .

Flames licking at her. The smell of incense. The howling of creatures.

Alex fought the memory. She tightened her legs around Reed's waist. *No . . . no . . . I want this . . .*

Crouching down, surrounded by underbrush, shrubbery. Hiding. The voice. The angry words she can't make quite out—

But then she does. They ring clearly in her head. Clark's words. Clark's voice.

"You want to know so bad. I'll show you."

A cry spilled past her lips. She realized she was crying.

"Alex? My God, are you all right?"

She blinked. Reed was breathing heavily, looking at her strangely. He'd stopped, his body already cooling.

"Did I hurt you? Sweetheart—"

"No." She began to tremble and rested her forehead against his. "Hold me. Please, just hold me."

He carried her to the living room; together they curled up under the blanket. For a long time, they lay like that, neither speaking. Clark's words replayed in her head. Words he had spoken today. In anger. In an implied threat.

Were they words from the past as well? Dear God, what was happening to her? Alex wondered. Was she jumbling together the past and the present? Or was she descending into mental illness?

"You ready to talk about it?" he asked quietly.

What could she tell him? If she shared everything, would he take her seriously—or think she was unstable, just like her mother had been?

Nothing she'd done since meeting him indicated otherwise.

Reed's stomach growled loudly. Saved, she thought, and tipped her face up to his. "Your pizza," she said. "I forgot all about it."

"Me, too." His stomach grumbled again.

"Liar." She eased out from under the blanket. "I'll reheat it."

"Don't bother." He caught her hand. "You ready to talk about it?"

"Can I have a little more time?"

He smiled lazily up at her. "They're your secrets. Take all the time you need."

A short while later, they sat on the floor eating the cold pizza and sipping on the warm beer. She'd slipped into his shirt; him his jeans.

"Good pizza," she murmured, reaching for a second slice.

"The best." He popped open another brew. "I had an interesting day. Max Cragan's house burned down."

"What?"

"Somebody torched it."

Flames. Surrounding her. The tentacles reaching for her, licking at her flesh.

"What's wrong?"

She blinked. It crossed her mind that she was glad they had been together. "Nothing. It's just so . . . shocking."

He frowned. "And that's it?"

"Yes . . . who would do that? It's so cruel."

"Cruel," he repeated. "That's an odd way to think about it."

Alex looked at him. "Because of Angie. She must be devastated. Losing all those . . . memories."

"She was." He fell silent a moment. "I spoke with Cragan's primary care physician today. He couldn't completely rule out Max being strong enough to hang himself that way, but doubted it."

"He was murdered," she said softly. "And his home burned down. My God."

"The Coroner established Cragan's time of death as between eight thirty and ten thirty P.M. You spoke with him during that time."

"Yes. He called me around nine. I showed you my cell's call register."

"That you did." He watched steadily. "Where were you that night, Alex?"

"Home. I told you that."

"Alone?"

She flushed. "Yes, alone. All night."

"No calls other than Cragan's? No visitors?" She shook her head. "Didn't run an errand?"

"No." She frowned. "I'm confused. Why is this important?"

"You may have been the last one to speak to Max."

"Not the last. He hung up with me to go to the door. I heard the bell ring."

"So you say."

She made a sound of disbelief. "I showed you my call log. I told you what happened. We made an appointment to speak the next morning. He said someone was at his door and hung up. He thought it was Angie."

"It wasn't."

"It could have been anyone."

"Yes," he said softly, "it could have."

She realized what he was saying and stiffened. "Why would I hurt Max? I hardly knew him!"

"I didn't say you did, Alex. Just doing my job."

"Were you just doing your job a half hour ago? When you were fucking me?" She scrambled to her feet, bringing the blanket with her. She stripped off his shirt and threw it at him. "Get out."

"Alex—"

"I felt safe with you. Until now."

"Don't you see, you're at the center of it all? Everything that's happened leads back to you."

"Not everything. In case you've already forgotten, I had an alibi for last night. I was in bed with you. Helping you do your job."

"Alex, you could be in—"

"Get out," she said again. "Whatever was going on between us is over, Detective."

Chapter Fifty

Saturday, March 13
8:00 A.M.

Alex had slept little. She'd tossed and turned, tormented by the events of the previous day—and each day since she had arrived in Sonoma.

And she couldn't let go of the way Reed had hurt her. She had been on the verge of laying herself bare to him.

As the dark hours ticked past one thing had become brutally clear: she was on her own.

But she wasn't about to run and hide, the way her mother had. She would face this head-on.

Something terrifying had happened to her, something fighting to be remembered. Dylan had been abducted and most likely murdered. Also murdered, a man with a tattooed image of vines and a snake on the bottom of his foot. Now, Max Cragan was dead. His home burned to the ground.

Why kill Max? Why burn his home to the ground? Each time Alex wondered, she became more certain of the answer: the record of Max's design creations. And who had commissioned them.

The secrets of the vines and snake.

She was part of those secrets. At the center of everything

that was happening. Just as Reed had said. All her life, her dreams had been nudging her, reminding her she had a brother whom she had loved. And lost.

Tim had called it avoidant coping. Memory loss that occurred after a traumatic, life-threatening event. An event so terrible or terrifying, the brain worked to hide it.

But the memory was still there, fighting to get out.

It'd come close twice. Both times, in a wine cave.

Whatever happened to her had happened in that cave.

Alex meant to find out what. The Sommer Winery began tours at 9:00 A.M., and she intended to be in the first group.

At 8:50 A.M., Alex parked her Prius in the winery lot. She saw that a number of other groups had already arrived. A good thing. She'd hoped to be able to blend in. She flipped down her visor to get a last look at herself in the mirror. She wore a baseball cap and dark glasses. She had pulled her hair into a ponytail that stuck out the back of the cap.

She didn't want the tour guide, if it happened to be the same one as the other day, to immediately recognize her.

And she certainly didn't want to run into Clark, or any of the other Sommers. To facilitate that, she meant to stay as far away from the tasting room as possible.

Alex bought her ticket and waited in the museum, this time only pretending to study the photographs. When the guide arrived, she was grateful to see it was a different woman.

"Come on then," the guide said, "let's begin at the beginning, with the grapes."

Alex followed the group, hanging back, pretending rapt attention as the woman described the collection and sorting procedure. Instead, what rang in her head was the rapidly increasing beat of her heart. The sound of her own shallow breathing. She wiped her damp palms against the sides of her thighs, acknowledging her anxiety. Determined to roll with it.

You have to do this, Alexandra. It's only a memory. It can't hurt you.

"The highest concentration of flavor is in the skins," the

guide was saying. "And this is a major way the fermentation of red and white wines is different. For reds, the skins remain with the juice. Not so for whites."

They stopped before the row of stainless steel fermenting tanks. "Here at Sommer we make two very good whites, a chardonnay and a pinot grigio, but our big, full-bodied reds are what we're known for."

She explained about punching down and the dangers involved; this time, however, Alex kept her mouth shut. The guide also explained that the wine was drained from the top to avoid dirt at the bottom of the tank, and that the spigot and hatch door at the bottom provided a way for the winemaker to check the wine's progress, and once the wine had been drained, for the tank to be cleaned.

She pointed to their left to a row of four much smaller tanks. "Those are used for some of our small production, reserve wines. We call those our tankquitoes."

That earned some laughs and a couple hurried across to take a picture. The woman posed by the tanks. "Oh my gosh, this one's leaking."

"Those tanks are empty right now," the guide said. "Now for the highlight—"

"No, she's right," her companion agreed, "it's open and leaking."

The group stopped and turned. The guide headed that way. "It might just have been cleaned," she offered, "so what you're seeing is probably—"

She bit the rest back.

Alex frowned. The hatch was cracked open and something was dripping from the edge and had formed a small dark puddle on the floor below.

The guide reached the tank. "Cleaning solution, I'm certain." She grasped the door handle and pulled. It opened. A tiny fist popped out, followed by an arm. The crown of a head, covered in baby fine wisps.

A child. An infant.

Not cleaning solution. Blood.

For one second the silence was complete. Then several screams rent the air. The guide stumbled backward, drawing back her hand, covered in blood.

Chaos ensued. Alex stood as if frozen, unable to drag her eyes away from the gruesome sight, the sounds of hysteria swelling around her.

"Someone get one of the family!"

"Call 911! For God's sake, someone call—"

"No, wait! It's a—"

Alex sank to her knees, struggling to breathe. It was so awful. She curved her arms around her middle, rocking. She heard Treven arrive, out of breath from running.

"Oh dear Jesus!"

Then Rachel. "My God! Has anyone called 911—"

"Sheriff's on the way. Ambulance, too!"

Clark, Alex recognized, gaze fixed on that tiny fist. So small and helpless. Like Dylan. Small and helpless. Innocent.

"You will not fall apart," Treven ordered, though whether to Rachel, Clark or someone else under his command was unclear.

"Clark, close the winery for the rest of the day. At least. No more tours. Get these people into the tasting room. Give them whatever it takes to calm them down."

"What if they want to go?"

"Absolutely not. I'm certain the police will want to talk to them. We need to manage this situation."

"Call Danny Reed. Let him know what happened. I want the best and I want a friend."

"Rachel, I do not want my brother down here. Do whatever it takes to keep him away."

"I agree. He's been through enough—My God. Alex? Is that you?"

"What's *she* doing here?" Clark asked.

Rachel responded by telling him just what she'd like him to do, then squatted beside Alex, laying a hand on her shoulder. "Alex? Honey, it's me, Rachel."

With what seemed like monumental effort, Alex dragged her gaze from the tiny fist. She opened her mouth to speak, then shut it when nothing came out.

Rachel frowned. "Are you okay? Can you walk?"

She nodded and Rachel helped her to her feet. "Come on, let's go to my office."

Chapter Fifty-one

Saturday, March 13
10:50 A.M.

Not a child. Not a gruesome murder.

A sick joke.

Reed had recognized the fake almost immediately. Almost, save for one agonizing second as his heart clutched in his chest. He glanced sideways, at Tanner. "Looks like the same kind of doll."

She nodded and fitted on gloves. "No doubt the same twisted jokester."

She tapped the red puddle, then rubbed the liquid between her fingers. "Same as last time."

He followed suit, then held it to his nose. It had a decidedly sweet smell. He looked over his shoulder at Treven, Clark and Rachel. "Somebody's playing a trick on you. A really sick one."

Treven frowned. "I don't understand."

"This is a doll, the blood is fake."

"An Ashton Drake doll," Tanner explained. "Very expensive. A collectible known for being lifelike, if you'll pardon the word choice."

The trio looked stunned. "But why?" Rachel said. "Why would someone do this?"

Treven stepped in. "Real child or not, now I've got a public relations nightmare on my hands. The last thing I want the Sommer label associated with is dead babies."

Dead babies. Two of them. First Dylan. Now this.

Reed felt Tanner's gaze and knew she had made the same connection.

"Let's focus on the good news, Uncle Treven," Rachel said, an edge in her voice. "Five minutes ago we thought someone had murdered a child and stuffed the body in one of our fermenting tanks. Now we simply have a public relations nightmare."

"It is pretty cold, Dad," Clark agreed. "You don't always have to be such a son of a bitch."

Tanner cleared her throat, Reed suspected, to hide a chuckle. For himself, he bit back a sound of surprise at Clark's uncharacteristic show of spine.

Treven flushed. "I have a business to run, Son. A bottom line to watch. If you plan to fill my shoes someday, you'd better toughen up."

Reed stepped in before Clark had a chance to respond. "We've seen this before, a couple weeks ago. A doll like this one was left mutilated and strung up in the Hilldale vineyard."

"This is the first I heard of it," Treven said. He looked at Clark, who shook his head, then at Rachel.

"I heard about it," she said. "Only because I'm friends with Betsy Dale."

Treven nodded, looking pleased. "That's good news. We'll work to keep this under the radar as well. Dan, can you help us out here? Can we keep it out of the papers?"

"Shouldn't be a problem." He glanced at Tanner for confirmation.

"Okay with me," she said to Treven. "You're the victim."

Something crossed his expression that left Reed feeling as if Treven Sommer hadn't appreciated that label.

"Who found it?" Reed asked.

"A couple from Illinois. They were taking a picture by the tanks."

He glanced at Tanner. "We question them first. Somebody goes to this much trouble and expense, they don't leave their work being discovered to chance."

Tanner agreed. "One of the deputies is gathering the names of everyone on the tour."

Treven looked at his watch, expression irritated. "If you'll excuse me, I have a dozen visitors I have to reassure and appease. Clark, Rachel, I could use your help."

"I'll be right there," Rachel said, the edge in her voice once again. "I need a minute."

Reed watched the father and son go, then turned back to Rachel. "Treven didn't seem too happy about your show of independence."

"He's an asshole."

Reed felt Tanner's surprise at Rachel's blunt expression. He admitted surprise himself. "You can speak freely around me, Rachel. Don't hold back."

"Sorry. That wasn't very professional." She let out a frustrated-sounding breath. "Grandpa had other ideas for the winery and Uncle Treven only got where he is because—" She bit the words back. "Maybe he should think of that the next time he decides to go all King of the World on us."

She jammed her hands into her pockets. "Look, I just wanted to let you know, Alex is in my office. She's pretty shook up."

At his obvious surprise, she added, "She was on the tour this morning. I'll be in the tasting room if you need me. Helping soothe those ruffled feathers."

Reed watched her walk away, then turned to Tanner. He found her watching him, eyes narrowed, expression speculative. "Interesting," she murmured. "The lovely Ms. Clarkson is in the thick of it again."

Reed collected his thoughts as he made his way to the administrative building and Rachel's office. Alex had been on the first tour of the morning. He found that odd. The obvious reason to take such a tour—to learn about the process and see the property—didn't wash. She could have asked Rachel, or several other family members, for a private tour.

But no, she'd bought a ticket to a group tour. The first of the day. A tour that turned out to be anything but routine.

"The lovely Ms. Clarkson is in the thick of it again."

Reed wished he could argue with the subtext of that comment, but couldn't. He'd said the same thing—to Alex herself—just last night.

The admin building was nearly deserted. All hands were no doubt in the tasting room doing damage control. He made his way to Rachel's office. The door was partially open; through the opening he saw Alex sitting slumped in a chair in front of Rachel's desk.

He tapped on the door. She wasn't alone, he saw. Krista, Rachel's assistant, was with her.

"Reed!" Alex cried, leaping to her feet and running to him. "Thank God!"

She threw her arms around him and held him tightly. "It was so horrible. That poor child . . . first Dylan, now—"

"It's all right, Alex." He awkwardly put his arms around her. "It was a sick joke."

She lifted her gaze to his. "I don't understand."

"It was a doll, Alex."

"But I saw"—her voice wobbled—"everyone did. It was so—"

"Real?" She nodded, throat working. "It's a very expensive type of doll known for its realism."

Tears filled her eyes. "Thank God . . . I was so, I couldn't stop thinking about what—"

As if suddenly remembering the night before, she stiffened and stepped away from him. She folded her arms across her chest. "Who would do something like this?"

He looked at Rachel's assistant. "Krista, could we have a few minutes?"

She left them alone and Reed motioned to the chair. "Sit down, Alex." When she had, he went on. "This has happened before. Once. Not that long ago."

She furrowed her brow.

"Same kind of doll. Also mutilated. But strung up in a vineyard."

"Crucifixion style."

He paused, frowning. "How did you know?"

She blinked. "I don't know. I just guessed."

"What were you doing here today?"

"Taking the tour, like everybody else."

"But you're not like everyone else on the tour. You have connections with the family. If you'd asked, any of them would have given you a private tour."

"I didn't want to bother anybody. It seemed so much simpler to just buy a ticket."

"That doesn't add up for me, Alex."

"Why am I not surprised by that?"

"Come on. Do you really blame me?" He crossed to stand directly in front of her. She tipped her head to meet his eyes. "You're here for this one tour, in the history of wine country tours, where a mutilated doll is discovered in a fermenting tank. And I'm not supposed to find that damn incriminating?

Before Alex could reply, Rachel stuck her head into the office. "How are you doing, Alex?"

"Better. Now that I know it was just somebody's perverse idea of humor."

"Tell me about it." She shifted her gaze to Reed. "Your partner asked me to tell you she'd like to speak with you, as soon as you're done here."

He nodded. "I'm done. For now." He looked back at Alex. "Are you going to be okay?"

Rachel answered for her. "She will. I'll make sure of it."

Chapter Fifty-two

Saturday, March 13
11:55 A.M.

Reed reconnected with Tanner outside the tasting room. "How are the tourists?"

"Happily inebriated. Or on the way to it." She glanced at her watch. "And all before noon."

"Anybody raise a red flag?"

"Nope. All staying at local hotels and B&Bs. All first-time visitors from out of state. All horrified, and not so secretly thrilled, by the incident."

Human nature, Reed thought. They could all go home with a vacation story to top all vacation stories, and knowing Treven Sommer, a cache of free wine as well.

"What about the family and employees? Nobody had better access."

"Deputies took statements. Running background checks on the transient help."

Reed nodded. "Got to cover bases, but the cost and availability of those dolls limits the suspect pool."

"My thought as well. What about Clarkson?"

Something in her tone set his teeth on edge. "She was understandably shaken."

"Did she tell you she's taken this tour before?" Tanner paused. "Yesterday. One of the guides remembered her. And a guard I spoke to found her in the caves, separated from the group. She told him she was claustrophobic and asked him to lead her out."

Reed frowned, remembering the episode she'd had in the cave the night of the party. She hadn't mentioned claustrophobia then. And why would she put herself in that situation not just once again, but today as well?

"There's more. Apparently, she had a run-in with Clark. He'd been drinking and got up in her face."

She hadn't mentioned that, either. Interesting. When he'd questioned her, she'd gotten indignant—like he was the one out of line, for being suspicious. Truth was, he'd be out of line for not being *more* suspicious.

What a dupe she'd played him for.

"What was the outcome of that?" he asked, voice tight.

"Treven came along, defused the situation. Settled her down. Or so he thought."

"What does that mean, or so he thought?"

"Maybe she placed the doll in the tank? Payback for him and the entire Sommer clan. For abandoning her."

He thought of the story his dad had told him about Patsy, what she had done. And how he, Treven and several others had run her out of town. And now this happened, two days later.

"Clark confirmed the story," she went on. "Was understandably sheepish about his behavior. She made a comment, he said, about the photographs in the museum. How none of them included her, her mother or Dylan.

"Let's look at this, Reed. A lamb is slaughtered, stuffed under Alex's bathroom vanity and left for her to 'find.' A bloodstained altar is discovered at Bart Park. Alex just happens to be an expert in alternative religious practices. Max Cragan hangs himself. Guess who finds the body? A second mutilated doll turns up—"

"And Alex is there to see it."

"Yes."

"And the first doll?"

"Check your calendar. Doll number one turned up on February 22, three days after Clarkson visits you at HQ."

He did the math and realized she was right.

"Tom Schwann is brutally murdered. Bizarrely, his murder is connected to Clarkson in two ways."

"The first, his tattoo and her ring. What's the second?"

"Alberto Alvarez, killed in the same manner as Schwann—"

"Twenty-five years ago. You're not suggesting a five-year-old child—"

"Committed the crime? Hardly. She's connected to it because she lived here at the time and occupied the bedroom across the hall from her brother the night he disappeared. For all we know, she might be the one who set Cragan's cottage ablaze."

"She wasn't."

"You're so certain? How?"

He met her eyes. "She has an alibi for that night. And for the night Schwann was killed."

For a long moment, Tanner simply gazed at him. When she spoke, her tone was measured. "I suggest you evaluate your priorities. And if I were you, I'd do it fast."

Reed managed to hold it together until he'd finished processing the scene. But even as he questioned winery employees and reviewed surveillance tapes and security logs, at the back of his mind, waiting to come barreling out, was his anger at Alex's duplicity.

He found Rachel in her office. "Has Alex gone?" he asked.

"An hour ago. At least. Is everything okay?"

"Fine. I had another question to ask her, that's all."

"She promised she was going home."

Reed thanked her and headed for his SUV. In typical wine country fashion, Saturday traffic was stop and go. It fueled his anger, and by the time he pulled up behind her Prius, he had to fight to keep it in check.

He climbed out of his vehicle and jogged up her walkway. He rang the bell, then, when she didn't appear, pounded. "Alex! It's Reed."

After several moments, she answered. She wore an oversized sweatshirt and jeans, her hair was sticking out in several different directions and her eyes were red.

"You took the Sommer Winery tour yesterday. You didn't tell me. Why?"

He'd caught her off guard, as he had meant to. She opened her mouth to speak, then closed it again.

"Why, Alex?"

She swung the door wider and stepped aside so he could enter. He did and she closed the door and faced him. "I started to last night—"

"I don't remember that. I remember you kicking me out because I dared to question you."

Color flooded her face. "I should have. I wanted to tell you everything—"

"But you didn't. Why, Alex?"

She jerked her chin up. "Because I knew how it would look! Okay? How it would make *me* look!"

"And how's that? Guilty?"

"No. Crazy."

That one caught him off guard.

"I had another episode, in the cave." She clasped her hands together. "It was worse this time. I had . . . I really panicked. I felt ridiculous after. And . . . shaken up."

She turned and crossed to her living room couch. She sank onto it and dropped her face into her hands.

"Why, Alex?" he asked, unmoved by her attempt to elicit his sympathy. "Why were you out at Sommer yesterday?"

For a moment she didn't respond, then lifted her face to his. "After you told me that story about my mom . . . I wanted to prove it wasn't true. I called your mother and—"

"My mother?"

"She'd offered to let me look through your family photo albums. Since I couldn't ask my mother the truth, I had to go looking for it. I figured the photographs couldn't lie to me.

"I ran into Ferris while I was there. He suggested I go out to the Sommer place, that there were photos there as well. Plus, I wanted to see Mother's painting, the one in the tasting room, behind the bar."

Reed knew the painting but hadn't realized Patsy had created it. "Why not ask Rachel or Treven to show you around?"

She spread her hands. "This was private. The last thing I wanted was to have to discuss it with one of them."

"And that's it?"

"Yes."

"Still covering up, Alex. Why?"

"I'm not!" She fisted her fingers. "You asked me a question. I answered it honestly."

"You and Clark had a confrontation."

"Yes."

"I saw you that night, you didn't mention it."

"Banging me doesn't give you an automatic right to my every thought and feeling."

"Is that what we've been doing? All we've been doing?"

She looked away. "It shook me up. He said something . . . about my mother, about wanting to know . . . He pinned me against the wall and when I struggled, he refused to let me go."

"Son of a bitch."

"Treven came along and sent Clark scurrying off. He was very kind to me."

Reed could picture that. "Anything else?"

She pulled in a shaky breath. "Let's see, other than your father making it clear that I was to stay away from his sons—"

"Excuse me?"

"Oh yeah, wouldn't want Patsy's tainted goods near his precious sons. I guess I'd give you cooties or something." She held his gaze. "Let's see, to continue with my really swell day—there was my emotional meltdown during sex and you questioning my motives. I think that sums it up."

He searched her expression, wondering if her story was

true. If it was, he felt both fool and brute, standing there, his accusations still hanging between them.

Reed crossed to stand directly in front of her. "So, why go back today, Alex? After all that, why go back?"

She didn't blink, though her eyes sparkled with tears. "Because I want to know the truth. Because I need to know it."

She was either being honest with him or was a liar of monumental skill. He drew her into his arms, against his chest. She melted against him, shuddering.

A part of him hated himself for this. For trusting her. For being here with her despite his partner's cautioning. Despite his own suspicions.

He'd never played the fool for a woman before; he wondered if he was now.

His cell phone went off and he dug it out of his pocket. "Reed here."

"It's Tanner. I connected with the tour guide from yesterday, questioned her in depth."

"She bring anything new to the party?"

"Yeah, she remembered Clarkson asking about Harlan Sommer's first wife and the accident that killed her. She also brought up Dylan's kidnapping. The guide found it weird and it made her uncomfortable."

"Thanks," he said, his gaze shifting to Alex. "Anything else?"

"From Schwann's phone. The odd number he dialed that night was a Red Crest Winery number."

"That makes sense."

"I thought so, too. Figured he got tired of waiting, dialed up to the party hoping to snag a ride. He connected with somebody, the question is who."

"I'll put that at the top of my list. Thanks." Reed ended the call and extricated himself from Alex. "I've got to go."

"What's wrong?"

"Have you told me everything, Alex?"

"Who was that?"

"Tanner."

"I see. So did she have some new incriminating evidence against me? Some suspicious thing I've held back?"

"She questioned your Sommer tour guide from yesterday. The woman said that on the tour, you brought up the death of Harlan's first wife and Dylan's disappearance."

"Was that a crime?"

He searched her gaze. "Why'd you do that, Alex?"

"I can't believe this."

"Why, Alex?"

"I don't know. I was mad. Pushing a point. In all those pictures in the Sommer museum, not one of me, my mother or Dylan." She tipped up her chin. "You couldn't understand."

"Try me."

She didn't respond. He sensed she was preparing her thoughts, sifting through them to find the truth. Her truth.

Or maybe he was simply naive. The duped homicide detective. Blinded when it came to a woman. He wouldn't be the first.

She began, speaking softly, "You can't understand because your roots go deep. You know who you are and where you come from. I don't have that.

"I feel a connection to this place. Sometimes the connection scares me. Like in the caves." She looked away, then back at him, expression raw. "This place is part of my history. I want to know the missing pieces. And I want to belong. Did I pass the test, Reed? Am I naked enough now?"

He stood and crossed to her, cupped her face in his palms. "Do you realize how bad all this looks?"

He could tell by her face that she didn't, not fully. "You being there two days in a row, you asking those questions, your confrontation with Clark—"

"I didn't leave the doll, Reed. I returned to Sommer today determined to take the tour again and figure out what the hell happened to me in those caves. And since you're wondering, I didn't slaughter that lamb and leave it for me to 'find.' Nor did I create that altar or kill Max Cragan. I may be nuts, but I'm not that nuts."

"I don't think you're crazy. But I need to know every-thing. From now on, total, brutal honesty." He searched her gaze. "The truth is, Alex, whatever's happening, you're a part of it."

Chapter Fifty-three

Monday, March 15
4:25 A.M.

Alex opened her eyes, fully awake. She held herself completely still, fear thundering through her veins. She moved her gaze slowly over the room. The darkness seeming to swallow it. The absolute and utter quiet.

Someone was in her house.

Slowly, she inched into a sitting position. She reached for her cell phone, resting on the bed stand. She closed her fingers over it, its cool weight reassuring. She let a breath out slowly, then listened some more.

Why was it so quiet? Where were the creaks and moans she had learned to associate with this old house?

She hadn't been dreaming. Something, someone, had awakened her.

Or had she been? A disgusted laugh slipped past her lips. Another nightmare. Shit. Would she ever sleep through the night again? She looked at the bedside clock and groaned. Four thirty in the morning.

Margo sat up, stretched and blinked at her. "Yeah, I know," Alex muttered, "I'm certifiable."

Her voice, the words, brought her and Reed's encounter crashing back.

She still hadn't been completely honest with him. She hadn't told him about her visions. Or her nightmares. She hadn't been able to bring herself to do it. They either made her look crazy, guilty, or both.

"Whatever's happening, you're a part of it."

But which part? she wondered. And why? She squeezed her eyes shut. *Remember, Alex. Remember. They're only memories. They can't hurt you.*

She breathed deeply, working to relax and let go. She focused on what her subconscious had already freed—the robed figures . . . the flames licking at her . . . the faceless baby screaming . . .

Suddenly, an image flooded her mind. The robed men circling her . . . Hands holding her down . . . terror . . . screams and laughter . . . a thrumming, thundering drumbeat . . .

Run . . . run . . .

Alex launched to her feet, her scream echoing in the empty house. She took a step, then stopped, quaking, terrified. It hadn't been real. A memory. Or a hallucination.

It was cold, she realized. A cold, damp breeze licked at her bare feet. She'd left her window cracked open. Alex reached for her robe, hanging on the bedpost, and shivering, slipped into it.

She closed the bedroom window, but still felt a breeze. Funny, she didn't remember having opened another window.

Goose bumps racing up her legs, Alex followed the breeze. The bathroom. The single window at the far end stood open. The gauzy drape stirred.

Not bothering with the light, she hurried across the bathroom, yanked the window shut and locked it.

She stopped and relieved herself, the toilet seat frigid against her backside, then started back to her bed. Her foot landed on something. Cold and soft. It squished beneath her foot and between her toes.

Fear took her breath. She pictured the slaughtered lamb, eye winking up at her.

With a cry, Alex flipped on the light and was momentarily blinded. Then she saw red. Smeared across the floor. On her foot and between her toes. Her heart leapt to her throat. A series of images played across her mind: the lamb, the bloodied doll in the fermenting tank, the altar, dried blood spilled across its top.

With a squeak of fear, she took a step back. More wet. More red. Bringing her hands to her mouth to stifle a scream, she realized what she was looking at.

Lipstick. The red she and Rachel had picked out.

How had it ended up on the floor?

The scream became an embarrassed giggle. Thank goodness no one but Margo was here to see her make such a monumental ass out of herself.

She bent to pick it up, then stopped. Red on her right hand, a stain. She studied it, frowning. Her writing hand. Along her forefinger, on the ball of her hand and thumb.

Slowly, she straightened. Turned toward the mirror. There, scrawled across it in Light Your Fire red, was one word: *Remember.*

Chapter Fifty-four

Monday, March 15
4:50 A.M.

With a cry, Alex turned and ran back to her bed. She flipped on the bedside light and threw back the covers. There, on the sheets, more red.

Alex stared at it in horror. Dear God, had she done this? Could she have?

She hugged herself, feeling as if she might be sick. What was happening to her? Was she crazy? She'd have to be, to have done that—and not remember. Like one of those people with multiple personalities.

She sank to the floor and hugged her knees to her chest. She'd always feared becoming mentally ill, like her mother. Now, it was happening.

No, God no. She'd just been telling herself to remember—had she dreamed it? Had she walked in her sleep? Could she have been? Maybe the someone in her house who had awakened her had been her.

She jumped to her feet, grabbed her cell phone and, clutching it to her chest, ran to the front of the house, flipping on every light on the way.

No more scrawled messages or open windows. Nothing different. Nothing out of place.

Call Reed.

No. He can't know this. Crazy . . . he'll think I'm—

Losing my mind, she thought. Is this what it'd been like for her mother? Had she even been able to recall destroying her art? Or had it played out like a nightmare or a fugue state?

Stop it, Alex. Stop. Think. Get a grip on yourself.

She made her way to the couch and sat. She struggled for calm. She concentrated on the in and out of her breath.

The window, she thought. It'd been open. Maybe someone had climbed in and . . . scrawled *Remember* on her mirror?

But why? And how did the lipstick get on her sheets and hands?

Hold yourself together. Consider the possibilities. Look at each event and—

A list, she thought. There in black and white, to manipulate and untangle.

She jumped to her feet and hurried to the work area she had set up in the corner of the room. Her dissertation research sat on the desk there, untouched since her first day in Sonoma. She rummaged through her supplies until she found an empty legal tablet, then took it and a pen back to the sofa.

At the top of the page she wrote: "Vision while making love with Tim. Robed figures. Baby screaming."

She followed with her panic attack in the Red Crest Winery cave. The smell of incense. The sound of people partying. Her scream.

Next, she listed the slaughtered lamb. Then the altar Reed had shown her, and meeting Max Cragan. She noted his strange behavior change after seeing the ring, then his even stranger call.

Then finding him dead of an apparent suicide. Reed sharing that her ring and the tattoo on the bottom of a murdered man's foot matched. Max's house torched. Beside that, she noted: Alibi/Reed.

And in the midst of all that, her morphing dreams. The forest setting. The sense of crouching, eavesdropping on something she couldn't understand.

Alex swallowed hard and moved on to the next event— her second vision in the Sommer Wine cave. She jotted down all the details: the smell of incense again, the flickering light becoming fire, its tentacles grasping at her.

The next day, the mutilated doll. And finally, this morning: *Remember* scrawled in lipstick on her bathroom mirror. The damning stain on her hands and sheets.

Alex gazed at the list, heart pounding. It was overwhelming. Frightening. A boatload of really weird, scary shit.

Why was she still here? Why hadn't she packed her bags and headed home? She recalled Reed's words: *Whatever's happening, you're a part of it.*

A part of it, what did that mean? That she was a catalyst? The center? The victim—or the perpetrator?

Head pounding, she went to make coffee. While it brewed, she studied the list. When the coffeepot had burbled its last, she filled a mug and sat at the table, going over every detail, recalling the date each event occurred, when she had learned of it. And her reactions.

The sandalwood scent. She had recognized it. It had triggered the first event in the cave. It had intruded upon her dreams. Of course. Alex stood, went for the package of Oreos and poured a glass of milk.

She returned to the table. Humans lived experiences through the senses. Studies had proved, of all the senses, the sense of smell was the most strongly associated with recovered memories.

Alex dunked a cookie in the milk, gaze fixed on the list, thinking back to her visions and dreams and how they had adapted to each new piece of information. The faceless baby, no longer faceless. The scent, now identified. And most recently, the angry voice, the words she had not been able to grasp.

"You want to know so bad? I'll show you."

Clark's voice. Even as a chill moved over her, she shook

it off, frustrated. Had it been Clark speaking all those years ago? Or had her confrontation with him, the implied threat simply triggered the memory?

She didn't know. She was no closer to an answer than when she had begun.

Could she be responsible for any of this?

She couldn't do this alone, Alex realized. She needed someone who knew her well, who wouldn't judge. Someone who would help her see through her emotions and ferret out the truth.

Tim. She needed Tim.

Alex dialed his number. It rang once, then twice. She prayed he'd answer. He did and relief rolled over her. "Tim, it's me."

"Hey, you." He yawned. "I'd wondered if you'd fallen off the planet."

She struggled to keep her voice from shaking. "I need to talk to you."

He yawned again. "What the hell time is it?"

"Early. It's important."

He must have heard the urgency in her voice, because he suddenly sounded wide awake. "What's wrong?"

"I think—" A hysterical-sounding laugh bubbled to her lips. Now she sounded as crazy as she thought she was becoming. "Tim, I think I'm losing my mind."

He laughed. "And you're just realizing that? Honey, you lost your mind a long time—"

"I'm not joking, Tim." She lowered her voice. "I need you to come here. Can you?"

"I guess, sure. I have classes until—"

"Can you cancel them?"

His silence said it all. Now he was worried.

"Please," she whispered. "You know I wouldn't ask if it wasn't an emergency."

For a long moment he was silent. Finally, he agreed. "I'll be there as soon as I can. Sit tight."

Chapter Fifty-five

The two hours' wait seemed interminable. She made another pot of coffee, showered and straightened the cottage. Still, every minute seemed like ten. When he finally pulled up, she ran to meet him.

He wrapped her in his arms. "My God," he said, "you're shaking."

"There's so much to tell you . . . so much has happened. I don't know where to begin."

"Slow down, honey. Take a deep breath. Start with today."

Alex breathed deeply, then said, "To start with today, I have to show you."

She led him into the house and through to the bathroom. She flipped on the light and stepped aside. She saw it through his eyes, the smears of garish red, the crudely written word, the underlying mania of it. As if it had been done in a frenzy.

He looked at her. "Holy shit, Alex. What is this?"

"I don't know, but I'm afraid . . . I think I might have done it."

For a long moment he didn't speak. When he did, he did

so carefully, his tone measured. "That's a fairly bold statement, Alex. One I don't think you should make lightly."

In his eyes, she saw real concern. "I'm not. I thought someone had broken in. The window was open. I was startled awake by something."

"Or someone."

"That's what I thought, but then I saw . . . my right hand was stained. From the lipstick." She held out her hands. "I showered. I probably shouldn't have, but . . . It was on my sheets, too. I could show you."

"It's okay. I believe you." He frowned and touched one of the smears, then rubbed it between his fingers. "I've never seen you wear red."

"Rachel and I each bought a tube of it. We were being silly."

He looked at her. "Who's Rachel?"

"My stepsister. I really like her." She rubbed her arms, suddenly chilled. "I need some sun. How about you?"

They ended up on the front porch, on the swing. On the way out, she'd grabbed the legal tablet and handed it to him now.

"What's this?" he asked.

"I made a list. Of everything that's happened. I hoped it would help me make sense of it all."

He took the tablet from her and began to read. While he did, she held her face to the sun. The morning was bright and lovely. The light angled across the porch, touching them as the swing moved. In the small oak tree at the end of the porch, two finches were busy building a nest.

After several moments, he stopped the swing and looked at her. "I want you out of here, Alex." As if anticipating her argument, he held up a hand to stop her. "You should have gotten the hell out when you found that lamb. Frankly, I'm a little concerned that you didn't."

"I thought the same thing this morning, when I took it all in."

"And?"

"They're not going to chase me off, Tim."

"Who?"

"I don't know, whoever's doing this. I'm not leaving until I learn the truth."

He angled toward her and gathered her hands in his. "What truth is that, Alex?"

"What really happened twenty-five years ago. To my brother. To me. Why my mother took me away and did her best to expunge my memory of the first five years of my life. What they've told me so far is a lie."

Tim frowned. "What've they told you?"

"That my mother had been seducing the teenage sons of her and Harlan's friends. It was a club, she publicly initiated them into sex. Then they all—"

She bit the last back.

"Then they what, Alex?"

She looked at him defiantly. "Took turns fucking her."

His eyebrows shot up. "Who told you that?"

"Wayne Reed. He and his wife were my mother and step-father's best friends. His oldest son was one of the boys." She cleared her throat. "After Dylan's abduction, he confessed it all to his father. Wayne Reed went to the other fathers, they confronted her and ran her out of town."

"And he just shared this out of the blue?"

"No. I was asking around about her ring, the one I found in her trunk."

"With the vines and snake motif?"

She nodded and he frowned. "I thought maybe it'd been from my father. Turned out she'd had it designed for herself. Her initiates got a tattoo of the same motif."

"And one of those 'initiates' turned up dead?"

She nodded. "They were afraid their secret would get out. They hadn't even told the boys' mothers. Or Harlan, he'd already lost so much. Plus, they didn't want it all dredged up for the boys."

"Nice and neat," Tim murmured. He tapped the list. "Except for all this. Why's it happening?"

A rhetorical question, she knew. Reed's words jumped into her head again. *"Whatever's happening, you're a part of it."*

Tim returned his gaze to hers. "Describe your wine cave experiences. Physically, how did they make you feel?"

"Both times, it was like having a panic attack. My heartbeat accelerated. My breathing. Palms began to sweat.

"Then the hallucination thing happened, though the two episodes were very different." She clasped her hands together. "The first time, I smelled incense and heard a group of people . . . I thought there was a group having a party. I called out, but no one answered."

Alex cleared her throat, remembering. "Some of the sounds coming from the group were . . . strange. Bestial. I lost it and screamed, though I had no recollection of doing it.

"My date found me," she went on. "I was so certain there were people partying in there, we searched together. But the cave was empty."

"I don't think this is about your mother, Alex."

She swallowed hard. "No?"

"No." He covered her hands with his. "Who's the sacrificial lamb?"

"I don't know what you mean."

"The slaughtered animal left under your sink was an actual lamb. The mutilated baby doll is its metaphorical parallel. Who in this story is the lamb?"

The one unfairly blamed for the acts of another. The one killed to further a cause.

"Dylan's the obvious choice," she whispered. "He's the faceless baby of my visions. Screaming. Children are often called lambs."

"Maybe. Who else?"

"My mother."

"Maybe the baby is you?"

She stared at him, heart thundering. "No. I would know it." At his expression, she added, "How could that be? I'm there in my vision. I'm the one seeing him scream."

"In dream interpretation, everything in a dream represents an aspect of the self."

"But these aren't dreams. I'm awake, Tim."

He tightened his fingers over hers. "Honey, this is about you. You're the sacrificial lamb."

She shook her head, not wanting to believe it. He pressed on. "Something happened to you, probably in the wine caves. And whatever it was, it was traumatic." He searched her gaze. "And either somebody else knows about it and is tormenting you. Or your subconscious is doing its damnedest—"

"To get me to remember," she whispered.

"Yes."

She didn't want to believe it, but it rang true. She started to shake. "That's why it was so easy for me to forget."

"I think so."

"I'm like her, aren't I? It's happened."

"No, Alex. You were a little girl and you were hurt. You're not unbalanced."

She laughed, tears filling her eyes. "Wow, that's not the way it feels."

"There's still so much we don't know, Alex. What's the rest of the story? How does your brother's abduction fit in? Or does it at all? What about your mother, that story about her? What about your father?"

She blinked, surprised. "My father? What could he have to do with any of this?"

"I don't know. Maybe that's the point." He lowered his voice. "I think it's time for you to come home."

Home, she thought. Away from all this craziness.

But how could she escape the craziness inside her?

"I can't run away," she said. "And I'm not afraid."

"I sure as hell am, Alex. Afraid for you." He leaned toward her. "Look, babe, whoever's doing this isn't screwing around. Somebody's dead. A house has been burned to the ground."

"I can't run away," she said. "You know I can't. If I don't stay to find the truth, the truth will find me."

His lips lifted. "Ever heard of therapy? A nice safe couch, a boring but intuitive counselor, two or three visits a week—"

"No. I'm not going."

"Think about it. Please?"

She opened her mouth to refuse, then shut it as a series of images filled her head: the mutilated doll, the blood of the lamb, Max Cragan's gentle countenance distorted in death.

She should be afraid. Terrified.

Why wasn't she?

"Okay," she said. "I'll think about it."

Chapter Fifty-six

Monday, March 15
7:40 P.M.

Alex and Tim sat at a window table at the girl & the fig. She had slept most of the afternoon. For part of the time, he'd laid with her, holding her. He'd made her feel safe.

"How are you feeling?" he asked.

"Drained."

"I'm glad you slept. You needed it."

"Thanks for watching over me." Emotion tightened her chest. "I'm a total screwup, aren't I? A real head case."

"Don't say that, it's not true. We'll figure this out."

"Alex?"

She looked up to find Rachel crossing to them. She got to her feet and hugged her. "This is Tim Clarkson. My ex-husband. Tim, my stepsister, Rachel."

He stood and held out his hand. Rachel took it. "Tim of the chopsticks," she said.

He glanced at Alex in question. "She admired the chopsticks you gave me."

"Oh." He smiled. "And you're Rachel of the really red lipstick."

"I guess I am. Although I prefer to think of myself as Rachel of the really wonderful red wine."

"That's right," he murmured. "You're one of the Sommer family."

"Would you like to join us?" Alex asked. "Please do."

"I'd love to, but I've got a date." She motioned to a striking, silver-haired man at the bar. "It's a first date, you know how tricky those can be. Nice meeting you, Tim. Call me," she said to Alex. "We'll have lunch."

They returned to their seats. Although Tim didn't comment, Alex could tell he hadn't liked Rachel. She told him so.

"It was that obvious?"

"To me."

He reached across the table and covered her hand with his. "You know me a little too well."

"That I do." She squeezed his hand, then slid hers away and reached for her glass of wine. "Why didn't you like her?"

He pursed his lips. "Too pushy."

"She is not. I asked her to join us, remember? Not the other way around."

"Fact was, she didn't like me. And she didn't waste a moment telling me who she was and why she was important. That says something about a person, Alex."

"The wine comment?" She rolled her eyes. "First off, here it's all about wine. If you are the wine, you let people know. Second, if you think she didn't like you, it's probably your own guilty conscience making you feel that way."

"My guilty conscience?"

"You're worried about what I might have told her."

She was teasing him, but he flushed. Obviously, she'd pushed a button. "She's possessive of you. It's not normal."

"That's not true."

"An entitlement thing. Like all those children of the vine."

"You've had too much to drink. Children of the vine, give me a brea—"

She bit the last back and brought a hand to her mouth. "Oh my God. I know what it means."

"What're you talking about?"

"What you just said. Children of the vine. Not children, boys. Boys of the Vine. That's what BOV stands for."

He reached for his wine. "I have no idea what you're talking about."

"My mother . . . the ring, its inscription . . ." Alex felt sick and got to her feet. "I have to leave. I need some air."

"Alex, what . . . wait—"

She ignored his attempts to stop her and hurried from the restaurant out onto the street. Even though it was a Monday night, the square hummed with activity.

Blindly, she started to walk. Her thoughts whirled. Her mother. It was true. It couldn't be, but it was.

It felt like losing her again. The few good memories, hopes and dreams that she had managed to cobble together, destroyed. She wanted to hate her. It would hurt so much less than this betrayal.

How could you, Mom? How could you be so low? So pathetic?

"Alex?"

She looked up, vision blurred with tears. Reed. With a woman. His partner, she recognized.

"Are you all right?" he asked.

"No, I'm—" She moved into his arms and clung to him.

His arms came around and she pressed her face into his chest. She tried not to imagine her mother with those young men, concentrating instead on the steady rise and fall of Reed's chest and how safe she felt in his arms. How reassured.

Tim called her name. He'd caught sight of her, she realized. And in that same moment, she realized how crazy she must look to Reed, his partner and anybody else strolling by.

"Alex, what's going on? Is that man bothering you?"

"No, it's—" She tipped her head back to look up at him. "The inscription on the ring, I figured it out, Reed. BOV means Boys of the Vine. My mother's boys. The story's true."

Chapter Fifty-seven

Reed watched Alex and her ex walk away. BOV. Boys of the Vine. It fit, that was for sure.

"What the hell are you doing?"

He looked at Tanner in question.

"You're a stand-up guy, Reed. Rock solid. And I like you. Clarkson, on the other hand, seems to be operating from a place somewhere left of center. She worries me."

She worried him as well. On several levels. Not the least of which was the way seeing her with her ex-husband made him feel.

The ex who hadn't acted like an ex. He'd been protective. And possessive. When he'd introduced himself, there had been a tone in his voice, a look in his eyes. That man-to-man sizing up of the competition. A challenge issued.

Reed had recognized it because he'd had the same tone, the same look. Obviously, Tanner had picked up on it.

He turned to her. "Mind if I bag on dinner? I'm going to run this BOV thing by a couple of old-timers."

"Want company?"

"Not this time." He started off. She stopped him by calling his name.

"Got your cell?" He indicated that he did, and she patted hers, clipped to her hip. "Use it, dude."

He did, calling ahead to make certain his dad was at home. He was. Luckily, his brother Joe was there as well. He parked behind Joe's big-ass Benz and climbed out.

His mom had seen the headlights and met him at the door. "This is such a lovely surprise, Dan."

He kissed her cheek. "For me, too."

"Your dad and Joe are in the library. Talking business, as always. Have you eaten?"

"No. And yes, I'd love to stay."

Reed made his way to the library and tapped on the partially closed door before sticking his head inside. "Am I interrupting?"

"Not at all, Son." His father waved him in. "Have a seat."

From Joe's expression, Reed suspected their father had been delivering news Joe hadn't particularly cared for.

Every once in a while, Reed compared his brothers' lifestyles to his own and wondered if he'd screwed up. The luxury vehicles and exotic trips, grand homes and designer clothing. Then he'd get a peek at what that lifestyle really cost his brothers and be thankful for his decision. He'd rather drive his battered SUV than be his dad's punching bag or puppet.

His dad poured him a glass of wine. "Particularly proud of this one," he said.

"What brings you out tonight?" Joe asked stiffly, refilling his glass.

Reed kept his eyes trained on his brother. "Boys of the Vine."

Joe seemed to freeze. "What did you say?"

"BOV. Boys of the Vine." Reed shifted his gaze from Joe's pale face to his father's flushed one, then back. "Joe? You recognize the name?"

His brother looked helplessly at his father. Reed found something in his expression trapped. And horribly lost.

He and his older brother had never gotten along that well, but he found himself feeling sorry for him.

"For God's sake, Dan!" his dad exclaimed. "This isn't the time or place—"

"You're right on one account, Dad. It's past time." He turned back to his brother. "Joe? You recognize it?"

"Yeah," he said, voice choked. "I recognize it. Boys of the Vine. That was us."

"Who?"

"Our posse. Me and Clark. Terry, Tom and Spanky. A couple others."

"That's all I wanted. Confirmation."

"Dinner is ready," Lyla said from the doorway.

"I'm not staying," Joe said. "I promised Cindi I'd be back in time to help with homework."

"But I thought—"

"Sorry, Mom. My bad." He kissed her goodbye, then without a word to either of the other two men, left.

Lyla looked from one to the other of them. "What was that all about?"

"Don't know, sweetheart." Wayne rubbed his hands together. "But that means more for me."

During dinner, his father was like another man. Not even a shadow of what had transpired seemed to cross his features. He was every inch the jovial, accommodating husband. The sympathetic father.

His father was a chameleon, Reed thought. Why hadn't he noticed before?

His mother interrupted his thoughts. "Have you made any progress on finding Tom's killer? I saw Jill the other day, poor thing looked devastated."

"The investigation's ongoing, Mom. But I'm glad you brought that up." He laid down his fork. "The night Tom died he made four calls in the seventeen minutes before his murder. One of them was to up here, to Red Crest."

His mother looked stunned. "My God, how awful."

"Did you happen to take that call?"

"No," she said, then turned to her husband. "Wayne, did you?"

He shook his head. "No, baby."

"He connected with somebody. The call lasted two and a half minutes."

His dad looked at him. "Maybe one of the staff answered?" he offered.

Something in his expression set Reed's hair on edge. What was he hiding? "Maybe. Why do you think he called up here?"

"Probably hoping to find a ride."

What he had thought. Until tonight.

His mother made a sound of distress. "If only I had answered, he might be alive today."

"I'll talk to the staff, see if one of them spoke to him," his father said.

"And I'll call the caterers," she added. "You never know."

You never did know, Reed thought a short time later as he and his dad walked to his Tahoe. He'd found his father's behavior tonight troubling. The chameleonlike quality, his evasiveness. Even Joe's unease and quick departure.

"I didn't appreciate that, Dan."

"What's that?"

His dad lit a cigar, then met Reed's gaze through a haze of smoke. "Coming up here, confronting your brother that way. Then questioning me and your mother."

"Too bad. Besides, Mom brought up Tom's murder."

"You will not disrespect me that way."

Reed stopped, turned fully toward his father. "Until tonight, I didn't realize how good you are at hiding the truth, Dad. You really have kept Mom in the dark about everything, haven't you?"

"What the hell's that supposed to mean?"

"Do you manipulate everyone? Your wife and kids? Business associates? Friends? Where does it stop?"

"You calling me a liar, Son?"

"You tell me, Dad. Are you?"

"Get the hell off my property. Nobody calls me a liar. Especially not one of my own children."

They reached the SUV. Reed unlocked his car door, then swung to face his father. "The night Dylan Sommer disappeared, you and Mom were having dinner with Patsy and Harlan."

He looked startled by the change in subject. "Yes."

"Where?"

"Here."

"You're certain about that?"

"Yes, dammit. I was sure of it then, I'm sure of it now."

So why, Reed wondered, did he think he was lying? "And Patsy, when did she do her Boys of the Vine thing?"

"When?"

"Yes."

"I don't know."

"You don't know? Joe didn't tell you?"

"It didn't seem that important. After they got out of school, I suppose. When we were all at work."

"Where'd they meet?"

"I don't know—Why does it matter?"

"How often?"

"Often enough to steal our boys' innocence!"

"Has it occurred to you that Dylan might have been stolen by one of the boys? One who was jealous? Or the family of one of the minors. Or Harlan himself."

"That's ridiculous. They were just boys."

"You took that call from Tom, didn't you, Dad?"

"The hell I did. I already told you—"

"And the Boys of the Vine thing, if it's not an outright lie, there's more to it. What aren't you telling me?"

"Go. Get off my property." His voice shook. "You're not welcome back until you're ready to apologize."

Reed opened the car door and slid behind the wheel, then looked back at his dad. "By the way, Pop, I choose my own relationships. Don't warn a woman away from me again."

Chapter Fifty-eight

Tuesday, March 16
2:30 A.M.

Alex opened her eyes to find Tim standing by the bed, staring down at her. A chill raced up her spine.

"Tim? What're you doing?"

"Watching you."

She looked past him, saw one of her kitchen chairs. "Have you been here all night?"

"It's not morning yet."

She glanced at the bedside clock and saw that it was still the wee hours of the night. "You need to go get some sleep."

He looked away, then back, expression rueful. "I'm still in love with you, Alex."

"Tim, this isn't the time for—"

"It's not about sex. It's not. Once upon a time, maybe. I'm stupid, I admit it."

He let out a strangled-sounding breath. "When you called me, I felt this incredible relief. I'd thought I'd lost you. Then tonight, when I saw you holding that other man, I felt . . . everything a man in that situation could. Jealousy and rage. Regret. Longing. Hatred."

She sat up, bringing the blanket up with her. "This is making me really uncomfortable."

"I don't mean to make you feel that way. I'm just—" He knelt beside the bed and gathered her hand in his, brought it to his lips. "I've missed you so much."

She wanted to argue with him. Wanted to remind him of all the reasons why they hadn't made it as a couple. She sensed she had better keep her thoughts to herself and swallowed hard.

He turned her hand over and kissed her palm. "Sitting here, watching over you last night, I realized something. This is what I'm supposed to be doing. Where I'm supposed to be. Watching over you, Alex."

She'd never seen him quite this way. The note of urgency and desperation in his voice was a surprise. It was unsettling. "I don't know what to say."

"Right now, don't say anything. I'm promising you, I'm here for you. Whatever happens. Whatever you need. You're not crazy, Alex. We'll get to the bottom of all this. We'll do it together."

"You're exhausted," she said softly. "You need sleep. And so do I. Let's pick this up in the morning? Okay?"

"Sure, babe." He bent and pressed a kiss to her forehead. "I'll be on the couch." He crossed to the door, then stopped and looked back at her. "I really do love you."

"I love you, too."

But as she scooted back under the covers, she acknowledged that there were many kinds of love. And the kind she had for Tim was more complicated than most.

The next morning, she awakened to the smell of coffee. And something baking. Cookies? Muffins?

Cinnamon rolls, she learned minutes later as she entered the kitchen, teeth and hair brushed, dressed in a pair of faded old jeans and a Cal State sweatshirt. Tim had just taken the pastries from the oven and was slathering icing on them.

He caught sight of her and smiled. "Morning."

She crossed to the coffeepot and poured herself a mug. "How long have you been up?"

"Long enough to run up to the corner market for the paper, some cream and a roll of the Pillsbury Doughboy's finest. Have a seat. I'll bring you one."

"Thanks." She sat at the table and curved her hands around the warm mug and sipped.

"There you go." He set a plate in front of her, then went back for his. A moment later, he sat across from her and dug in.

She watched him eat a moment, then shook her head. "What's going on, Tim?"

"Nothing. Why?" He took a huge forkful of the warm roll.

"You're not a morning person."

"This morning I am." He got to his feet, refilled his cup, then returned to the table. "I've got to head back today. I've got a faculty meeting this morning."

Tim was leaving? The realization shouldn't have shaken her, but it did. "Do you have to?"

"It's a command performance."

"I don't know what I'll do."

He grinned. "That's what I like to hear."

She meant it. What would she do? There was no need to ask any more questions about the past or her mother—she knew more now than she wanted to.

Boys of the Vine.

She wished she could go back. Wished she had left all this alone. Stayed in San Francisco, clinging to the photograph of her mother and Dylan and her foolish belief that her mother had been as much of a victim as Dylan had been.

"I know what you need." She cocked an eyebrow and he laughed. "No, I didn't mean *that*, though you probably do need it. A spa day."

She burst out laughing. "Right. A spa day."

"The Kenwood Inn and Spa is just down Sonoma Highway. My first wife adored the place. We spent one Valentine's Day weekend there."

"I can't afford that."

"I'll pay."

"I can't accept that."

"Too bad, it's already done."

"What do you mean, already done?"

"Just what it sounds like. I booked you a spa day. It's paid for in full. Consider it a birthday gift."

A birthday . . . and then she remembered, tomorrow was her birthday. With everything that had been happening, she'd forgotten. "I can't believe you. When did you do this?"

"Last night. While you were in the ladies' room at the girl & the fig."

"Sneaky. Very."

He stood and crossed to her. He laid his hands on her shoulders. "I'll know you're safe. That's really important to me. Then I'll be back tonight. We'll figure this out."

She searched his gaze. The truth was, having him to turn to and lean on had been a relief. He knew her. He understood how to support without smothering. She trusted him completely.

And he didn't think she was crazy.

Maybe that was the biggest relief of all. She would hold tightly to that, because the way things had been going, that could change in the blink of an eye.

Chapter Fifty-nine

Alex reclined on a chaise in the spa lounging area. Bundled up in a thick terry cloth robe, she'd been warmed, wrapped and rubbed, exfoliated, hydrated and perfumed. Soothing new age music mingled with the tinkle of water fountains and she drifted, ridiculously relaxed, the events listed on her legal pad pushed to a far back corner of her brain.

Her thoughts lit on Tim's middle of the night profession of love. She knew Tim. Understood him. He didn't mean it. Not in a forever kind of way. Not an I-want-to-be-faithful-to-one-woman-until-we're-old-and-gray kind of way.

He was a little like Peter Pan, refusing to really grow up. And that was okay. It just wasn't what she needed.

And just like the child who only wanted to play, he didn't want to share, either. And he had seen her with Reed.

Reed. His image filled her head. She allowed herself to linger on it a moment. Linger on the memory of his arms around her. And the way they had made her feel.

She pushed both away. She wasn't ready to think about Reed or what her feelings for him might be. How could she?

He half believed she was responsible for all the craziness going on.

Of course, she half believed it, too.

Deep in her robe's pocket, her cell phone vibrated. She'd tucked it there, though having it with her was against spa policy.

Except for the attendant who came and went, she was alone in the lounge. Alex dug the device out of her pocket. It was Tim, she saw.

"'Lo," she answered, voice thick with relaxation.

"Alex? Is that you?"

"You can't call me here. Any minute Helga's going to pop back in and bust me."

"I really thought I'd get your voice mail."

"I sneaked the phone in." His voice sounded strange. "Where are you?"

"On the road. Look, Alex, there's something I need to tell you."

"Shoot." She reached for her glass of wine. "Better hurry, though. I think I hear Helga."

"Something your mother said," he went on. "About your dad."

Alex set the wine down with a thud. Some of the golden liquid splashed over the rim. "My dad? She said something to you about him and you didn't tell me?"

"Don't be mad—" His voice faded. It sounded like he had his convertible top down. "It was during one of her episodes. She'd crashed . . . you know what she was like then. The crazy things she would say. I didn't think any of it was grounded in reality."

"What, dammit? What did she say?"

"Miss, there's no cell phone use in the spa."

Alex held up a finger. "What did you—"

"—called him a bad man. Really bad, she said—"

"Ma'am, our rules are specific, while inside the spa, all cell phones must be off and stowed in the locker room."

"—she left Sonoma to get away from him . . . keep you away from"—his voice faded in and out—"a liar. Lied about her. I'm wondering, that story about the boys . . . who told you?"

"Wayne Reed. Tim, pull over. I'm only getting part of what you're saying."

". . . blamed him for Dylan . . . his fault—"

The spa attendant huffed loudly and held out her hand for the phone. Like Alex was a two-year-old playing with something she shouldn't.

Alex looked at her. "Excuse me, this is quite urgent. And it's not like I'm disturbing anyone but you."

The woman's expression registered shock, then anger. She turned on her heel and stalked out. Alex suspected she would be back directly—with reinforcements.

"You have to go . . . I'll tell you more tonight—"

"No, wait—"

"I'm turning off my cell."

"No! Tim—"

"Relax, doll. We'll talk later."

He hung up. She immediately dialed him back, but true to his promise, he had turned off his cell. It dumped her into voice mail.

She was leaving him a sharply worded message as the attendant and spa manager entered the lounge. The manager approached her, a perfect smile pasted on her plastic face. "Ms. Clarkson, I'm afraid I have to ask you to stow your cell phone with the rest of your belongings. I apologize for any inconvenience, but our goal is to provide you a luxurious and total relaxation experience. I hope you understand."

Alex did, but she wanted to argue anyway. She wanted to shout that she had waited all her life to learn who her father was, and because of their rules she would have to wait hours more.

But she suspected they wouldn't care. And that she would come off as the crazy woman she so feared becoming.

"Of course," she said, getting to her feet. "I'll do it now."

Her thoughts raced with what Tim had revealed. He knew something about her father. He had known for some time.

And he hadn't told her.

How did she wrap herself around that? Tim, more than anyone, had known how much finding her father meant to her.

Alex opened the locker but didn't make a move to stash her phone. She stared at her neatly folded garments, the liquid relaxation of earlier little more than a memory.

Her mother "blamed him for Dylan."

What did that mean? There were many reasons to place blame. For real sins—and imagined ones. Did that mean she thought he'd abducted him? If so, surely she would have gone to the police. A bad man, Tim had said. Really bad. A liar Alex had needed protection from.

Screw this, she decided. Relaxation was the last thing on her mind. Instead of stowing her cell phone, she grabbed her clothes and dressed.

Chapter Sixty

Tuesday, March 16
4:30 P.M.

Tim had beat her back to the rental, Alex saw. His candy ap-
ple red Chrysler Sebring sat parked in front, top still down.
She had tried him twice since leaving the Kenwood; both
times she had been rolled over to voice mail and neither time
did she leave a message.

She parked behind him, climbed out and hurried to the
front door. She let herself in, then stopped, surprised. The
small dining table had been set with white linen and china.
A bottle of champagne sat chilling in a bucket, two flutes
beside it.

Went for food. Help yourself to the bubbly.
P.S. Don't be mad. I have news.

Alex stared at the setup, bemused. The man was nothing
if not a suck-up. He knew she was mad and intended to coax
her out of it. He'd even provided the opportunity for her to
get started doing that without him.

She crossed to the champagne and poured a glass. She'd

have a little surprise for Mr. Clarkson when he returned. No way was he going to wiggle off this particular hook.

She carried her wine out to the front porch to wait. And wait she did. Ten minutes became twenty, became thirty. Where was he? There were a number of good restaurants within walking distance. Which one had he chosen? She dialed his cell and found that he still hadn't turned it back on.

She let her breath out in a short, frustrated huff. At this rate, she'd be drunk before he returned with the food.

No doubt, that was his plan. Tim didn't like emotional scenes. That's why he'd called when he had—thinking he'd leave a message and avoid the messiness of a face-to-face.

There would be no avoiding it, she thought. She would drill him until she knew every detail of what her mother had told him. She wanted the when and where, the date and the circumstances.

And she wanted to know how, under any circumstances, he could have thought it was okay to keep the information from her.

Wineglass empty, she stood and went for a refill.

Meowing, Margo darted out of the kitchen. "Hey, girl," she said and scooped her up. Purring, the cat nuzzled her shoulder.

"Tim's in big trouble, isn't he?" she asked. "He's a big traitor."

Margo meowed again, leapt out of her arms and onto the linen-covered table. "Margo, no! Off the . . ."

The words died on her lips. Margo had left paw prints on the linen. Alex shifted her gaze to the wooden floor. A trail of prints led from the kitchen to where she stood. She lowered her gaze to her shirtfront. Her white, long-sleeved T was smeared with red.

Blood.

She stared at it with a growing sense of horror. And denial. No, wine. Margo had toppled an open bottle. She had done it before, while she and Tim had been married. Not blood, she thought again. Wine.

Blood wine. The sharp smell of sandalwood stung her nose. Her glass slipped from her fingers, hitting the floor and shat-

tering. A thrumming filled her head. Light . . . flickering . . .
blood . . .

A scream, high and terrified. Hers. She ran toward the
kitchen, pushed through the door. She slipped, landing on
her hands and knees in something. Blood, she saw.

She shifted her gaze. Tim. On the floor, on his back.
Something shiny sticking out of his throat. Chopsticks, she
saw. The ones he had given her.

She crawled the rest of the way to him, sobbing, praying
it wasn't too late. She placed her hands on his chest, over his
heart. *Nothing.* She pressed her ear to the spot, then her fingers to his wrist.

Nothing . . . nothing . . . Dear God . . .

Alex backed up, sobbing, hysterical. She became aware
of her own voice, her repeated pleas. She was covered with
blood, she realized. It was everywhere. Her hands and hair.
Her clothes.

No . . . no . . . Whimpering, she tried to rub it from her
hands, but it only smeared more. Her fault, she thought.
She'd brought Tim into this. If not for her—

What to do? She dug her phone out of her pocket, dialed
911.

"Help," she whispered, when the dispatcher answered.
"Please. Tim's . . . he's been . . . stabbed. I think he's . . .
Oh my God, he's dead!"

Chapter Sixty-one

When Reed arrived, Alex sat huddled on the floor, Margo on her lap. Her hands, face and clothes were stained with blood. She stared blankly ahead.

A deputy stood nearby. Reed met the man's gaze with the briefest nod, then crossed to Alex and squatted down in front of her. "Alex, honey. Are you okay?"

She blinked, as if seeing him for the first time. "Reed," she said. "What are you doing here?"

"You asked for me. When you called 911."

Her gaze shifted to a point behind him. The kitchen, he thought. Location of the victim.

"He's dead," she said. "Tim's dead."

"Yes, I know. Are you all right?"

She frowned. "What do you mean?"

"Are you hurt?"

"No."

"Can I get you anything?"

"No."

He heard Tanner and Cal arriving. "I have work to do now, but I'll be close by. If you need anything, including to talk to me, just ask Jim here." He pointed to the deputy, who nodded in acknowledgment. "Jim will get it for you."

Reed stood and exchanged another glance with the deputy. He understood his duty: do not let her out of his sight, even to go to the bathroom.

Cal had gone on to the kitchen to inspect the victim; Tanner waited behind for him. When he reached her side, she murmured, "This is complicated for you."

"I know what I have to do." He heard the edge in his voice and regretted it. He was the one who was out of line, not Tanner.

"Do you?"

She held his gaze. He worked to control a rush of anger. He wasn't even certain who he was angry with—her, for questioning his professionalism; or himself, for being in this mess in the first place.

He leaned toward her. "Yes, dammit, I do. Just give me the chance to process the scene and question her, then I'm out."

"Agreed."

They moved into the kitchen, careful to step around a puddle of blood. The first responders had done their job: secured the scene, established the outer and inner perimeters and isolated the suspect.

Cal had already begun photographing the scene. The Coroner's detective would take their own shots and would need to do it before the body was touched in any way.

"Coroner's Office has been notified?" Reed asked the deputy standing watch.

"On their way."

Reed nodded and signed the inner perimeter log. "What do you have so far?"

"Woman's name is Alexandra Clarkson. The man was her ex-husband. When we arrived, she was hysterical. Babbling about finding him. I asked her about the blood. She said she ran to help him. That's all she could remember."

"Did she touch the body?" Tanner asked.

"Yes. Pressed her ear to his chest, then tried his pulse."

"Throat or wrist?"

"Wrist."

Reed shifted his attention to the scene. Judging by the amount of blood, whoever stuck him had hit the jugular. Blood would have literally shot out. Death would have come quickly, in a matter of a couple minutes.

The cottage was old and had settled to the northeast corner. The blood had sought the lowest point, pooling in front of the kitchen door. That would explain the prints, human and feline, that circled the area. It appeared as if both the cat and Alex had moved through it. On the floor near Clarkson's head was one perfect imprint of a hand.

"He wasn't a tall man," Tanner commented. "Coroner will get an exact measurement, but I'm thinking five foot six, maybe seven?"

Reed pictured him from their meeting the night before, recalled he and Alex walking away and thinking he wasn't taller than she was.

"That'd be my guess. Why?"

She shook her head. "No sign of a struggle."

"Bottle of red open on the counter."

"It's a good one," Cal said. "I already checked. "Seghesio Rock Pile Zin. It seems wrong to let it just go to waste."

They ignored him and studied the bottle and two glasses on the counter beside it. One was full, the other empty.

Tanner leaned closer, carefully inspecting the full glass. "Looks like he filled this one, but didn't drink from it."

"He was pouring," Reed murmured, "his assailant came from behind, reached around—"

"And planted the chopsticks neatly in his throat. Would've been messy."

"Strike two against the pretty head case in the other room," Cal offered.

Reed ignored that and squatted near the body, inspecting the wound. "Stainless steel chopsticks. Is that unusual?"

"Not really," Tanner said. "They sell them a number of places, including the Sur la Table."

He looked at her and she shrugged. "I was in the market. But I think I'll pass now."

They made their way out to the living area. Alex, Reed saw, hadn't moved. Neither had Margo. The cat was busy cleaning herself.

The table in the dining alcove had been set for a romantic dinner for two. Reed experienced a quick jab of something he didn't care to analyze.

"Watch it," Tanner said, touching his arm. "Broken glass."

He bent and inspected it. A broken champagne flute. It'd been empty—or nearly so—the floor around it dry.

"Take a look at this."

Went for food. Help yourself to the bubbly.
P.S. Don't be mad. I have news.

He and Tanner exchanged glances. A note from Clarkson to Alex? Or the other way around? One had been angry at the other. But why?

Time to find some answers. Wordlessly, they parted. Tanner would begin processing the scene for physical evidence and he would question Alex.

He asked the deputy to take notes of the interview. He wanted Alex to feel relaxed, like it was just the two of them talking, and his taking notes would get in the way of that. In addition, should it come to it, he didn't want the information gathered to be tainted by his relationship to the suspect.

He sat on the floor in front of her, mirroring her Indian-style position. "Tell me what happened, Alex." When she looked confused, he added, "How did your ex-husband end up dead?"

"Someone killed him. Stabbed him"—she touched her throat; he saw that her hand shook—"here."

"Did you kill him, Alex?"

That penetrated her glassy-eyed shock. Her eyes widened. "No!" She shook her head as if for added emphasis. "I couldn't . . . I found him like that."

"Okay, sweetheart, take a deep breath. I need you to tell me exactly what transpired. Moment by moment."

She did as he suggested and took several deep breaths, then began. "He had a faculty meeting this morning. At San Francisco State."

"He's a professor there?"

"Yes. He bought me a spa day . . . I wouldn't have accepted it, but it was for my . . . birthday."

"Is today your birthday?"

Her eyes filled with tears. Reed plucked a tissue from the box on the floor beside her. She took it and pressed it to her eyes. "Tomorrow."

"What spa was it?"

"The Kenwood Inn."

"Go on," he said gently.

"I was there when he called me. I wasn't supposed to have a phone . . . it's the rules, but I'd slipped it in my robe pocket. I don't know why. Instinct, maybe."

She fell silent for a long moment. So long he was about to nudge her when she spoke again. "He was surprised when I answered, said he meant to leave a message. He said he"— she crumpled the tissue in her fist—"knew something about my . . . dad. My mother had told him . . . back when he and I were still together."

She fell silent; he prodded her. "What did she tell him about him?"

Alex lifted her stricken gaze to his. "I could hardly hear! He was driving and the spa attendant . . ."

The convertible parked out front.

"I couldn't believe he hadn't told me before . . . all the time that's passed. I could have known something, Reed."

Her eyes filled once more, tears spilling over and rolling helplessly down her cheeks. He ignored the catch in his chest, denied the urge to take her in his arms and comfort her.

"He promised he would tell me more tonight . . . and now—" She grabbed another tissue and blew her nose. "I was really pissed. So I left."

"The spa?"

"Yes."

"And you came here, looking for him. Angry?"

"Anxious," she whispered, rubbing her arms. "I mean, I was hurt and mad that he had known something about my dad he'd kept a secret . . . but I couldn't sit still." She rubbed her arms.

"What happened next?"

"I got here. Saw his car. The whole dinner setup. Read the note."

"What did you think when you saw the table and champagne?"

She shrugged. "You have to know Tim. He doesn't like entanglements. Doesn't like messy emotional scenes. I figured he was managing me."

"What does that mean?"

"Predisposing me not to be mad anymore."

"So he wrote the note." She nodded and reached for another tissue. "He said he had news, Alex. What about?"

"I don't know."

"Any guesses?"

"With Tim, it could be anything. That he'd taken the week off to help me, or gotten acknowledged by the dean at the faculty meeting."

"Both of those are about him, Alex. What about you?"

"I don't understand."

"Could he have had news for you? About your father?"

She stared at him as if she hadn't considered the possibility before this moment. Apparently, her ex was an all-about-me sort of guy. "My God, I never . . . Do you think . . . Could he have?"

"What happened next?"

"I poured a glass of the champagne and went out front to wait."

"How long were you out there?"

"Thirty minutes. Maybe a little longer." She cleared her throat. "I'd finished my drink and come inside for a refill. Margo came along . . . she jumped into my arms. That's when I . . . when I saw . . ."

She began to tremble. Her eyes widened and he knew she was reliving the moment.

"You can do this," he said softly. "You are up to it, Alex."

She nodded, visibly struggling with her emotions. "I panicked and ran to the kitchen, I saw Tim . . . I fell, slipped and—" She held up her hands, her palms red, a look of horror on her face. "It was everywhere. They wouldn't come clean."

"Did you touch him, Alex?"

"Yes. I put my hands on his chest . . . then my ear. I didn't hear his heart, so I checked his wrist. For a pulse. There was nothing."

"And then?"

"Called you, I guess. I didn't know what else to do."

"You did the right thing, Alex. You did. I have just a couple more questions.

"What was your relationship with your ex-husband?"

"We were friends."

"You weren't in love with him?"

"No." She shook her head.

"You weren't reconciling?"

"No." She lifted her gaze to his, pleading. "We were friends, that's all. I called him."

"Why?"

She hesitated; he wondered why. "Because of all the stuff that's been happening. I was sort of . . . I knew he could help me put it in perspective."

"And that's it?"

"Yes."

He didn't buy that but didn't push it. She clasped her hands in her lap.

"Okay," he murmured, "here's what happens next. I'm going to have to take you in for an official statement."

"Take me in?"

"In a situation like this, there's no way around it."

She nodded as if she understood, but he sensed she didn't. That she was still operating on autopilot.

"Can I change first? Get cleaned up?"

"I'm sorry, but I can't let you do that. Not yet."

For a fraction of a moment, he thought she was going to ask when. But then she understood. It moved across her features like a cloud. "Do I need a lawyer?"

"You have the right to one. You're not under arrest, Alex. But because of the circumstances, you are a suspect."

"A suspect?"

"Yes, in the murder of your ex-husband."

"Oh my God." She brought a hand to her mouth. "But I didn't do . . . I couldn't do . . . this."

"Because of our relationship, I can't bring you in. But nice Deputy Jim here will do that. Right, Jim?"

"Yes, Detective."

"I'll be right behind you. With you all the way. Do you understand?"

"Yes. What about Margo?"

"She'll be fine. I'll have Tanner keep an eye on her, make certain she has food and water before they leave. I don't think you'll be gone that long."

He smiled to reassure her, though he didn't know how honest he was being. Depending on what went down at HQ, she could be charged and processed today.

He got to his feet and held out a hand to her. "Are you ready?"

"Some clothes?"

"Sure, tell me where."

She did and he collected a fresh set, grabbing things that looked comfortable. Of course, if the worst case scenario came to pass, she wouldn't be needing a change of clothes—she would be wearing a blue jumpsuit.

He slipped his jacket over her shoulders, as much for warmth as to shield her from the curious stares of the crowd that had surely gathered outside. It would include neighbors and passersby, tourists drawn by the flashing lights and the press.

A photograph of her drenched in blood would make a great front page, but innocent or not, it could harm her chances for a fair trial—in court, or in the court of public opinion.

When they reached the front door, he stopped and looked

at her. "One last thing, Alex. From here on out, I can't help you with this. Because of our relationship, I'm going to have to excuse myself from the case. And because of my badge, we won't be able to see or even talk to each other. Do you understand?"

She did. He saw it in the panic that raced into her eyes. As if she had just realized how much trouble she might be in—and that she was completely alone.

And in that moment, he realized just how much he hated it being this way.

Chapter Sixty-two

Tuesday, March 16
9:20 P.M.

Half a dozen people gathered around the video monitor, watching the interview in progress. They'd been going at Alex for some time and she looked a hairbreadth from falling apart.

When they'd arrived at the Barn, the deputy had gotten Alex set up in an interview room. Reed had connected with his sergeant, explained the situation and recused himself from the case. Unfortunately, because of the way current events crisscrossed and possibly linked to Alex, it left a new detective with a whole lot to familiarize himself with. Mac had not been happy about it.

Reed glanced at the sergeant now; he was frowning. "Her story hasn't altered, Mac. Not from when she first relayed it to me."

The assistant D.A. agreed. "You know the drill, boys, charge or release."

"Okay," Lieutenant Torres said, "let's get Detective Saacks back in here." While Mac retrieved the detective from the interview room, the lieutenant went on, "What've we got, Team? Lay it all out there."

Tanner began. Mac and Saacks slipped into the room. "We've got a motive. She admits she was angry with him."

"Spa employees confirmed. They overheard her leaving a nasty message for someone—"

"Clarkson, the deceased."

"We've got that." Tanner replayed it: *"Dammit, Tim! Pick up! I can't believe you would do thi—"*

"That's it, she didn't finish," Tanner said. "My guess is that's when the spa attendants came in and busted her."

"She sounded pretty upset." Lieutenant Torres looked at the assistant D.A. "She left in a huff, before she'd even finished her prepaid services."

"But she didn't threaten him in any way," Reed murmured. "And by her own account, she was angry. She didn't try to hide that."

Tanner went on. "And depending on the timeline, we've got opportunity."

Detective Saacks jumped in. "We're working on establishing a firm timeline."

Bob Ware, the Coroner's detective, spoke up. "He hadn't been dead long when we got there. Lividity was under way, but just under way, and rigor mortis hadn't even started. By the time I got him to the morgue, body temperature had only dropped by three degrees. Factoring in transporting the body and investigative time, that doesn't leave a lot of wiggle room."

The D.A. agreed. "We can make that stick. No doubt."

Saacks spoke up again. "A neighbor confirmed her version of events. He saw her on her porch about four forty-five P.M. Drinking wine. They didn't speak. He heard her scream a short time later and was dialing 911 when he heard the first responders' sirens."

"Did he happen to notice, was she covered in blood?"

That brought a chuckle from the group.

Cal tapped on the closed door, then poked his head inside. "Tanner, Reed, a moment, please."

They excused themselves and met him out in the hall. "What's up?" Tanner asked.

"Thought you'd be interested." He handed them each a pair of Latex gloves. While they fitted them on, he continued, "Found this in the suspect's bedroom. It's a list of all the crazy shit that's happened since she arrived in Sonoma."

He handed the yellow legal tablet to Tanner. "She notes having an alibi for one item." He looked at Reed. "Sorry, man."

"Not your issue, Cal. But thanks."

He and Tanner reviewed the list. Reed stopped on the item that read: Max's house torched. Alibi/Reed. His stomach sank. That didn't look good.

"What's this?" Tanner asked. She tapped the very last item on the list: "*Remember* scrawled in lipstick on bathroom mirror. Stain on hand and sheets."

Another bizarre occurrence on Alex's doorstep. "First I heard of it," he said.

"In her statement, she never mentioned the list or this 'Remember' thing."

"She's had a little on her mind."

Tanner narrowed her eyes. "Watch it, Detective, your loyalties are showing."

"Playing devil's advocate. Look, the list makes sense. She said she called her ex-husband to help her put everything that was happening in perspective. Looks to me like she was trying to put it in perspective on her own first."

"Let's let the team get a look at it."

They did, and after the group had pored over it, discussion resumed. "It's an incomplete list," the D.A. said. "Neither Schwann's nor Clarkson's murder is noted."

The lieutenant agreed. "In my opinion this supports her version of events."

Mac spoke up. "I'm bothered by her mentioning her own alibi. That's just off."

The D.A. looked at Saacks. "How reliable is the neighbor who saw her on her porch?"

"Seemed lucid. Sixtyish. Wearing glasses."

The D.A. took over. "We've got motive. And depending on our timeline, we've got opportunity. What about evidence?"

"Processed the scene," Tanner said. "Collected a ton of blood samples, prints and other miscellaneous pieces of physical evidence. It'll be awhile before we get results back; however, what we do have is a physical scene with no overt evidence of anyone's presence besides the deceased's and suspect's. We also have a suspect well covered with the victim's blood and a handprint near the body that she confirmed is probably hers."

Saacks added, "And we have the weapon, high-quality, stainless steel, two-gauge chopsticks."

"Prints on them?" Lieutenant Torres asked.

"Wiped."

Reed frowned. "That's interesting. Why would she carefully wipe the weapon and leave a big bloody handprint on the floor?"

"He has a point," the D.A. agreed. "I don't like the neighbor. Without that witness, I'd go for it right now. But the picture of Clarkson calmly sitting on the front porch, enjoying a glass of wine, blows it for me. And I strongly suspect for a jury as well." She turned to Reed. "Any chance she'll disappear? You have a relationship with her, what do you think?"

They all looked at him. It was a damn awkward position to be in. Either way, he was putting himself on the line. "She's not going anywhere."

"She hasn't lawyered up yet, but will. At any moment is my guess and that'll just prolong this. We could keep her forty-eight hours, but if she's not a flight risk, why force her hand?"

The lieutenant looked at him. "I want you to take another crack at her, Reed. Bring the list in. She trusts you. Use that to see if you can get us anything else."

He nodded and exited the room. In the hall, his cell vibrated. "Reed here."

"Dan, thank God! It's Rachel. What the hell's going on?"

"I can't talk now."

"I drove by Alex's . . . I saw a body being brought out—"

"I really can't tal—"

"Is it Alex?" Her voice rose, taking on a hysterical edge. "Is she okay? No one will tell me anything!"

"She's fine," he said, glancing at his watch, aware of the team in the other room waiting for him. "She's here. We're questioning her."

"Then who—"

"Her ex-husband."

"Oh my God! I'm coming down there—"

"No! There's nothing you can do. I have to go, Rachel."

He ended the called and entered the interview room. He steeled himself for his first look at Alex—and for what her response to him would be. The truth was, he was afraid he would give himself away.

She didn't kill Clarkson. The evidence might be damning, but his gut said otherwise. And he still trusted his gut—foolish or not. Which was why, rightly, he was off the case.

"Hello, Alex," he said softly.

She looked up, her immediate expression of relief becoming one of hurt. "How could you think I did this?" she asked, voice cracking. "How could any of you? Forget the fact that I could never do that to anyone, let alone someone I loved—"

She fisted her fingers, as if fighting for strength. "Forget all that and consider that I waited all my life to learn something about who my father is, and you all think I might have killed the one person who knew something about him?"

He crossed to the table and sat in the chair across from hers. "No, Alex, I don't think you killed your ex-husband." His lieutenant and the others watching would think he was working her. Problem was, he meant it. "Are you okay?" he asked softly.

"I am now."

He imagined the groans and guffaws in the viewing room at that. He leaned slightly toward her. "I need to find out who did kill him. And I want to make certain that he doesn't hurt you. To do that, I need your help."

She nodded and wiped the tears from her cheeks. "Why are they letting you talk to me?"

Tough question. He went for partial honesty. "Because they know, if anyone can help, it's me. And frankly, you look like you've had it."

"I'm so tired."

"I know, sweetheart."

"I can't believe Tim's dead. It's like a bad dream. All of it. Everything that's happened since I got here."

"There's been a lot of bizarre stuff going on, and it all seems to revolve around you." He laid the legal tablet on the table between them. "I need you to tell me about this."

She stared at it, paling. "It's a list."

"Yes. Why'd you make it?"

She swallowed audibly. "I was trying to get a grip on what was happening. You know, to put it all together."

"I get that," he said. "But what about this—Max's house torched. Alibi/Reed?"

"Because we were together. I knew I couldn't be responsible for doing that."

He cocked his head frowning. "But you worried you were responsible for the others?"

"Yes," she whispered. "Because of the word on the mirror."

"*Remember*," he said.

"Yes." She cleared her throat. "I awakened that Monday, suddenly. I thought someone had been in my house. But then it was so . . . quiet. I figured another nightmare had awakened me."

"Another nightmare?"

"I've always had them, but lately . . . they've been bad. It's this place, I think." She leaned toward him, expression pleading. "I think something bad happened to me . . . I don't know what—So I struggled to remember, concentrated on trying to . . .

"Suddenly this vision filled my head. Robed men holding me down. I knew I had to run and did. I ran to the bathroom. That's when I saw it."

"*Remember* written on the bathroom mirror?"

She nodded. "The window was open, I thought someone had climbed in, but—"

"What, Alex?"

"My hands. They were stained with the lipstick. It scared me. I wondered if I could have written that myself and not . . . remember doing it. That's why I called Tim. I knew he could help me figure it out."

"Why didn't you call me, Alex?"

"Because . . . I didn't want you . . . to think I was . . . crazy."

"What did Tim think?"

"That someone was messing with me. He was going to help—" She bit that back and leaned forward, eyes widening. "That last call from Tim, why'd he make it?"

"I don't follow."

"He didn't expect me to answer. He knows spa rules, he's had more experience with them than I have. He even said he was surprised when I answered, that he thought he would leave me a voice mail."

"Okay, go on."

"He called to tell me about my dad. That's all he said." She leaned forward. "Why, Reed? Why then?"

"You tell me."

"My mother told him my father was a really bad man. That she left Sonoma to protect me. And that she blamed him for what happened to Dylan."

"Whoa, wait. Did she accuse your father of harming Dylan Sommer?"

"I don't know for sure." She dragged a hand through her hair. "We never got a chance to talk further."

"So, what are you saying, Alex?"

"She didn't care if they told lies about her. If they reviled her after she left."

Reed thought of his father, his story about Patsy. And of their conversation the night before, the way his father had acted. The way he had effortlessly changed personas.

At his silence, Alex added, "The BOV, Reed. That story about her. Maybe he killed Tim."

"He, who?"

"My dad. Maybe he's behind it all." Her voice rose.

"Maybe they did it. Maybe they took Dylan, too! The real BOV. Whoever they are." She held out a hand, pleading. "Don't you see. It makes sense."

He gazed at her, heart sinking. She was irrational. "No, Alex. It doesn't make sense. I'm sorry."

He glanced up at the camera with a small shake of his head, then stood. "I'm going to see what I can do about getting you out of here. Hold tight a little longer."

She reached out and caught his hand. "I'm right about this." She lifted her chin. "I know I am."

He opened his mouth to reason with her, then said instead, "We'll figure this out. Whoever did this, we'll get him."

Chapter Sixty-three

Tuesday, March 16
10:10 P.M.

They released her with the warning she was not to leave the area. She almost laughed out loud at that. Where would she go? The only two people she had called family were gone now.

Tears flooded her eyes. Where *did* she go now? She was alone. On her own with no one to turn to.

"Alex!"

Alex turned. Rachel. Hurrying across the Sheriff's Department waiting area. Alex ran to meet her. She still had Rachel, she thought. Thank God.

"I've been beside myself," Rachel cried, hugging her tightly. "I saw the squad cars and Coroner's wagon . . . My God, that could have been you!"

"But it was Tim," Alex whispered. "Maybe it should have been me."

"Don't say that." Rachel held her at arm's length. "Look at you. They didn't let you clean up? I'd like to give that Danny Reed a piece of my mind."

Alex didn't bother telling her that they had—after photographing her, they'd allowed her to change clothes, though they had kept hers as evidence.

"It's my fault he's dead. He came to help me. I asked him to come because—"

She bit the last part back and Rachel searched her gaze. "Because of what, Alex?"

She shook her head, "It doesn't matter, does it? He's gone now and they think I did it."

"No!"

People were looking their way. She caught Rachel's hand. "Get me out of here, please."

She did, hurrying to her Infiniti coupe. She opened the passenger door for Alex. "You're staying with me. No arguments."

Like she would argue, Alex thought, sinking into the leather seat. She had nowhere else to go.

"What about Margo?" she asked.

"We're going to go get her. And anything else you need."

Alex shuddered. "I don't think I can go back in there. Not ever."

"I'll do it," Rachel said. "I'll take care of everything."

She did. While Alex waited in the car, Rachel collected everything she needed, including a traumatized Margo. In what seemed like no time at all, Rachel had Alex installed in the guest room of her charming cottage on the winery grounds. From her bedroom window, she could just make out the entrance to the caves.

"Your place is lovely," Alex said as she wandered into the kitchen. She'd showered, changed clothes again and felt almost alive.

"Thank you. I love it here."

"Do you ever get . . . enough of it?"

"It?" Rachel asked, pouring her a glass of wine.

"The winery. Your family. Living here, working here. Don't you ever just want to get away?"

She thought a minute, then shook her head. "Oddly, no. I truly couldn't imagine myself anywhere else. I'm connected to this place, to the vines, the wine. And my roots run really deep."

"You're an old vine, then."

Rachel laughed and handed Alex a glass of red wine. "It's not one of mine," she said. "I'm constantly trying other house's wines. This one's a Bordeaux-style blend from a boutique outfit in Napa Valley, Fleury. The winemaker's also the owner and this is his flagship wine, Passionne."

Rachel sipped. "Good balance of fruit and spice. Nice, full body. Long finish. I need to watch this one."

Alex sipped but didn't comment. It could have been vinegar for all she cared right now. She couldn't shake the image of Tim, on her kitchen floor in a pool of blood, out of her mind. Or the detectives' questions, the way they kept pounding at her.

"I figured you would be hungry," Rachel was saying, "so I pulled together some cheese and pâté. I didn't know if it would be enough, but worried that something too heavy would—"

"It's perfect, Rachel. Thank you."

They carried it all to the living room. Alex curled up on the end of the couch and watched as Rachel lit the gas fireplace.

"Do you have the energy to talk about it?" Rachel asked.

Alex shook her head.

"I'm sorry." Rachel cupped the wine bowl in her palms. "You seemed to care a lot about him. Everyone I know who's divorced would do a victory dance if—You know."

"He was always . . . there for me when I needed him. Maybe not on my timetable, but eventually. And he . . . understood me."

"I've never been in a relationship like that. Truthfully, that night I met him, he seemed sort of . . . shallow."

"Tim of the chopsticks."

Rachel's words from that night at the girl & the fig rang in her head, followed by Tim's response.

"Rachel of the really red lipstick."

The chopsticks, buried in Tim's throat. The red lipstick, scrawled across her mirror.

A sick sensation settled in the pit of her stomach. One of revulsion and denial. No. It didn't mean anything, she told

herself. Rachel was her friend. She was the only one she had
left.

"What's wrong?" Rachel asked.

Alex realized she was staring at Rachel and looked away.
"I can't talk about him anymore. I just . . . I can't."

"I'm sorry." Rachel sounded distressed. "Is there anything I can do for you?"

Alex looked back at her, vision swimming. What she was
thinking, that Rachel was implicated in all this, wasn't true.
It couldn't be. "You've already done so much. If you hadn't
shown up tonight, I—" She paused, as if in thought. "How
did you know to come get me? Tonight, when you did?"

Rachel blinked. "How? Danny called me."

That made sense, didn't it? Alex ran a hand across her
brow. "I hope I don't seem ungrateful, but would you mind
if I went to bed? I'm not very good company right now."

"No problem." Rachel got to her feet. "Take your wine
and a plate of—"

"I'm not hungry."

"I insist. And look, I have sleeping pills—"

"I won't need that."

"Just in case. I'll get them."

Dutifully, Alex collected her plate and glass and carried
them to her bedroom. A moment later, Rachel was at her
door with a bottle of pills and a small, Priority Mail box.

"I almost forgot. This was on your porch."

She handed the box to Alex. It was from Rita Welsh,
Alex saw. It had been sent to her San Francisco apartment,
then rerouted here. What, she wondered, could it be?

"Who's it from?" Rachel asked.

"A friend of my mother's."

She held out the vial of pills. "Directions are on the label,
just in case. They're super mild and nonhabit-forming, so if
you need one, really, don't hesitate."

Alex swallowed hard. "Thanks, Rachel. I can't tell you
how much you being here means to me."

Rachel hugged her, then stepped back. "If you need anything, I'm just down the hall."

Alex thanked her again and closed the door. She stared it a moment, feeling incredibly, achingly alone.

"Tim of the chopsticks."

"Rachel of the really red lipstick."

No. Not Rachel, she thought, crossing to the bed and sinking onto it. Please God, not Rachel.

She looked at the box in her hands, wondering again what it could be. Acknowledging the only way to find out, she pulled the tab, then opened the lid. Inside was a note card and a tissue-wrapped item.

Alex opened the card. It read:

> Dear Alexandra,
> I hope you are well. I discovered this while I was packing for my move to Oregon. (To be near my daughter and grandchild.) This was left behind the last time I babysat for you. I set it aside, thinking your mother would come for it, but she never did.
> Peace and love,
> Rita

Alex carefully unwrapped the package. A silver baby brush, she saw. The silver was tarnished, though considering the years that had passed, not as badly as she would have expected.

She gazed at it a moment, tears blurring her vision. She had so few mementos from her early years; she had always wondered why. And had always felt unwanted because of it.

She ran her fingers over the soft bristles, heart in her throat. She turned it over—and found it was engraved. She rubbed at the engraving with the hem of her T-shirt.

Beloved Alexandra—Daughter of the vine—March 17, 1980

She stared at the words in a combination of excitement and distaste. And a sense of destiny fulfilled. Like Rachel and Clark. Like Dylan. She was one of them—a daughter of the vine. Why else would she have been given that brush, engraved that way?

One of them, she thought again. Her father had been from a wine family.

But was he also a killer?

Suddenly cold, she stood and drew back the covers, then crawled into the bed. She cradled the brush to her chest, though a sour taste filled her mouth as she recalled the things that Tim had said about her father: *He was a really bad man . . . Your mother left Sonoma to protect you from him . . . blamed him for Dylan . . .*

What did you do, Tim? she wondered, eyes burning. Try to play hero? Figure you could charge in with your psychobabble and good intentions, and what? Talk it out? Turn him around?

Could he have connected with him? His note had said he had news. The champagne suggested the news had been good. Celebratory.

News about her father. Maybe.

Could he have known more than he'd told her? Probably. Maybe even a name. She squeezed her eyes shut, trying to remember everything he'd said, the questions he'd asked and her responses to them.

At one point, Tim had asked her where the BOV story had originated. In that short conversation, why would that have mattered?

The story. About the boys and her mother. Of course. Her mother had called him a liar, warned that he had told lies about her.

Wayne Reed.

The realization hit her and she sat up. Wayne Reed had passed the story to his son. He'd made no secret of his dislike for her, his wish that she would go away.

His warning to "stay away from my sons" took on new meaning, and she brought a hand to her mouth. She and Reed could be brother and sister.

Surely not. Surely, somehow, on some instinctual level, they would have known.

But, God, it made sense. All of it—the elder Reed's dislike, the BOV story, his desire for her to be gone. His concern that she would become involved with one of his sons.

Unable to sit still, she climbed out of bed and began to pace. Could Reed be her brother? She couldn't focus on the horror of that, not now. She needed to discover if Wayne Reed really was her father. And if he was—had he killed to keep his secret safe?

As she paced, her thoughts whirled. Again and again, she analyzed the things she knew to be true—and those she didn't. The minutes ticked into an hour, then two. But the same questions remained. Plus others.

How did she prove it? Where did Dylan's disappearance fit into the scenario? If the Boys of the Vine had been a lie, what did BOV mean? And the image of the vines and snake?

She couldn't do this alone. But who could she turn to? Not Reed. Tim was dead. Rachel, she realized. She was the only one she had left.

"Tim of the chopsticks."

Alex hesitated. her stomach seeming to crawl up to her throat. What did she choose to believe? That's what it came down to.

And in her heart—and gut—she believed Rachel was on her side.

She had no one else. *Do it. Now.*

Alex started out of the bedroom, then hesitated. What if Rachel thought she was crazy, the same as Reed did? What would she do then? Who would she turn to?

She couldn't worry about that now. She had to do this.

Alex exited the bedroom and hurried down the hall to Rachel's. She rapped on the door. "Rachel," she called. "It's Alex. I have to talk to you."

The light popped on and Rachel responded with a thick-sounding "Come in."

Rachel was sitting up in bed, bleary-eyed with sleep. "What's wrong?"

"I need your help. I know who killed Tim."

Rachel's eyes widened. "My God, who?"

"My father. Wayne Reed."

For a long moment, Rachel simply stared at her. "Do you know what you're saying?"

"Yes, unfortunately."

"And you're certain? You have proof?"

Alex shook her head. This was the point it got tricky. "I think I'm right. The pieces fit, but—"

"But you have no proof?"

"No."

Rachel held her gaze. "Then, what *do* you have, Alex?"

Chapter Sixty-four

Wednesday, March 17
1:40 A.M.

They agreed to meet in the kitchen in five minutes. Rachel claimed she couldn't think without caffeine and Alex used the time to collect the baby brush and prepare her thoughts.

When she entered the kitchen, Rachel was already there, preparing lattes at a high-tech-looking machine. She wore a fuzzy robe and Uggs. She shuffled across to the breakfast counter with the two drinks. "Quad shot for me," she said. "Single for you. You look like you're already wide awake."

She was, Alex acknowledged. Her every nerve ending seemed to be humming. Truth was, even a little caffeine might be too much.

Rachel sank onto one of the bar stools. "Hit me with it, Alex. Whatcha got?"

Alex launched in. She started at the beginning, sharing everything, every event, thought, comment and feeling. She told her about Rita Welsh and what she had learned about her mother from her; she shared the BOV story—her voice growing thick with emotion. She described her visions, her nightmares and the details of her panic attacks in the caves.

Rachel finished her latte and made another. She listened attentively, rarely commenting.

Alex explained how she had recognized the sandalwood scent and learned it was Lyla Reed's favorite. And how Clark's aggression in the winery had made its way into her dreams.

"How so?" Rachel asked, standing and crossing to the coffee machine for a sprinkle of cinnamon.

"His voice. And something he said—'You want to know so bad. I'll show you.'"

Rachel didn't reply, and she went on. Deciding to hide nothing, lay it all out for the other woman to examine, Alex shared that she and Reed had become lovers.

Finally, she explained why she had called Tim. How she feared for her own sanity, then about his call to her at the spa, detailing the things he'd said about her father, and finally describing returning to her rental and finding Tim dead. Her grueling interview by the police.

Alex took a deep breath. "That package you gave me last night was from that old friend of my mother's, Rita the librarian. My silver baby brush. My mother left it the last time Rita babysat for me and she'd found it while packing to move."

Rachel still stood at the espresso machine, back to her. "Rach?" she asked. "Are you okay?"

"Fine." The other woman turned. Alex thought she looked strange. Her latte sloshed over the rim as she carried her beverage to the table.

She handed Rachel the baby brush. She watched as Rachel unwrapped it, turned it over in her hands, then read the inscription. Her expression altered slightly. She lifted her gaze to Alex's. "So, why Wayne Reed?"

"Mainly because the BOV story originated with him. But the rest works as well. He wanted me to go away. He warned me away from his sons. He's the scion of an old wine family. The strong scent from my episode in the cave was Lyla Reed's scent."

Completely spent, she laid her head on her arms, folded

on the counter in front of her. Wordlessly, Rachel set about making them toast, pouring juice.

The horizon lightened; they ate the simple meal in silence. The food helped, delivering a small burst of energy. Alex looked at Rachel. "Reed doesn't believe me. He thinks I'm crazy."

"I don't think you're crazy," Rachel said softly. "I know you're not."

"How, Rachel? How do you know?"

"Because I lived through the same nightmare."

The same nightmare. Of course. Rachel was implicated—because she was a part of it as well. Alex experienced an almost dizzying relief.

She wasn't alone. Not anymore. This wasn't just about her, it was about Rachel, too.

Because of Dylan. Because of what happened to him.

"Why now?" Alex asked. "After all these years—"

"Because he was found! His remains. That was our brother who was dug up in that vineyard. Our brother who had been stuffed into a wine crate and buried."

"I didn't think he'd been positively identified. When—"

"Dad ID'd them. He's positive."

Reed hadn't told her.

"Dylan's killer is out there, Alex. And I think you being here is making him nervous."

"Why?" she asked.

"Because you know who he is. You saw something that night, something you repressed."

Alex shook her head in denial, though she knew in her gut that Rachel was right.

Rachel grabbed her hands. "First that night in the cave at Red Crest, then later here, in this one, something happened to you. Something terrifying—and terrifyingly real. We both know why."

Alex swallowed and nodded.

"The police found blood outside the cave entrance."

"Dylan's?"

"His type. DNA wasn't what it is now, but it was presumed that, yes, it was his."

Alex felt sick. "From what I told you, do you think my father killed Tim?"

"I don't know. Why else would someone want Tim dead?"

Alex shook her head. "He didn't know anybody here but me. He was murdered in my kitchen, nothing was stolen, so—"

She bit back the last and looked at Rachel. "No wonder they think I did it. I'm the obvious choice."

"But you *didn't* kill him. And his last communication with you was about your father."

"No," Alex corrected, "it was his note. He said he had news for me."

"So, unless you're lying to me, we've got a no-brainer here. The question is, could Wayne Reed be your father?"

They fell silent. Alex thought of Reed, her feelings for him. The time they had spent together. How he would—

"Oh my God," she said, suddenly remembering. "At Red Crest, the night of the launch party, Lyla was giving me a tour of the family trophy room. We were looking at the photographs on the walls . . . there was one of Wayne Reed with Robert Mondavi. She mentioned him by name."

"The Robert Mondavi Winery, that's where your mother was working when she met your dad."

"Yes." Alex dropped her face in her hands. "This can't be happening."

"It is," Rachel said tersely. "You're going to have to deal with your personal feelings later. Right now, we figure out what happened. When we do, then we go to the police."

Alex squeezed her eyes closed. The image of the robed figures filled her head. The men, their arousal . . . hands holding her down. The fire, its tentacles reaching for her. The screams.

"We can do this, Alex. You can do this."

She snapped open her eyes. "How?" she whispered. "How do we make me remember?"

"You already know. You tried it yourself."

She did know. *The wine cave.*

Alex's heart beat heavily. She struggled to breathe past the sudden, overwhelming fear that balled up in her chest. Was she up to this? Was she strong enough?

It's what she had set out to do. Unearth her past. Fill the empty place inside her, the one where those memories used to live. Find her father and identify her brother's killer.

Was she strong enough? she wondered again.

Alex shuddered and Rachel caught her hands. "I'll be right there with you. I'll talk you through it."

"A reenactment," she whispered. "That's what we need to do."

"Yes."

"When?"

"Tonight. Late. I'll prepare everything. You try to get some rest."

That would be easier said then done, Alex acknowledged. She was completely terrified already, and she hadn't yet set a foot in the cave.

Chapter Sixty-five

Wednesday, March 17
11:40 A.M.

Reed sat at his desk, staring blankly at his computer screen. He'd been unable to stop thinking about that last interview with Alex. He had replayed the things she'd said about Clarkson's last call to her, the things about her father.

"Maybe my dad's behind all of it. Even Dylan."

She had come off as desperate and irrational. To him— and the entire team. Guilty of murder or not, they'd written her off as a first-class whack job.

That's what he wanted to believe. His gut told him other- wise. Or were his personal feelings interfering with his pro- fessional judgment? In terms of the case, it didn't matter. He was off it. But on a personal level, it bugged the hell out of him.

He wasn't one of those guys, wasn't one of those cops. He didn't get personally involved. Didn't let his emotions get in the way of rational thinking. So what the hell was going on here?

"Maybe my dad's behind all of it. Even Dylan."

A missing piece of the puzzle. One the investigators at the time wouldn't have considered. Unless alerted by someone.

Patsy. She was the only one who would have been able to do that. Instead, she had run away. What had Harlan said? That Patsy had been overcome with guilt and despair.

The guilt fit now. She had suspected Alex's father's involvement, but had kept her mouth shut. Out of fear. Maybe. For her young daughter. For herself?

On a hunch, he picked up the phone and dialed information, retrieved San Francisco State's number. The main office directed him to the College of Behavioral Sciences. There, the department secretary confirmed his hunch.

Tim Clarkson hadn't had a faculty meeting the day before.

So, where the hell had he been? Why had he made certain Alex was out of the way for the day?

Her father. She'd been right. About it all. That's why Tim had called her at the spa, meaning to leave a message for her. To prepare her.

Reed's thoughts raced forward to the note her ex had left for her. *I have news.* Clarkson's meeting with Alex's father had been successful. Or so he had thought.

Why kill Clarkson?

Reed answered his own question. To keep his secret safe. Of course. But what secret? That he was Alex's father? Or something more ominous?

"You okay, Reed?"

Tanner stood in his doorway. He motioned her in. "I'm good. And you're just the person I needed to see."

She wandered in, sank onto the chair across from him. "What's up?"

"Followed a hunch and gave San Francisco State a call. Clarkson didn't have a faculty meeting yesterday."

"So one of them lied."

"My bet's on him."

"That doesn't surprise me."

He ignored that. "The question is why."

She nodded. "Thanks. We'll work on that. Cell records will help there." She leaned forward. "Got some interesting information from the Ashton Drake people. Apparently, each doll is unique and comes with a serial number and adoption papers."

She paused. "You adopt your baby. It's all very official. They've got 'adoption' documents going back to the seventies."

"Tell me you've got a name."

"Not yet. By the end of the day."

She stood and stretched. "Sorry you're off the case."

"How's Saacks doing?"

"He catches on fast. He's trying to nail down who at Red Crest took Schwann's call. I'll keep you updated."

His cell vibrated. He glanced at the display and saw that it was his father. They hadn't spoken since two nights ago, when his dad had told him to get off his property.

He thanked Tanner, then answered. "Hello, Dad."

"I need to see you. Can you come over?"

"When?"

"Now?"

"Where are you?"

"My office."

Reed frowned. His father sounded strange. Shaken. "What's this about, Dad?"

"I'll tell you when you get here."

Chapter Sixty-six

Wednesday, March 17
12:45 P.M.

When Reed arrived at Red Crest, he headed back to the offices, which he found deserted. Everybody, it seemed, was at lunch. He passed Eve's desk, making his way to his dad's office.

The door was closed; he tapped on it. "Dad, it's Dan."

Wayne called for him to come in; Reed did and closed the door behind him. His father stood at the window, gazing out at the vineyards.

At the snap of the door, he swung to face his son. "I heard about that murder."

Reed slipped his hands into his pockets. "What did you hear?"

"That she most likely did it."

"She?"

"Patsy's girl."

He couldn't even say her name. Why? Reed frowned. "You mean Alexandra?"

"You know I do."

"Then why not say her name?"

He glared at him. "I hear you let her go."

"Didn't have enough to charge her, Dad. And I don't make those decisions. D.A. called it."

"You know where she is?"

"I might. Why?"

"She's been busy." He crossed to his desk, snatched up an envelope from his desk and held it out. "Take a look at this."

Reed crossed to his father and took the envelope. Inside, folded, was a single sheet of paper. On it, in what appeared to be twelve-point Helvetica, were two simple sentences: *I know your secrets. I will make you—and the others—pay.*

He read it twice, then returned his gaze to his father's. "You think Alexandra sent you this. Why?"

"Who else would have?"

He searched his father's expression, noting the way he couldn't hold his gaze for more than a few seconds, the subtle flush across his ruddy cheeks. "What secrets is the letter writer referring to?"

"How the hell should I know? She's crazy with a capital 'C.' Just like her mother."

Reed narrowed his eyes. "You're lying, Dad. We both know it, so can the bullshit outrage and tell me the truth."

For a moment, it looked as if his dad was going to argue anyway, then he shut his mouth and went around his desk and sat. He dropped his head into his hands.

Reed watched him a moment, waiting. "What secrets, Dad?" he prodded finally.

When he still didn't answer, Reed took a shot. "It's that story you told about Alex's mother, about the BOV. It was a lie, wasn't it?"

He nodded but didn't look up.

"Why'd you lie?"

"To cover up the real truth of the BOV. In the hopes that she would stop asking questions, go back to San Francisco and just let the past die."

"Are you Alexandra's father?"

He looked stunned by the question. "God, no! Why would you even ask that?"

Reed ignored the question. "What does BOV really stand for? Not Boys of the Vine?"

"No. Brethren of the Vine." He sighed, the sound heavy. "It started out innocently. On the Spring Equinox, a costume party. A mock Dionysian ritual. Patsy arranged the party. She invited the group we routinely partied with. She went all out, studied the myths and rituals surrounding the god. We had a mock altar, candlelight, incense. Wine and more wine.

"We were wild back then. Full of ourselves. Wine was becoming the legal drug of choice, and California was the supplier. We thought no one could touch us. That we were invincible.

"The party became a monthly thing. It got wilder, more out of control. As if we'd begun buying into it all, taking it seriously." His father's voice cracked. He passed a hand across his forehead. He didn't look Reed in the eye. "It started innocently. A touch that should have been rebuffed, but wasn't. A drunken kiss between friends that became anything but platonic, a revealing glimpse of breast or belly . . . I don't remember exactly the moment it happened or which incident went from blurring the line to crossing it."

Reed stared at his father, struggling to come to grips with what he was telling him. "You're talking about wife swapping and group sex?"

"Try to understand, Son. We were living in this small world. We were the beautiful people. Everybody wanted to be us . . ." His dad looked ill. "It grew on us. It became like a drug. For all of us. If one had called a halt, I think we would have all stopped, but—"

"No one did."

He shook his head. "It was insidious, like a spider. The forbidden. Our secret. The sex. Soon we were all ensnared in the web of our own making."

Reed turned his back to his father, unable to look at him.

"That's what we were all doing the night Dylan disappeared. We were all in the cave."

He swung back to face his father. "You lied to the police, the FBI."

Wayne got to his feet. "Don't you understand? Our reputations were at stake! If this had gotten out, we would have been ruined!"

"Don't *you* get it? Any one of you could be the one who killed Dylan."

"No." He shook his head. "We were all together in the cave."

"And no one could have slipped out unnoticed? Between the wine and the orgasms, Dad, who was paying attention?"

No one was. The blood drained from his father's face and he sat back down.

"Do you know who killed Alberto Alvarez?"

"Who?"

"The Sommers' gardener. The one murdered with a secateur."

"No! Why would I know that—"

"Who was involved? What families besides you, Patsy and Harlan?" When he didn't immediately answer, Reed began ticking them off. "The Schwanns. The Townsends. The Bianches. Who else?"

"Max Cragan and his wife. For obvious reasons, we kept it small."

Max Cragan. Who'd designed the ring. And who was now dead.

"Joe and his friends, were they involved?"

"No! God, no. I'd never—"

"Then why'd Tom Schwann have the tattoo?"

"I don't know."

"That's bullshit!"

"It's not! I don't know!" He launched to his feet once more, quivering with some strong emotion. "I—" Suddenly, he seemed to crumble. "They found out, somehow. Not everything, not about the sex . . . but they . . . started their own group. That stopped, too, after Dylan was abducted."

"I've got to go. Give me the note." His father hesitated and Reed crossed to the desk and snatched it up. "Are you lying about this, too?"

"No. I promise I'm not."

Without another word, he started for the door.

"Son"—his father stood—"I'm begging you. She knows. I think she means to kill me."

Reed stopped, hand on the doorknob. "I really doubt that. But you know what, right now I could almost kill you myself."

"Wait!" Wayne held out a hand, his expression pleading. "What are you going to do?"

"I don't know yet."

"Please. Think of your mother. Your brothers. I never meant for this to happen."

Reed took in a deep breath, then released it slowly, counting to ten. "When you told that story about Patsy and all of the sons, your little speech about being sickened every time you thought of it was very convincing. You're quite an actor."

"I am sickened, when I think of what I exposed my family to. How I brought such evil into our lives. If I could go back, I would. We all would."

"We had our differences, Dad. But even so, I always respected you. Until today."

A sob escaped his father as he fell back onto the chair and dropped his head into his hands.

Reed gazed at him, unmoved. "You were so worried about your precious reputations. About the truth ruining you. You didn't see that you'd already been ruined and that the truth was the only thing that could have redeemed you."

Reed let himself out. He glanced down the hall and saw his brother Joe, standing in his office doorway, expression stricken. They stood that way a moment, gazes locked. He should question him, Reed knew. And he would. Just not right now. He didn't have the stomach for it.

Moments later he stepped outside and into the brilliant day. He breathed deeply, using the moment to steady himself. He tipped his head to the sky, squinting against the light. Would he ever be able to look at his mother and father the same way? What of their friends? How did he put this behind him?

He opened his cell, dialed Alex. It went straight to voice

mail and he left a message asking her to call him. Next he dialed Rachel.

"Hi, Rachel," he said when she answered. "It's Dan Reed."

"Hi, Danny. What can I do for you?"

"Is Alex with you?"

"Not at this moment, I'm at work."

"When did you see her last?"

"This morning. She stayed with me last night. She called a bit ago and said she was going to pick up some things at her place. You might try there."

"Thanks, I will."

"Wait, Danny! What's up?"

"Nothing, just looking for her." He ended the call, acknowledging that he hoped it was nothing.

Chapter Sixty-seven

Wednesday, March 17
4:55 P.M.

Reed found Tanner and Saacks in the break room. He dreaded what he had to tell them. He felt responsible.

Alex had bolted. He had done an hourly drive-by of her rental: no Alex and no Prius. He had left several voice mails for her without a callback and had checked in with Rachel twice, exacting a promise that she would call if she heard from Alex.

Tanner saw him first. Her greeting died on her lips. "What's wrong?"

"I think Clarkson's gone."

Saacks swore and jumped to his feet. "I thought you said she wouldn't run."

"Apparently, I was wrong."

"Are you certain?" Tanner asked.

He crossed to them and handed Tanner the note his father had received. She read it and passed it to Saacks. "What's that all about?"

Reed told them. When he'd finished, he pulled out a chair and straddled it. He looked from Tanner to Saacks and back. It seemed he had temporarily shocked them silent.

"Wow," Tanner finally said. "A wine orgy. Kinky."

Saacks cleared his throat. "When did you learn this?"

"Couple hours ago. Been trying to find Clarkson ever since."

"Without luck, apparently."

"She stayed with Rachel Sommer last night. When I couldn't reach Alex on her cell, I tried Rachel. She said Alex had called her and said she was going by her rental. She suggested I try there. Which I have, repeatedly. No sign of her or her vehicle."

Saacks looked at him. "Do you think she's dangerous?"

Reed laughed without humor. "You're asking me? I said she wouldn't bolt."

They all stood. "Let's get out an All Vehicle Alert for her plate," Saacks said. "If she's anywhere in the valley, we'll find her. And Reed, I suggest you tell your old man to watch his back."

Chapter Sixty-eight

Wednesday, March 17
7:00 P.M.

"Alex? It's time. You need to wake up."

Groggy, Alex dragged herself from sleep. She blinked against the light streaming in from the hallway. "Rachel? What time is—"

"Seven. Have you been sleeping all day?"

She had, Alex realized, and sat up. She climbed out of bed, feeling wobbly-legged. She still wore the jeans and sweatshirt she had thrown on in the middle of the night.

"I took one of your pills," she said, pushing the hair out of her eyes. "I figured I'd need some rest before tonight."

"Good girl. Why don't you get cleaned up and I'll make us something to eat?" Rachel started off, then stopped and looked back. "Wear something warm. It'll be cool in the cave."

Twenty minutes later, Alex joined her in the kitchen. The other woman stood at the stove, making omelets. A bowl of strawberries and plate of croissants sat on the counter. Tonight, Rachel's ever present bottle of wine was missing.

"It smells divine," she said, slipping onto one of the counter stools.

"Thanks. I didn't want to make anything too heavy, but figured you had to eat something."

"If I wasn't starving, I don't think I could eat a thing. I'm too anxious." Alex reached for a strawberry. "Any questions about me today?"

"At least a hundred." Rachel met her gaze. "Sorry."

What had she expected? She dropped the unfinished strawberry on the plate. "How bad did I look?"

"Let's put it this way, you make for a good headline."

Rachel eased one of the omelets onto a plate and slid it across the counter. "Please, don't wait for me."

Shaking off her unease, Alex dug in.

"Everything's ready," Rachel said, expertly flipping her eggs. "I'm due to do some barrel tastings, so if someone should happen to see us go into the cave tonight, they won't think a thing about it."

She checked her omelet, then slid it onto a plate. "Are you ready for this?"

Alex had to honestly admit that she was not. "But I'm doing it anyway. I'm not going to run away from the truth. I won't be like my mother."

They finished their meal in silence. Together, they straightened the kitchen, then donned jackets. Rachel handed her a flashlight and they stepped outside. The stars and moon, obscured by clouds, turned the night a deep black. Rachel led the way, moving slowly, deliberately toward the cave entrance.

Alex's heartbeat quickened; fear turned the inside of her mouth to ash. As if she knew, Rachel caught her hand and laced their fingers together. The way they had when they were kids. And the way she had at five years old, Alex clung to it.

The cave was secured by both iron gates and a chain and padlock. Rachel unlocked both; they slipped through the gate and into the cave. Once inside, Rachel snapped on her flashlight; Alex followed suit. Training the beam dead ahead, they moved forward.

Alex caught Rachel's hand, clinging to it. With each step deeper into the cave, Alex's fear grew. The walls and ceiling closed in on her, the dark became heavier, more impenetrable. Her heart beat wildly, her every instinct screamed she should run. Her steps faltered. She couldn't do this, she thought. She couldn't.

Rachel tightened her fingers. "Stay with me, Alex. We're almost there."

"I don't know if . . . I—" Her voice rose. "I don't—"

Rachel cut her off. "Yes, you can. Do it for Dylan. Do it for Tim."

And for her mother, Alex thought, marshaling her courage. No more running. No more searching for what was missing.

She would finally know.

They wound deeper. Every so often the lichen would catch on her hair or brush her face and she would squeak in terror. She squeezed Rachel's hand so tightly, she knew it must hurt. She told herself to ease up, but found she couldn't respond.

"Talk to me, Rachel. Please, just talk—Oh my God, it's happening. I smell it! Sandalwood!"

"It's okay." Rachel said softly. "It's real, I set the stage. We're almost there."

Alex stumbled; Rachel steadied her. The smell grew stronger. A thrumming filled her head, like a chant. She wanted to run, but was frozen in fear.

Rachel tugged on her hand. "C'mon, Alex, just a few more steps."

Her words seemed to be coming from a great distance. Alex obeyed woodenly. They turned. In the distance she saw a circle of flickering light. With each step it grew bigger, more brilliant, its pull on her stronger.

"You're five years old, Alex," Rachel said softly. "You didn't mean any harm . . . you just wanted to see what was happening . . ."

And then Alex realized: Rachel was a bigger part of the nightmare than she had let on. She looked at her. "I followed you, didn't I? That night, I followed you into the cave."

"Yes," Rachel said softly.

Alex brought a hand to her mouth, not so much remembering as putting the pieces together. "You hated it when I followed you around. But I did it all the time. I adored you."

Alex put herself back there, imagining that night. "I hear you sneak out and decide to follow."

"You brought Dylan with you."

"Yes. I would have known I couldn't leave him alone."

Alex pictured her five-year-old self standing on tiptoe, scooping Dylan up out of his crib. He would have been heavy for her. She imagined her determination. Her fear of dropping him.

"You went into the cave."

"Yes," Rachel agreed.

Alex looked ahead, at the flickering light pouring out of an alcove up ahead. From candles, she realized. "And I followed you even though I was terrified of the cave."

Again, Rachel agreed.

"At some point I must have heard sounds. Like the ones from my visions. And seen the flickering lights."

Alex wetted her lips, dry from breathing heavily through her mouth. She realized she held her arms as if cradling a baby. She moved forward, toward the lit opening, Rachel beside her.

She stepped into the room, her gaze going immediately to an opening in the cave wall. She crossed to it. "You were peeking through an opening. This opening."

"You called my name," Rachel said. "When I saw you, I was so angry. Because I was scared. I knew how much trouble I could be in. Then Dylan started to cry."

Rachel reached out as if to take a baby from her arms. "I took him. To try to get him to stop. What did you do then, Alex?"

Alex shifted her gaze to the opening again. "I wanted to see what you were looking at." She crossed to the opening. With her mind's eye, she saw herself, drawn to the flickering light, like tentacles of fire reaching for her, pulling her in. She peered through the opening.

And the past hit her with the force of a wrecking ball, the

memory of what she saw flooding back. Men in long, hooded robes. Women, too, but some naked . . . Dancing sensuously in the candlelight. Touching themselves. Being touched. The grunting, howling noises from her dreams. Not strange creatures—the sounds of wild sex.

Sex. Her mother, Alex remembered. Naked. Spread out on an altar, a man on top of her. Riding her.

Rachel came up behind her. "You started to scream. I put my hand over your mouth, like this."

Rachel covered her mouth and jerked her away from the opening. "Go back to bed," she hissed. "And if you tell anyone what you saw, I'll hurt you. I promise I will. I'll do to you what those men are doing to your mommy!"

Rachel released her and Alex stumbled backward, away from the opening. She sank to the cave floor, and brought her hands to her face, feeling ill. Candles, incense and an altar. All the trappings of a religious ritual. The orgy in progress. She wouldn't have had any frame of reference for what she was witnessing. No place to put it. How frightened she must have been.

It explained so much about her. Her studies, relationships and periods of promiscuity. She had spent her life trying to make sense of it all.

"Alex," Rachel said softly, kneeling in front of her. "Let's finish this."

Chapter Sixty-nine

Alex searched Rachel's expression. In it she saw steely resolve—and regret. "What are you thinking?" Alex asked.

"I'm sorry I said that to you. I was just a kid, I was terrified of what Dad would do to me if he found out. I'm so, so sorry."

Alex let out a deep, shuddering breath. "I'm not sure I can do this anymore."

"Yes, you can. I want to be free. Don't you?"

She did. *Dear God, she wanted it more than anything.* She squeezed her eyes shut, opening the door in her mind: a naked man howling, fully aroused . . . her mother spread out on the altar, bodies writhing together . . . springing away . . . Rachel's hand over her mouth, the hissed words in her ear . . .

"Go back to bed. And if you tell anyone what you saw, I'll hurt you. I promise I will. I'll do to you what those men are doing to your mommy!"

She opened her eyes, looked at Rachel. "I ran, didn't I?"

"Yes. But you didn't go back to bed, did you?"

"No." Alex swallowed hard, reliving those terrifying minutes. "I started to. Then I hid. Behind some barrels."

"Why?"

"I don't know. I was scared. I wanted to see—To wait for you."

"You didn't wait long, did you?"

"No. You had Dylan. You were hurrying." Alex swallowed hard; she rubbed her damp palms against her jeans. "I waited a minute, then followed. I couldn't see you anymore. Then I heard Dylan crying again. You screamed.

"I ran then. You were at the front of the cave. There was a group of robed men . . . they were all around you."

Alex brought her hands to her mouth. "They took Dylan and . . . Rachel . . . they grabbed you and dragged you beyond where I could see."

She was crying, Alex realized. She wiped at the tears with the heels of her hands. "I peeked around . . . they had you on the ground, holding you down. You were fighting, but they were too strong, there were too many . . .

"Your T-shirt, they yanked it up over your face. I couldn't move. I couldn't make a sound. But inside . . . I was screaming."

Alex couldn't stop the words, they poured out of her in a rush. "He raped you, Rachel. The others were cheering . . . laughing . . ." God, she hated this. It hurt saying the words, but she had to. "He wasn't the only one. The others . . . after him—"

"Two others," Rachel whispered.

"Yes. Then, you didn't move anymore. I knew that was bad. I wanted to find our parents, but I was afraid. I couldn't go back in there . . . I was too scared!" Her voice caught on a sob. "I'm sorry, Rachel. I'm so sorry."

"How many, Alex? How many were there?"

She struggled to remember. "Five, I think. One ran away. One just helped hold you down. They teased him about it but—"

She looked at Rachel. "Oh my God, the first one, before he raped you, he said—"

"'You want to know so bad,'" Rachel murmured, "'I'll show you.'" She caught Alex's hands. "You said that in your dream, it was Clark's voice. Was it?"

"I don't know for sure, Rachel. I'd just had that confrontation with him. Maybe that's why it was his voice."

"What about Dylan?" she asked.

"He was there, on the ground, not far from the cave entrance. Crying and crying—"

"And then he stopped. Why, Alex?"

She fought to remember. "I don't know. Something . . . Suddenly all but one was gone. They ran away."

They ran away. Frightened. They were just boys, she realized. Teenagers. Like Clark.

She looked directly at Rachel. "I ran, too. But then stopped, and looked back. His hood had fallen away—"

Alex grabbed Rachel's hands, squeezing them tightly. "It was Clark. The boy who raped you first was Clark."

Chapter Seventy

Moments passed; neither moved. Alex kept ahold of Rachel's hands.

"Clark," Rachel said, voice shaking. "That son of a bitch. I always wondered, but—"

"I'm sorry, Rachel."

"I'm not. I'm thrilled." Rachel freed her hands and stood. "I'm going to take care of this right now."

Alex followed her to her feet. "What are you going to do?"

Rachel didn't hesitate. "I'm going to kill him."

Alex wanted to laugh. It started to form on her lips, uncomfortable and inappropriate. "You're joking, right?"

"I've got a gun, Alex. I bought it specifically for this. And I'm going to use it."

Alex's heart lurched. "Don't do this, Rachel. It's not worth it. He's not worth it."

"You don't think so? All my life I've lived with what they did to me. I hid it away, shoved it into the deepest, darkest corner of my mind. Because I didn't know who. I do now. And he's going to pay."

She started off; Alex went after her. "Wait! What about Dylan?"

Rachel stopped but didn't look back.

"After I saw Clark's face, I ran. Back to my bed," Alex said. "What happened to our brother?"

"He was gone." Rachel turned. "When I could move, I dragged myself over to where he had been, but he wasn't there. There was blood."

The blood the police and FBI found.

"Why didn't you get help? Why not go to your dad or—"

"And tell them what? That I was spying on them? Tell them what those boys did to me—I was ashamed! I was scared! I didn't know what to do! I—"

She tipped her face to the ceiling, fighting tears. "I thought . . . I hoped, Dylan was back in his bed. Who would hurt him? He was such a sweet baby. So I crept back to the house and cleaned myself up. I didn't even check his crib because . . . I couldn't. I prayed he would be there in the morning. I promised myself he would be."

But he wasn't.

"I can't change that, Alex. And I've lived with it for twenty-five years. Helpless to change anything. But I can change this. I'm not helpless anymore."

She turned and started off. "Wait!" Alex called. "What about justice for Dylan? Let's go to the police. Let's—"

"This is justice for Dylan," Rachel said without looking back. "Who do you think killed him? Who did you see standing there?"

"I can't let you do this."

"You can't stop me."

She turned. Alex caught her breath. She had a gun; she was pointing it at Alex.

"What are you doing?"

"I'm sorry, Alex. I have to do this."

"You're going to shoot me?"

"Only if I have to."

"We're stepsisters. Friends—"

"Clark and I are cousins. That didn't stop him, did it?"

"You're better than he is! Dammit, Rachel—"

"I'm going now. Don't follow me."

She meant it, Alex realized, watching as Rachel walked away. She had to stop her. Had to find a way.

"What about the vines?" she called after her, sounding as desperate as she felt. "What about your wines, your legacy?"

Rachel didn't answer. The bobbling beam of the flashlight disappeared from sight. Alex counted to ten and started after her—same as she had all those years ago.

She moved as quickly and quietly as she could, forgoing the flashlight for stealth. Her heart pounded, but not with fear this time, with determination.

She wouldn't let Rachel do this.

Up ahead, she heard Rachel at the cave entrance. Heard the creak of the gate closing and the clank of the chain and padlock.

Rachel was locking her inside the cave.

Alex snapped on the flashlight and ran. She was too late. Rachel had fastened the gate. She stood waiting for Alex, expression apologetic.

"They'll find you in the morning," she said. "Don't be scared."

"Please, think this through, Rachel. Please, don't—"

"I've spent my whole life thinking this through."

"Rachel—" Alex reached through the metal rails. "I don't want to lose you."

"Before I go, I have to tell you something. That baby brush, I have one just like it."

"What? You—"

"Wayne Reed's not your father." Rachel caught her hand, brought it to her mouth, kissed it. "Goodbye, Alex."

Chapter Seventy-one

Wednesday, March 17
10:30 P.M.

They'd located Alex's car. The Rohnert Park Walmart parking lot. A search of the store had produced no sign of her; they were in the process of getting the store's security tapes.

Reed shown his flashlight inside the Prius. No sign of a struggle. No left behind articles that might suggest a criminal act. No shopping bags.

He didn't like this. His earlier presumption that she'd bolted felt wrong. All along he'd seesawed between suspecting she was behind events and worrying she was in danger from them. The seesaw had just tipped—he feared for her safety.

Reed looked at the deputy who had called it in, working to keep his cool. "Report."

"Doing a routine sweep. Recognized the car from the Alert, checked the plate number to confirm, then called it in. Performed the same check as you."

Tanner and Saacks arrived. They climbed out and crossed to him. "You have a visitor." Tanner motioned to the car. "Your brother Joe. Came to the Barn looking for you. Says it's about Clarkson and what's going on. Wouldn't talk to us."

Reed's heart seemed to stop. He nodded and headed for

the car; Joe stepped out as he reached it. His normally pressed and creased brother was a mess. "I don't want to talk to them," Joe said, motioning to Tanner and Saacks. "Just you."

"Can't help you there, Big Brother. We're a package deal."

"Forget it then. I'm not talking."

Reed snapped. "No problem. Because I'll haul your ass in and book you for obstruction, which is a felony. And then you'll talk, only it'll be in a nine by twelve windowless room with a lock on the door. Don't test me, Brother."

Joe paled. He moved his gaze from Reed to the other detectives and back. He looked like he might puke. "It's about that night. The night Dylan disappeared. We raped her. We raped . . . Rachel."

Standing in the middle of a Walmart parking lot, Reed could have heard a pin drop. His brother dragged a hand through his thinning hair, the movement jerky. "I didn't. I . . . couldn't. I ran away. But the others—"

"Who?" Tanner demanded.

"Clark and Tom. Spanky and Terry.

"I ran, but I didn't do anything to stop them. I didn't go for help. Nothing."

He hung his head. Reed gazed at him, feeling nothing but contempt. "Where?"

"The Sommer place. Outside the wine cave."

Reed and Tanner exchanged glances. "The night Dylan disappeared."

"Yes, he was there. Rachel had him. He was crying."

Reed felt sick to his stomach. "What about Alex?"

"Didn't see her."

Tanner's cell phone went off. She checked the display, then excused herself.

"Did you go to Dad, tell him any of this?"

He shook his head. "Never told anyone. Until now." He started to cry. "All these years, I've hated myself . . . that I let them do that to her." He lifted his gaze to Reed's, expression pleading. "But she turned out okay. Right, Reed? She's good."

"That was Cal," Tanner said, returning to their sides. "He

heard back from the Ashton-Drake people. The two dolls, they both belonged to Rachel Sommer."

Reed realized two things simultaneously—they combined to take his breath away: Rachel was definitely not okay and worse, Alex was with her.

Chapter Seventy-two

Wednesday, March 17
10:55 P.M.

"No! Rachel, come back here! Help! Help! Somebody!" Alex grabbed the gate and shook it. "Dammit, Rachel!"

Her voice caught on the night air, was lifted and dispersed. She kept calling out anyway, until she was hoarse. Throat raw and voice gone, she shone her flashlight toward the main house, flipping it on and off.

A figured emerged from the path, hurrying toward her.

Treven, she saw. She cried out in relief. "Thank God—"

"Alexandra, what are you—"

"She's gone to kill Clark! We have to stop her!"

"Kill Clark?" He fumbled with the locks. "Who?"

"Rachel. She has a gun."

He got the padlock open, then the gate. "That's crazy. Why would Rachel—"

"He raped her. The night Dylan disappeared."

He looked at her as if she had sprouted horns. "That's insane. I don't know what you think you're doing but—"

"Trying to save your son's life! Where is he?"

"I'm calling the police."

"Good. Yes, call them." She grabbed his arm. "But by the

time they get here, it may be too late. Do you know where Clark is?"

He gazed steadily at her, as if sizing her up, weighing his options.

She tightened her grip on his arm. "I remember everything, Treven. About that night. What was going on. I was there! I'd repressed it all . . . Rachel helped me remember. That's how she learned that Clark was—"

He shook off her hand. "I stood up for you. When Reed and others called you crazy. But now, you're calling my son—"

"Where is he! Home? Out somewhere? All Rachel would have to do is call him, ask to meet, say it was an emergency."

She was getting through to him, Alex saw. She lowered her voice. "What do you have to lose by believing me?"

"He's here," Treven said. "In his office."

Alex started to run. Treven with her. Light shone from the winery offices. In the parking area beyond, Treven's BMW and Rachel's Infiniti were parked, side by side.

They reached the building's entrance, found it unlocked. "This way," Treven said. They started forward; a shot rang out.

"No!" Alex cried and ran.

She reached the office and stopped dead. *She was too late.* Clark lay in a crumpled heap on the floor, a pool of blood slowly spreading around him.

"Clark!" Treven cried, rushing to his son's side. He bent and checked his pulse, then looked up at Rachel's stricken face. "He's dead. You killed him."

"I had to do it, Uncle Treven. Don't you see?"

"Give me the gun, Rachel." He stood and crossed carefully toward her, hand out.

"He raped me, Uncle Treven. And tonight, he laughed about it. He said—"

"Give me the gun."

"He called me stupid. And weak."

Treven took the weapon from her and Rachel slumped against him, crying. He looked at Alex. "Close the door, would you?"

Confused, she did as he asked. He motioned her over. "Check Clark's pulse again. I thought I saw him move."

Alex hurried to do it. Squatted beside him, she pressed her finger to his wrist, then throat. Nothing. She looked back up at Treven. And found him holding Rachel, one arm across her throat, the gun to her head.

"Treven?" Alex started to stand. "What are you—"

"Shut up. Stay exactly where you are."

She froze. Heart thundering, she struggled to breathe evenly, think clearly. She wanted to look at Rachel but was afraid of what he might do if she did.

"Do you have any idea how sick I am of you?" He readjusted his grip on Rachel. Alex used the moment to peek at the other woman. She looked terrified. "I never should have gotten involved with your mother. Of course, I didn't know what a complete whack job she was."

Treven was her father. The family resemblance. The baby brush.

He smiled at her expression. "Shocking, isn't it? Our plan was perfect. She would marry my brother, then break his heart. All the while remaining my mistress."

"Why?" she asked. "What did you hope to gain—"

"It would hurt him," he said simply, as if it was the most logical thing in the world.

He hated his brother that much, Alex realized, shuddering. Her mother had been right to run.

"Problem was," he went on, "she fell in love with the twerp, then gave him a son."

"But it all turned out much better, didn't it?" Rachel managed, voice tight with fury. "You were able to completely destroy him by killing his son."

"You," he said with a sound of regret, "I'm going to miss. You are an excellent winemaker. Clark, on the other hand, brought nothing special to the party."

"You're completely evil."

He laughed. "Perhaps. Let's get on with this thing."

"Wait!" Rachel said, struggling to find her voice. "That night, Dylan, how—"

"I bashed his head in," he said so matter-of-factly Alex's blood ran cold. "It was so perfect. I was able to swoop in and save the day. Take over the business for poor, devastated Harlan. The way it should have been all along." His voice hardened. "It should have been mine. I'm the oldest son! Me!"

Rachel struggled and he tightened his grip. "That's what I want you to do. Fight me. Make it look good. After all, you killed Clark. Then Alex. I tried to stop you—"

"No one will believe you!"

"You're crazy, Rachel. The rape left you unbalanced. You hid it all these years. Until poor little Dylan was dug up—"

The fire alarm's piercing shriek rent the air. It mingled with the sound of a shot going off. Alex launched to her feet; a searing pain speared through her.

The office door burst open. Harlan charged through, swinging a wine bottle.

A wine bottle? Alex thought, light-headed. She brought a hand to her side; it came back wet. And red. She fell to her knees. As if from a great distance, she heard the wail of sirens.

"Alex! No!"

Rachel. Holding her. Crying.

The thunder of feet. Voices. Shouting.

"Jesus! Somebody! Get the EMTs—"

"On their way."

"Hold on, sweetheart."

Reed. She opened her eyes. He came into focus. She tried to tell him not to worry, but the words came out a jumble.

He leaned close. "Hang in there, baby. It's going to be all right. You're going to be just fine. I promise . . ."

Alex smiled and closed her eyes, serenity flowing over her. She believed him.

Chapter Seventy-three

Thursday, March 18
11:10 A.M.

Alex opened her eyes. She hurt. Her mouth was dry, her limbs heavy.

"Hello, dear. Welcome back."

A woman came into focus. *A nurse.* The room followed. *A hospital room. IV. Monitors. Flowers.*

She returned her gaze to the nurse. "Was I dead?"

The woman chuckled. "Luckily, not even close. How about a sip of water?"

"Yes, please—"

"I'll take care of that."

Alex turned her head. Rachel stood in the doorway, equally weighted by a vase of flowers cradled in one arm, a bottle of wine in the other.

Alex managed a weak smile. "Can't drink while I'm on pain meds."

"But you won't be on them forever." She strolled into the room, exchanging a glance with the nurse as the woman slipped out. "Besides," she said, setting the bottle on the bedside table, "you lay this baby up, it'll only get better."

Alex shook her head, thinking how much she liked her.

Cousins, she thought. Amazing. And despite everything that had happened, wonderful.

She found the remote and raised herself up to a forty five-degree angle. "Treven shot me."

"He did." Rachel held the cup of water and straw to her lips. "Could have been a lot worse, if not for Dad's quick thinking. I'm so proud of him."

Alex took another sip, then lay back against the pillows, exhausted.

"Reed had called him. Asked him to check on me." She pulled the chair over and plopped onto it. "He saw the light on in the winery and went to investigate."

Her voice thickened. "He heard it all, Alex."

Alex reached out her hand. Rachel grasped it. For a long moment, they sat that way. Lost in their own thoughts, drawing comfort from the other. At least Alex knew she was.

"We need to talk," Rachel said finally.

"Am I up to this?"

"I hope so." She freed her hand from Alex's, then immediately looked sorry she had. Instead, she folded both hands in her lap. "I did some things I'm not proud of. Things I hope you can forgive me for. I didn't do them to hurt you, you have to believe me . . . I just wanted to . . . stir things up. Make them, the ones who raped me, nervous. I wanted them, and Dylan's murderer, to know that their secrets weren't going to stay buried forever."

"And you needed my help?"

She looked away, then back. "Yes."

"You scrawled *Remember* on my bathroom mirror."

"Yes."

"And you butchered those baby dolls."

"Yes."

"The lamb?"

"Not me. That one . . . my guess is Clark or Treven. In the hopes of scaring you off."

"We'll never know for sure, will we?"

"Actually, we just might." At Alex's expression, she grinned. "Clark's alive."

"That's not . . . How . . . I checked his pulse."

"Not well enough, apparently." She leaned forward. "The bad news is, I'm a lousy shot. The good news, I didn't kill anybody. Our family lawyer's hooking me up with a top criminal attorney. He thinks that, considering the circumstances, I won't be charged."

"What about Treven?"

"In jail. Charged with the murder of Dylan Sommer."

"Am I interrupting?"

Harlan stood in the doorway, also carrying wine and flowers. She had to laugh, though when she did it really hurt.

When she was done grimacing, Alex waved him in. "Of course not."

He crossed to the bed, deposited his gifts, then hugged his daughter. "I'm so glad I still have you," he said.

He turned toward Alex. His eyes, she saw, were wet. "And you, too, Alexandra."

"Our hero," Rachel said. "But Dad," she said, "what were you thinking? It was a 2000 Stag's Pass Reserve. A magnum of it."

"You're worth it. Both of you."

Rachel smiled and kissed his cheek. "Enough crazy talk from you."

He bent and pressed his lips to Alex's forehead. "Thank you. I finally know . . . It's almost unbearable to think about, but at least—"

He choked on the words and Alex grabbed his hand. "I know," she whispered. "I feel the same way."

He squeezed her hand. "When you're better, let's talk. I'd like you to come work for us. After all, it is a family winery."

Chapter Seventy-four

Monday, May 3
5:45 P.M.

Good men were like pennies from heaven, Alex thought, falling against Reed's chest, totally spent. And she had found the best one of all.

She pressed her lips to his shoulder, then neck, loving the feel of his heartbeat against her breast, the stirring of his breath against her ear. But most of all, she loved the way he gave himself to her. Wholly and without doubts.

They had left both their doubts and regrets behind.

In the weeks that had passed, their wounds had begun to heal. Her physical wounds had seemed so easy to overcome, the emotional so difficult. One day she was on top of the world and seemingly on the road to recovery, the next ripped wide open, raw and hurting.

It had been just as difficult for Reed. And Rachel. Perhaps more so. Because they faced their parents—and their parents' sins—every day.

Alex had considered refusing Harlan's offer and leaving the valley, but had realized that all her life she had longed for family, history, and roots that ran deep. She had that now, she wasn't about to run away.

She wasn't like her mother. Alex knew that now. And for the first time in her life, she felt rock solid.

"What're you thinking?" Reed asked softly, stroking her back.

"About you. How happy you make me."

"I like that." He grinned and rolled onto his side, taking her with him so they lay facing one another. "I have something that will make you even happier."

She arched her eyebrows. "Love the thought. Can I have ten minutes to recover first?"

He laughed. "Not that. D.A. offered Clark a plea deal in exchange for information. Clark's singing like a bird."

Alex propped up on an elbow. "I can't believe it. After all these weeks."

"Apparently the idea of life in prison wasn't appealing. Since at the time of Dylan's murder, Clark was a minor and under his father's influence, his guilt is reduced in the eyes of the law. He'll still go to prison, but he won't rot there. He's offering up all kinds of details, including ones about the murders of Tom Schwann, Alberto Alvarez, and your ex-husband."

"Tim," she whispered, voice catching.

"According to Clark, your ex-husband contacted Treven and started asking questions. Turns out your mother had shared more with Tim than you knew. She'd told him that 'your father had gained everything from her and Harlan's loss.'"

Tears stung her eyes. "He was trying to help me find my dad. And it got him killed."

Reed caught one of her tears with his index finger. "Like the rest of us, he didn't have a clue what Treven was capable of. He probably figured your mother had exaggerated how bad he was."

Knowing Tim and her mother, it made sense to her. "That he found my father, that was the good news he was going share with me."

She rested her forehead against Reed's. "I feel responsible."

He kissed her. "Don't, sweetheart. Leave the blame where it should be, solely on Treven Sommer's head."

"He killed Tom Schwann. Why?"

"Schwann was cracking under the pressure. Making noises about going to the police. Treven wasn't about to chance that. He saw the opportunity and took it. Same as he had twenty-five years ago." Reed paused. "There's more."

She tipped her head back to look him in the eyes. "More?"

"Treven's decided to change his plea to guilty."

She caught her breath. "That means no trial."

"That's right, just sentencing. I can't lie, it's a big relief."

They had managed to keep the most salacious details of the case out of the media. The valley wine community was a tight one and those involved had been extremely powerful, but once the trial had begun, no amount of influence would have kept the muck from flowing.

"As angry and disappointed as I am in my parents and brother, I dreaded our name being dragged through the mud."

"What have you decided about Red Crest?" she asked, referring to his brothers' request that he join them at the winery. "Your dad's stepping down in just a few days."

"I haven't decided yet."

She wound her arms around his neck. "The vines are in your blood, you know. You can't escape it."

He rolled her onto her back. "You're what's in my blood, Alexandra. And I have no intention of going anywhere."

Read on for an excerpt from Erica Spindler's next book

Watch Me Die

Coming soon in hardcover from

St. Martin's Press

Tuesday, August 9, 2011
9:40 am
New Orleans, Louisiana

At any given moment, the demons could descend upon Mira Gallier. Sometimes she marshaled the strength to fight them off, denying their dark, tormenting visions. Their taunts and merciless accusations.

Other times, they overpowered her and left her scrambling for a way to silence them. To obliterate the pain.

Last night they had come. And she had found a way to escape.

Mira lay on her side on the bed, gazing blankly at the small rose window she had created in secret, a wedding gift for her husband-to-be. In the tradition of the magnificent gothic windows, she had chosen brilliant jewel colors; her design had been complex and intricate, combining painted images within the blocks of color. For her, the window had been a symbol of her and Jeff's perfect love and a new, beautiful life together.

She had never imagined how quickly, how brutally, that life would be ended.

It hurt to look at it now and Mira rolled onto her back.

Her head felt heavy; the inside of her mouth as if it were stuffed with cotton.

Eleven months, three weeks, and four days, shot to hell by one small, blue, oval tablet.

What would Jeff think of her now? Even as she wondered, she knew. He would be deeply disappointed.

But he couldn't be more disappointed in her than she was in herself.

On the nightstand, her cell phone chirped. She grabbed it, answered, "Second level of hell. The tormented speaking."

"Mira? It's Deni."

Her studio assistant and friend. Sounding puzzled.

"Who'd you expect?" she asked. "My husband?"

"That's not funny."

It wasn't, she acknowledged. It was angry. And sad. Jeff was dead, and she had fallen off the wagon. Neither of which had a damn thing to do with Deni. "I'm sorry, I had a really bad night."

"You want to talk about it?"

The roar of water. A wall of it. As black and cold as death, brutal and unforgiving. Jeff's cry resounded in her head. Calling out for her to help him.

But she hadn't been there. She didn't know what that last moment had been like. She didn't even know if he'd had time to cry out, to feel fear, or if he had known it was the end.

And she never would.

He was dead because of her.

"No. But thanks." The last came out automatically, what she was supposed to say, even though gratitude was far from what she was feeling.

"You used, didn't you?"

No condemnation in Deni's voice. Just pity. Still, excuses flew to Mira's lips, so familiar she could utter them in her sleep. They made her sick. She was done with them.

"Yes."

For a long moment Deni was silent. When she finally spoke, she said, "I take it I should reschedule your interview?"

"Interview?"

"With Libby Gardner. From Channel Twelve, the local PBS affiliate. About the Magdalene window. She's here."

Mira remembered then. The interview appointment. Her work on the Magdalene restoration being included in a sixth anniversary of Katrina series the station was planning. "Shit. I forgot. Sorry."

"What should I tell her?"

"How about the truth? That your boss is a pill head and basket case."

"Stop it, Mira. That's not true."

"No?"

"You suffered a terrible loss. You turned to—"

"The whole city suffered that same freaking loss. Life goes on, sweetheart." She spoke the words harshly, their brutality self-directed. "The strong thrive and the weak turn to Xanax."

"That's such bullshit." Deni sounded hurt. "I'll see if she can reschedule—"

"No. Get started with her. Explain how the window ended up in our care, describe the process, show her around. By the time you've done that, I'll be there."

"Mira—"

She cut her assistant off. "I'll be in shortly. We can talk then."

Mira ended the call and hurried to the kitchen. She fixed herself a cup of strong coffee, then headed toward the bathroom. When she caught sight of her reflection in the vanity mirror, she froze. She looked like crap. Worse even. The circles under her hazel eyes were so dark, her pale skin looked ghostly in comparison. She was too thin—her copper red hair like the flame atop a matchstick.

She wore one of her husband's old tees as a nightshirt: GEAUX SAINTS the front proclaimed. Mira trailed her fingers over the faded print. Jeff hadn't lived long enough to see his beloved NFL team win the Super Bowl.

It's your fault he's dead, Mira, the voice in her head whispered. *You convinced him to stay. Remember what you*

*said? "It'll be an adventure, Jeff. A story we can share with
our children and grandchildren."*

The air conditioner kicked on. Cold air from the vent
above her head raised goose bumps on her arms and the
back of her neck. No, she told herself. That was bullshit.
Wasn't that what her shrink, Dr. Jasper, had told her? Jeff
had been a fifty-percent partner in the decision. If he had felt
strongly they should leave, he would have said so.

His family blamed her. Her and Jeff's friends had been
subtle in their accusations—she read condemnation in their
eyes.

She stared helplessly at her reflection. The problem was,
she blamed herself. No matter what her shrink said or what
the facts were.

She moved her gaze over the destruction of her
bathroom—drawers emptied, make-up bags and carry-ons
rifled through.

As if thieves had broken in and turned her home upside
down in search of valuables.

But she had done this. She was the thief. And the eleven
months, three weeks, and four days she had robbed herself
of couldn't be replaced.

Her cell phone went off. She saw it was Deni—no doubt
calling to say the reporter had taken a hike. "Pissed off another one, didn't I?" she answered.

"Something really bad's happened, Mira."

She pressed the device tighter to her ear. "What?"

"It's Father Girod, he's . . . dead. He was murdered."

An image of the kindly old priest filled her head. He had
approached her after Katrina about his church's stained-
glass windows, decimated by the storm. In the process of
restoring the twelve panels, she and the father had become
friends.

Grief choked her. "Oh, my God. Who could have . . .
When did—"

"There's more, Mira." Deni's voice shook. "Whoever did
it also vandalized the windows."

* * *

Homicide detective Spencer Malone angled his vintage, cherry-red Camero into the spot between the coroner's wagon and crime scene van, stopping sharply. Coffee sloshed over the rim of his partner's coffee cup and onto his paisley-print shirt.

"Crap that's hot! Drive much, Malone?" Detective Tony Sciame blotted the spot with the back of his tie. "And here I wanted to look good for my party."

Malone cut the engine and shot a grin his way. "No worries, Tony, it blends right in." He and Tony had been partners for better than six years. Their partnership worked despite the differences in their ages, investigative styles and—thank God—fashion sense.

Had worked. Today was Tony's last day on the force.

"Was that a shot?"

"Hell no, partner. Just a fact." Spencer slung open his door, then looked back at Tony. "You're still going to look real 'purty' for your party."

"Kiss my ass, Malone."

They climbed out of the Camero, slamming their doors in unison. A couple of uniformed officers looked their way.

Located on Carrollton Avenue at Fig Street, Sisters of Mercy Catholic School and Church straddled two distinctly different areas of the city—Uptown and Mid-city. Unfortunately, as the years had passed, the affluent had begun moving farther uptown, leaving Sisters of Mercy to the middle class and the working poor.

Still, it was a beautiful campus occupying a massive amount of land for an urban location. Its buildings, with their stone construction and barrel arches, owed more to Romanesque architecture than the fanciful Creole style the city was known for.

"Always wondered what the inside of this place looked like," Tony said. "And what do you know? Last day on the job and I get to find out."

"You're livin' right, Tony. No doubt about it."

They reached the exterior perimeter. Malone recognized the log officer—he and his brother Percy used to raise some serious hell together.

That was the thing about being a Malone—with three brothers, a sister, and various other extended family members on the force—he was always running into someone who had a connection with one of his nearest and dearest. Not all of that history was the kind one wanted to be reminded of.

"Yo, Strawberry," he greeted the man, nicknamed for the birthmark on his ass. "How you doin', man?"

"Not so bad." He held out the log. "Hear you're getting married. Never thought I'd see the day, dude. It's like the end of an era."

Tony guffawed. "Trust me, kid, he's only a legend in his own mind. What've we got?"

"Vic's in the sanctuary. Priest got whacked. Can you believe that shit? Who does that?"

"That's what we're here to find out." They ducked under the tape and followed the walk to the massive double doors and into the church narthex. The interior was cool and hushed. Through the open doors directly ahead, the sanctuary was bathed in colored light.

Malone stepped through. Stained-glass panels lined both side aisles. They were beautiful, but that wasn't what had him sucking in a sharp breath. Someone had taken a can of spray paint to them.

"Holy Mary, Mother of God," Tony muttered.

Malone silently seconded the sentiment, then turned his attention to the scene. Twelve glass panels, he counted. The tall, narrow windows looked to be about twelve by five feet; each depicted a scene from the life of Christ.

He backed up, taking in the graffiti on the first window to the left of the entrance, then swiveled slightly to take in the next, gaze moving from one panel to another until he had visually circled the room. Scrawled on each of the first eleven panels, buried among random marks and shapes, was a single word. On the twelfth, the perp had drawn a smiley face.

"Take a look, Tony. He left us a message—He - will - come - again - to - judge - the - living - and - the - dead."